A Convenient
Arrangement

What Reviewers Say About Jaime Clevenger's and Aurora Rey's Work

Aurora Rey Reviews

You Again

"*You Again* is a wonderful, feel good, low angst read with beautiful and intelligent characters that will melt your heart, and an enchanting second-chance love story."—*Rainbow Reflections*

Twice Shy

"[A] tender, foodie romance about a pair of middle aged lesbians who find partners in each other and rediscover themselves along the way. ...Rey's cute, occasionally steamy, romance reminds readers of the giddy intensity falling in love brings at any age, even as the characters negotiate the particular complexities of dating in midlife—meeting the children, dealing with exes, and revealing emotional scars. This queer love story is as sweet and light as one of Bake My Day's famous cream puffs."—*Publishers Weekly*

The Last Place You Look

"The romance is satisfying and full-bodied, with each character learning how to achieve her own goals and still be part of a couple. A heartwarming story of two lovers learning to move past their fears and commit to a shared future."—*Kirkus Reviews*

The Inn at Netherfield Green

"[Aurora Rey] constantly delivers a well-written romance that has just the right blend of humour, engaging characters, chemistry and romance."—*C-Spot Reviews*

Lead Counsel—*Novella in* The Boss of Her

"*Lead Counsel* by Aurora Rey is a short and sweet second chance romance. Not only was this story paced well and a delight to sink into, but there's A++ good swearing in it and has lines like this that made me all swoony because of how beautifully they're crafted."
—*Lesbian Review*

Recipe for Love

"So here's a few things that always get me excited when Aurora Rey publishes a new book. ...Firstly, I am guaranteed a hot butch with a sensitive side, this alone is a massive tick. Secondly, I am guaranteed to throw any diet out the window because the books always have the most delectable descriptions of food that I immediately go on the hunt for—this time it was a BLT with a difference. And lastly, hot sex scenes that personally have added to my fantasy list throughout the years! This book did not disappoint in any of those areas."—*Les Rêveur*

Autumn's Light

"This is a beautiful romance. I loved the flow of the story, loved the characters including the secondary ones, and especially loved the setting of Provincetown, Massachusetts."—*Rainbow Reflections*

Spring's Wake

"[A] feel-good romance that would make a perfect beach read. The Provincetown B&B setting is richly painted, feeling both indulgent and cozy."—*RT Book Reviews*

Summer's Cove

"As expected in a small-town romance, *Summer's Cove* evokes a sunny, light-hearted atmosphere that matches its beach setting. ...Emerson's shy pursuit of Darcy is sure to endear readers to her,

though some may be put off during the moments Darcy winds tightly to the point of rigidity. Darcy desires romance yet is unwilling to disrupt her son's life to have it, and you feel for Emerson when she endeavors to show how there's room in her heart for a family."
—*RT Book Reviews*

Crescent City Confidential—*Lambda Literary Award Finalist*

"*Crescent City Confidential* is a sweet romance with a hint of thriller thrown in for good measure."—*Lesbian Review*

Built to Last

"Rey's frothy contemporary romance brings two women together to restore an ancient farmhouse in Ithaca, N.Y. ...[T]he women totally click in bed, as well as when they're poring over paint chips, and readers will enjoy finding out whether love conquers all."
—*Publishers Weekly*

Winter's Harbor

"This is the story of Lia and Alex and the beautifully romantic and sexy tale of a winter in Provincetown, a seaside holiday haven. A collection of interesting characters, well-fleshed out, as well as a gorgeous setting make for a great read."—*Inked Rainbow Reads*

Jaime Clevenger Reviews

Three Reasons to Say Yes

"This was a really easy story to get into. I sank right in and wanted to stay there, because reading about other people on vacation is kind of like taking a mini vacation from the world! It's sweet and lovely, and while it has some angst, it's not going to hurt you. Instead, it's going to take you away from it all so you can come back with a smile on your face."—*Lesbian Review*

All the Reasons I Need

"What a fantastic follow up to what was one of my favourite books from last year. I hope this isn't the end for this series. I'm so invested now and can't wait to read more from these characters."—*Les Rêveur*

Just One Reason

"*Just One Reason* by Jaime Clevenger is a great age gap, workplace romance that kept me entertained and invested in a happily ever after for both main characters. ...The storyline glides along with ease and Clevenger's great dialogue lets the reader see how Sam and Terri are hardwired. The story is told from both Sam and Terri's points of view so getting to know them happens naturally. This is the third book in the Paradise series, but it works as a stand-alone. ...This book checked all the boxes on my list of what I want in a good book. I got to bond with two intriguing main characters. The plot had enough angst to make me question if there'd be a happily ever after (Hint: it's a romance), and the sex was hot. From any way you look at it, this story's a winner."—*Lesbian Review*

Party Favors

"Like the old CYOA (choose your own adventure) books, *Party Favors* is written in the second person so that the reader is the main character. ...I'm not sure what I expected when I started this book, but it ended up being way more fun and hot than I'd imagined. All paths head towards some kind of sexual encounter, and no two encounters are the same. ...If you like erotica and books that are seriously fun, definitely check this one out, and even better—read it with a friend."—*Smart Bitches Trashy Books*

One Weekend in Aspen

"Who'd have thought a book about a sex party would be full of suspense? I couldn't put One Weekend in Aspen down. I had to know what would happen next. I would have read it in one sitting if life had let me, but as it is, I had to stop reading for a whole day. Yet, now that I have turned the last page, I'm sad it's over. I really didn't want it to end. …With this book, Jaime Clevenger did something that I didn't think was possible, not to that level: she wrote an incredibly hot story that will, at the same time, give you all the feels."—*Les Rêveur*

"Jaime Clevenger is on my automatic list of authors to read so when I realized she had a new release, I already knew that I was going to read it. But when I read the blurb, it definitely caught my attention. I'm happy to say that I wasn't disappointed. …I knew that Clevenger can write awesome sex scenes since I've read her erotica book Party Favors followed by her Paradise Romance series. So I wasn't surprised to see that One Weekend in Aspen was seriously hot. No, scratch that, this book is smoking, sizzling hot. …So, if you are looking for some serious steam in your romance you should add this book to your list."—*LezReviewBooks*

Visit us at www.boldstrokesbooks.com

By the Authors

By Jaime Clevenger published by Bella Books:

The Unknown Mile

Call Shotgun

Sign on the Line

Whiskey and Oak Leaves

Sweet, Sweet Wine

Waiting for a Love Song

A Fugitive's Kiss

Moonstone

Party Favors

Three Reasons to Say Yes

All the Reasons I Need

Just One Reason

One Weekend in Aspen

Published by Spinsters Ink:

All Bets Off

By Aurora Rey

Cape End Romances:

Winter's Harbor

Summer's Cove

Spring's Wake

Autumn's Light

Built to Last

Crescent City Confidential

Lead Counsel (Novella in The Boss of Her collection)

Recipe for Love: A Farm-to-Table Romance

The Inn at Netherfield Green

Ice on Wheels (Novella in Hot Ice collection)

The Last Place You Look

Twice Shy

You Again

Follow Her Lead (Novella in Opposites Attract collection)

A Convenient Arrangement

by

Jaime Clevenger and Aurora Rey

2021

A CONVENIENT ARRANGEMENT

ISBN 13: 978-1-63555-818-0

This Trade Paperback Original Is Published By
Bold Strokes Books, Inc.
P.O. Box 249
Valley Falls, NY 12185

First Edition: November 2021

CREDITS
EDITOR: CINDY CRESAP
PRODUCTION DESIGN: SUSAN RAMUNDO
COVER DESIGN BY TAMMY SEIDICK

Acknowledgments

Jaime Clevenger would like to thank Corina McKendry for being both a rock star beta reader and amazing partner on so many life adventures. Thank you especially for being willing to listen to writer woes at any hour of the day and for always giving the best story advice! Jaime would also like to thank Aurora Rey for being a fabulous co-author. This project was even more fun than expected. Also many thanks to editor, Cindy Cresap, as well as everyone at Bold Strokes Books and Bella Books for bringing a two-book co-authored project to readers. And thank you, dear reader, for turning the page.

Aurora Rey would like to thank Jaime for the adventure of turning these wacky ideas into two really fun stories, and for proving her wrong about group projects. Huge thanks to Leigh Hays for beta reading and Cindy Cresap for the stellar editing and hilarious sidebar commentary. Also, much gratitude to Bold Strokes Books and Bella Books for letting us team up on these projects. And, as always, deepest gratitude to the readers who make it all worthwhile.

Chapter One

"Cuffing?" Jess Archer schooled her face into a neutral expression that hopefully gave away nothing of where her mind had gone. Which might have involved her headboard and having her wrists bound to it.

"Yes. It's where you jump into a relationship in the fall but break up before spring. It's been a straight thing for a while and is catching on with lesbians." Her boss, Donna—ten years older but at least twice as hip—gave her a pitying look. "Keep up, Jess."

She cleared her throat. "So, you want me to write an article about this...phenomenon?"

The withering look turned into a sly smile. "Actually, I was thinking more of a series for your column. Told from the first person."

Meaning took hold and Jess shook her head. "No. Absolutely not."

"Look, I don't want it to be some fluff piece about the top ten things to do during cuffing season or how to 'draft your team.' That's been done."

She couldn't decide which was worse—the idea of writing those stories or the fact that someone already had. "You want me to fake date someone for, what, three months and write about it in my column?"

Donna frowned. "When you say it like that, it sounds sketchy."

"Ya think?" She didn't even try to hide the sarcasm in her voice.

"I'm not saying you have to get any more involved than feels natural. Or even have sex with the person."

She hadn't even considered the sex part—having it or writing about it. "I appreciate the caveat, even if it's mostly covering your ass for HR."

Donna pressed a hand to her chest. "I'm hurt."

Jess gave her a bland look because she very clearly wasn't.

"You've been saying you want to do something immersive."

She had. Maybe not some hard-hitting investigative story, but something meaty. Something that mattered. She loved that her job at Sapphisticate didn't come with the pressures of the twenty-four-hour news cycle, but it sometimes came at the expense of serious journalism. "This isn't exactly what I had in mind."

"This is relevant for our demographic, more so than U-Hauling these days. We need to explore it, get into the perks and pitfalls. And we need to do it smart, fresh, and with heart."

Jess blew out a breath. After more than five years of working together, Donna knew exactly what buttons to push to get her to say yes. "Why me?"

Donna didn't answer right away, leaving Jess to imagine her putting together the perfect compliment about her writing style and authentic voice. Eventually, she lifted a shoulder. "You're single."

Her mouth fell open but she didn't care, didn't bother closing it. Because Donna wasn't kidding. "I don't even know how to respond to that."

"It's not an insult, or a liability even. You can do this, literally, with no strings attached." Donna offered her a wink. "Besides, you might even have a little fun for a change."

She scowled. "I have fun."

That earned her a raised brow. "Teaching aerobics doesn't count as fun."

"Maybe we have different ideas of fun. Besides, barre isn't aerobics." She hated herself for sounding so petulant.

Rather than reply, Donna folded her arms and said nothing. Seconds ticked by.

"My dating life shouldn't be any of your business, you know." Not that Donna made a habit of sticking her nose in inappropriately. It was just that publishing and maintaining the hottest lesbian lifestyle site wasn't a typical office environment. And Jess's column, about the ups and downs of being an up-and-coming—and coincidentally single—professional in her early thirties kind of put her personal life on display. "How in the world am I supposed to do this?"

Donna shrugged. "You don't have to say yes. I'm sure Katie would happily take it on."

Speaking of buttons. Of course Donna would have to go and mention her nemesis. Okay, maybe nemesis was a bit too strong of a word, but it wasn't completely off the mark. Katie was in her mid-twenties, pushy, perky, and pretty much everything Jess found irritating in a colleague. And they didn't even work out of the same office. "I didn't say no."

"I didn't think you would." Donna smiled that smile she saved for when she'd effectively gotten her way. Which, in Jess's experience, was pretty much always.

"You're an evil genius. You know that, right?"

Donna didn't even bat an eye. "But I use my powers for good, so it's okay."

Jess shook her head.

"So, is that a yes?"

She really shouldn't. At least not without thinking it through. Especially whether or not sex would be part of the equation. Oh, and figuring out how the hell she'd go about setting something like this up. And with whom. "Yes."

"Excellent. Do you think you can have your first column ready for next week's posting?"

Fuck. "Um."

Donna lifted a hand. "Just an intro. What cuffing is, how it works, why you want to give it a try."

"I'm guessing 'because my boss told me to' isn't going to fly?"

Donna gave her a bland look.

"Kidding." She was, but also absolutely wasn't.

"You're grumbling now, but you're going to thank me. This is going to turn your column into the must-read for every lesbian on Sapphisticate."

The ego stroke wasn't enough to overcome the uncomfortable pressure in her chest. Unable to sit still, she got up and started to pace Donna's office. "It feels kind of unethical."

"Not at all. It would be if you went in under false pretenses. You're not going to do that."

Well, that was true. She absolutely refused to be dishonest, especially in matters of the heart. "So, I get to do this my way? No well-intentioned meddling?"

Donna made a face like Jess had just insulted her children. "When have I ever?"

She pulled up her mental Told You So file. "What about the cruise?"

Donna winced. "I knew you were going to bring that up. But you have to admit, it made for a great article."

It hadn't been Donna's fault that the five-day jaunt around the Caribbean had included a norovirus outbreak. But since she'd been the one who wound up puking for four of those days, she considered it her prerogative to bring it up anytime it bolstered the point she was trying to make. "Which is easy for you to say. You weren't on the S.S. *Stomach Bug*."

Donna angled her head and smiled. "Hopefully, you'll get some nice cozy dinners out of this one and you'll manage to keep them all down."

She groaned at the memory. She wasn't sure she'd ever been that sick.

"I'll see you in the morning, Archer."

She made to leave but turned back. She bit her lip, hating herself for asking even before the words were out of her mouth. "Are you sure this is going to work?"

"Of course it will. All you have to do is run along and find the right girl."

She opened her mouth to reply, but Donna's phone rang and she was shooed along before a who, what, where, or how could escape her lips. Fuck.

As inclined as she might be to stew—or reassure herself with research or try to write her way out of it—she had a class to teach and just enough time to go home to feed Rascal and change. So she grabbed her bag, shoved her laptop in it, and left.

❖

By the time Jess walked into the gym an hour later, she'd gone from convinced Donna was out of her mind, to thinking the whole idea was kind of genius, and back again. Twice. Each time she nudged herself into thinking she could pull it off, a single reality came crashing down. She couldn't do it alone.

On the heels of that revelation came the prospect of trying to find a suitable candidate. Bars. Apps. Setups by well-meaning but completely incompetent matchmaking friends. She'd survived all three. Not for the sake of a column, of course, but she had a hard time imagining the added layer of complication would make things better rather than worse.

She checked her class list, noting a few familiar names and some newbies, before heading to the barre studio. Inside, she turned on her warmup mix, then pulled out a mat and the props she wanted for the day. She did a mental run-through of each section of class, planning the poses and moves she'd use.

"Hey, gorgeous. Plotting the day's torture?"

She turned to find her roommate, Finn, hovering in the doorway. "Maybe. You going to let me torture you today?"

Without even a second of hesitation, Finn shook her head. "Nope. Fool me once, shame on you. Fool me twice…"

She trailed off rather than finish the adage, making Jess smile. "Come on, you're in excellent shape. You said so yourself."

"Yeah, and my ass hurt for four days. So, no, thank you."

Much like the guys who wandered into her class, expecting something fluffy they could coast through while ogling women, Finn had agreed to give it a try. Well, not the ogling part. Finn was classier than that. But she hadn't stopped complaining about it since. "Baby."

"Yup."

"At least you're honest."

Finn nodded affably. "I try. You okay? You looked like you were in need of a punching bag when I walked by."

She let out a sound somewhere between a sigh and a growl. "Just a weird day at work."

Finn came the rest of the way into the studio. "Oh, no. Trouble at L Word Denver?"

Despite the funk, Finn's nickname for Sapphisticate made her smile. "My boss wants me to write about cuffing."

Finn grinned. "Kinky."

"Not that kind of cuffing."

"Wait. There's another kind?"

She explained the newfangled version, leaving out the fact that she'd only learned about it herself a few hours prior. "And I let Donna talk me into it even though it's got disaster written all over it."

Finn frowned. "I'm confused. So, you meet someone, start dating, but both agree going in it's only going to last until spring?"

"I think so? I mean, I'm not sure everyone does. Some people probably just jump into a relationship and then break it off when the weather turns nice and they want their freedom back. I'm obviously not going to do that." She straightened her shoulders. "I have some integrity."

Finn nodded slowly, more like she knew better than to argue rather than agreed. "Right. So, who are you going to do this cuffing with?"

She lifted her chin and made a show of looking Finn up and down. "You interested?"

Finn went from teasing and a little smug to deer in the headlights in about two seconds flat. "Uh…"

"Kidding. I love you, but I don't want to date you."

Finn smiled. "We know each other too well to put up with each other's shit."

"Exactly." Although she'd been the one to suggest it, she was happy Finn wasn't interested. Talk about complicated. "Would you consider cuffing with someone else?"

"No way. If I have to suffer through another date, I want it to be the start of something serious."

"Huh. Okay. Well, good for you." She wasn't there yet but didn't begrudge any of her friends who were.

"It's only good if I can find the right girl."

Before she could answer, the first of her students trickled in. Finn offered a playful salute and went on her way. Jess greeted her regulars, introduced herself to newcomers, and tried to get in the mindset of teaching class.

But as warmup gave way to arms, arms to thighs and seat, and seat to core, Donna's words echoed in her mind. Ironically similar to Finn's plight. *All you have to do is find the girl.* Easier said than done, if her overall track record with dating was anything to go on. Just the prospect filled her with a dull but persistent dread.

Dread or not, she'd said yes. And so whatever teasing she'd lay on Finn, she was kind of in the same boat. Well, not quite the same. She wasn't looking for Ms. Right, after all. What she needed was a viable Ms. Right Now. Preferably one she could stand spending time with for the next three or four months.

Chapter Two

W hat is all over your face? Chocolate?" Cody hoped it was chocolate while her mind scrolled through the other possible options. She scooped Ben up and hugged him anyway. "Missed you."

"We made cookies," Ben said triumphantly. "Oatmeal chocolate chip. I got to add the chocolate chips."

"Do I want to know how many you ate in the process?"

Ben's brow furrowed. "Probably not."

"Hey, Cody." Amelia poked her head out of the kitchen and waved an oven mitt. "I'm about to take the last batch out of the oven. Come on in."

"You've got to try one, Mom," Ben said, wiggling out of her arms and tugging her to the kitchen.

"Excellent timing." Amelia, who'd recently broken her foot in a car accident, leaned on one of her crutches and slid a warm cookie off the sheet onto Cody's outstretched palm.

"This is where I should say we're supposed to have dinner before dessert." Cody took a bite and didn't hold back a moan.

"Told you she'd be impressed." Amelia winked at Ben. "You can come help me bake anytime."

Ben's chest puffed up and Cody again thanked the universe that Amelia's number had appeared on her phone when it did. She'd been in dire need of a babysitter for a last-minute meeting with her department chair that afternoon and none of her usual sitters were available. Thankfully, Amelia had instantly volunteered. Cody had been so relieved she forgot to ask why Amelia had called in the first place.

"Can I have another one?" Ben eyed the platter Amelia was busy filling and looked hopefully at Cody.

"That'd be your third," Amelia said. "Maybe dinner first?"

"Good idea. And since I'm going to want another cookie after dinner too, we better think of something healthy." Cody bumped Ben's shoulder with her hip. "What are you making me for dinner?"

"Hmm. Healthy." Ben pressed his index finger against his chin. "How healthy are we talking?"

Cody laughed. He'd not only managed to mimic her thinking pose but also phrased the question exactly as she would have. "I'm thinking cheesy broccoli and chicken nuggets."

"We had that three days ago."

"You know, for a five-year-old, you have a really good memory. But why can you never remember where you left your shoes?"

"If you want a night off cooking, I've got leftover chili in the fridge and there's plenty for all of us," Amelia offered.

Ben started nodding before Amelia even finished. "Please can we stay, Mom?"

"You're picking chili over cheesy broccoli?" Cody asked, her voice full of mock disbelief. Chili happened to be his favorite.

"It'll be nice to have company." Amelia hefted her casted foot in the air and made a sour face. "With this thing, I've been stuck here at Nana's and my social life has basically consisted of Nana and Percy."

"What about Veronica?" Amelia's accident had actually been crashing the U-Haul she'd been driving to move in with her girlfriend. The accident, and the requisite time off work, was the main reason Amelia had been able to watch Ben at three in the afternoon, and Cody felt a pang of guilt at not visiting her sooner.

Amelia made a face of frustration laced with resignation. "She's in New York."

"Ah." From her calculations, Veronica would have had plenty of time to hightail it back to Denver by now. But it wasn't her place to say so.

"For work."

"Sure."

"Can I go play with my LEGOs until dinner?" Ben asked, clearly bored of the grown-up conversation.

One nod from Cody and Ben tore off to the living room.

"He's such an easy kid," Amelia said. "I want ten just like him."

"Wait till you've had one. You might change that number." As much as Cody loved Ben, parenting was more work than she'd ever imagined, especially solo. One was definitely enough. "Speaking of, how are things with Veronica?"

Cody had met Amelia's new girlfriend shortly after they got together, and the next thing she'd heard, they were talking about moving in together and researching sperm donors. As much as she wanted to be happy for Amelia, Cody couldn't help thinking Veronica seemed all wrong for her.

"She's been so busy with her work in New York we haven't had much time to talk. Honestly, I've seen more of Finn in the last week than Veronica."

"Finn?"

"You know, the paramedic."

"How could I forget?" Finn, the paramedic who'd taken Amelia to the hospital after the crash and then showed up to visit her, too. "Does she have a crush on you?"

"No, no," Amelia said quickly. "We're only friends. But Finn's been great visiting me and she and Nana have become friends."

"Of course they have." Edith, Amelia's grandmother, was a spitfire.

"That's actually why I called you this afternoon. Finn's working a Halloween festival at the fire station this weekend. I thought Ben would like it."

"And you need to borrow a kid or you'll feel weird showing up just to see Finn?" She made her expression playful so Amelia wouldn't take it the wrong way.

Amelia's blush said everything. "Maybe it's a bad idea."

"How about the three of us go? Ben would love it and I have no plans. Besides, I want to see this knight in a shining ambulance who's wooing you."

"Not wooing. Friends. Like you and me." Amelia waved the spatula in her hand to make her point. "She's keeping me company while Veronica's busy. That's all."

"Yeah, but we're friends because we tried dating and realized it didn't work for us. You said this paramedic was hot, right?"

"I'm going to ignore the suggestion that I can't be friends with someone I'm attracted to because it's ridiculous." Amelia cleared her throat. "And now I'm skillfully changing the subject. How's work? How'd the meeting with your department chair go?"

"Ugh."

Amelia laughed. "That well?"

"Ralston's this old guy who should have retired ten years ago. He doesn't think women belong in the sciences and I know he'd rather I didn't get tenure."

"Did he say that?"

"Not in so many words. What he said was, quote, 'somehow you've managed to publish a few decent papers.' For the record, I've published seven and all in good journals. My student reviews are solid. Tenure should be a done deal."

"But it's not?"

Cody lifted a shoulder. "Ralston doesn't like me."

"What about that big grant you got?"

"Ralston doesn't think I should be the one in charge. He doesn't think a woman should be running a lab with a million-dollar NSF grant. And he made some comment today about how my priorities should be taking care of Ben."

"Seriously?"

"Said he'd understand if I wanted to step back and take care of my parenting responsibilities." Cody glanced to the living room where Ben had set up his LEGOs on the coffee table. He was happily constructing something that resembled a yellow pterodactyl. "One of the other chemistry professors told me Ralston said it'd be better if I were married."

Amelia cocked her head. "He does know you're a lesbian, right?"

"I don't make any secret of it. Which may be part of the problem." Not that who she liked made any difference considering she hadn't gone on a date in years.

"And this Ralston guy gets to decide your tenure?"

"Technically, the tenure and promotion committee makes a recommendation to the president of the university and the board of trustees and they make the final call. But Ralston could do a lot to sabotage things for me. He has to summarize my whole file and recommend me for tenure. Or not."

"That's crazy. I had no idea." Amelia had gone to the fridge, but she paused, not opening the door. "Isn't the president of your college a lesbian?"

"Yeah. Why?"

"You need to make friends. Go around your department chair and get on her good side."

Cody shook her head. "It's not that easy."

"Because Dr. Cordelia M. Dawson has her hands full with that spanking new million-dollar NSF grant not to mention raising a son? Or because making friends is hard?"

Cordelia might be her legal name, but she didn't let many people get away with calling her that. Amelia was only doing it to get a rise out of her now. "I don't have time to make friends."

"Of course you don't, but this is important. You're a genuinely nice person who deserves—"

"I'm not going to make friends to get what I've already earned. My work should stand on its own. I want to be judged on that, regardless of being a single parent or a lesbian."

"You do realize how sweet and naive that sounds, right? And you know who would probably agree with you? The president of your college. But I bet you haven't taken the time to even introduce yourself."

"She knows who I am. I think." Reality was, the president likely wouldn't be able to recall her name if pressed. She was one junior faculty member out of several hundred.

"You need to talk to her. There has to be some way. Could you schedule a meeting with her?"

"There is this dinner thing I have to go to at her house in a couple of weeks…" Cody shook her head, not believing she was even considering the plan. "It's for grant recipients and faculty who have won awards. Things that make the university look good."

"Perfect. All you need is a date." Amelia flashed a smile. "Know any cute single women?"

"You said I only needed to talk to her. Why do I need a date?"

"Because. You aren't going to walk up to the president of the university and whine that you're being treated unfairly."

"I don't get what that has to do with me bringing a date."

Amelia let out an exasperated huff. "You've got to finesse the situation. As soon as the president sees you with a woman, she'll want to know more about you. Let's be real, there aren't that many of us out there. She'll ask around and find out you're up for tenure. Then she'll find out how cool you are and all these things you've done. Or she'll introduce herself to you at this dinner and you can get chummy."

"I don't do chummy." Her stomach clenched just thinking about socializing with President Toller.

"Which is why you need a date. Or, even better, a girlfriend."

"Between teaching, running a lab, and taking care of Ben, I barely have time to sleep. You think I can swing a girlfriend? Exactly when?" Cody slumped into one of the chairs at the table. "Besides, I'm not the world's most eligible bachelor. I'm a thirty-five-year-old divorced single parent."

"Who is smart and good-looking. A pain in the ass and stubborn as shit, but some people are into that." When Cody didn't respond to the dig, Amelia hobbled over to the table and sat down. "Hey. I know you're doing everything you can. And you're doing an awesome job, with Ben and with your work. But wouldn't it be nice if you didn't have to worry about this tenure thing on top of everything else? Finding a date won't be that hard. There are apps for everything."

"A fake date seems ethically wrong."

"So be upfront about it. You'd be surprised how many women would be up for a random hot night out."

"With me?" Cody held out her arms.

"Whatever. You turn heads all the time. Not that you'd ever notice because you're too busy being busy."

The last comment hit Cody more than anything else. She met Amelia's gaze. "I'd like to be less busy someday."

"Would getting tenure help?"

"It'd be one less stress." A big one.

"Then bring a date to the president's house. And think about getting a girlfriend. You know what they say about all work and no play."

❖

Cody unlatched Ben's seat belt and lifted him out of the booster seat. His head dropped onto her shoulder, but he didn't make a sound. Still, she didn't quite believe he was asleep. "You're getting too heavy for me to carry."

"You're strong," he murmured. "You'll always be able to carry me."

She chuckled. "Not always."

Cody fished for her keys, balancing Ben in one arm and her laptop case in the other. No one greeted them when they came in. That still bothered her, though it'd been years since her dog, Evie, had passed. More than once she'd thought of getting a dog for Ben. Well, for Ben and for her. But her excuse was the same as for everything else. No time.

She headed up the stairs, not bothering to turn on the lights. The old staircase creaked reliably on the fourth step, as if to cue Ben's sleepy yawn. He snuggled closer in the hollow of her neck.

"I want oatmeal cookies for breakfast tomorrow."

"Not gonna happen, buddy."

"Why not?"

"Because they're for dessert." She toed open his door and laid him gently on the bed. He tugged a blanket over himself and she decided not to hassle him about pajamas. At least she'd managed to get him to brush his teeth with a spare toothbrush Amelia had.

"Amelia has cookies for breakfast. She said so."

"Well, she's a grown-up. She can make those choices."

"You're a grown-up. You could make those choices, too. I like oatmeal cookies." Another yawn.

"Well, I like you, but I'm not eating you for breakfast." She settled on the edge of the bed and tucked Ben's teddy bear next to his pillow.

"You don't like me. You love me," Ben said, his voice getting groggier with sleep.

"Turns out, I can like and love you."

"I like and love oatmeal cookies."

"Still no." Cody brushed a fingertip over Ben's forehead, pushing a few curls that had fallen forward back into place. He had

Anastasia's hair. Blond ringlets. His curls were a shade lighter than hers and softer. Silky like angel hair, at least when he was freshly bathed. Which he wasn't tonight.

"Tell me a story."

"It's late."

"Please?" His blue eyes closed. "I want to hear about the Granuches again."

"The Granuches? I thought you said they were scary."

"You're scared of them. I'm not." Ben held out his hand, palm up. Cody clasped it. Sticky fingers that needed to be washed gave hers a gentle squeeze. "Granuches are only an inch tall, Mom. Besides they're only pretend."

"Did you know they're completely green? All the way from their heads to their tiny little toes. Even their tongues are green."

Ben nodded knowingly.

"Did you hear about the trouble they got into last night?"

"No." He yawned again. "Tell me."

Cody didn't have to tell a long story. Ben was softly snoring in five minutes. She eased her hand out of his grip, kissed the top of his head, and tiptoed to the door. Before she made it out of the room, her phone buzzed.

"Hello?" She answered only when she'd made it to the hallway and Ben's door was closed.

"Professor Dawson?"

By the tremor in his voice, Cody knew it was one of the new students she'd added to the lab at the start of the quarter. "Yep. What is it?"

"It's Rashad. Sorry to call so late, but I can't figure out how to turn off the spectrometer. I did all the steps Keith told me to do, but it isn't working. The light keeps blinking. Maria didn't answer when I tried calling her. I didn't know who else to call."

"It's fine, Rashad. Just leave it on. I'll check it first thing tomorrow. Sometimes it's a little glitchy. You probably did everything right." She'd inherited the spectrometer from the retiring professor she'd replaced and fully intended on upgrading it—as soon as the grant money was in her account. "You're there late. You okay locking up?"

"Yes, ma'am. I mean Professor."

"It's okay to call me Cody. Everyone in the lab does."

"Okay, Professor. Sorry. Cody. And thanks." Rashad paused. "Also, I wanted to say that I really appreciate you giving me a chance. Never thought I'd be working in a lab this cool my sophomore year."

"I'm happy to have you on my team. And you earned the spot. See you at the lab meeting tomorrow."

When the line clicked, Cody leaned against the doorway. Despite the long hours and all the stress, she wouldn't trade her job for the world. Mostly because of kids like Rashad who made it about so much more than atmospheric chemistry. And as soon as she got tenure, she could stop worrying about losing everything she'd worked for.

Amelia's advice filtered to the front of her thoughts. If bringing a date to the grant recipient dinner put her in good favor with the president, maybe the inconvenience and time would be worth it. And a girlfriend wouldn't be awful even if she had no time to spare. Maybe she could find someone equally busy…

But she had Ben to think about. She hadn't dated anyone since Anastasia left three years ago. Every other time she considered dating again, she told herself it was too soon. Too soon for him to get attached and have them leave all over again. But how long was she planning on waiting?

Chapter Three

Jess stood back and studied the booth she and Finn had just finished setting up for the annual Halloween festival at the local fire station. "I think we're good."

Finn spread her arms. "Of course we are. We've run the best ring toss operation in town three years going."

"We certainly have." Finn had started volunteering at the festival because, as a paramedic, she had so many firefighter friends. She'd roped Jess in one year when her partner bailed at the last minute and Jess had been coming ever since. One, because cider donuts were her weakness. Two, because kids in costumes made her smile and they hardly got any trick-or-treaters at the apartment.

She came back into the booth and adjusted a few of the bottles while Finn started making tidy stacks of rings. "How's Operation Handcuffed? Any takers yet?"

Jess glowered. "It's cuffing, not handcuffed. And I'm pretty sure you know that."

Finn shrugged. "You might get more readers if you call it handcuffed."

"It's not that kind of story." Though she did have her share of fantasies about handcuffs. Or rope. Or any other manner of bondage. But she wasn't about to tell Finn that. Finn would tease her mercilessly and Donna would have her reporting on location from a sex dungeon.

"Fine, fine. How's the story you're really writing?"

She rolled her eyes and groaned. "I don't want to talk about it."

"Second thoughts?"

She'd not resorted to the apps—yet—but her other attempts, including putting feelers out to friends and going to a bar with a couple of her colleagues, had been beyond disappointing. "If by second thoughts you mean fear of a complete crash and burn on takeoff, then yes."

Finn cringed. "That bad?"

"When did I get so terrible at dating?"

That got her a look of sympathy and a pat on the shoulder. "You're not bad at it. You just haven't found the right person."

"Well, I'd settle for anything in the vicinity. I'm running out of time and Donna is—"

"She's here."

"Who? Donna?" Even as she said it, she realized it made no sense. Donna had kids, but even if she had somehow wandered into this festival, Finn had no idea what she looked like.

"Amelia."

"Oh." They'd discussed Amelia at length—Finn playing hero at the hospital, how beautiful Amelia was, the unlikely friendship Finn was developing with Amelia's grandmother. Oh, and the fact that Amelia had a girlfriend.

"Dark brown hair, red sweater, clunky boot on her right foot."

Jess found her in the crowd. Not to mention the gorgeous woman she appeared to be with. "Pretty. Who's the hottie with her? The girlfriend?"

Finn shook her head. "I don't know but definitely not the girlfriend."

"How do you know?"

"The girlfriend isn't nearly that butch." Finn squinted. "And I know she doesn't have a kid."

Which meant the kid probably belonged to whoever Amelia was with. Jess sighed. Too bad. Well, not too bad. She liked kids well enough. But a kid meant the mystery butch was probably married, or at least in a relationship. Which all made perfect sense, since she seemed to be attracted to women who were unavailable, unsuitable, or both.

"What?"

The question broke into her mental kvetching. "Nothing. Are you going to go talk to her?"

Finn shook her head. "Not yet. I don't want to seem too eager."

Jess gave her an elbow to the ribs. "Even though you are."

"I'm not eager. I'm…"

When Finn didn't immediately finish the sentence, she happily filled in, "eager."

"You're no help," Finn grumbled.

She glanced in the direction Finn now refused to look. "Sure I am. I'm going to tell you Amelia is coming this way instead of letting her sneak up on you."

"She is?"

"Mm-hmm. And your face? One hundred percent eager."

"Okay, I'm going to go talk to her." Finn glanced down like she was double-checking her appearance and groaned. "Why did I let you talk me into dressing up like a banana again?"

"Because it's cute. And it complements my pineapple." She struck a pose, trailing one hand up the brown tights covering her legs and using the other to accentuate the pointy top perched on her head. "Obviously."

Finn rolled her eyes. "Obviously."

"Besides, I didn't think either of us would be doing any flirting."

"Mm-hmm." Finn ducked out of the booth and met Amelia halfway.

Jess allowed herself one more appreciative glance at Amelia's friend and turned her attention to the kids who'd gathered, asking them about their costumes and handing over stack after stack of rings to toss. She clapped and congratulated, gave out coloring books, and picked up the dozens that landed on the ground. And then she did it all over again. Finn might have laughed at their fruit-themed costumes, but at least they were loose and a little stretchy for all this bending. Even if she hadn't taught barre that morning, she'd be getting her workout.

Finn returned with news Amelia and her friends were going to have lunch then come over. Jess teased her, mostly to distract herself from asking questions about the mystery woman. But Finn volunteered details anyway, probably to make herself seem slightly less obsessed with Amelia. Her name was Cody—which instantly made Jess want to know if it was a nickname or short for something or what—and she was a high school friend of Amelia's and her son's name was Ben.

"I didn't see a ring, though, so who knows what the deal is."

She narrowed her eyes, wondering if Finn was trying to insinuate something. But before she could ask, or elbow her again, their booth got swamped by a group that identified themselves as Brownie Troop #833. She gave them her attention and, honest to God, didn't think about Cody again until she looked up and found Cody smiling right at her.

She hated those lines about throats going dry and being at a loss for words, but that's exactly what happened to her. Something about the smile, paired with those blue eyes and that perfect, rugged but preppy jeans-and-flannel package struck every chord she had. It was all she could do to manage a casual, "Hello."

"Hi. We hear you have the best coloring books at the festival."

She nodded and tried to shift her attention to the kid. "We do. Especially for big red dogs."

He made a face. "I wanted to be Clifford but I'm hot."

She could empathize. "It is a lot of fur. What's your name when you aren't Clifford?"

"Ben."

"Well, it's very nice to meet you, Ben. I'm Jess." She held out a stack of rings. "Would you like to give it a try?"

He lifted a shoulder and seemed reticent.

"Go on, buddy." Cody put a hand on his shoulder, then made eye contact with her. "He's just a little tired. It's been a full day."

It sounded like maybe there was more to it than too much stimulation from the festival, but it certainly wasn't her place to presume or ask. She leaned in and whispered loudly. "If you don't want to, it's okay. You can still have a coloring book."

The idea that he didn't have to—or maybe didn't have to do it well—seemed to perk him up. "No, I wanna."

"Go for it." She handed him the rings and he started tossing them with more intense focus than she'd have expected.

Cody smiled at her again. "Thank you. I'm Cody by the way."

She resisted saying she already knew and extended a hand. "Jess."

"Nice to meet you, Jess."

She wanted to ask so many questions—what Cody did, if she was married, if she might be interested in grabbing a drink later—but held her tongue. If she was going to get to know anyone right now, it needed to be a candidate for the Cuffing Chronicles. And Cody definitely wasn't that.

Ben didn't ring any bottles, but Jess gave him his coloring book as promised, which he accepted with a polite "thank you." He studied it for about half a second before handing it to Cody in exchange for the cup of cider she'd been holding. Since Finn and Amelia were still chatting away, she racked her brain for something to say. She usually had an easy time with kids, but Cody left her flustered and a little annoyed with herself for always wanting things she couldn't have.

She'd just settled on asking if Clifford was Ben's favorite book character when Ben spilled the nearly full cup of cider all over himself. He didn't say anything, but his eyes got huge and instantly filled with tears. Since Cody stood behind him, it took a second for her to realize what had happened. But then she sprang into action like only a parent can.

"Oh, buddy. It's okay."

"But. My. Costume." Each word was punctuated with a choppy intake of breath.

Jess snagged the roll of paper towels tucked under the booth. "Here. Start with these."

Cody accepted them and started wiping the floor. Jess hurried around to join them. "I'll do that. You take care of him."

"Get it off." Ben started tugging at his costume and his voice took on an air of desperation.

To her credit, Cody didn't seem fazed. "We will. Just give me a second."

"The bathrooms are over behind the bounce house." Then, without really thinking, she added, "I can show you."

"You don't have to—"

"I don't mind." She tossed the sopping paper towels in a nearby can and gave Ben an encouraging smile. "Come on, Ben. This way."

Ben sniffed, looked to Cody, and they both followed her.

"It's a good thing you aren't really Clifford or we might have to take the hose to you."

He didn't laugh, but she was pretty sure he cracked at least a hint of a smile.

At the bathrooms, Cody and Ben disappeared inside. She hovered for a moment, wanting to be helpful, but not sure how. But then she decided hovering made her look too attentive—or maybe too invested—so she headed back to the booth.

Finn had her hands full with a gaggle of princesses and Jedis, leaving Amelia off to the side. Amelia was ostensibly watching the kids, but Jess caught her sneaking peeks at Finn. She stepped back into the booth and took a ticket from a taco with purple-framed glasses, handing over a set of rings.

"Did you two make out all right? I know those bathrooms can be tricky." Finn's eyebrow waggle lacked even the premise of subtlety.

"Whatever. I was being nice."

"Uh-huh. Come back to my place kind of nice, maybe."

"Jesus, Finn. She has a kid. Who was right there. I wasn't trying to pick her up."

Finn lifted both hands in defense. "If you say so."

She rolled her eyes. "Go talk to Amelia. I got this."

Finn frowned. "I already talked to her."

"Well, go talk some more. She's standing over there by herself pretending not to look at you."

"She is?" Finn's eyes darted in Amelia's direction, but quickly returned.

"Oh, my God. Go."

The cajoling worked and Finn ducked out once again. Jess returned her attention to her customers, handing out coloring books and puzzle games whether they managed to technically win or not. She tried—and failed—to keep her gaze from wandering to where Finn and Amelia stood, and in the direction of the bathrooms. It wasn't long before Cody and Ben rejoined them, with Ben looking much happier in jeans and T-shirt than he had in his costume. Cody glanced her way and totally caught her looking.

"Fu—or the win!" She threw her hands in the air, celebrating the fact that she managed not to swear more than the ring that landed over a bottle in the middle row.

The mom of the ballerina in question raised a brow but didn't say anything. Jess handed over two coloring books and blew out a breath. Close call.

"Thanks again for your help earlier."

She'd been so busy congratulating herself, she'd missed Cody come right up to her. She let out a yelp—not a cute and girly one, either—and barely resisted a facepalm.

"Sorry." Cody offered a sheepish smile that somehow made her even more attractive.

"No, no. I'm sorry. My mind wandered." And Cody absolutely didn't need to know where.

"Happens to me all the time."

Cody was likely just saying that to be nice, but at this point, she'd take it. "Everything turn out okay?"

Despite the mundanity of the question, Cody smiled. "Yes. He picked out that costume, but I think it was much hotter and itchier than he bargained for. After I assured him it could be washed in time for trick-or-treating later, he was happy to take it off."

"The best costumes are always the least fun to wear."

Cody made a show of looking her up and down. "Are they now?"

Somehow, she'd lost track of the fact that she was dressed as a giant pineapple. Any illusions she had about Cody taking her seriously, much less finding her attractive, went out the window. She patted the puffy front. "This one is surprisingly comfortable."

Cody nodded, her expression serious. "Good to know."

Now aware of how ridiculous she must look, it was all she could do not to tug at the fleece or adjust the spiky hat affixed to her head with bobby pins. "I mean, it's no banana."

The reference to Finn's costume got Cody to chuckle. "But what is, really?"

"Exactly."

"So, um, anyway. We're heading out. I just wanted to say thanks again for earlier."

"It was nothing." Only another case of not thinking before speaking and accidentally inserting herself into a situation that wasn't hers to begin with.

"We could have found the bathrooms, but you managed to distract Ben. I'm pretty sure you singlehandedly prevented a complete meltdown."

She had enough experience with nieces and nephews to know—and appreciate—what Cody meant. "Well, then I change my answer to you're welcome."

"Good. We'll maybe see you around sometime?"

She had no idea when or how that might happen, but she liked the idea of it. If Cody was as close to Amelia as she was to Finn, maybe it wasn't so outlandish after all. Finn might argue otherwise, but she was smitten. And from what she'd seen of Amelia, the feeling was mutual. "That would be great."

"Good luck with the rest of the day. I hope you make it out of your costume before it loses its charm."

There was nothing suggestive about the comment, but that didn't stop her from imagining what it might be like to have Cody undress her. Not from her current outfit, of course, but more generally. And vice versa. Christ, what was wrong with her? She cleared her throat and, with it, the very un-PG images from her brain. "Thanks."

Cody offered a wave and headed over to where Finn seemed to be entertaining Ben with a dancing banana bit. Despite the Finn and Amelia thing, it was entirely possible she'd never see Cody again. Which was maybe for the best, all things considered. But as they walked away, Ben and Cody holding hands, all she could manage to feel was disappointed.

Chapter Four

Technically, the Atmospheric Dynamics class could have gone worse. It also could have gone much better, and of course, it was the one time Ralston picked to review Cody's class. As soon as she'd seen him slip in to back of the lecture hall, his expression dour as always, she'd lost her train of thought. "Traces of mercury have been found in...uh..."

Dammit. Cody knew the subject matter as well as the order of spoons and knives in her silverware drawer. And it was important stuff. Every other time she'd taught the course, she'd nailed the lecture and had the students clambering to stop air pollution before it was too late. But this time most of the faces shining back at her looked sleepy. Worse, some looked truly confused. One kid was even snoring.

Everyone had clearly partied too hard that weekend to pay attention to anything but their navel at eight in the morning. And on the Monday after Halloween, what did she expect? Ralston left before the class was over which was fortunate because for the first time, no one stayed late to ask questions.

Cody gathered her things and flipped off the lights, thinking a walk might clear her head. For better or worse, she had twenty minutes free before her lab meeting. She stepped out into the sunshine and took a deep breath of the crisp fall air. At least it was a gorgeous morning.

"Jess?"

The woman froze midway up the stairs. For a moment, Cody worried she was wrong. Why would Jess—the pineapple woman from the ring toss—be on her campus?

"Cody?"

Cody nodded, moving out of the doorway as a student hurried past. "You look different. I almost wasn't sure it was you."

"Without the pineapple topper?" Jess cocked an eyebrow and then smiled. "Turns out I do wear ordinary clothes sometimes."

These were ordinary clothes? Cody did her best not to outright ogle, but Jess in *ordinary clothes* was breathtaking. Everything from the heels up commanded attention—black tights, stylish short skirt, and a snug sweater all accentuating a trim figure and sexy curves. Her auburn hair fell in soft curls past her shoulders, and if Cody let her eyes linger a moment longer, she'd be spellbound. Had she really flirted with this woman? Fortunately, Jess probably hadn't realized she'd been trying to flirt. With Ben as a distraction, it wasn't like she'd been that overt.

"Do you teach here?"

Cody closed her mouth, realizing she'd let it hang open as she'd appraised Jess. She managed a nod and then added, "Do you? I've never seen you on campus before."

"No. I'm here to interview President Toller." Jess reached into her purse and pulled out a card. "I'm a journalist—well, it's one of my jobs anyway. I'm doing a piece on local women in leadership."

"President Toller is amazing." Cody eyed the card. She wished she could say that she recognized the site name, or even better had read one of Jess's articles, but the only things she read lately were picture books with Ben and academic journals. She planned to change that now. "Can't wait to read your article."

Jess nodded at the card. "Actually, that card's for Sapphisticate, my main job. This piece will be in the *Denver Voice*."

"Well, I'll make sure to look up both."

Jess nodded. She bit her lip like she was thinking of saying more and then thought better of it. "I should let you go. You seemed to be in a hurry when you were coming out."

"I was only in a hurry to get outside," Cody admitted. "But you've got an interview with the president. I don't want you to be late."

Jess glanced at her watch. "I've got ten minutes. I like to be early."

"Were you meeting her in Platt Hall?" Cody couldn't recall the last time she'd seen President Toller inside the earth sciences building. Although she was an outspoken supporter of the sciences, she rarely made an appearance on the north end of campus.

Jess's eyebrows bunched together. "Platt? I thought this was Emporium Hall. The president's office is in Emporium, right?"

"Well, yeah, but Emporium's clear on the other side of campus."

"Shit. You're sure?" Jess shook her head. "Of course you're sure. I'm terrible with maps. And sorry for swearing, but I hate being late."

Cody hitched up her messenger bag. "You're fine. I work with college students not kindergartners. You should hear what they say when they fail my exams." She stepped past Jess. "Come on. If you want to make it on time, we've got to hustle."

"You're taking me there?" Jess started after Cody.

"I could give you directions, but it's kind of tricky and if you thought that was Emporium Hall"—Cody thumbed at the building behind them—"I think you need my help."

"Thanks." Jess quickened her pace. "Should we run?"

"Maybe. But then we'd get there all sweaty and out of breath."

"Not the best look for an important meeting. But wouldn't be the first time." Jess cussed again. "I really hate maps. I've never been good with spatial things. I'm way better with oral."

Cody barely resisted the urge to laugh.

Jess slammed to a stop. "I can't believe I said that. Verbal. I meant verbal not oral. You know like how some people are visual learners and others are verbal?"

"I got it. Verbal not oral." Cody cleared her throat. She most definitely did not need to think about Jess's oral skills at the moment. "We really should hurry."

"Right." Jess broke into a half jog. "How far?"

"I'd guess about a half mile. But we don't have to run. You're in heels."

"I can run in heels. Left or right?"

The path ahead split, carving out a space for the North Pavilion. In the spring, it was one of the favored gathering places for the students to sunbathe and throw frisbees, but this morning only a handful of students stood around chatting. "Left."

Both ways got to Emporium Hall but the path to the right went in front of one of the cafés and was always crowded between classes. Besides, the path on the left was lined with an assortment of elm, ash, and maple, all in varying degrees of fall colors. The leaves were stunning, and if Cody wanted to show off the scenic side of the campus, this was it. Not that Jess was in any position to pay attention to the sights. She had a panicky look on her face, suggesting chitchatting wasn't going to happen.

Even if they had time for a leisurely walk, Jess would probably want to talk about something more hip than pretty foliage. Cody wondered what normal single people talked about. It'd been so long since she'd gone on a date that she couldn't think of what topic she'd even bring up. Kids and work weren't likely to kindle any flames, and that was literally her entire world.

Jess started to veer to the left when the path split again and without thinking, Cody reached out and caught her hand. "We go right this time." She let go of Jess as soon as her body gave her a reality check. Grabbing a beautiful woman's hand was a bad idea if she wanted to retain her cognitive abilities in the near future.

"Are we close?"

"Well, closer." The campus was spread out between city streets which complicated getting anywhere in a hurry. "We have to cross the main road and then it's about three more blocks."

"Three blocks? How did I screw up the directions that much?"

"I'm honestly not sure. Maybe you had the map upside down?" They'd reached the intersection and had to stop to wait for the light.

"That was a rhetorical question."

"I know. But I was trying to make you feel better. And I didn't think I should bring up the thing about your oral skills again."

Jess laughed. "Thanks. You know, ordinarily, I'd have some snarky comeback, but I can't think of anything right now because I'm too worried about being late."

"In my experience, President Toller typically runs about twenty minutes late for her appointments."

Jess eyed her watch again and grimaced. "I'm never late. It was the damn map."

"We all have things we're not good at. Could be worse. You could be good at visual but bad at oral."

"I meant verbal." Jess laughed again. "Oh well. That's what I get for trying to impress anyone at nine in the morning."

"Who were you trying to impress?" Cody realized the answer as soon as the words left her mouth. She felt her cheeks get hot. "Oh."

"At least you're the one blushing."

If Cody had been at all suave, she would have said something about how Jess had already impressed her at the Halloween festival. Not only had she managed hordes of screaming kids at the ring toss, she'd sported a pineapple costume like a pro. And she'd been amazing with Ben. But when Jess gave her a knowing smile that was equal parts sweet and sexy, she couldn't think of anything to say.

The light changed and Jess hopped off the curb. Cody caught the blur of a bicyclist hurtling toward Jess and immediately yanked her back. The bike hung a right, narrowly missing Jess, and then sped out of sight.

Without missing a beat, Jess shook her fist in the air and let out a string of curse words.

"I don't think he can hear you." Cody's heart was still racing, however. The cyclist had been flying and she didn't want to think of what might have happened if her adrenaline hadn't kicked in.

Red-faced, Jess turned to her. "He didn't even look my way. He nearly killed me."

"Total asshole. I hope he gets a flat tire."

Jess's expression softened. She looked as if she might laugh. "That's your best curse? A flat tire?"

"I'm not very good with curses," Cody admitted. "And I've got a five-year-old. I'm kind of out of practice with the swearing thing. Asshole was a big step."

"Well, good job then. I'm sorry I overreacted. I got scared."

"You didn't overreact. That was a close call. On the bright side, I'm convinced you know all the swear words the college kids use." Cody tried a smile. "And in a fight, my money's totally on you."

"Now you're just trying to make me feel better." Jess puffed out a breath. "It's working. Thank you for saving me, by the way." She glanced at the light which had changed back to a flashing red hand. "Dammit, I'm gonna be so late."

"I know a shortcut. It doesn't smell good, but we can cut through the alley where they keep the dumpsters."

Even if Cody had been feeling brave enough to ask Jess out, she didn't get the chance. They'd arrived at the president's office with one minute to spare. Jess turned to her, breathed out a thank you, and then disappeared inside. Cody wanted an excuse to follow her but had no reason to be at Emporium Hall at nine thirty on a Monday morning. And she had a lab meeting to run.

The rest of the day flew by and she couldn't help her good mood. Even Ben asked why she was smiling so much when she'd picked him up from school. She'd told him it was because of the surprise she had planned for dessert—brownies she'd picked up on a whim—but mostly it was because of the fifteen minutes she'd had with Jess. And now, twelve hours later, Jess was even more on her mind.

Cody opened her laptop and pulled up the website printed on Jess's business card. She scrolled past message boards and articles until she found a picture of Jess and a listing of all her posts. The top post under her name was "The Cuffing Chronicles" and without thinking about the subject, Cody clicked on it.

About halfway down the page, meaning sank in. She stopped reading and pushed back in her chair. Cuffing had nothing to do with handcuffs and Jess was looking for a date. Not a girlfriend but a short-term fling. In fact, Jess had spelled out a convincing argument for why long-term relationships were overrated and Cody agreed on every point.

So why did she feel so disappointed? *Because.* For a moment she'd entertained the idea of asking Jess out. She realized how dumb that was now. Jess might have flirted, and her hand might have felt incredibly good to hold, but she was smart, pretty, and clearly too cool for Cody.

Cody closed her laptop and rubbed her face. The day's exhaustion settled in and she decided against the hour of grading she'd planned to do that night. She picked up Jess's business card and considered tossing it. That's what she should do. Forget their chance meeting on campus, un-bookmark Sapphisticate, and go back to thinking her life was full and she was happy enough.

One thing she knew for sure was she couldn't put Ben through a fling. He'd already gone through a divorce with one parent moving halfway across the country. She didn't need his little heart to get trampled again.

But was she really going to wait until he was in high school to date again?

No. That was too long. If she'd learned anything from meeting Jess, it was that her libido might have gone dormant, but it hadn't died altogether. Waiting until Ben was a teenager who could understand things like dating might seem like a good idea, but she wanted to get laid now. Or at least soon. As crass as that might be, it was the truth. She didn't want to wait ten years to enjoy the company of a woman. The flirting, the long conversations that weren't about work or kids, the hand-holding...

Suddenly it hit her—she could date without telling Ben. He was only five, after all. She was so used to being open with him that she hadn't considered not, but she could introduce someone like Jess as only a friend. And friends come and go. He knew that. One of his classmates had already moved away only two months into kindergarten.

Someone like Jess? Or could she actually ask Jess out?

Without stopping to think about it, she reached for her phone and tapped in the number from the business card. The line rang three times and Cody nearly hung up. Then voice mail picked up and she steadied her breath.

"Hey. This is Cody. You know, the one who sucks at cursing?" She felt her throat tighten and decided to get right to the point before her courage failed. "So, I, uh, read your article about cuffing and I was wondering if you'd found anyone yet. To cuff with, or whatever you call it. I'm not sure I'd be what you're looking for and there's some limiting conditions on my end that we'd need to discuss but...wow... okay, this is weird. Probably what I should say is that it was nice seeing you again and I'm sorry about that bicycle almost hitting you. Hope you got over the shock and your meeting with President Toller went okay." She took a deep breath. "And, yeah, I was wondering if you'd like to go out on a date with me. This Thursday. At six. Anyway. I thought it might work since you want to date someone for your article and I kind of need a date." Cody closed her eyes wishing she could take back her last sentence. "Can you tell I don't do this very often?"

Yes, Jess would be able to tell that she didn't call women up very often. Or at all. She managed to blunder through a good-bye and hang up, then stood and paced the room. Maybe she'd have a date to the grant recipient dinner after all. Or maybe she'd managed to sound like a complete idiot. Either way, at least she could tell Amelia she'd tried.

Chapter Five

Jess stared at her phone screen, narrowing her eyes and willing it to tell her what to do. When it didn't, she tapped the play button to listen to Cody's message for the tenth or so time. She could practically mouth the words along with Cody, a fact that made her feel obsessive and not in a good way. This was ridiculous. She was ridiculous.

She'd been obsessing since first hearing the message last night. She'd played it for Finn, who tried to be supportive but mostly focused on the fact that Cody was a friend of Amelia's. In other words, no help. She listened to it before bed and again when she woke up, then twice in the car.

In so many ways, it was perfect. And yet. What?

Part of it was that last statement, the one about Cody needing a date. Given her own situation, it shouldn't bother her. Maybe it was just curiosity. Wedding of an ex? That was literally the only thing she could think of. Which would be fine, right? Uncomfortable, perhaps, but it would make for a great column.

Jess sighed. No, it wasn't really that. It was Cody's mention of issues, which had to be code for the fact that she was a single parent. She at once hesitated over that and hated herself for hesitating.

She stood, sending her desk chair rolling clear out of her station and into Silpa's. When it bumped—barely—into the corner of her desk, Silpa scowled. "Hey."

Jess lifted both hands. "Sorry."

Silpa rolled her eyes and shook her head before returning her attention to her computer. She glanced at Frida, whose desk faced hers, and cringed. Frida pressed her lips together, but her eyes were laughing. Silpa took her work, and herself, very seriously. She was pretty sure Silpa resented the fact that her magazine—the *Mile High Business Journal*—had deigned to share office space, HR, and IT support with Sapphisticate, leading to many jokes with Frida about being the lesbian hussies in the cubicle next door. Only the open concept floorplan meant they had to share one big space, leaving Silpa with nary a wall or door of her own.

Her phone buzzed and she snagged it, knowing Cody would unlikely message her again until she replied, but having that thought nonetheless. What she found was an IM from Frida. *She had to waste nine seconds of her workday thanks to you and your unruly desk chair. How dare you?* Then, *Hussy.*

She let out a snort and typed back *Wheeled chair, don't care* before heading across the large open area where the writers worked to Donna's office. When she got there, Donna was on the phone. She paced around a bit, listened to Cody's message one more time, and checked her calendar. Unfortunately, the last hour had not brought a break in the time/space continuum and her next cuffing column remained due in six days.

"Archer, get in here."

Donna's voice made her jump and she scurried to the doorway. "Good morning."

"Good morning, indeed. Have you checked the traffic stats on your column? They're up twenty percent from your usual views."

She hadn't checked. She'd been too busy fretting over what the second installation would hold. Oh, and attempting to write a serious article on homophobia in hiring practices. But Donna loved stats and so she nodded. "I hadn't but that's great to hear."

"Have you found your target yet? Time's a ticking."

"About that." She stepped the rest of the way into the office. "I may have, but I have some reservations."

"Are they dinner reservations?" Donna chortled at her own joke before looking at her expectantly.

"Not yet, but they could be. I had a woman ask me out."

"And? What's the problem? Not smart enough for you? Too femme?"

Even if she'd be inclined to take offense, Donna's assessment of her preferences were spot-on. "She's a college professor, so I'm pretty sure she's smarter than me. And she's definitely my type."

Donna threw both hands in the air. "Then what the hell is the problem? Don't tell me you're getting squeamish."

Jess blew out a breath. "She has a kid."

Donna blinked a couple of times. "So?"

"So, that makes things more complicated."

"She's the one who asked you out. She's obviously interested in dating. Are you afraid she wants something serious?"

She should have known Donna would be stingy in the sympathy department. "She's actually read the column, so she knows what she'd be getting into."

"She didn't email you from the site, did she? That's the one thing that I might give you a pass on. We love our readers, but we don't want to *love our readers*." Instead of another chuckle, she tipped her head back and forth and shifted her shoulders suggestively.

It helped to know Donna had some boundaries, even if they didn't help her in this situation. "No, no. Nothing like that. I met her in a perfectly natural way."

Well, aside from the pineapple costume, perhaps. But Donna didn't need that detail. Or just how lost she'd gotten herself at the university, for an assignment not even for Sapphisticate.

"So, I'll ask again. What's the problem?"

For all her fretting and handwringing, it hit her there was no problem. If she was going to do this, Cody might be her best bet: smart, attractive, funny, kind. And the complications she mentioned in her message probably had to do with the kid. As long as Cody wasn't looking for a babysitter or a stepmom, Jess could handle a kid. She liked kids. "You know what? Nothing. I'm going to go call her right now."

Donna beamed. "That's the spirit."

"Right. I mean, what's the worst that could happen?"

Donna seemed to take the question to heart before shrugging. "You fall for someone with a kid."

She'd already turned to leave, but Donna's words stopped her fast. "Wait. What?"

Donna gave that nonchalant shrug she usually reserved for springing a big project with a tight deadline. "You fall for her and become a mom way faster than you planned to."

Donna had three kids and she'd carried them all herself. Her column about lesbian parenting was pretty much what launched Sapphisticate. It was hilarious, heartfelt, and brutally honest. She didn't drop hints about becoming a mom lightly. Unlike Jess's mom, who mentioned grandkids at least once every few weeks. "You know that's not on the table, right?"

Another shrug. "When it comes to falling in love, things are never on the table until they are."

"Falling in love isn't on the table, either. You're the one who gave me this assignment. Cuffing. Don't you know how it works?"

"Sorry, sorry." Donna lifted both hands again, more concession than exasperation this time. "You're right."

"Are you saying I shouldn't call her?"

"Oh, you should definitely call her."

She nodded, despite hoping for some concrete reassurance. "Because the whole premise of this is transparency and good boundaries."

"Sure." Donna seemed to be suppressing a smile.

"No?"

"I was thinking more that your next column goes live in less than a week and, unless you're keeping them from me, you don't have a lot of alternatives."

She pinched the bridge of her nose. "You're the worst. You know that, right?"

The insult didn't seem to stick. If anything, Donna seemed to take it as a compliment. "Let's see if you feel the same way when your column becomes more of a must-read than mine."

Before she could even contemplate a response, Donna's phone rang. Probably for the best, given the number of curse words flitting through her mind. She headed back in the direction of her desk, hoping to commiserate with Frida. Only Frida was gone, probably interviewing some hot, newly out pro athlete.

She flopped in her chair, careful to angle herself toward the window and not Silpa's desk. She took out her phone and pulled up her voice mails once more. Her finger hovered over the play icon. There was no point, really. She knew exactly what Cody had—and hadn't—said. She glanced at Silpa, who had earbuds in and a laser focus on her computer screen.

Just a slight shift of her finger to the right and she tapped the call button. Like Donna said, time was ticking and she didn't have a lot of options.

"Cody Dawson."

The terse greeting, paired with Cody's sexier-than-she-remembered voice, had her fumbling. "Um, hi. This is Jess Archer from Sapphisticate." She waited a beat. "And the pineapple costume and the frantic dash across campus."

Cody's laugh managed to put her at ease and just a hair more on edge at the same time. The good kind of edge. The kind that came with flirting. "Hello, Jess Archer."

"I got your message." Why was she nervous? Cody had been awkward as all get-out. That should make this easier.

"So I gathered."

"And I was wondering if you wanted to get together to talk." She hesitated. "About the terms."

"And my—how did I phrase it?—limiting conditions."

Breathe, Jess. Jeez. "Yes, those conditions. We definitely need to discuss those."

"One of them is obviously that I have a kid. I just want to make sure that's not a deal breaker before we go to the trouble of getting together."

Donna's words echoed in her mind. Well, less of an echo and more of a flash, complete with red lights and warning bells. "It's not, though I'd like to get a clear picture of how much he'll be—"

"He won't. If this is some temporary thing, I don't want him getting attached."

"Oh." Why did relief feel so much like disappointment?

"I mean, I'm sure you'll see him, but I'm planning to tell him we're just friends."

"Okay. Yeah." It made sense. And she respected Cody for being protective of him. Which made the arrangement a good thing.

"Sorry. Not the most romantic way to set up a first date."

Despite the scattered state of her thoughts—not to mention feelings—she laughed. "I'm sorry, too. This whole situation is a little strange, to be honest. Not the you part, but the cuffing part. And the writing about it part."

Cody laughed in return. "Thanks. I think."

At least they seemed to be on the same page about it being weird. That—weirdly enough—made her feel better. "So, we should talk more."

"Right. Because you're all about the oral."

She groaned. "Okay, that was not my finest moment."

"I liked that moment, actually. But I shouldn't poke fun. I promise I won't bring it up every time we see each other."

The fact that Cody could poke fun, but that it wasn't her only MO, added a few more points to the plus column in her mind. "I don't mind some teasing, for the record."

"Good to know. Because I do plan on bringing it up at least every other time." Cody paused, but then continued. "Are you a yes to Thursday then?"

"Thursday?"

"I wasn't sure if I should have called it a date. Do we have to work up to that? Or were you just being nice when you said I wasn't part of why this was so weird?"

The date. Right. "No, no. Sorry. I lost track of the question."

"Ah."

"Yes. It's a yes." She grabbed her mouse and toggled to her calendar before Cody could have second thoughts. "Thursday sounds great." And it technically gave her something to write about in the meantime if things went sideways.

Cody cleared her throat. "I don't want to get ahead of myself, but I was wondering if you're also free the following Tuesday evening. I have a work dinner and, I mean, assuming we decide to go ahead with this, I was hoping you'd go with me."

Even as Cody answered one of the questions in her mind, several new ones popped up. Like, what kind of work dinner? And did Cody need a date more than she wanted to go out with Jess specifically? She resisted asking any of them, though. Some things were better discussed in person. And it wasn't like she was in any position to judge why Cody might be looking for an atypical dating arrangement. "I'll pencil it in."

"Thank you." Cody seemed relieved, but also genuinely happy with the answer. "For Thursday, would you prefer to meet somewhere, or should I pick you up?"

She appreciated that Cody asked her preference. "Let's meet. That seems easier."

"And gives you an out in case you decide I'm a weirdo and want to leave."

"Are you a weirdo?" She was mostly teasing. From what she'd seen so far, Cody was anything but. In fact, Cody had so much going for her, she had quite a bit of wiggle room in the weird department for her to even rank.

"It's relative, no?"

She laughed because it was true, but also because having that awareness was typically a decent insurance policy against being too much of one. "Good point."

"Do you know Mahogany in Capitol Hill?"

She did—great food with a casual atmosphere. Another point for Cody. Not that she was keeping score. "One of my favorites."

"So, Thursday at six?"

"Perfect." Was it as easy as that?

"Excellent. We have a date."

Apparently, it was. "I'll see you soon."

"Looking forward to it. Bye."

"Bye." She pulled the phone away from her ear and stared at the screen as though it might reveal something more than the list of her recent voice mail. "Huh."

She wasn't quite sure why the interaction left her sort of surprised. Was it because it had gone so smoothly? Or because, aside from the kid complication, Cody was shaping up to be a much better fake girlfriend prospect than she'd let herself hope for?

Wait. Correction. Temporary, not fake. Anyway.

Definitely one of those things. Because she didn't have lingering reservations about doing this in the first place. Right? Right.

CHAPTER SIX

Cody realized she was tapping her foot and made herself stop. "We're meeting to discuss terms and conditions. I'm guessing it won't take longer than two hours. Less if I say the wrong thing and she pulls out of the deal."

"I thought this was a date." Amelia's brow furrowed. "Sounds more like a business meeting."

"That might be closer to the truth." Cody pulled at her necktie, loosening the knot. "Probably I overdressed."

"Stop fussing. You look good." Amelia gave Cody a disapproving look when she took off the tie. "You look good in a tie."

"I'm not sure what the heck I'm doing. This all seemed like a great idea until about an hour ago." Cody tossed the tie on the counter and glanced at Ben. As soon as they'd gotten to Amelia's— well, technically Edith's—Ben tore off to the kitchen to start on the promised cupcake icing project. He hadn't hesitated to pull up a chair right in front of a bowl of candy and several tubes of frosting.

"Mom! Look! It's a monster with one eye." Ben held up the cupcake he'd slathered in orange frosting. One green M&M dotted the middle. "Can I eat it now?"

"Not yet." Amelia picked out another chocolate cupcake and deftly exchanged the one-eyed monster for a new plain cupcake on a fresh paper plate. "You've got forty-seven more to decorate and we haven't even cracked open the sprinkles."

"Sprinkles?" Ben's face lit up. He looked at Cody, likely anticipating that she'd tell him not to eat the sprinkles straight out of the jar as he was wont to do. "You can go anytime, Mom."

Cody chuckled. "Okay." She walked over to the table and ruffled his curls. "I love you."

"Love you, too. I'm gonna make you a ghost." He reached for the white icing, nodding to himself. "But I won't make it too scary."

"Thanks, buddy." She kissed the top of his head. Already he smelled like a sugar high waiting to hit. "I'll see you in a couple hours. Be good for Miss Amelia."

Amelia followed Cody to the door. "Try to have a little fun." She handed Cody the tie she'd left on the counter. "You look good without it but better with."

Cody hung the tie around her neck but didn't bother tying it. She'd only take it off as soon as she got to her car anyway. "Thanks again for watching Ben."

"You know I love having him. And any excuse to eat cupcakes. Now go be charming. Lesbians everywhere are going to be reading about this tomorrow I'm sure."

"Ugh. Don't remind me."

Parking was notoriously tricky in the neighborhood around the restaurant. Partly it was all the trendy restaurants and shops in Capitol Hill, but there was an Art Walk going on which didn't help matters. Cody started to worry about being late after the fifth loop she made searching for an open spot. She finally found a place, but it was several blocks from the restaurant. "Nothing like a sprint to start out the evening."

Dodging ambling art walkers on the crowded sidewalks proved trickier than anticipated, and she ended up taking a longer route to avoid the main road. As soon as the restaurant came into view, she stopped running, doubled over, and caught her breath. The loose ends of her tie flopped in her face.

"Dammit." She'd forgotten to leave the tie in the car and now she'd have to stuff it in her pocket or actually tie it correctly. In a minute. First, oxygen. She didn't want to show up panting and clammy-palmed from sweating in the brisk air.

"Cody?"

She shot up, the breath she'd just caught now gone from her lungs. "Uh, hi." She tried to slow her breathing, but her pulse was a lost cause. One look at Jess and her heart rate had doubled. How did Jess get more attractive each time they met?

"You all right?"

"Yeah. For sure." Cody cleared her throat. "Would you buy it if I said I wanted a little run before dinner?"

Jess smiled. "No. I'm thinking you couldn't find parking and ended up in the garage over on Sixteenth Street."

"That would have been a good idea. But no. I parked all the way over on York. And I knew you'd be on time."

"I'd have given you a five-minute grace period." Jess reached out and flicked one end of Cody's tie. "Especially if I knew you were tying this."

"Sh-oot. Forgot about that." Cody tugged the tie off her neck and shoved it in her coat pocket. If her cheeks weren't already red from running in the cold, they were certainly crimson now. "So much for starting out suave."

"Shoot? Do you not swear at all?"

"Oh, I have a half-full swear jar back home. I'm trying to get better so I don't have to go to the bank for another roll of quarters. Ben doesn't let me slide."

"I need one of those. But I'd definitely run out of quarters. As far as the suave thing, you haven't blown it. You look good even without the tie. And you were on time." Before she had a chance to respond, Jess gestured to the sign over the restaurant. "Shall we?"

She was happy to be saved from further embarrassment, but as they walked, the reality of being on a date kicked in. She wanted simply to be excited, but she was rusty at the dating game. And Jess clearly wasn't. Cody didn't need to know her history to figure that out. She had a flirty confidence that was as intimidating as it was a turn-on, and one look at her in the leather jacket, knee-length dress, and boots had Cody second-guessing if she could even pull off dinner with someone like her. Not to mention a relationship where everything that happened would likely make it into one of Jess's articles.

If only Jess wasn't quite so hot. And didn't write a weekly column with relationship and other life advice.

The door to the restaurant opened and a boisterous group spilled out, all talking at once. Cody stepped close to Jess to let them pass.

She held her breath, trying to ignore how her body vibrated with the feel of Jess inches from her. But then her mind chose to remind her of how nice it had felt to hold Jess's hand, too. She'd reached for her accidentally as they'd rushed to the president's office, but how would it be to take her hand intentionally?

Once the group had passed, Cody took a step back and faced Jess. "By the way, you look really nice. I wanted to say that as soon as I saw you, but the whole tie thing kind of threw me off track."

"Thank you. Gotta make a good impression on a first date." Jess winked.

Did the wink mean this wasn't a real date? Or was Jess telling her to relax? Cody told herself not to overthink it and reached for the door. She stepped to the side, waiting on Jess. "I'm going for a good second impression."

"Second impression, huh?" Jess looked Cody up and down. It was either a reprimand for thinking she should open doors for Jess or an arousing once-over. Unfortunately, Cody couldn't tell which.

"Third?" She cleared her throat. "Should I not open doors for you?"

"You can if you want." Jess walked past Cody and murmured, "I was thinking about you in a tie. Someday I'd like to see it on you, properly tied."

Properly tied? A hint of Jess's perfume combined with the feel of her brushing close, and Cody couldn't manage any comeback. Instead, all she could think of was what it'd feel like to kiss Jess. Maybe have Jess untie her tie. From there, her imagination jumped to the two of them in bed with the sheets tangled around their legs. She took a deep breath and followed Jess inside, wishing her hormones would give her a break.

A hostess asked about their reservations and promptly showed them to a table. No time for awkward silence but also no chance for Cody to get her head fixed back on her shoulders. How could she be completely unprepared for a basic date and at the same time leaping to the possibility of shucking clothes?

When the hostess left, Jess picked up her menu but set it back down. "Can I ask you something? It's about the column. Well, it's about cuffing anyway. And what we both want out of it."

Cody lowered the menu she'd just picked up. "Okay. Is there a contract or something you want me to sign?"

"No. I don't think we need a contract to date." Jess hesitated. "Unless you think we do? I'm going to be writing about you, but I promise I'll change your name and it'll mostly be about my experience, not your life story or anything like that. In fact, I can omit any details you tell me to."

"Then I think we're good. A contract would be weird."

Jess blew out a breath. "Great."

"What was it you wanted to ask then?"

Their server, Reggie, arrived with a warm greeting and the wine list, and Jess seemed to take the moment to gather her thoughts. Or her courage. She was clearly anxious about something. Which only made Cody more worried about what she wanted to know.

They each ordered a glass of the house red and the server slipped away again. She looked at Jess expectantly. The longer the delay, the more she wondered why she hadn't done any real research on cuffing. She was the one who checked every available review before buying a toaster. And yet she'd gone into this only with the information from the few paragraphs she'd read of Jess's article.

"I don't want to make a big deal out of nothing," Jess said finally.

"I'm better when people are direct."

"Okay." Jess nodded resolutely. "You mentioned limiting conditions in your message. I think we should start with what those are before we get any further. I know you said one part of it was Ben. Which I completely understand. In fact, I want you to tell me more about that so I don't make any mistakes. But I'm wondering about the other conditions. You kind of froze up when I stepped close to you earlier. It occurred to me that you might not be comfortable with this being a physical relationship. Given everything, I'd understand. But if intimacy is something you don't want, you should tell me now."

Jess had seemed to race to get the last few sentences out, and Cody needed a moment to process what she'd said. *Intimacy.* A completely reasonable thing to want to discuss, considering the circumstances, and yet her brain immediately snapped back to the image she'd conjured of Jess in her bed. With no clothes between them. She swallowed, trying to think of an answer that wouldn't make her sound horny. Before tonight, she'd only focused on how convenient it would be if things worked out and she had a date for the president's dinner. "You want to know if I have any problem with sex being part of the arrangement?"

"Basically, yes. I understand if you want this to be platonic because I'll be writing about what happens. Or maybe because of your kid. Or maybe because this is a temporary thing." When Cody didn't volunteer an answer, Jess added, "Or maybe you're Ace? Plenty of people don't like sex and that's fine." She sucked in a breath. "I'm rambling. Feel free to cut in anytime."

"I'm not Ace." Cody fought back a smile. She suddenly felt like the confident one at the table. Maybe she was rusty, but back when she'd had it regularly, she'd been good at sex and didn't figure there'd be any problems getting back on that horse. "But I am enjoying watching you sweat this one a bit."

"You are, aren't you?" The table wasn't big, and Jess had no trouble leaning across it to swat her hand.

Cody laughed. Getting swatted by Jess wasn't a bad thing at all. And she loved that Jess could dole it out as much as she could playfully take it. She held Jess's gaze for a moment, knowing by Jess's coy smile that she wasn't the only one who could feel how the electricity sparked between them.

"The only reason I froze earlier was because I was thinking about what it'd be like with you." She lifted a shoulder. "And then I realized that was inappropriate because this is only our first date."

"Now you tell me."

"I'm not sorry. I like this kind of icebreaker conversation. My two concerns are my kid and my job. Those are my priorities and I need to protect them both."

"Of course. Is there another parent in the equation or…"

She appreciated that Jess didn't make assumptions one way or the other. "Ben has another mom. My ex. His birth mom, actually. But she lives in California and isn't in the picture much."

"Okay." Jess looked like she wanted to ask more but didn't. Or maybe wanted to pass judgment but wasn't sure if she should.

"She realized parenting wasn't for her and neither was living in Colorado." It had become a stock answer, one that didn't paint

Anastasia in the best light but not the worst either. Which was how she tried to think about Anastasia most of the time.

"So she left?"

"I promise she's not a bad person." Cody considered leaving it at that, but one look at Jess's still furrowed brow and she knew more explanation was needed. "She's got a career that's fast-paced and super demanding. It's exciting, and she loves it, but the work's in LA and it doesn't mesh with being a parent—or having a partner with a tenure-track job in Denver. You don't really need to know all of that except it means I have Ben pretty much all the time."

Again, Jess seemed to debate follow up questions but eventually said, "Okay. Thank you for the context."

"I'm okay with you mentioning I have a kid, just nothing identifying about him."

"Of course. Like I said before, I won't mention any personal details. You can even read my column before I submit it each week if you'd like."

Cody shook her head. "That'd be a little too much like reading your journal. I think it's probably better if I don't know what you write from here on in. As long as you promise that no one will suspect it's me, we're fine."

"Well, if you change your mind about that, I won't blame you. I am putting it all online after all." Jess paused. "Also, I completely respect that you're planning to tell Ben we're only friends. If I had a kid, I'd probably do the same."

Cody didn't need that confirmation, but it was nice to hear Jess understood she had to watch out for Ben. Above all else.

"Do you have any questions?"

Plenty. Did Jess like foreplay? What about toys? And how many dates before they discussed an overnight? Cody knew her body was getting ahead of things. As much as she wanted to let loose and enjoy what came, she had to be grounded and make sure whatever happened didn't affect Ben or jeopardize her chance for tenure. "How long does this last? I'm guessing you have an expectation for your article. Does cuffing season have an expiration date?"

"Three months would be ideal. That's my goal anyway."

Cody had to admit the timing would be perfect. She'd know if she got tenure by mid-January. "So, we break up right before Valentine's Day."

"Sounds super romantic, doesn't it?" Jess smirked. "From what I've read, that is actually the most common time for cuffing relationships to end. It seems crazy but…"

"This whole thing is a little crazy."

Jess pursed her lips. "I wouldn't hold you to dating me that whole time if you're not enjoying yourself."

"I didn't mean it that way." Cody scratched her head, trying to figure out how to restate and not dig her hole deeper. She settled on simply being honest. "I'm goal oriented. I can do three months. And the truth is, I could really use a girlfriend for that same amount of time. But what if we like each other at the end of it?"

"That's definitely a risk. Why do you need a girlfriend?"

"I'm up for tenure and my department chair doesn't like the fact that I'm a single parent."

Jess straightened. "Are you kidding? That's bullshit. Not to mention illegal. Did they tell you that directly? You can't discriminate against someone for being a parent. Or for being single."

That Jess had flown right to her defense was sweet. And her obvious will to fight the system made her even sexier. But Cody didn't have the energy, or the time, to fight the system.

"Trust me, I'm not happy about it either. But I can't exactly tell the powers that be to suck it right before my review."

"So, you need a pretend girlfriend?"

"Temporary. Like cuffing."

Jess folded her arms. "Arguably, I'm glad you need me as much as I need you. But that doesn't mean I approve."

"Should I tell you about the work obligation I need a date for next Tuesday?"

"Only if you can make it sound romantic."

"As romantic as cuffing?" Cody chuckled. "You know, I had to reread the first paragraph of your article a few times because I was trying to figure out if cuffing involved handcuffs or some other kind of restraint. At first my response was—wow, Jess writes about BDSM? How cool is that?"

Reggie appeared with their wine. He must have heard the mention of BDSM but skillfully feigned ignorance as he set down their glasses. "Are you two ready to order or would you like a little more time?"

"We need another few minutes, please." Jess didn't miss a beat. "We got a little distracted by each other."

He blushed, stumbled over an apology for interrupting, and promptly walked away.

"You added that distracted bit on purpose, didn't you? To make him squirm."

"Me?" Jess cracked a mischievous smile. "Right about now he's wondering which one of us is going to be tied up. Actually, so am I."

"You're trouble." Cody laughed.

"You say that like it's not happening. I thought you understood what cuffing was about." Jess raised an eyebrow as she reached for her wine. "We should probably decide what we're going to eat before he comes back or we'll really make him uncomfortable."

CHAPTER SEVEN

Jess didn't expect to linger over dinner, exchanging bites of seared steak and chicken marsala, but that's exactly what happened. She didn't expect Cody to suggest they share dessert, either. But when Cody asked how she felt about tarte tatin, she admitted she felt very positively about it and they ordered a slice to share.

"Coffee?" Reggie eyed them warily, perhaps worried they'd start discussing bondage again.

"Decaf for me, please," Cody said.

"I'll have tea if you have anything herbal." Jess tried for a friendly smile.

Reggie nodded. "I'll bring you a selection to choose from."

"Perfect."

Reggie disappeared. Cody folded her arms and leaned forward. "Preference or are you old like me and can't have caffeine this late?"

She offered a single nod. "Yes."

Cody chuckled. "I'm glad I'm not the only one."

"It's pretty much been since college for me. But I don't complain because it means a cup of the real stuff first thing still works its magic." And she seriously needed that magic most mornings.

Cody tipped her head. "That's an excellent point."

"So, morning person or night?"

Their dessert arrived as Cody considered. After thanking Reggie, she said, "Reluctant morning."

Jess laughed. "Doesn't that make you a night person?"

"Not really. I've been a parent for five years, so I've been rocking the morning thing for a while. And since I'm technically still a junior faculty member, I often get the eight a.m. sections. I don't always love it, but I've made peace with being productive first thing. What about you?"

"Definitely night. My job is pretty free and loose when it comes to regular business hours. I mean, I could argue that I'm working right now." The second the words were out of her mouth, she wished she could take them back. Fortunately, Cody didn't seem offended.

"Not a bad gig."

"Not at all." And this particular assignment was shaping up to be much less awful than she'd started to fear. She lifted her cup. "Here's to good gigs and our fake, I mean temporary, relationship."

Cody lifted her cup but paused. "I'm leaning toward thinking of it as a marriage of convenience."

She knew what Cody meant, but couldn't resist raising a brow.

Cody's eyes got huge. "But not a marriage. Just, like, that's a familiar phrase. Concept. Not actually a marriage. Obviously."

"Obviously." She smirked, not quite able to help herself, before tapping the edge of her cup to Cody's and taking a sip of her tea.

"You know," Cody set down her own cup and tapped a finger on the table, "I think it's a good sign we can joke about it. Keeps things light."

Light. Right. Because that's what they'd just spent the better part of two hours agreeing to. "Exactly. And having good rapport will make us more convincing at your work thing."

"Right." Cody's expression turned serious, like maybe she was having second thoughts about that part.

"What? Changing your mind about having me be your plus-one?"

Cody shook her head. "No, not at all. Honestly, I'd been focused on the idea of having a date and sort of dreading it and now I'm thinking how nice it will be to go with someone whose company I enjoy."

She appreciated the honesty, especially since her feelings weren't so different. Those were her predominant feelings, after all. Not what it might feel like to kiss Cody. Or whether Cody's comment about having sex meant they would.

Sex would make her foray into cuffing more authentic, that's for sure. But it might make things a hell of a lot more complicated, too.

No more complicated than Cody having a kid, though. Or the fact that she'd be writing about their dates and posting it online for anyone with an internet connection to see.

Before she went too far down that rabbit hole, Reggie appeared with the check. Cody insisted on paying. She acquiesced, but only after getting Cody to promise they could take turns. As they exited the restaurant, she began to wonder whether they should shake hands or hug. She'd like a kiss but probably that was rushing things. Even for cuffing.

"May I walk you to your car?"

Cody's question pulled her out of the daydream and launched her deeper into it at the same time. "You don't have to do that."

"But we're on a date, aren't we?"

Were they? She'd gone back and forth. Though, they'd just tentatively agreed to spend the next three months in a relationship, so probably better to put it in the date column. "Yes, but we already agreed to do this. You don't have to try to impress me."

Cody gave her a quizzical look. "Do you think that's why I'd offer?"

She resisted scrubbing a hand over her face. She had no desire to admit what that question said about her recent track record when it came to dating. Not to herself and definitely not to Cody. "I just don't want you to feel obligated."

"How about this? I'll feel like an ass if I don't. You don't want me to feel like an ass, do you?"

Jess tapped a finger to her lips. "I do not. Especially since merely saying 'ass' is probably traumatic for you."

Cody grinned. "Exactly."

"All right, then." She hooked a finger in the direction of her car. "I'm that way."

"Right. Because you parked in the garage like a sane person."

This relaxed, charming, just a tiny bit flirty version of Cody was making it harder to think about keeping things platonic. But if they had sex, she'd have to write about it. Ugh. "Well, if I'm being honest, my shoes played into the decision."

Cody glanced down at her heeled boots, but her gaze made the trip back to Jess's eyes more slowly. "I don't see anything wrong with that."

It was the sort of compliment that should have landed and rolled off like water hitting an umbrella. Maybe it would have, if Cody hadn't paired it with that knowing, appreciative look. "That's generous, but I'll take it. Especially since winter is coming and I only sometimes make responsible decisions with regard to footwear."

"You'll be happy to know I'm prepared to provide door-to-door service anytime we go somewhere together."

She felt a smile tug at the corners of her mouth. "I'm not sure I would have pegged you for the chivalrous type."

Cody's shrug seemed almost sheepish. "I wouldn't go that far."

The banter, while flirtier than many first dates she'd been on, felt safer than where her thoughts—not to mention her body—wanted to take her. "You know all I want to do now is ask how far you would go."

The rise of color in Cody's cheeks said more than any words. "I guess we'll have to wait and see, won't we?"

Indeed they would.

The walk wasn't long, but Jess was almost surprised to arrive at her car. Silly, really, since she'd been the one to lead them there. She fished her keys from her purse. "Not to be cliché, but I had a nice time tonight."

"Me, too. Better than I thought I would." Both of Cody's hands came up. "I mean, not that I thought it would be bad. I just figured the negotiation part would be awkward."

She put a hand on Cody's arm. "Don't apologize. I know what you mean because I feel the same."

Cody nodded, her relief evident. "Okay, good."

"So, I'll see you Tuesday?"

Another nod. "Yes. I'm officially looking forward to it. Which is saying something, since these things can be pretty dreadful."

"I think we'll manage to have at least a little fun."

Cody smiled, a genuine smile that brought out little creases at the corners of her eyes. "I think we will."

"Does my door-to-door service kick in for this?"

"I would love to pick you up."

She told herself it was logistically easier more than wanting another display of that chivalry Cody had been reluctant to own. "I'll text you my address."

"Perfect." Cody hesitated for a moment. "I'm glad we bumped into each other."

Cody's tone implied so much more than her words. "I am, too."

She still wanted that kiss, but she wasn't going to be the one to initiate it. Cody didn't move in, but she didn't turn to leave, either. Jess looked down for a second, her way of deferring. The only problem was not knowing whether Cody would pick up on it. Well, that and not knowing whether a lack of response had to do with not picking up on it or not wanting to.

But when she looked up, Cody's eyes were steady on hers. And before Jess could decide what to do, Cody leaned in and placed a kiss on her cheek. It lingered just long enough to make it clear Cody would have happily kissed her for real. It was, she realized, the perfect compromise.

"Have a good night," Cody said.

She nodded, buying time for her brain to string together words. "You, too." Okay, not a reply that should have taken conscious effort. But despite the tameness of the kiss, her pulse raced and her skin tingled.

Since she was in danger of standing there with a goofy look on her face all night, she clicked the fob to unlock her car. Cody reached for the door before she had a chance. She slid into the driver's seat, letting Cody close her in with yet another of those weak-in-the-knees smiles.

Because Cody was standing right there, she didn't indulge in sitting and staring out the windshield like she might have otherwise. She fastened her seat belt and offered a friendly wave, then headed home. When she pulled into her usual spot next to her building, she cut the engine but didn't get out right away.

Huh.

She was going to have to come up with a hell of a lot more than that for her column, but for now, that's pretty much what she had.

"'What started out as a business meeting ended with a touch of chivalry and at least one of us wishing for a good night kiss. Not bad for a first date of any ilk. We're off to the races, dear readers. Consider this girl cuffed for the season.'" Donna looked up from her screen, beaming. "It's a triumph, Jess. An absolute triumph."

She wasn't prepared, as Cody would say, to go that far, but she'd been pleased with the column. She'd managed to find that elusive balance between cheeky and heartfelt which, in the case of this particular assignment, felt essential. "I'm glad you're pleased with it."

"Pleased? The column hasn't been live twenty-four hours and you've already surpassed the pageviews of your intro piece. I think we need to talk about moving some of your content behind the paywall."

She knew it was a compliment, even if she had mixed feelings about restricted access to her work. Not that her writing was some hard-hitting news the public deserved access to. She'd given up notions of doing that kind of work. "I don't know."

"Not the whole column, of course. I'm thinking bonus content. Personal details. That sort of thing."

It was a typical model for their site and others like it. Providing enough material for free to bring in and maintain an audience but offering a paid premium subscription with exclusive articles and stories. Often, they offered extended versions of pieces on the public side of the site—celebrity interviews, the real-life experiences behind Donna's column.

Jess's column was popular, but not that popular.

"You don't have to be PG behind the paywall." Donna wagged her eyebrows with about as much subtlety as a cartoon character.

Oh, God. "Uh."

"I'm not saying you have to, at least not yet. But think about it. Try writing a supplement to your next installment and let's see how it goes. It doesn't have to be racy."

Donna would never force her to do something she was truly uncomfortable with, but she could be all sorts of persuasive when it came to gray areas. Like this whole cuffing experiment to begin with. "I will. Think about it, that is."

Donna offered a decisive nod and returned her attention to her computer, basically ending the conversation. Jess returned to her desk and considered putting the finishing touches on her non-cuffing piece for the week. It wasn't due for a couple of days, though. And she had her second date with Cody that night. Maybe a little noodling instead.

She opened the folder in her Dropbox labeled "Cuffing" and created a new document. But instead of starting to type, she toggled over to the web browser she'd minimized earlier and pulled up her first installment. She closed her eyes, took a deep breath, and scrolled down to the comments.

It wasn't that she never read the comments on her columns. Okay, it was. People were crushingly free with their opinions on the internet, even after the site's filters scrubbed out the trolls. And even if nice comments outnumbered the mean ones, it was invariably the mean ones that stuck. Especially when it came to writing about her personal life.

She opened one eye, then the other. Skimming first, then doubling back to read more thoroughly.

Huh.

She didn't like to think of herself as easily dumbfounded, but once again, this project left her at a loss for words. People were into it. Sure, there were some naysayers and curmudgeons thrown in, but for the most part people were fascinated, amused, and encouraging.

She set her elbow on her desk and propped her chin on her fist. Donna's compliments—uncharacteristically gushing—echoed in her mind. Cody's comment about wondering what it would be like if they slept together joined in. And the memory of her body humming the entire drive home after Cody's arguably platonic kiss.

Maybe this would turn into a mess of epic proportions. Or maybe, just maybe, it would work out after all.

Chapter Eight

I had no idea you and Jess were together. She's lovely."
President Toller—Gillian—abruptly switched the subject
from Cody's research with a nod in Jess's direction.

"She is lovely." While that was certainly true, together might
be a stretch. Still, Cody couldn't correct the assumption. Technically,
they were dating—if only temporarily. Did that count as together?

Maybe the fine print didn't matter this time. Jess seemed to be
enjoying herself anyway. At the moment, she was animatedly chatting
with the president's wife, Shannon, and either she genuinely liked
dinner parties or she was good at faking it. Either way, Cody was
impressed.

Jess's social skills weren't the only thing that was easy to admire.
For the past hour, Cody had alternated between hoping Jess might
truly be into her for more than business reasons, and then thinking
someone so charismatic and beautiful couldn't possibly see anything
in her. Every time she looked at Jess, she felt a rush. With her hair
down and her black cocktail dress hugging her figure, she was truly
a knockout.

"I think Shannon may have made a new best friend. I can only
imagine what plans those two will come up with for the four of us."
Gillian clinked her glass against Cody's. "We better forge an alliance
now."

"They do seem to be scheming." Shannon had leaned in to
whisper something to Jess and when she pulled back, both looked
over at Cody and Gillian.

"I love it." Gillian lowered her voice and added, "Shannon has to suffer through more than her fair share of boring social events as the wife of the president. It's nice to see her truly enjoying herself at one, instead of pretending to be interested in one of the old faculty member's grumblings about grading or their teaching load."

"Grievances about grading don't make for the most titillating conversation."

"Exactly." Gillian sighed. "But it's all part of my job. I don't think she realized what she was in for when we got together. Between fundraising events, entertaining speakers, hosting the Board of Trustees, and"—she waved her hand at the gathering in the living room—"the odd faculty dinner, we have an engagement twice a week at least."

"I'd die."

Gillian laughed. "Trust me, I have moments when I think I might. You wouldn't believe how dull it can be at times. I've secretly wished one of the faculty banquets could be held at a dance club. Maybe with a drag show."

"Even I'd come then."

Gillian laughed again. "I don't see you often at faculty dinners. I assume it's the single parent thing?"

"Uh..." Cody scrambled. Was an apology in order? Clearly, Gillian had done some research on her guests for the evening. Earlier, she'd brought up the work Cody's lab was doing, and even asked good questions about the grant. None of that was a shock. But had she also kept tabs on Cody's social appearances—or lack thereof? And she knew Cody was a single parent?

Gillian touched Cody's arm. "I don't mean to call you out. I'm sure you have even less free time than I do. It's amazing to me how much you've accomplished given that you have a little one. Although he's probably not that little anymore. How old is Ben now?"

Cody tried to hide her surprise that Gillian knew her kid's name. "Five. Well, five and three-quarters according to him."

Gillian smiled. "It's good to be precise. I'm not going to add the three-quarters to my age, however. Jess seems like the type of person who'd be a magnet for little kids. I bet Ben loves her."

Before she could think of what to say, Shannon and Jess walked over. Shannon said something to Gillian and then motioned to one of the caterers as Jess subtly linked Cody's arm with hers.

"Doing okay over here?" Jess asked quietly.

"Mm-hmm." She had to steady her breathing when Jess's fingers played on her forearm.

Jess tilted her head as if not quite believing the answer. "You sure?"

"I'm not the best at these things." Whispering probably wasn't necessary considering Shannon and Gillian were chatting with the chef, but Cody didn't raise her voice.

"So far, you're doing just fine. I'll tell you later what Shannon said to me." Jess squeezed Cody's arm in the crook of hers. "Oh, and we may have to talk about our 'how we met' story to get everything right."

"Does that mean I can't tell everyone you were dressed as a pineapple when I first saw you?"

Jess rolled her eyes. "You would want to hold on to that one detail."

"It makes for a good story. Plus, you were a sexy pineapple."

"We'll talk about it."

Gillian rang a little bell to get the group's attention. "If everyone would please move to the dining room, the chef's informed me that dinner is ready."

Gillian led the way to the dining room, but Cody noticed Shannon surreptitiously moving place cards before the others entered the room. With the switch, she'd ensured Jess was on one side of her and Cody was directly opposite by Gillian. If making herself known to the president was Cody's only goal, the evening could be over. But as she sat down and Jess smiled across the table at her, she realized how much she didn't want it to be over.

"Well, that went better than expected." Cody unlocked the car and opened the passenger door.

Jess raised a brow. She rested a hand on the edge of the door but didn't get in. "Wasn't too dreadful to spend the evening with me?"

"As it turns out, no." Cody laughed, more relaxed and happier than she'd been in a long time. The wine probably didn't hurt, but she'd only had one glass. Mostly, it was Jess. Being around her made everything feel more exciting. With one flirty look, Jess awakened desires she'd given up for lost. But it wasn't only the arousal part. It was as if she'd walked into a room with extra oxygen. She wanted to take a deep breath and not leave any time soon.

"Good." Jess seemed to take her answer at face value, but Cody wanted to give her more.

"To be honest, I've been looking forward to seeing you so much that I've had trouble focusing on anything else." Not a lie. Her daydreaming about Jess had almost been a big problem. She'd nearly deleted two months of data on the ambient oxidized mercury project because she'd been so distracted. "What I wasn't looking forward to was a stuffy dinner with the president."

"Gillian's not stuffy. Neither is her wife."

"I know. I was wrong."

"Hmm." Jess brushed her hand down Cody's tie. "I like someone who can admit when they're wrong. And can rock a tie."

Cody held her breath when Jess took a step closer instead of getting in the car.

"You look nervous all of a sudden."

"I suddenly am." She looked at her shoes and chuckled. "I don't know why."

When she raised her eyes to Jess, she wanted to kiss her more than anything. Her heart raced, egging her on, but she didn't make a move and Jess only held her gaze. The heat between their bodies ratcheted up. She was almost certain a kiss would be welcome. On the second date, people kissed. She knew the rule. But she'd been somehow transported back to her high school self and dumb insecurities about kissing skills piled on top of the persistent question of whether Jess was truly into her. Was this all an act for the article?

"Should we talk about why you're nervous?" Jess gave Cody's tie a subtle tug.

"No. I'll get over it. Don't worry." She tried a smile.

Jess's eyes narrowed. "You're one of those strong silent types, aren't you?"

"That depends. Will you give me a pass if I say yes?"

Jess rocked her head side to side. "Only because I'm in a good mood." She let go of Cody's tie and shifted back a step. "Just don't think I'll always let you off so easy."

"Noted." Cody wanted to kick herself. As soon as Jess stepped back, the window of opportunity on a kiss had closed. What was wrong with her? "Tonight was nice. Thank you for saying yes."

"Thank you for inviting me. I quite enjoyed myself." Jess mimicked Cody's formal tone.

"Does that mean I might get another date with you?" Despite their agreement, nothing felt certain. Jess could find someone more capable, and easily more experienced. Hell, she couldn't even manage a kiss at the right time.

"I hope so. Maybe something chill?" Jess smoothed the skirt of her dress. "As much as I love an excuse to wear something nice, it'd be even better to just hang out."

"How does a movie sound?"

"Sounds nice. Your place?"

Cody hesitated. "Ben will be there."

"Right." Jess nodded slowly. "Do you never have friends over?"

"Well, Amelia has come over a few times. And my buddy Paul comes over with his son, Luke, but that's more of a playdate for the kids."

"So, grown-ups don't get playdates?"

"Well, I suppose they could." Sooner or later, she'd have to face this hurdle and she knew Ben would rather not have a sitter. "Actually, it'd be great if you're really up for it. Most of the time he's in bed by eight anyway."

"Perfect. I promise to be on my best behavior with the swearing thing."

"I'll loan you quarters."

"Then it's settled. Grown-up playdate at your place." Jess paused. "Shannon told me I'd snagged the city's most eligible butch. Did you know you had a reputation?"

"You've got to be joking."

Jess laughed and shook her head. "I'm completely not. She was gushing about you. It's a good thing she's married or I might have to worry about the competition. Oh, and I promised her that I'd convince you to go to the annual fall faculty banquet."

"You did?"

"I thought it'd be a good thing. You know, because of your work and wanting to make a good impression." Jess frowned. "If you don't want to go, I only told her that I'd see what I could do."

"The banquet's next week." The banquet always fell around midterms and Cody never understood why no one had thought to change it to a better time. Then again, the faculty that went probably gave multiple choice exams and had their TAs do the grading.

"Too soon?"

"I'm gonna be slammed with grading. It's midterms."

Jess's brow furrowed. "Well, we could make a quick appearance and then you can teach me how to grade sciencey exams."

"I wouldn't put anyone through that. But making an appearance is probably a good idea."

Jess smiled. "I'm full of them. I also wouldn't mind another excuse to see you dressed up."

Cody chuckled. "Does that mean I have to wear a tie again?"

"A tie would be a good decision for multiple reasons." Jess glanced at the car and then back at Cody. "You still nervous? I'm not above talking about the weather while I wait for you to kiss me."

Cody couldn't hold back her smile. "Please, anything but the weather."

Jess was undaunted. "It's a lovely evening for mid-November, isn't it? Unseasonably warm."

"I'm actually not nervous anymore." In fact, her body zinged with happy anticipation.

"What are you waiting for then?"

Cody would have laughed again, but the look in Jess's eyes stopped her. Simple, unapologetic desire. Cody swallowed. No more waiting. No second-guessing.

She reached for Jess's hand and a flare shot through her. God, it'd been too long since she'd kissed someone. Really kissed.

One step and she closed the distance between them. Jess's lips met hers and Cody's breath slipped away. She fell into the kiss, wondering how it was she'd held herself back from something so nice for so long. The supple warmth, the call and answer—all of it familiar and as comforting as it was arousing.

But there was something new in kissing Jess. Something she hadn't felt with Anastasia or the half dozen women who'd come before her. A challenge. When Jess parted her lips, she yielded while at the same time daring Cody to go further. And her hunger kept pace with Cody's. She couldn't get enough.

A staggering desire to satisfy her every want swept over Cody. Jess definitely wasn't acting. That question was almost laughable now. Cody touched the warm smooth skin at Jess's neck, then slid her hand through her hair to pull her in deeper. She didn't want to stop kissing. Could she take Jess home? Would it be crazy to suggest that? Her hormones argued that she had nothing to lose as Jess's tongue danced against hers.

Then she registered a ringing. Distant, at first, but insistent. With a start, she realized her phone was not only ringing but vibrating in her pocket. That meant only one thing. Ben's babysitter. She broke away from Jess's lips and scrambled to answer before the call went to voice mail.

"I'm so sorry to interrupt your dinner."

"It's fine, Trevor. What's wrong?" Cody's stomach turned at the distress in his voice.

"Ben said he had a stomachache when he went to bed. I didn't think it was anything more than maybe too much Halloween candy, but he woke up twenty minutes ago crying for you. I don't think he has a fever, but he won't stop crying. I didn't want to bother you, but—"

"It's okay. Tell him I'll be home in a half hour. In the meantime, can you read him the book on his nightstand? He'll calm down as soon as you start reading."

"Thank you." Trevor's relief made Cody's heart ache even more. Not only was he one of Ben's favorite people, he'd been the usual babysitter for two years now. If Trevor couldn't console him, there definitely was a problem.

Cody hung up and turned to Jess. "That was terrible timing for a phone call. I'm sorry."

"Ben's sick?"

"Hopefully it's only too much Halloween candy. I've been parceling it out slowly, but I forgot to mention that to his babysitter." She sighed. "I really wanted to suggest a way that we could continue things."

"Maybe it's better if we take things slow." Jess's lips turned up in a tentative smile. "That was some first kiss."

"Yeah. I'm a little shaky."

Jess laughed. "You're shaky? I think my knees gave out halfway in." Her smile widened. "You need to get home to your sick kid. I'll call a rideshare so you don't have to worry about dropping me off."

"No way. Not even up for debate. If I was really worried, I'd take you home with me and you'd have to deal with a sick kid on our second date. But I'm not that worried." Cody pointed to the passenger seat. "Get in." At Jess's raised eyebrow, Cody added, "Please. We could argue but it would only take more time and I'd win."

Jess got in and Cody went around to the driver's side. She turned on the car but could tell Jess was waiting to say something. "What?"

"Strong, silent, and stubborn?"

Cody pulled out of the parking place. "Pretty much. You might as well know now."

"Then you might as well know that I'm only going to put up with one of those three," Jess returned. "And I do have a preference on which."

"Stubborn?"

"Wrong." Jess stared out her window.

"Silent?"

"Wrong again."

"In that case, I think I better work on my bench presses." Cody tried for a charming smile.

"I felt your arms. I think it's more the emotional growth you need to work on."

"Ouch." But she laughed.

They crossed through the center of town, the trees already aglow with holiday lights, and pulled onto the highway. The feel of Jess's lips lingered on Cody's mouth, and despite Trevor's call, and the worry about Ben, her body still thrummed with desire. "You know sometimes stubborn can be a good thing."

"Considering the way you kiss, I have no doubt."

Jess kept her gaze trained out the window, but her words lit through Cody. There was nothing sexy about dealing with a sick kid and that was her reality tonight. But some evening she intended to show Jess all the benefits of a stubborn lover.

Chapter Nine

J ess emerged from her room to find Finn on the sofa with the television on. Rascal looked up but didn't move from her spot pressed against Finn's leg. Since she didn't need to leave for half an hour, she joined Finn, flopping unceremoniously onto the couch. "I didn't even hear you come in."

"You were in the shower. I was going to get in right after you, but I haven't managed to get up." She looked pointedly at the dog, who merely raised one eyebrow then the other.

"Resistance is futile."

Finn chuckled before looking her up and down. "Don't you have a date tonight?"

"Yes, but it's a stay-in movie date."

Finn's eyebrow wag was more suggestive but decidedly less charming than Rascal's. "All the more reason to show a little skin."

"Ben is going to be there. I'm not going to dress like I want to have sex when a five-year-old is going to be present."

Finn angled her head. "Does that mean you aren't wearing sexy underwear even?"

They'd been friends and lived together long enough for Finn to get away with saying things like that. Still. "That's none of your business."

"I knew it." Finn pointed at her for extra effect. "You're hoping for a little nooky after the kid goes to bed."

She'd certainly entertained the possibility. Even as she'd put on jeans and a relatively innocuous sweater, she hadn't been able to quash the optimism of something sexy underneath. "No comment."

Finn folded her arms. "That pretty much answers my question, you know."

"For the record, I wear silky and lacy things because they make me feel good." Which was true, if not the entirety of the truth.

"And you also have sports bras and granny panties. I live with you. I've seen your laundry."

She rolled her eyes. "Has anyone ever told you that you act like an annoying little brother instead of a grown woman sometimes?"

Finn shrugged. "Just you."

She reached over Rascal and gave Finn's shoulder a shove. "Jerk."

"Wait. Toni called me a teenage boy the other day when I got half a dozen donuts for breakfast. Does that count?" Finn lifted a finger. "Though I'd like to point out I was prepared to share. It's not my fault she only eats healthy crap."

Jess pressed her lips together but didn't try too hard to hide the smile. "It's a good thing I love you."

"I love you, too. And I hope you get to make out, at least, especially after the kissus interruptus last time." Finn hefted herself up, much to Rascal's chagrin. "And maybe get to second base."

"You're such a child," Jess said to Finn's back as she headed in the direction of the bathroom. It was a retort on principle though, because really, she hoped she did, too.

Just thinking about it conjured the kiss she and Cody shared after the dinner at the president's house. Three days had passed, but it took virtually no effort to feel Cody's mouth on hers—hot, skilled, and full of pent-up wanting. Even with the interruption, it was the best kiss she'd had in as long as she could remember. The prospect of a repeat—and maybe more—had her skin tingling and other parts of her, well, also tingling.

She checked her watch again. Between talking to Finn and fantasizing about Cody's mouth, she'd managed to kill twenty minutes. She hoisted herself off the couch and pulled on her coat and boots, trying not to think about how much she'd like to kiss Cody, and more, without interruption.

❖

Jess balanced the pizza box in one hand and used the other to ring the bell. Even through the door, she could make out the sound of running feet. The door swung open, but no one stood in front of her. At least no one at eye level.

"Hi, Miss Jess." What Ben lacked in height, he made up for in enthusiasm.

"Hi, Ben. It's good to see you again."

Ben continued to smile but let out a sigh. "I thought you might be dressed as a pineapple again, but Mom said you probably only wore that for Halloween."

"Your mom is pretty smart. Most of us grown-ups only get to wear fun costumes on Halloween."

He shook his head, disappointment evident. "When I'm a grown-up, I'm going to wear whatever I want."

Before she had the chance to ask him what that might be, Cody appeared, looking gorgeous but also slightly disheveled and out of breath. "Sorry. We were just, um, tidying before you got here."

She smirked, unable to resist. "I hate to say it, but I'm afraid your hair didn't get the memo."

Ben looked up at Cody and giggled while Cody frantically combed her hair with her fingers. Then she blew out a breath and shook her head. "Since the ship of impressing you has sailed, why don't you come on in?"

"I wouldn't say that." She stepped into the entryway and handed Cody the box. "You make it sound like I'm difficult to impress or something."

Cody frowned. "I'm sorry. I didn't mean—"

"No, I'm sorry. It's just that you're cute when you're flustered, and I couldn't pass up the chance to tease you." She gave Cody a wink before reaching down to unzip her boots.

"You're welcome to take your shoes off, but you don't have to," Cody said, still holding the pizza.

She eyed both Ben's and Cody's sock-clad feet. "It's wet out. Besides, I wore fun socks."

"You did? What kind of fun socks?" Ben stared at her feet with rapt attention.

"How about we let our guest take off her boots and coat and get comfortable before we discuss her socks?" Cody nodded to a coat rack behind the door. "Feel free to hang your coat there."

"Thanks." Jess set her boots next to a pair of bright green galoshes and hung her coat next to Cody's black North Face windbreaker. "It's starting to feel like winter out there."

Cody shook her head. "Don't say that. I'm not ready."

"I don't disagree, but I think there were flurries mixed in with the drizzle."

"Snow! Snow! I love snow!" Ben danced around to his made-up tune.

Cody ruffled his hair. "It's not going to make Christmas come any sooner."

Jess shook her head. "I'm with you, buddy. I love the snow."

Cody made a show of sighing. "Outnumbered already. I should have known. Well, at least you brought dinner. Thank you for that, by the way."

"I literally passed the place on my way here. Happy to."

"And you really won't let me give you any money?"

She let out a sigh that mirrored Cody's from a moment before. "I really won't. Besides, if this is my turn, I'm getting off cheap."

Cody looked to be on the verge of a clever comeback, but Ben asked if they could eat already because he was starving. They headed to the kitchen, where the table was set with two regular plates and a Cookie Monster one. She made a joke about being excited to get the Cookie Monster plate and Ben asserted it was his, but that he'd share.

They lit into the pizza and the conversation that ensued reminded Jess of spending time with her nieces and nephews. Her pizza socks were a hit and led to a discussion about whether it was cooler to have food or animals on one's socks and underwear. She laughed at a truly terrible knock-knock joke and had this image of Cody and Ben at her family's big Thanksgiving weekend in Breckenridge. Which was silly, because surely Cody had family that she spent the holiday with.

After dinner, Ben made a show of asking what movie she wanted to watch. She deferred back to him and they settled on *Frozen*, all the while debating who'd seen it more times. Ben asked if she liked the middle of the couch or the end. Despite wanting to sit next to Cody, she got the distinct impression the middle was his favorite, so she picked the end.

"We share the blankets and pillows." Ben handed her a dark blue throw pillow that felt like velvet.

"That's very nice of you." She smiled at Ben before making eye contact with Cody.

"It's how cuddle piles work," Cody added.

Ben nodded. "And we're friends now, so we get to cuddle."

"I like the sound of that." And she liked the idea of it almost as much as she liked little boys being raised to show affection without hesitation.

They situated themselves on the sofa, Ben curling up against Cody, but sticking his feet out so they touched Jess. She leaned in slightly and rested her hand on his legs, happy he was so comfortable with her already. The shift brought her just close enough to Cody that Cody's outstretched arm reached her shoulder. The lazy circles Cody traced with her thumb managed to relax her and turn her on at the same time.

By the time the credits rolled, Ben was sound asleep. Cody gave her a hopeful look. "This gets me out of story time. If you're not in a rush to get home, I'd love to chat or maybe watch something not G-rated."

Had she not already been hankering to stay, Cody's hopeful expression would have swayed her. Well, that and it was barely eight o'clock. "I'd like that."

In a way that seemed both practiced and effortless, Cody stood and scooped Ben into her arms. His limbs dangled, making it clear the move didn't wake him in the slightest. "I'll be right back. Make yourself comfortable."

Cody disappeared up the stairs, leaving Jess to wonder what to do with herself. She gathered the cups and popcorn bowls from the coffee table and brought them to the kitchen. Since doing dishes felt more presumptuous than thoughtful at this point, she returned to the living room, homing in on one of the bookcases flanking the television.

The lower shelves were all LEGOs and children's books, as she'd expect. The upper ones managed to surprise her, though. Fiction—both popular and literary—mingled with biographies, history, and even some self-help. She loved the variety almost as much as she loved how they were all crammed in together. For some reason, she'd expected Cody to have a precise, if not downright scientific, system.

Besides the books and a few knickknacks, pictures of Ben took up a good deal of space. Ben as a baby, Ben in a snowsuit so puffy it reminded her of the little brother in *A Christmas Story*, Ben and Cody posing by a waterfall—it all painted a picture of a perfect little family. It made her wonder again about Cody's ex and her choosing the exciting career over parenting. Cody had said her ex wasn't a bad person, and she didn't know enough about the woman to be judgmental. But still. How could she not want to be part of Ben's life?

"No comments on my stylish look in that waterfall picture?"

Jess turned to find Cody coming down the stairs at a jog and all thoughts of Cody's ex vanished. In their place, appreciation of the gorgeous woman in front of her.

"I was carrying Ben in one of those hiking backpacks and didn't realize until we stopped that he'd stuck a bunch of leaves in my hair from the trees we'd passed. Had to stick my head in the waterfall to get them all out and got half drenched in the process."

She leaned close to study the picture in question and smiled. "I think you missed a few leaves. But you look pretty good half drenched."

Cody lifted a shoulder in a way that seemed almost bashful. "You don't have to say that. I know exactly how goofy I look in that picture."

It would be so easy to forget Ben was sleeping right above them. "You say goofy, I say sexy."

"Something tells me not to argue with you."

It was her turn to shrug. "You can argue, but I'll win."

Cody chuckled. "We'll see about that."

"I brought the dishes to the sink, but I didn't want to overstep." Why did she feel the need to explain herself? Was it because Cody had caught her poking around?

"That was thoughtful. Thank you." Cody came to stand next to her, close but not close enough to touch. She stuck her hands in her pockets. "So."

If they hadn't shared such a hot and heavy kiss the last time they were together, the hesitation would have given her pause. Tonight, it merely made her wonder if Cody simply didn't have a lot of practice navigating dating and parenting at the same time. "So."

Cody ran a hand up the back of her neck. "Did you want to put on another movie? There's Netflix and stuff. I also have a bunch of old black-and-white ones on DVD."

"Do you? Like what?"

Cody smiled. "Lots of Cary Grant and Katherine Hepburn. That sort of thing."

One more thing she wouldn't have pegged Cody for. "Interesting."

"In a good way, I hope."

"Oh, very good. And I think that sounds perfect." She angled her head. "Assuming, of course, we get to cuddle."

The comment seemed to help Cody relax. "Of course. I mean, friends cuddle. It's a thing."

Jess bit her lip, thinking of doing all sorts of things with Cody besides cuddling. "Right, right."

"Can I get you anything? More popcorn? Wine?"

"I think I'm good, thanks."

Cody nodded and went to a drawer under the TV. "Do you want to pick?"

She returned to her spot on the sofa. "Surprise me."

In a matter of minutes, they were curled up together under one of the blankets. She might have wanted more, but she'd be hard-pressed to complain about the way Cody's arm felt around her shoulder or the way Cody stroked her hair without seeming to know she was doing it. It was so much closer to girlfriend territory than so many of her previous attempts at actually having a girlfriend.

She lifted her head to say as much to Cody, but before she could, Cody's mouth was on hers. A little less urgent than the last time, but no less hot. Jess sank into it, letting herself acknowledge just how badly she'd been wanting Cody to kiss her again. She shifted so she could face Cody fully, but Cody didn't stop there. She guided Jess onto her back and braced herself in a way that gave Jess a delicious taste of what it would be like to have Cody's body over hers in bed.

Cody's thigh came between hers, creating just enough friction to have her craving more. She arched into it even as she inched her fingers under Cody's shirt in search of skin. Cody's free hand did the same, creeping up Jess's torso and grazing the underside of her breasts.

"Fuck." It came out breathless, barely above a whisper, but she slapped a hand over her mouth anyway. "Sorry."

Cody smiled. "It's okay. He can't hear you. It was a good fuck, though, right?"

Hearing Cody swear made her snicker. "So good."

"I know it's too soon, but I hope you know a really big part of me wants you to stay."

Was it too soon? She'd had hookups by the third date plenty of times. Though, this was unlike any dating situation she'd been in before. Between that and Ben sleeping upstairs, she had to agree. Even if her body begged to differ. "Yeah."

Cody sat back and blew out a breath. "I'm sorry if that was too much. Or too fast."

"It wasn't. I promise. We're definitely on the same page."

Cody nodded and seemed to relax, as though she'd needed that confirmation. "Okay. Good."

"Which means I should probably go." Because if she stayed, she really didn't trust herself not to tear Cody's clothes off.

Cody snagged the remote and paused the movie. "Yeah."

The reluctance in Cody's voice made her smile. "But maybe we should accept that sex might become part of our arrangement."

Cody's expression turned serious. "Honestly, I think it will make all of this feel more natural."

Natural. Not the word she'd have used, but Cody had a point. Both her column and Cody's desire to have the appearance of a girlfriend would benefit from taking their relationship to the next level. For some reason, it was easier to focus on that more than the off-the-charts chemistry they seemed to have. "You make a good point."

"I mean, I'm not saying we have to go there, but I'm open. More than open."

Again, she would have expected Cody's slight awkwardness to be a turnoff. But Jess couldn't help but find it endearing. Maybe because there was nothing awkward or hesitant about the way Cody kissed her. If anything, the combination of the two made for an almost irresistible package. "I'm glad we agree."

Cody nodded but then glanced at the television and frowned. "I feel bad having you go before the movie is over."

"It's okay. I've seen it enough times to know how it ends."

"Right." Cody smiled, but her eyes held disappointment.

"Or we could agree to finish watching and just cuddle."

"Really?"

As much as she wanted Cody to take her to bed, there was something to be said for being curled up in her arms. "I'm game if you are."

"Okay, great."

Cody sat back in her original spot and picked up the remote. Jess cuddled up to her and tried to focus on the television and not the heat radiating from Cody's body or Cody's muscular arm around her. It didn't really work, but she managed to stay mostly still and keep her hands to herself. She had a fleeting thought about how she'd describe it in her next column and spent the rest of the time wondering when—more than if—sex would be on the table.

Chapter Ten

A melia let out an audible sigh. "I love hearing you sound so happy. Really I do."

"But?" The truth was, very little that Amelia could say would put a damper on Cody's mood. Jess was on her way over, Ben was playing LEGOs while keeping an eye out for Trevor, and dinner was done. She squeezed the phone between her shoulder and her ear as she pulled the lasagna out of the oven.

"I keep thinking Valentine's Day is going to come quick. That's when it's all over, right? Are you really going to be able to walk away then?"

"Valentine's Day is a rough timeline." Which was not an answer to Amelia's question. She didn't want to think about an end, however, when things had barely gotten started. Speaking of getting started, Cody wished Jess could be coming over for another evening at home. It was silly to leave a perfectly good lasagna.

Amelia let out a longer sigh. "Cody, I'm worried about you. We both know you fall in love fast."

"Ha. Coming from you, that's—"

"Funny. Yeah. I know. And completely off topic. We're talking about you and your heart—not me crashing a U-Haul en route to move in with a woman I'd only known for six weeks."

Cody chuckled. "Well, me and my heart are fine. I got this."

"Do you really? I don't want to bring up Anastasia, but—"

"Great. Let's not bring her up then." Thinking about Anastasia was worse than thinking about Valentine's Day. "For the record, you were the one who encouraged me to go on a date."

"A date, yes, and I thought this cuffing thing would be a good idea, but now you're acting like Jess is the real deal just because she's good at kissing."

"Really good at kissing. But that's not all I like about her. We click. It feels easy to hang out—way easier than anything ever was with Anastasia, since you brought her up. And I'm having fun." In fact, that's the only thing Jess and Anastasia seemed to have in common—a fun, adventurous spirit that could pull Cody out of her tendency to be too serious about everything.

"I'm not saying you shouldn't have fun, but you also need to protect your heart." Amelia paused. "What if you're only an assignment for her?"

"Then I'm hoping she wants extra credit." Cody chuckled but Amelia only grumbled. "Seriously though. I'm more mature than I was with Anastasia. I'm not going to do anything like impulsively decide to become a parent."

"I don't know what to do with you. Have you read her latest article?"

Before Cody could answer, Ben came barreling into the kitchen. "Is it done yet?" He hopped up and down trying to get a peek over Cody's arm. "I want to eat. I'm so hungry. Oh, Trevor's here."

"Hold up, Amelia," Cody said into the phone. She looked down at Ben. "Did you let Trevor in?"

"No. He didn't knock. But I heard a car." Ben pushed closer to the lasagna. He waved his hand over it like a little chef trying to catch more of the aroma. "It smells so good. Can we eat now?"

"First you gotta let Trevor in." Cody pointed to the hallway. "Go."

Ben took off, again at a run, and Cody glanced at the clock. "Amelia, I have to go. I promise I'll cross my heart or whatever it is you want me to do."

"Protect your heart. But whatever. I know you won't anyway."

Wouldn't she? Sure, it was fun to get swept up in the moment, but she'd learned her lesson. And feeling that spark again wasn't the same think as falling in love. "Thanks for the vote of confidence. By the way, tell your grandma thanks for the lasagna. Ben and the babysitter are eating it tonight and I'll be having leftovers tomorrow."

Cody ended the call and turned at the sound of clicking heels. *Jess.* "You're not Trevor."

"Not the last time I checked. By the way, you might need to fire your security guard. This kid let me right in." Ben was in Jess's arms grinning like he'd won a prize and Jess looked just as happy.

"I let you in, but then I attacked you with killer hugs," Ben argued.

"Killer?" Jess laughed at Ben's enthusiastic nod. She spun him in a circle and he cackled with glee.

The sight of them together made Cody's chest unexpectedly tight, and a lump formed in her throat. Was it simply that she hadn't seen another woman hold Ben since Anastasia left or was it how perfect they looked together? Either way, Amelia's admonition echoed in her ears. She promptly shoved both the feeling and the warning aside.

Jess's gaze lighted on hers. "Hello, by the way."

"Hi." She wished she had Ben's confidence. Although she'd skip hugs and go right for kissing. When a smile curved Jess's lips, it was as if she'd read Cody's thoughts. Cody cleared her throat. "You look nice. Again. You seem to keep doing that."

"You, too. But where's the tie?" Jess's subtle wink sent a warmth through Cody.

The doorbell rang and Ben wiggled out of Jess's arms. "I want to tell Trevor we're having lasagna. It's his favorite."

"He's got a lot of energy, doesn't he?"

"Yes." No denying it. Was his energy too much for Jess? Did it matter if this was only going to last another three months? "Fortunately, he does fall asleep eventually. And he likes to sleep in which is a plus."

"Definite plus." Jess stepped forward and tilted her head up to meet Cody's lips.

Cody could have savored Jess's kiss all night, but Ben's greeting for Trevor carried down the hall and she knew it wouldn't be long before they had company. When she pulled back, Jess made a little moan that convinced her she wasn't the only one pining for more.

"Oh, hi." Trevor stepped into the kitchen and immediately blushed. Ben had clearly pulled him all the way from the front door to the kitchen, jabbering away about the lasagna. Cody barely had time to step away from Jess, and she knew Trevor could guess what he'd interrupted.

"Jess, this is Trevor. Trevor, this is my friend Jess."

Trevor's blush only reddened. He opened his mouth as if to say hi and then nodded instead. Normally, he was talkative, but Jess seemed to leave him at a loss for words.

"Trev." Ben tugged Trevor's arm, trying to regain his attention. "We get lasagna for dinner. Your favorite. Look."

"Uh-huh." Trevor closed his mouth, swallowed, and looked at Ben. "That's great."

"But you didn't even look."

"At what?"

Cody nearly laughed. Trevor lived next door with his parents and was in his first semester at the local community college. As far as Cody knew, he hadn't been on a date yet and she'd wondered if he might be gay considering how little he mentioned girls. Although by the way he'd turned to mush at the sight of Jess, she figured he had enough interest in women to be at least bi.

"Okay, you two, we're going to head out. Enjoy your lasagna. There are cookies for dessert." Cody kissed Ben's head and then clapped Trevor's shoulder. "Also, I got a new Playstation game for you boys to try out. Be good."

Cody waited until they stepped outside to reach for Jess's hand. "So, do guys often forget how to talk around you?"

Jess rolled her eyes. "No."

"Mm-hmm. Why do I not believe you?" Cody unlocked Jess's door and reached for the handle. Before she could open it, Jess stepped forward and pressed her against the car. Her lips stole all the thoughts from Cody's mind.

When Jess pulled back, her expression was decidedly smug. "It was hard waiting to do that. By the way, Ben's a sweetie. You have a good kid. And Trevor seems nice, too."

She should say something in response. Unfortunately, no words were possible at the moment.

When Jess slipped around Cody to open the door, her hand caressed Cody's midsection. She dropped into the seat. "Apparently, guys aren't the only ones who forget how to talk around me."

"I deserved that." She closed Jess's door and went around to the driver's side. "And I do have a good kid. I know I'm lucky. But it's nice to have some grown-up time that doesn't involve working."

"You do remember we're going to your work thing, right?"

"Yeah, but it'll be different with you there." Cody backed out of the driveway and pulled onto the street. "Although if it's an option, I wouldn't mind skipping the banquet and going to your place."

"As much as I want you to play hooky so we could, I want you to get tenure even more."

"I should probably thank you. But playing hooky is fun."

Jess shook her head. "So I've heard. I think I'm too much of a good girl to enjoy it."

"Do you mean you've never done it before? Not even back in high school?"

"Never. I loved school."

Cody laughed. "Good thing we didn't know each other back then. I played hooky a lot and would have tried hard to get you to join me."

"You? The soon-to-be chemistry professor? I would have figured you'd never miss class." When Cody lifted a shoulder, Jess narrowed her eyes. "Okay, now I want to know what you played hooky to do."

"I don't kiss and tell."

Jess laughed. She reached over the console and set her hand on Cody's thigh. Cody tried to keep her foot steady on the gas, but when Jess's hand inched higher on her leg, she nearly slammed on the brakes. Except they were on the highway. She cursed under her breath as Jess's hand strayed up the inseam of her pants.

"Heard that. You don't have a swear jar in the car, do you?"

"Nope."

A car swerved around Cody and Jess pulled her hand away. "I better let you focus. Gotta keep up my good girl reputation."

As much as Cody wanted to argue that she could multitask, she didn't want the first time with Jess to be in the car. She wanted to do things right. That realization was promptly followed by a reprise of Amelia's warning. Wanting to have sex didn't necessarily have anything to do with love, and yet Amelia wasn't completely wrong. She had fallen for Anastasia fast, and if she didn't watch herself, she could end up liking Jess a lot more than Jess liked her.

They'd no sooner walked into the banquet hall then she gave in to the urge to ask, "How long do we have to stay?"

"We just got here." Jess caught Cody's hand and gave it a squeeze. "There's your boss. Pretend you like me."

"As if I could pretend I didn't."

Lines creased around Jess's eyes when she smiled, but her gaze stayed on the approaching President Toller. "Focus. She's coming this way."

"If you hadn't noticed, it's hard for me to focus on anyone else when you're around."

"I have noticed and it's flattering, but I also want you to keep your job." Jess's smile widened as she let go of Cody's hand and stepped forward to hug President Toller. "Gillian, lovely to see you again. Where's Shannon?"

"Chatting with the chair of the economics department." Gillian lowered her voice and added, "I know she'd love to be rescued. But I'm trying to avoid the entire economics department tonight."

She gestured with her chin across the banquet hall to where Shannon was cornered by Tim Jaysworth, the economics chair notorious for forgetting the point of long-winded stories, and two other professors. Jess gave Gillian a conspiratorial wink. "If you'll both excuse me, I need to talk to Shannon about something that can't wait a moment longer."

"You're a dear," Gillian said, clearly thankful. She turned to Cody when Jess left and added, "I don't know where you found her but hold on tight to that one."

Cody hoped a smile would suffice. She couldn't outright lie nor admit there was already an expiration date for their relationship.

"I hear you're also a big fan of Avis DeVoe. Shannon told me that she and Jess already discussed getting tickets for her next concert so the four of us can go together."

"Oh. Um, yeah. That sounds great." She'd heard of the singer, but it was the first she was hearing about possible plans.

"News to you?" Gillian laughed. "I'm glad I'm not the only one who feels like I'm out of the loop half the time. And now that they're texting each other, we're really in for it. Who knows what they'll sign us up for?"

"I can only imagine." Cody wanted to be excited. A double date sounded fun. And she had no problem with Jess texting the president's wife. But if they got close, it was entirely possible Jess's article and their fake—or temporary—relationship would come to light. Even if that didn't happen, she couldn't help worrying what Jess might accidentally say. Or forget to tell Cody. The whole situation could get sticky. Stickier than it already was.

Cody dropped her keys and wallet in the basket by the door and shrugged off her coat. She was happy to be home, at least, and happy Jess had come inside instead of saying good-bye in the driveway. But she wasn't sure about what would happen next, and it was her fault.

"I want to talk about the concert thing, but I can tell you don't," Jess said.

"It's not that I don't want to talk about it—"

"You don't. I can tell." Jess crossed her arms. "But I think we should anyway."

Cody knew better than to argue. "Okay."

Jess settled on the couch while Cody paid Trevor. Now, with her heels kicked off and her legs stretched out, she looked decidedly hot as hell, which only made Cody regret even more that she'd started what might turn into their first fight.

On the drive home she'd admitted she felt sideswiped not knowing any of the details of a double date to the concert of a person she'd never listened to—but supposedly loved. Jess apologized, but spent the rest of the drive quiet, leaving Cody to feel bad for bringing it up in the first place. Now Jess wanted to resolve things, and while years of therapy had taught Cody that was a good sign, tonight she would have traded resolved conflict for simply making out.

"Are you upset that Shannon and I have been texting?"

"It's totally fine." She wasn't upset about it, but Jess had to realize there was a risk. Shannon would figure out the truth about their relationship if they got close. Cody hated worrying about being discovered, but even more hated feeling dishonest.

Jess's eyebrows bunched together. "You sure?"

"Yep. Want something to drink?"

"I think we might have two different definitions of 'totally fine.'"

Cody sighed. "Is that a yes to a drink? Or a no?"

Jess pursed her lips. "Water would be great."

If only they could rewind the evening. Dinner had been perfect. Despite the fact that they were surrounded by other faculty, Jess had successfully kept Cody from thinking about work. Time slipped away as they chatted about road trips. And movies. And favorite childhood memories. She'd enjoyed herself entirely—something that seemed impossible at a faculty banquet—and then she'd gone and screwed everything up.

Cody returned to the living room and handed Jess a glass of water. "I know we aren't done talking, but I have to go check on Ben. You okay here for a minute?"

Jess nodded. "I feel a little silly making you talk."

"It's probably good for me."

"Okay. Go check on Ben."

Cody headed upstairs wondering if there was any chance Jess would consider tabling their disagreement. How were they already fighting anyway?

She stopped in the hallway when she noticed light under Ben's door. Not a great sign, but when she opened the door, he didn't move from his curled-up position and his eyes stayed closed. She crossed the room to turn off the bedside light, but before she got to it, Ben yawned and stretched.

"Is Jess still here?"

"Hey, buddy. What are you doing still awake?"

"Trevor said Jess could read me a book if I was awake when you got home."

"He did, huh?" Cody tried to keep the frustration out of her voice.

"I got sleepy, but I kept myself awake counting my toes. Then I counted the lines on my pillow, but I messed up at twenty-four and had to start over again."

Cody sat on the edge of the bed. "I love you. But I wish you hadn't kept yourself awake."

"Is Jess still here?"

"Yeah. She's downstairs. But you should have been asleep an hour ago."

"It's not fair that you got to spend all the time with Jess and I only had Trevor."

Cody couldn't argue. She'd take Jess over Trevor too. "Jess went with me to a work thing, buddy. It wasn't any fun."

"Please can she read me a book? Just one?"

Cody bit her lip, wondering if Jess knew what she'd bargained for when she decided to date someone with a kid. "Promise to go right to sleep after one book and not ask for two?"

He nodded and stuck out his hand, pinky extended.

Cody locked his pinky with hers. "Okay. I'm holding you to this."

Jess looked up as Cody came down the stairs. "Everything okay?"

"Any chance you'd be up for reading a picture book? You were specially requested."

"He wants me to read to him?" Jess sounded surprised but also a little pleased.

"Kept himself up counting his toes and hoping you'd say yes."

She sat up straighter. "His toes? Okay that's really cute."

"And the stripes on his pillow."

"There's absolutely no way I can say no to that." Jess stood. "Do I get to pick out the book?"

"You're excited about this?"

Jess gave Cody an incredulous look. "Are you kidding? Of course, I am. I'm excellent at doing voices. My nieces and nephews rave about me."

Cody grinned. So much for worrying that Jess would find it a bother. "Can you maybe not be too excellent? I want him to go to sleep after one book."

"You got it." Jess stopped on the first stair and turned to Cody. "By the way, this doesn't mean you're getting out of our conversation."

Cody blew out a breath. "I figured."

"Also, you're distractingly sexy. I've spent all evening wondering what it'll be like with you and I'm bummed we're arguing instead of getting naked."

"You tell me all this right before you read my kid a book?"

"With voices." Jess kissed Cody's cheek. "You can handle it."

Chapter Eleven

Jess walked into Ben's room and found him sitting up with a book clasped to his chest. "I heard you waited up for me."

Ben nodded. "I counted to stay awake."

"Maybe next time we could read a book first so you don't stay up past your bedtime." A sentiment she would embrace even if it didn't mean interrupting things with Cody.

"You sound like Mom."

She couldn't help but smile. "Your mom is smart."

He nodded, as though being asked to weigh in on the matter. "Yeah."

"So, it looks like you've got one picked out already." A fact that was about as adorable as his dinosaur pajamas.

"It's my favorite." He handed it over proudly.

"*The Mousetronaut*. I can't believe I've never read it."

Ben shrugged. "Well, it is for kids. You probably read grown-up books without pictures in them."

"Sometimes. Although I love picture books, too. And I love outer space."

"You do?" He seemed incredulous.

"I do. I thought I was going to be an astronomer when I grew up."

He frowned. "What's an astronomer?"

"It's someone who studies stars and planets."

He looked at the spacesuit-clad mouse on the book cover, then at her. "Like an astronaut?"

"But an astronomer does it from the ground."

He nodded slowly, as though trying to make sense of why someone wouldn't want to go into outer space.

"I always loved the stars and the solar system, but my tummy doesn't like things that go very fast."

The nod became one of understanding. "I like fast rides, but sometimes my tummy hurts in the car."

Poor kid. She could empathize. "Me, too."

"Do you want to read something else?"

It melted her heart a little that he'd ask. "Oh, no. I meant what I said. Astronauts are very cool. Mice are, too, as long as they're not scurrying across my kitchen floor."

He giggled at the last part and scooted over so she could settle in next to him. She did, wondering if Cody was going to join them or see how she'd fare with Ben on her own. She turned to page one and fell into the world of Meteor the mouse and his quest to join a space mission. And maybe she did a few voices, but it was kind of impossible not to.

"The end." Jess closed the book and looked at Ben. His eyes were sleepy, but he was still awake. "Thank you for letting me read you a story."

"Can you read me one more?"

The combo of sleepy and hopeful was too much. She'd say yes to all sorts of things she shouldn't if he kept looking at her like that. "Well—"

Before she could cave, Cody appeared in the doorway. "What did we agree to?"

"Uh." Had she agreed to something and forgotten? It wouldn't be the first time.

Ben let out a sigh. "That if Jess read me a book, I wouldn't ask for another."

"Oh." Jess cringed.

"It's okay. You didn't know the rules, but this one did." Cody hooked a thumb in Ben's direction.

"Sorry." His sheepish apology was probably well rehearsed, but she bought it hook, line, and sinker.

"It's okay, buddy. Maybe we can read together again soon."

He nodded, then thanked Jess before giving her a hug and wishing her good night. Jess extricated herself from the bed and tried not to hover awkwardly as Cody tucked Ben in and kissed his forehead. Out in the hallway, Cody pulled Ben's door most of the way shut. "Thank you for that. You were definitely a hit."

"Thanks." She'd felt it, but having Cody confirm it was nice.

But despite the compliment a second before, Cody took a deep breath and looked uncomfortable. Did she regret letting Jess read Ben a story? Was it too much? Jess looked down at her feet and braced herself for some version of the it's not you, it's me about so much kid time. "I guess we should go back downstairs and finish our fight."

It was hard to say what was more ridiculous—the level of her worry or the extent of her relief. She pressed her lips together to keep from smiling. "We're not fighting."

Cody raised a brow and managed to look suspicious on top of uncomfortable. "No?"

"No. But we should finish our conversation. And probably not right outside Ben's door. Is he okay, you think?"

"Hopefully down for the count."

Had Cody truly been looking to avoid talking, she could have played the "I need to stay close" or the "He's a light sleeper so we should call it a night" cards. The fact that she didn't gave Jess hope. "Okay."

Cody took her hand to lead them downstairs—totally unnecessary yet totally nice. They settled on the couch and Jess couldn't help but think about what they'd been up to the last time they'd been there, complete with Ben asleep upstairs. But as much as she'd like to pretend Cody hadn't been stiff and awkward on the ride home, and make out instead, they needed to clear the air.

"So." Cody looked at her expectantly.

"So, I apologized for not telling you about the concert plans, but you still seem upset."

Cody blew out a breath. "I'm not upset."

"You are. You have a terrible poker face."

Cody winced, but it turned into a sheepish smile that reminded her of Ben's. "Yeah."

"I need to understand why. Because I thought the whole point of this was to be convincing, but now I'm not so sure."

"I do want us to be convincing. I…" Cody opened her mouth but didn't continue.

"Am I not intellectual enough?" It wouldn't be the first time a girlfriend had said as much. Or that her job was frivolous, and she should aim higher if she wanted to be taken seriously.

"God, no." Cody seemed genuinely mortified by the insinuation. "If anything, I worry that my academic life is too boring for you."

She reached over and grabbed Cody's knee. "I told you I can handle work functions with the best of them."

"Right."

"What is it really?"

Cody shrugged. "I guess it's one thing to have a date at work events. It's another thing entirely to go on double dates with the president and her wife."

"But isn't that a good thing? Having a personal connection to the college president has to be good for your career."

"It is, but it makes the stakes higher. Spending time with them outside of work means opening the door to personal questions—how we met, how long we've been together, everything."

Was that really what this was about? "So, we spend some extra time getting to know each other. Research is your middle name. Mine, too, if in a completely different way. We got this."

"But what if they ask about your work?"

A ripple of shame started in the pit of her stomach and radiated out. "So, I'm smart enough, just too—what? Low brow? Unambitious?"

"Jess, no. God. That's not what I meant at all."

Shame gave way to ire, fight and flight now warring with one another. "No? Then what did you mean? Do you not want to do this anymore?"

Cody closed her eyes and took a deep breath. "You interviewed Gillian, so she already knows you're a journalist. What if they ask you what else you write? Or if she or Shannon googles you? They'll find your column. Which will make it clear you and I are cuffing. And that will make me look even more unstable than being single would."

Cody scrubbed a hand over her face, looking like she wanted to disappear, or at least like she wished she could take back her words. Only she couldn't take it back and Jess was the one who wanted to disappear. Shame returned as a more general sort of embarrassment. How often did her enthusiasm get the better of her? At work, in relationships. She got carried away and acted impulsively and got herself into trouble. And Cody couldn't afford that kind of trouble. "I'm sorry."

Cody took her hand. "No, I'm sorry. I overreacted. You were just trying to do something nice."

She had been. But she also hadn't stopped to think about the potential consequences. "I didn't mean to put you in that position. I swear I didn't."

"I didn't think you did. Which was why I wanted to let it go."

It would have been easier for sure. Would it have been better? Hard to say. She didn't like that she was prone to getting carried away and getting into exactly the kinds of situations Cody worried about. She liked even less that Cody's top priority was her career and how their relationship could damage it. Which was utterly unfair considering Cody's career was her whole reason for agreeing to be in this pseudo relationship in the first place, but she still didn't like it. Or that her own feelings for Cody had less and less to do with her column. But none of that fit with what they'd agreed to and she'd already overplayed her hand once tonight. "Yeah, okay. Let's do that."

Cody regarded her with concern. "Are you sure?"

"I am." She nodded with more enthusiasm than she felt. Even if things didn't feel entirely resolved, she was more than ready to be done with the conversation. "Do we get to kiss and make up?"

"Depends. Will there be actual kissing?"

Just the idea had her body ramping up and her mind wanting to pretend nothing had ever happened. "I hope so."

Cody leaned in. So did Jess. There was nothing impulsive or unexpected about it. But the moment Cody's mouth covered hers, Jess would have sworn she saw stars. The intensity of her reaction to Cody was no less potent than the last time. Neither was her desire to get under Cody, preferably naked.

"Mom, I'm thirsty."

Ben's sleepy little voice might as well have been an air horn for how quickly she and Cody jumped apart. She had a moment of panic, but Cody's dramatic cringe, followed by a grin, softened the blow.

"Coming, honey." Cody stood, but before she turned away, she mouthed "sorry."

Cody headed to the kitchen and Ben came the rest of the way downstairs. "Are you going to marry my mom?"

"What?" Surely she'd misheard.

"I saw you kiss her."

Fuck. Fuck fuck fuck. Good thing mental cussing didn't require payments to the swear jar. "Um."

He blinked at her with that unstudied curiosity only kids could pull off.

"No. We're just friends."

Blink.

"Who kiss. Some friends kiss." She had an image of him planting one on his classmates. "Grown-up friends, that is."

He wrinkled his nose. "Gross."

The matter-of-fact declaration, laced with little boy disgust, had her biting back a laugh. She coughed to cover it up, and to buy time. It did, just enough for Cody to return with a plastic Scooby-Doo cup.

"What are you doing downstairs?"

Ben gave her a sheepish look. "I wanted to say hi to Jess again."

Cody handed him the glass and pointed. Ben pouted but only for a second. He wished them good night again and headed back upstairs.

When she was sure he was out of ear shot, she said, "He asked if we were getting married."

Cody balked. "What?"

"He saw us kissing and I guess that somehow equates to getting married?" She shrugged. It felt like a leap but was the best she could come up with.

"Damn Disney movies. What did you say?"

"That we were friends who kissed." She cringed at her own absurdity. "And that grown-up friends do that sometimes."

Cody tipped her head back and forth like it maybe wasn't the best answer but definitely wasn't the worst. "Okay."

"I mean, I think he believed me because he was pretty grossed out. And then you came back and spared me before I dug myself any deeper."

Cody chuckled. "Sorry about that."

"No, I am. We agreed he'd see us as just friends."

Cody shrugged, not nearly as upset as Jess would have expected. "He still does. We're just friends who kiss."

"And that's a thing in his mind?"

"Apparently. No less logical than equating kissing to marriage, right?"

Jess shook her head. "If you say so."

"He'll develop suspicion soon enough. Right now, he mostly believes what adults tell him. Adults he trusts at least." Cody smiled at the last part.

"Then I'm going to put this in the gift horse category and leave it at that." And try not to think too much about what it meant that Ben trusted her so easily.

"Sounds like an excellent idea."

Now that the moment had passed, with no real fallout, she let herself appreciate how funny it was. "He reminds me of my nephew, Joshua. He's always keeping my sister and her wife on their toes. Well, so do my nieces."

"How many nieces and nephews do you have?"

She smiled at the thought of them. "Six, though two are in college already. My brother married a woman with children from a previous marriage."

"So you have one brother and one sister?"

It occurred to her this was the kind of conversation they might have had on their first couple of dates had they not been negotiating terms and expiration dates. "And two siblings is plenty. When we all get together, it gets a little wild with the kids running around."

"I bet."

She imagined Ava and Addy—her sister's twin girls—doting on Ben the way they doted on their brother Joshua. "I think they'd like Ben."

Cody nodded. "I've always been a little sad that Ben doesn't have cousins his age."

"You know, if you two don't have plans for Thanksgiving, you'd definitely be welcome to join my family." The words tumbled out before she'd thought them through—yet again. And if the look on Cody's face was anything to go on, she'd overstepped. "I mean, you probably do have plans, but we're one of those the more, the merrier kinds of families and I think you'd get along with them, too. My sister-in-law is an economics professor and always has good stories of academic life."

Cody nodded slowly, making it hard to tell if Jess's rambling was making things better or worse.

"Anyway. That was probably more information than you needed. And maybe more of an invitation than you wanted. But the offer stands. We rent a couple of cabins up in Breckenridge and it manages to be slightly rowdy but also super laid-back."

Cody stopped nodding and smiled, though it was one of those smiles that gave nothing away. "Thank you for the invitation. Is it okay if I let you know?"

"Of course." If Cody was even considering saying yes, it meant she didn't have definitive plans already. It made her wonder about Cody's family situation beyond her absentee ex-wife. She wanted to ask, but it didn't feel like the right time. And since she'd already stuck her foot in her mouth more than once this evening, maybe she should quit while she was ahead. "I guess I should probably head home."

Cody looked disappointed, which shouldn't have made her feel better but did. "Yeah. I'm sorry things went sideways tonight."

"Stop apologizing. They didn't. At least not really." Just because her libido was having a field day and she had no prospect of relief on the horizon.

"You don't have to say that."

"Well, if they did, it was as much my doing as yours." She kept her tone light, going for self-deprecating over self-loathing.

"How about we call it even?"

"I'd like that." About as much as she'd like to go back to making out and pretending they were just a normal couple with amazing chemistry.

"Then it's a done deal." Cody stuck out her hand. It reminded her of their first date, when they agreed to be significant others like it was a business arrangement. They hadn't shaken on it then, but maybe they should have. She took Cody's hand, but instead of shaking it, Cody brought it to her lips. Then she used the connection to pull Jess close and kiss her for real.

It was easy—too easy—to sink into Cody. The heat and strength of her body, the way she got all confident and sure once they actually started kissing. And the kissing itself. God, Cody was good at kissing. She could lose hours kissing Cody and not regret a single second. As if to prove the point, when Cody pulled away, she whimpered.

"Sorry," Cody said.

"Sorry?"

"Yeah. You said you wanted to go home and here I am holding you hostage."

Her first thought was that Cody could hold her hostage anytime she damn well pleased. But since she'd already gotten herself into trouble for being too forward, she settled for, "I'd be hard-pressed to complain."

"Good to know."

Cody walked with her to the door, sticking her hands in her pockets while Jess put on her shoes and coat, like a reminder to keep her hands to herself. It made Jess smile, even if questions and worries and a whole lot of pent-up longing swirled around in her mind. "I'll text you about getting together again?"

"Not if I text you first."

The comment—for all its cheesiness—eased some of the worry. But it didn't put a dent in how much she wanted Cody. Wanted Cody to kiss her again. Wanted to know if Cody did other things as well as she kissed. She chuckled, more at herself than the line.

"It's nice of you to humor me."

"Huh?"

Cody angled her head. "I know that was a totally dorky answer. I said it was nice of you to humor me."

Right. Humoring her. That's what Jess had been doing. "You're cute."

Cody's eyes narrowed slightly. "Thanks?"

That got her to laugh in earnest. "I mean it. Now I'm going to leave before I start making out with you again."

"Fine." Cody's forlorn face was about as subtle as Ben's.

Jess picked up her purse and pressed a quick kiss to Cody's mouth. "Good night."

Cody opened the door and Jess stepped onto the small porch. "Hey, Jess?"

Why did Cody have to go and make her name sound so freaking sexy? "Yeah?"

"Text me when you get home?"

She could have teased Cody about such a protective, parental sort of request. But the truth of the matter was she found it sweet. "I will."

Cody nodded, as though knowing the trajectory of her thoughts. "Good night."

She offered a parting wave and headed to her car. Of course, Cody waited until she'd started the engine and backed down the driveway to close the door. She and Cody weren't half a dozen dates in and she was already having all sorts of feelings she had no business feeling. And if tonight was anything to go on, Cody wasn't anywhere close to being on the same page. Sadly, her track record of wanting more than she could have was holding steady—real relationship or arranged.

CHAPTER TWELVE

A real astronaut suit!" Ben ran straight for the glass cabinet. He stared at the outfit, mouth agape for a long second, and then spun in a circle before landing on his next target. "And a spaceship!"

"That's the Lunar Module we were reading about. Ooh, look, we can peek inside. So cool." Jess followed on Ben's heels, heading for what Cody would have also called a spaceship.

For months, Ben had hounded her about seeing real astronauts. After reading *The Moustronaut* with Jess, his pleading had decidedly amped up. The Space Foundation, an hour's drive from Denver, was the closest thing Cody could come up with to satisfy him, and as soon as she'd shown him the website, he insisted Jess would want to go as well. He'd worked on convincing Cody for two days before she finally relented and texted Jess with an invite. To her surprise, Jess instantly agreed, leaving her with a week of worrying if it was a good idea.

The drive had been full of space talk—most of it from Jess—and when they'd arrived at the Space Foundation, her enthusiasm only increased. But even now she wondered if Jess had any idea what she was really in for, spending the day with an energetic five-year-old. At least she seemed truly excited about the space part.

Cody made her way over to the Lunar Module right as Jess leaned over the rope designed to keep kids from climbing on it. "If you set off an alarm, I'm going to laugh my butt off."

"I won't set off an alarm, but check this out." Jess pointed to a panel of instruments. "These panels open up and the landing gear comes out down here. It's so rad we can look inside. Can you imagine this thing landing on the moon?"

"Not really. But honestly, I'm still trying to get used to the idea of you as a space nerd. By the way, I love that you use the word rad."

Jess cocked her head. "The atmospheric chemist is calling me a nerd?"

"Well, I always knew I was a nerd, but you seemed like a cool kid."

"Whatever. I am cool. Anyway, Ben understands." Jess scanned the area, her brow furrowing with concern. "He was just here."

She pointed to a rocket explosion simulator adjacent to the Lunar Module where Ben was busy pressing all the buttons at once. Lights lit up on the wall in front of him, followed by the recorded rumble of a rocket. "Spend time with little people and you get amazing peripheral vision."

"Damn, he moves fast."

"Yep. Do you want to take a break for a while?" She nodded at a bench in the middle of the room. "I can chase after him if you want a breather."

"No way. This is the most fun I've had in weeks."

Cody wondered if that were true or if Jess was only trying to prove she could keep up. Jess didn't give her a chance to ask. She headed right over to the rockets and asked Ben to show her how to work the simulator.

A few minutes later, they returned to the Lunar Module, but this time climbed up on a platform to get a better view of the astronaut's workstation. Cody snapped a picture as they both pressed their faces up against the plexiglass to peer inside.

"Real astronauts were in there?" Ben asked. "Where'd they sleep? There's no beds."

"No beds. This was the docking hatch." Jess stepped back to read a plaque alongside the module.

"But where'd they sleep? And where'd they go pee? Can we see that part?"

Jess shook her head. "I wish. You know what else I wish? That we could go to the moon."

"I'd want a bathroom. And a bed."

Undaunted, Jess continued. "Did you find where the landing gear comes out?"

Ben shook his head.

"See where your mom is standing?"

Cody raised her hand and waved.

"Where she's standing would be the moon. The landing gear comes out here." She pointed and he nodded, mouth hanging open. "And do you see this little compartment over here?"

Ben squinted in the direction Jess was pointing. "Yeah?"

"That's the control panel. One of the astronauts stood right there when this thing landed on the moon and made sure the hatch opened at the right moment. A moment too late and they would have crashed. Can you imagine what it must have felt like?"

"I bet it was bumpy." Ben slipped his hand in Jess's. The simple gesture was enough to send Cody's heart to the moon.

"Maybe. Or maybe it felt like landing on pillows 'cause there's not as much gravity on the moon." Jess glanced at the photograph of the moon's surface hanging above the display. "It'd be so cool to walk around up there."

"I wouldn't walk. I'd jump." Ben took a tentative hop, then checked to see if she'd tell him to stop. When she didn't, he hopped again and the platform they were standing on banged noisily against the metal railing.

"You can jump. I'd dance." Jess twirled in a circle, still holding Ben's hand and taking him hopping along with her.

"I'd jump and dance," Ben said.

The platform rattled more and Cody wondered if some space curator was going to appear to chew them out. But she couldn't help smiling at the scene. After a moment, Jess stopped dancing and leaned down to get eye level with Ben. "We'd be the best astronauts." Her face was flushed and a smile stretched from ear to ear. "But we better stop jumping and dancing or one of the guards is gonna come and chase us out of here."

Ben looked around for an approaching guard. "Hey, what's that?" He jutted his chin at what looked like a big white box propped up on metal stilts.

"That's a Mars Viking Lander. Forget the moon, that little guy landed on Mars."

"Really?"

"Want to check it out?"

Jess didn't really need to ask. Ben was already halfway down the stairs. As the two of them went to check out the Viking Lander, Cody hung back by the Lunar Module. Clearly Jess had been serious about her interest in space. What surprised Cody more, though, was that she truly seemed to like spending time with Ben.

The Mars Lander didn't hold Ben's interest for long, but Jess stayed, reading all the placards after Ben went back to the rockets.

Cody walked over and bumped Jess's hip. "Hey, space girl."

"Hey, yourself." Jess didn't look up. She read a section aloud from the sign next to her about the Mars landing and then shook her head. "It still boggles my mind that we've taken photographs on Mars. I mean think about it. Mars."

"I'm trying to think about it, but I'm distracted by something else."

"By what?" Jess's eyebrows bunched together.

"Not something, really. Someone."

"Someone more interesting than Mars?" Jess folded her arms, but a smirk played on her lips.

"Yes. And she keeps getting more interesting, and sexier, the more I get to know her."

"Hmm. You better watch out. She might be a cool kid."

Cody laughed. "She is. But for some reason she's decided to hang out with me—a total nerd."

"Better watch your step. She sounds like trouble." Jess slipped her arm around Cody's waist. "Any chance we can convince Ben to watch the planetarium show?"

"I don't think you'll have any trouble convincing him." Cody stole a quick glance at Ben, making sure he was still entranced by the rockets. "Would it be entirely inappropriate if I kissed you here?"

"Entirely." Jess narrowed her eyes. "Besides, good things come to those who wait, and the planetarium show starts in five minutes. We should get in line now so we get good seats."

❖

Ben fell asleep not long after they pulled on the freeway. After the planetarium show, they'd gone to a nearby park with a playground so Ben could blow off some steam before the drive. It'd seemed like a good idea and Cody had packed a picnic, anticipating that'd be easier than braving a restaurant with a boisterous kid, but it'd been windy and cold.

For most of the hour they spent there, Cody and Jess huddled under a picnic blanket trying not to freeze as they ate sandwiches while Ben bounced between them and the swings. Under other circumstances, the picnic blanket cuddling would have been sweet, and maybe even sexy. But Ben hovered close, keeping one eye on them even as he circled the playground, and then literally flopping on top of them every time he took a break.

The other problem was that Jess seemed distant ever since the planetarium show where Ben insisted on sitting between them. She guessed Jess was no longer enjoying herself but didn't want to ask. If the problem was that Jess wanted a relaxing day without a kid, she shouldn't have agreed to the field trip. Then again, Cody probably could have done a better job warning her exactly what would be involved when she'd invited her.

Either way, she'd hoped they might have some time to talk in the car. Only now that they did, Jess didn't seem interested. If it was the kid thing, Cody wished she'd come out and say it. As much as she hated it, she had experience in that department. With someone thinking a kid would be fun and then changing her mind. She might still resent Anastasia for making that decision, but she wouldn't begrudge Jess.

She should have put up clear boundaries from the start, but it seemed too late now. As much as she'd thought she could keep their dating separate from her life with Ben, she realized she'd done a terrible job of it. Probably it wouldn't have worked anyway. Being a parent was part of who she was. She couldn't pretend otherwise. More than that, after seeing Jess and Ben dancing together and pretending they were on the moon, it hit her how much she wanted whoever she dated to like Ben.

To be fair, Jess really did seem to. But she hadn't signed up for an insta-family. And they still hadn't even had sex. The more Cody considered the situation she'd put Jess in, the worse she felt. Maybe she needed to offer her an out.

When they finally cleared the traffic in Colorado Springs and picked up speed, she snuck a glance at Jess. She was looking out the window at the passing fields—long stretches of rangeland interspersed with bunches of cows and an occasional farmhouse.

"Should I ask what's wrong?"

Jess's gaze snapped from the window to Cody. "What do you mean? Nothing's wrong."

"You sure? You've been pretty quiet for the last hour."

Jess took a deep breath and let it out slow. "Sorry about that. I've been thinking. Today made me do a lot of thinking."

"You don't need to apologize. In fact, I think maybe I need to apologize."

Jess tilted her head. "For what?"

"Well…" She glanced at her rearview mirror to make sure Ben was still napping. "You gave up a whole day to have an adventure with a kid. I'm pretty sure cuffing doesn't typically include that."

"Today was amazing. I loved everything about it. And I loved that you and Ben included me." Jess paused and lifted a shoulder. "I also love how much he likes me."

She felt a rush of relief. Jess didn't want out of their arrangement—at least not because of Ben. "He's quite smitten."

Jess smiled. "I know. He's like you—easy to tell exactly what you're thinking."

"Okay, so maybe help me out and tell me what you've been over there thinking about since you're not obvious and the rest of us aren't mind readers."

Jess sighed. "Life choices. You know, roads not traveled and that sort of thing."

"Regrets?"

Jess raised a shoulder. "Maybe?" She shook her head. "No, I don't think it's regret. I'm happy. I like the choices I've made."

Cody waited, sensing Jess would offer more if she didn't press. But she knew all about regretting things even while being happy. *Happy enough.*

"I failed organic chemistry. Twice." Jess shifted in her seat, turning to face Cody. "I kind of hate admitting that to an atmospheric chemist."

"Organic chemistry is hard. Don't beat yourself up about it. I'm guessing that was a required course for something you wanted to do?"

"I wanted to get a degree in astronomy. When I was ten, my grandpa gave me a telescope for my birthday. Best present ever. I spent hours looking up at the stars and trying to pick out all the planets. I thought for sure I'd work for NASA one day." She sighed. "Then came chemistry. I had no problem in physics. Or calculus for that matter, but chemistry was like my kryptonite. So, my third year of college I reevaluated my life. I was dating this English professor and decided on journalism. Thought I'd do investigative reporting for the *New York Times*. That didn't happen either."

"Hold up. You were dating an English professor?"

Jess grinned. "Turns out I like professors."

"Yeah, but you were a student?"

"She was a brand-new professor. Only twenty-eight. And I was twenty-one. So it's not as scandalous as it sounds, but, yes, it was a mistake. Anyway, as it turned out, all she wanted to do was talk about poetry. Don't get me wrong, I like poetry. But at twenty-one I wanted to do more than talk."

"There was something better her lips could have been doing?" Cody winked.

"Exactly. Want to know the worst part? She was terrible at kissing and didn't really like sex." Jess's cheeks colored with the hint of a blush. "That makes me sound awful, doesn't it?"

Cody laughed. "Being good at kissing is important."

"She was so hot, too. It was a shame."

"I dated someone like that once. It didn't last long."

"Thanks for making me feel less shallow." Jess chuckled. "The truth is, I really am happy about the choices I've made. I love my job. I love my side gig teaching barre, too, but I do wonder how things would have turned out if I'd passed organic chemistry."

"Too bad you didn't have me as a tutor. I'd have made sure you passed."

"Well, I definitely would have studied hard." Jess glanced in the back seat. "He's really cute when he's sleeping."

She registered the shift in conversation but didn't comment. "He's cute all the time. And a lot of work. You sure today wasn't too much?"

"No. Not at all. I love kids and you've got a good one." She paused. "I just haven't had a day like this in a long time."

"What do you mean?"

Jess hesitated. "A day that made me step back and think about my life. Realize what I have. And what I want."

Cody waited for Jess to go on, but this time she didn't. Her hand settled on Cody's thigh, but her gaze drifted back to the window and the passing view. After a moment of back and forth, Cody settled on keeping things light. "Is it sex?"

Jess's eyes creased with her smile. "That's definitely part of it." Her hand inched up higher on Cody's thigh. "Do you have plans tonight?"

"I want a telescope," Ben said.

Jess yanked back her hand and her eyes widened. Cody almost laughed at how fast she stiffened. "It's fine," she mouthed.

She met Ben's gaze in the rearview mirror. "We thought you were sleeping back there, buddy."

"I was. You woke me up talking." He yawned. "Jess, was your grandpa an astronaut?"

"No. But he likes the stars almost as much as me."

"He's still alive?" Ben's shock was evident. "How old is he?"

"Eighty-nine and definitely still alive."

"I don't have a grandpa."

"Well, you can borrow mine if you want. He loves kids. And space. And I don't mind sharing. As far as grandpas go, he's pretty great."

"I don't have any grandparents at all." Ben sounded more resigned than sad.

"Really?" Jess looked over at Cody, clearly surprised.

"My parents both passed away before Ben was born and Anastasia's parents...well, it's a long story."

Jess seemed to understand that she didn't want to explain more. She returned her focus to Ben. "I'm definitely sharing my grandpa with you."

"Will he be at your family's Thanksgiving? Maybe we can meet him then. If the invitation still stands."

"The invitation definitely still stands. And Grandpa will be there. Probably arguing with my dad over how to carve a turkey." Jess paused. "I wasn't sure if you were really considering coming."

She'd been hesitant, but that seemed foolish, all things considered. "Usually, we join up with a few colleagues for Thanksgiving, but I'm sure they won't mind if we skip this year."

"Then you should come to Breckenridge. I'd love you two to meet my whole family."

"What do you think, Ben? Want to go meet Jess's grandpa?"

"Yes!" He clapped his hands together.

"Then I guess it's decided." She looked at Jess. "Thank you for the invite. We'd love to come."

"I'll bring my telescope."

Was it weird to be planning a trip before they'd even slept together? Maybe, but that certainly wasn't the only thing that made the relationship different from any other she'd had. Cody relaxed and focused on the road as Jess explained to Ben what they might see with the telescope. Hopefully, different was a good thing for Jess too.

Chapter Thirteen

I don't understand."

Jess pinched the bridge of her nose, wishing she hadn't decided to call her mom from work. "You know I've been seeing Cody. She and her son don't have a lot of family. I invited them to join us. It's not rocket science."

Mentioning rocket science had her mind wandering back over the day she spent with Cody and Ben at the Space Foundation. Ben's infectious enthusiasm. Her own nerdy delight. Cody's genuine amusement over the whole thing, followed by the gentle prodding to open up and talk about her feelings. Pretty much the last thing she expected in terms of a date, and yet one of the most perfect days she'd had in a long time.

Though, did it count as a date if Ben was with them the whole time? And if it did, how the hell was she supposed to write about it?

"Jessica."

"What?" Usually, Mom only used her full name if she was in trouble.

"I asked you a question."

Shit. "I'm sorry. What?"

"Are you calling me from work? Multitasking?" Mom didn't even try to hide the sniff of disdain. "What have I told you about multitasking?"

"That it's not really a thing and that giving two things half your attention means you're probably doing them both poorly." Mom had very strong and very longstanding feelings on the matter.

"Then stop clicking around in your email or call me back when you're able to have a real conversation."

They were close enough that Jess laughed rather than taking offense. "Sorry, sorry. I wasn't answering email, I promise. My mind wandered is all."

Mom sniffed again, clearly unconvinced. "I asked if Cody was the person you're dating for work. Is Cody Carrie?"

She sighed. Her mother—the biggest fan of her column as well as pretty much everything else she'd ever written—already knew the answer to that. She'd changed Cody's name and enough details to protect her privacy, but it wasn't like she was dating multiple people. Certainly not multiple people who happened to be single parents. "She is."

"Well, then, that's what I don't understand. Don't get me wrong. We'd be thrilled to have you bring home someone you're seeing. Lord knows it's been a while. But why would you do it with someone you know you're going to break up with?"

"It's complicated." She knew she wouldn't get away with that but figured it would buy her time to come up with something more convincing.

"Do you feel sorry for her? Is that it?" Despite the probing nature of the question, Mom's tone had already softened. "I'm sure it's hard if she doesn't have much family."

"It's not that." Though, to be honest, Ben's declaration about not having grandparents and the look in Cody's eyes as she explained had pretty much melted her heart into a soupy puddle. "I like Cody. I like her son almost as much. And maybe we're only dating as a matter of convenience, but I think maybe we can stay friends after. Spending time with them is good for me. And I like to think I might be good for them, too."

Seconds ticked by and Mom didn't say anything. Jess tapped her fingers on her desk arrhythmically, earning her a glare from Silpa. She stopped.

"Are you developing feelings for her?"

It was a gentler question than the one she deserved—about whether she was falling for Cody—but it landed in her chest with almost the same impact. "I mean, I don't really do anything with no feeling. That's not how you raised me."

Rather than getting her off the hook, the parenting compliment earned her a few tuts. An upgrade from the sniffs, though, so there was that.

"I'm serious, Mom."

The tuts gave way to a sigh. "You know I love your big, tender heart."

Jess blew out a breath and stared at the ceiling. "But not my tendency to dive in headfirst without checking to see if the water is deep enough."

It was a metaphor for her life, but also a mistake she'd made literally as a child. Fortunately, the tooth she'd knocked out that time had been a baby one. She'd learned her lesson when it came to swimming. Matters of the heart were a different creature.

"Do you think Cody feels the same way?"

Despite wondering the same thing on a nearly hourly basis, she said, "It's a little early to be going there. We've been dating less than a month."

"What about the little boy? What's his name again?"

"Ben." Just mentioning him made her smile. Probably a goofy smile. Or at least a smushy, sentimental one. But Mom didn't need to know that. "He's great. Not exactly what I had in mind for this project, but I really like spending time with him."

"I'm sure he adores you, too. You're a natural with kids. But that means there's a third heart on the line in this whole thing."

Ben's question about whether she was going to marry Cody still clanged around in her mind. Not that there was a chance in hell she'd be sharing that story now. "He thinks we're friends."

"Friends."

"Who kiss."

The absurdity seemed to break some of the tension because Mom laughed. "Of course."

"It's not a lie." It really, really wasn't.

"What should I tell your father?"

He was just as supportive but asserted dad prerogative when it came to not reading her column. Aka, when it came to her sex life, ignorance was bliss. She didn't want to saddle him with TMI, but she also didn't want him getting overly attached. "Tell him we're dating but with the agreement to keep it light. And that I'm writing about it."

"Okay, dear."

"You know you sound like Grandma when you say that."

Mom didn't miss a beat. "I am a grandma now."

A fact that helpfully kept the pressure off her to reproduce. If only she could extend that to the pressure to find the one and live happily ever after. "You're right. Are you going to take up knitting, too?"

"Not on your life. Does Cody ski?"

Huh. "You know, I don't know."

"Well, be sure to ask her. If she doesn't have her own pair, find out what size she is. We might have some that would work."

As people in her family outgrew ski equipment—either due to size or skill—her parents' garage had become a catchall for gear anyone might need to borrow. "Thanks, Mom."

"We're really looking forward to seeing you." Mom paused. "And meeting Cody." Pause. "And Ben."

"It's going to be great. Don't worry." Though, even as she said it, her own apprehension ticked up a few notches.

"It will be. The more, the merrier. Love you, honey."

"Love you, too."

She ended the call and resumed drumming her fingers. The more, the merrier. She'd used that exact phrase with Cody. And making sure everyone had a nice place to go for holidays was part of why people cuffed in the first place, right? It would be fine. More than fine. Fun.

"Do you mind?" Silpa's voice pierced the bubble of her thoughts.

"Sorry, sorry." She lifted both hands in a show of apology but also to get them away from the surface of her desk.

Silpa rolled her eyes and shook her head, then resumed typing. Jess looked longingly at Frida's empty desk, wishing her back from her latest field trip. She grabbed a pen to scribble a reminder to ask Cody whether she skied. Then she turned to her computer. She didn't last thirty seconds before snagging her phone once more.

I need to tell you something. She hit send and started the follow-up text, but Cody replied before she could type it out.

What's wrong? Are you okay?

Cody's immediate concern made her feel bad and yet smile at the same time. She cut her longer message in progress to offer assurances and apologies.

No, I'm sorry. I swear I wasn't always this much of a worrier. Followed by, *I'm lying. I've always been a worrier :)*

Now she was smiling full on. She pasted the partial message she'd started and finished the thought. *I'm just not sure I fully disclosed the amount of big, rowdy, nosy, noisy family you were signing up for. You should be allowed to make an informed decision.*

Cody didn't respond immediately, so she tried to turn her attention to her column. The one she'd started at least half a dozen times. There was the draft where she questioned her life choices. The one where she mused about becoming a parent. Oh, and the one where she admitted to wishing for a sleepover despite her own exhaustion, a looming deadline, and Cody's early class the next day. Not one of them was right. The last one was closest, but it felt like cheating to focus on the sex she didn't get to have after spending the day with Cody and Ben. She closed her eyes and tried to channel WWDD— what would Donna do?

Before she came up with any answers, her phone pinged. *Is that your polite way of rescinding the invitation?*

Jess cringed and typed furiously. *No, no, no.* Send. *Absolutely not.* Send. *I just got off the phone with my mother.* Send. *She's very anxious to meet you.* Send.

Cody responded with a smiling emoji and the blinking dots promising a more thorough answer. *I'm not sure if I should be excited or worried about that last part, but I confess my overall sentiment is excited. We never get to do big family holidays. So, as long as you're still sure, we're still a yes.*

The sensation spreading through Jess in that moment resembled relief, but it was tinged with excitement. It might be a terrible idea, but she wanted to spend Thanksgiving with Cody and Ben. More, she wanted to introduce them to her family. Grandpa, of course, but everyone—Grandma, her parents and siblings, her nieces and nephews.

Any chance you're free for lunch?

She blinked at the screen, trying to register meaning. *Like, today?*

LOL. Yes. I had a meeting canceled and have a magical two hours to myself. Then, *You're probably busy but I thought I'd ask.*

Busy was a relative term. Did she have a column due in under twenty-four hours? Yes. Had she promised Donna an extra column that could be hidden behind the paywall? Yes. But seeing Cody sounded like a much better way to spend her time. And, technically, spending time with Cody counted as work. She sent a yes, complete with exclamation point, and an offer to meet closer to campus so they'd have more time.

While waiting for Cody to suggest a place, she took another look at her most recent draft:

> ...After the most perfectly nerdy field trip ever, we stopped at the park for a picnic and some play. Well, kid play. Carrie and I huddled under a blanket and tried to stay warm.
>
> Is it wrong to want to get it on with someone under a blanket in a public park? Debatable. But wanting it while the other person's kid runs around a few feet away is not ideal. The pseudo snuggle was nice, though, even if it left me wanting. Hard to go home to my empty apartment and even emptier bed.
>
> Still wanting, readers. Still wanting.

It wasn't all bad. She let out a sigh and put her computer to sleep. Maybe an impromptu lunch date would provide inspiration as much as distraction. Just like inviting Cody to Thanksgiving with her family, it was a sound journalistic decision. Right? Right.

CHAPTER FOURTEEN

Cody straightened as Jess pulled up to the curb. Her pulse quickened and her libido sprang to attention the moment Jess got out. *Chill. It's only a lunch date.*

But damn if Jess wasn't gorgeous all over again.

She let her eyes linger on the curves Jess's tight jeans highlighted. She was searching her purse for her keys, and as far as Cody was concerned, she could take her sweet time. If only they could skip lunch and explore the back seat of Jess's car instead. Not that she wanted their first foray to be in a cramped Mini Cooper but still. Her body was getting impatient.

Jess finally found her key fob, hit the lock button, and stepped onto the sidewalk. "Thanks for saving a spot for me."

"No problem." Jess didn't need to know how many cars she'd had to chase off to keep the spot for her.

Jess pecked Cody's cheek and then hooked arms. "I love that you broke me out of my office on a boring Thursday. Let's get inside. It's freezing out here."

A blast of warm air greeted them when Cody opened the door. The bistro smelled like tomato soup—the special of the day according to the chalkboard in the waiting area—and pickles. It was a strange combination but one that had Cody's stomach rumbling.

"Two for lunch?"

Cody nodded at the server.

"Follow me."

Jess unhooked her arm but caught Cody's hand. Heat spread through her at the touch. A few diners glanced their way as they passed, but Jess didn't loosen her hold. In this part of town, two women out on a date wasn't an anomaly, and Cody was ninety percent sure the twenty-something handsome server they were following was gay, too. Still, Cody didn't blame anyone for staring. If she didn't know Jess, she would have stared too—probably awkwardly.

After they'd been seated and the server left to get waters, Jess cleared her throat. "There's something I've been thinking about."

"Uh-oh. You know that's not the first time you've started one of our dates with a sentence like that. This time I don't feel quite as nervous, but I think you better tell me what it is before I decide on soup of the day or a club salad."

"Sex. I want to sleep with you."

"Oh, only that?" Cody raised the menu, pretending to study it intently. "In that case, I'm going with soup."

Jess reached across the table and pushed Cody's menu down, a smile playing on her lips. "Very funny. But this is serious. We need to talk about how it's going to work. 'Cause I'm going crazy over here. And I can tell I'm not the only one. You gave me a once-over outside that has me so hot and bothered, I'm not even hungry anymore."

"How big is the back seat of your car?"

"Not big enough. Hold on, were you thinking of making out in the back seat of my car when you were waiting for me?" Jess wagged her finger as Cody laughed. "I thought you had a guilty look when I kissed your cheek."

"It's possible I may have considered it." No point arguing. "But I don't actually want our first time to be in a car."

"Good. Me neither. So, how does this work? Do we schedule it? Because it needs to happen."

"Or else?" Cody grinned. Jess's insistence was a mix of sexy as hell and endearing. It was even better that she was willing to discuss it all in public—not that anyone was listening.

"Or else this." Jess stood up, leaned over the table, and planted a huge kiss on Cody's lips. When Cody started to pull back, knowing they were going to have people gawking, Jess caught the front of her shirt and pulled her in for another crushing kiss. She forgot about the other diners then, parting her lips as Jess took it deeper.

God, she wanted more than kissing. Jess's mouth had her whole body on fire. Could they walk out of the restaurant right now? Forget the car. With Ben at school, they'd have the house to themselves.

Without warning, Jess pulled back and dropped into her seat, a smug look on her face. "So. How do I get on your calendar?"

Cody laughed. She could hardly believe Jess was for real.

The server reappeared. "Are you two ready to order? Or should I give you a little more time?"

"I don't need more time." Jess gave the server a polite smile before returning her gaze to Cody. Not subtle at all and totally sexy. "I'll have the club salad."

"And for you?" The server turned to Cody. "Would you like what she's having?" He lowered his voice and added, "I'd say yes if I were you."

"Yes, please. And I'll take a cup of the tomato soup, too." She handed off her menu, smiling her thanks.

"Actually, I want soup as well," Jess added.

"Perfect." He jotted their order on his little notepad. "I'm pretty sure half the restaurant wants the same thing you two are getting."

Cody looked at Jess and couldn't keep herself from grinning.

"I'll be right back with your soups." He slipped the pencil behind his ear and pocketed the notebook. "Or should I take my time? I may play for the other side, but there's nothing like two women kissing."

"Go on, cutie-pie. I'm hungry." Jess waved him off and he went, chuckling to himself.

"Well, you made that guy's day," Cody said.

"I'd rather make your day."

Jess had already done that. And then some. "This is the best Thursday I've had in I don't know how long."

"We could make it even better. What are you doing after this?"

"I have to teach." With Jess looking at her the way she was, and her own lips still buzzing from their kiss, Cody wished she could cancel class. As it was, she didn't know how she was going to sit still through the rest of lunch. "The back seat isn't the worst idea."

"In the middle of downtown Denver? No. The last thing we need is someone taking a picture of us and posting it online. I mean it might be good for hits on my column, but still."

"Okay. You're right." She tried to tamp down her arousal. Getting Jess naked wasn't happening today even if they found a quiet parking lot somewhere. But damn did she have ideas for what she wanted to do with her. "I'm not usually free in the middle of the day, but I could make it happen. I'd need a little planning time."

"What about an overnight at my house?"

Cody hesitated. As much as she wanted to agree to it, she'd never left Ben alone with a babysitter for a whole night. What if he woke up and needed her?

"Or maybe it'd be better at your house because of Ben?"

"Yeah, but then there's always the possibility that he'd wake up. It doesn't happen often, but would you be okay with that?"

Now it was Jess's turn to hesitate. "Maybe not for our first time."

Cody understood, but as their options dwindled, doubt nudged in. It was ridiculous that they had to schedule their first time together and yet she didn't see how it could be helped. How many times now had they almost started something only to have to stop? "I could get a babysitter for an evening and instead of going out we can stay in—at your place. We could have plenty of time together."

Jess nodded slowly. She didn't seem thrilled, but it was the most plausible compromise. "When?"

"Next week?" Cody wished she could offer that evening, but she had to work on tomorrow's lecture, and finding a last-minute sitter was never easy. And the weekend was shot. She'd promised to look over her two senior students' research reports and she had to make time at some point to grade the exams she'd given that morning. But saying she didn't have time for sex wasn't going to fly. "We could go big and get a hotel room."

"Next week is Thanksgiving."

"Oh. Right." Cody dropped her gaze to the varnished wood tabletop.

"You're giving up that easy? I didn't figure you for the quitting type." Jess tipped Cody's chin up and then smiled when she met her eyes.

"I'm not quitting."

"Good. A hotel room sounds like a lot of fun. I'd want you for the whole night, but it'd feel like we were sneaking off and doing something naughty if it was only for a few hours. And it'll give me good material for my column." She winked and shifted back in her seat. "So, how's two weeks from now look on your schedule?"

"I'll make it work. And get us a room." Two weeks was too long, but Jess's smile convinced Cody she'd be worth the wait.

"Deal."

Excitement gave way to doubt when she remembered that whatever happened would end up in Jess's column. "Would you want to have sex with me if you didn't need something to write about?" Cody hated voicing those thoughts—and the insecurity that came with the question. But if Jess only wanted something that would give her webpage more clickbait, she needed to know the truth going in.

"Are you kidding? Where were you when we kissed? Maybe you didn't notice, but that's me really fucking turned on."

"I did notice but—"

"Cody, I've been very good at keeping things in check, but only because I've had to. I can't wait to have my hands on you. Even more than that, I can't wait to be in your hands. I know how you kiss. And I know you want me just as much as I want you. You can't hide it and I love that."

"You're right and I shouldn't have suggested—"

"I'm not finished." Jess held up her hand. "I get why you asked. It's a fair question, especially because I brought up the column. I was trying to be funny. But wanting to sleep with you isn't a joke and it definitely has nothing to do with my job."

Cody's heart hammered in her chest. Either Jess was an amazing actress or she was telling the truth.

"And if you're half as good kissing naked as you are dressed, I'm going to be a very lucky woman. Which is why we're scheduling it." She punctuated her last sentence with a jab at the table.

The server appeared, balancing two cups of soup and two bowls of salad. "I don't know what she wants to schedule, but you'd better say yes. You want to keep this one happy."

"Thank you." Jess leaned back in her chair and spread her hands. "Apparently, I need some backup convincing her. And this is something I know she wants."

"Oh, girl, I have the same problem with my boyfriend. Hot but too damn hard-headed for his own good. We should talk."

Jess agreed, laughing. When he'd gone off again, she squared her shoulders and took a bite of soup. "So. Thanksgiving. My parents have the cabins rented from Wednesday through Saturday and we can stay as long as we like. What are you thinking?"

Right. Thanksgiving. How the hell was she going to spend all that time with Jess and not jump her? "Honestly, I'm still thinking about you and me in a hotel room."

Jess smiled. "I'm not going to stop you from planning that one out in your head, but in the meantime, do you ski?"

Chapter Fifteen

Jess pulled into Cody's driveway, parking her car next to Cody's SUV. Cody and Ben were already in the driveway, ostensibly loading up. She didn't want the first thing she noticed to always be how Cody looked, but damn if she didn't look good in jeans, hiking boots, and a puffer vest over a dark green sweater.

She'd barely cut the engine and was still getting out of the car when Ben came running over. "Jess! We're all ready to go. I packed clothes and pajamas and my toothbrush and snow pants and my pillow because Mom said it's sometimes nice to have something from home."

She tipped her head back and forth as he listed things. "Mm-hmm, mm-hmm. Sounds pretty good. But did you remember to pack underwear?"

Ben dropped his shoulders dramatically. "Who forgets underwear?"

She hung her head but then looked up with a grin. "I did once. And I had to go without."

Ben looked utterly horrified. "You didn't wear underwear?"

"I know. It was very uncomfortable."

"Maybe I should double-check." He let go of the handle of his Spiderman suitcase and started unzipping it.

"You remembered. I promise." Cody picked up the suitcase before he got it open and set it in the back of the car.

Ben still looked worried, so she slung an arm around his shoulder. "If your mom says you remembered, I'm sure you did."

"I'm going to check my backpack." He hefted open the door and scrambled into the back seat.

After a glance at Ben, Cody leaned in close. "And I'm going to make you promise to tell me more of that story sometime."

"I'm afraid it's not as charming or sexy as you might imagine."

Cody offered her a sideways smile. "I'll be the judge of that."

She covered her face with her hand, but more on principle than any real, lingering embarrassment. "After a couple of glasses of wine, maybe."

"I'll take it."

She pressed the button on her key fob to pop the back hatch. "Are you sure you're okay taking your car?"

Cody grabbed the bag from the back of Jess's car and set it next to Ben's. "Absolutely. Mine's roomier and has Ben's booster seat already in it."

"I don't disagree, I just didn't want you to feel obligated." Though it was nice to be having this conversation as a matter of consideration and not whose car was less likely to kick it in the middle of a trip—a reality of her not-too-distant past.

"I don't. Besides, your back seat probably isn't littered with Cheerios and Goldfish crackers and ours already is."

She laughed. Probably a more appropriate response than her first thought—that having kid flotsam in her car wouldn't be the worst thing.

"Goldfish? I want Goldfish." Ben's head appeared over the back seat from where he'd started to arrange books and action figures and whatever else he'd packed for his car ride entertainment.

"It's nine in the morning," Cody said without missing a beat. "And you had breakfast an hour ago."

"You said we could have snacks because it's a road trip."

"We aren't on the road yet," Jess said. She didn't doubt Cody's ability to manage Ben's requests but being part of the team made her happy. Happier than it should, perhaps, but that was for overanalyzing another time.

"What she said." Cody hooked a thumb in her direction.

"Fine." Ben's voice had all the angst of a thwarted teenager, which proved quite adorable.

"There's coffee in the kitchen if you'd like a cup for the road." Cody angled her head toward the house. "I confess I've already got one made up and ready."

"Well, if you're offering." She'd had a cup while packing but having a mug to sip leisurely while they drove felt like a treat.

"How do you take it?"

"Cream and sugar. Lots." She closed her eyes for a second, imagining the aroma as much as the taste.

"I wouldn't have pegged you for that."

She opened her eyes to find Cody regarding her with curiosity. "Well, it's vacation."

"I see."

"Not that I don't always want cream and sugar. I usually just refrain from lots."

Cody chuckled. "Noted."

"I can keep an eye on Ben if that's all you still need from the house." Even though she'd like to steal a kiss or two, it seemed like the mature thing to say.

"I appreciate that, but this is not my first rodeo." Before Jess could ask what she meant, Cody turned to Ben. "Almost time to go, buddy. Let's hit the bathroom one more time."

"Oh. Right." The comment was more to herself than anyone else, but Cody caught it and grinned.

"I don't need the bathroom," Ben insisted.

"Yeah, but we're going to try anyway." Cody closed the back hatch. "And you? Do you need the bathroom?"

Cody's tone was teasing, but the mere suggestion had her second-guessing herself. She offered a playful shrug. "I should at least try."

They filed into the house, taking turns in the bathroom and getting coffees and a juice box ready to go. Cody locked up and got Ben situated, then they were on their way. "Sorry if that took longer than you were expecting," Cody said.

"Not at all. You seem to have this down to a science." A fact that managed to make Cody even more attractive, for better or worse.

"Oh, no. I'm a scientist. Science has order and rules and predictability. Getting out of the house with a kid in tow is an art. And I still feel like a novice most days."

She reached over without thinking but caught herself in time to give Cody's knee a friendly pat instead of a squeeze. "Could have fooled me."

Cody glanced at her briefly, the smile reaching her blue eyes. "Thanks."

They cleared the congestion of the city and Cody quizzed her about her family. Ben talked them into a rousing game of I Spy before nodding off. The hour and a half seemed to pass faster than her typical twenty-minute commute. She directed Cody from the main road to the winding drive that led to the cluster of cabins.

"So, you do this every year?"

"Get together? Yes. We only started doing the cabin thing when my sister, Lacey, and her wife had the twins. My parents decided everyone would be more likely to show up if we weren't all crammed into their three-bedroom ranch. And since Jake and Ayana alternate years with her family, they can come up for the weekend and it still feels festive."

Cody pulled in next to Mom's old Subaru. "And that's what's happening this year. Jake and Ayana are coming with the two in college and their youngest on Friday."

"Yes." She smiled at how seriously Cody took learning the names and details. "But also, how are you so good at this?"

"I'm a teacher."

"Right." She thought of Cody as more of a fancy scientist than a teacher, but she loved that Cody identified that way. And referred to herself as a teacher instead of a professor.

"And I'm going to bond with Keisha, Lacey's wife, over that." Cody winked, then reached into the back seat to put a hand on Ben's leg. "Hey, Ben. Wake up. We're here."

Ben blinked a few times and rubbed his eyes. When he looked out his window, his mouth dropped open. "Are we staying there?"

Jess couldn't help but grin. "We are."

"It's so big."

"Well, there are a lot of us, so we need lots of room."

He nodded, understanding but no less in awe. "It's like in a movie."

Cody ran a hand through her hair. "We clearly don't get out of the city enough."

She laughed, reminding herself to focus on the pending introductions and not how absentmindedly sexy Cody looked when she did that. She turned to Ben. "Do you want to go see the inside?"

He nodded eagerly and unbuckled himself. "Yeah!"

"I love that he's not nervous," she whispered to Cody.

"He can be shy sometimes, but he's been dragged to enough things with me that new environments don't spook him. I always feel bad about it, but maybe there's some good."

"For sure."

Ben stomped around in the snow while they grabbed the bags. Cody handed him his backpack and he put it on, even though they were only about ten steps from the house. They hadn't hit the front step before the door swung open.

Mom stepped onto the wide plank pine porch. "You're here."

"Hey, Mom." She let herself get pulled into one of those hugs that made everything seem right with the world.

Mom released her more quickly than she would normally and turned her attention to Ben. "And you must be Ben."

Ben took a step closer to Cody but managed a smile and a hello. Cody introduced herself and extended a hand, which of course made Ben want to shake hands, too. Inside, Jess suggested they head upstairs first to drop off their things and use the bathroom. She figured it would give both Cody and Ben a minute to settle before the barrage of introductions and questions and conversations her very well-meaning but very loud family could dish out.

They'd no sooner come downstairs when the front door swung open again, this time with her grandparents on the other side. Ben, who'd opted to hold her hand, stopped in his tracks. The tug on her hand made her stop as well. "You okay, buddy?"

Ben looked at her, eyes wide and full of wonder. "Is your grandpa...Santa Claus?"

He said "Santa Claus" with that exaggerated whisper five-year-olds have, and it took every ounce of self-restraint not to laugh. Because, clearly, he wasn't joking. She leaned in to whisper her reply. "He isn't, but he could play Santa in a movie, don't you think?"

Ben nodded, his awe only slightly tempered. "He could."

Ben continued to stare and Cody leaned in with a whisper of her own. "I'm pretty sure he thinks it's a cover-up and he's looking at the real Santa in street clothes."

She snorted before she could help herself, then attempted to mask it with a cough. Cody smiled conspiratorially. Meanwhile, Mom was giving her the quizzical brow from across the room. More flustered than she cared to admit—by both—she cleared her throat and launched into introductions. Introductions spilled into lunch, the traditional pre-Thanksgiving sandwich buffet.

She joined the line with Cody and Ben, plopping a couple of slices of seven-grain bread onto her paper plate. "I hope this is okay. We always do sandwiches for the first day since people get here at all times. I promise tomorrow's cooking will make up for it."

After putting a sub roll on her plate and a piece of wheat bread on the one she was building for Ben, Cody gave her a questioning look. "What's not to like? It's a meal I didn't have to think up, plan, put together, or make kid-friendly."

"Okay, okay. When you put it that way. I had this flash of dinner at the president's house and thought maybe you were used to something fancier."

Cody laughed. "Maybe one day I'll tell you how often we eat chicken nuggets for dinner."

"With broccoli and cheese sauce," Ben added, shuffling along the length of the kitchen island between them.

It still caught her off guard how often Ben was paying attention to their conversation. She'd thought it had to do with being afraid she would say something inappropriate for five-year-old ears. But seeing Ben stay close to Cody while her nieces and nephew sat at the kids' table talking amongst themselves made her realize her childhood had been the latter. Enough siblings and cousins milling around that she rarely had to resort to adult company. Not that there was anything wrong with adult company, but she hoped Ben got along with Joshua and the girls and didn't need to bother with grown-ups, at least for a little while.

"Turkey or ham?" Cody asked him.

"Turkey, please."

They finished making their sandwiches, debating the relative merits of Cheetos versus potato chips and agreeing pickles should count as a vegetable. She was just about to ask Ben if he wanted to sit with the other kids when Cody beat her to it. When he agreed to join the kids' table without hesitation, her heart swelled with pride she probably had no business feeling.

After eating, she had a faint inkling that a nap would be nice. Which made her think about what it would be like to curl up with Cody. Like they did on Cody's sofa, but in bed. With fewer clothes. But before she could entertain the idea any further, or rein herself in, Lacey stood from the table. "Who wants to go sledding?"

"I do! I do!" Ben jumped up and down in unison with Joshua.

At Ben's unbridled enthusiasm, Lacey cringed and shot Cody an apologetic look. "Sorry, I should have asked you first."

Cody stood as well, waving her off. "No worries. I think sledding is a fantastic idea, especially after so much sitting still this morning."

Lacey tapped her ginger ale to Cody's glass of water. "Here's to tiring them out and sleeping through the night."

Cody lifted her glass. "I'll drink to that."

"Can I drink to that, too? In solidarity?" Because tiring Ben out had its own merits.

"Absolutely." Cody clinked with Jess.

Lacey followed suit. "But that means you're on equal kid duty with the rest of us for the next three days. Especially if someone wants something at six in the morning. No shirking."

Cody put a hand on her arm. "I wouldn't ask—"

Jess lifted her free hand to cut Cody off. "Nope. I accept all the rights and responsibilities of being the cool aunt slash grown-up. You can't take it back now."

Rather than get overly serious, which she thought Cody might do, Cody laughed. "Oh, I'm not taking anything back. I'm wondering if I should get you to sign a contract."

Lacey roared with laughter, though it might have more to do with knowing that her and Cody's entire relationship was basically a contract. Cody offered a friendly shrug, then rustled up Ben so they could go change. She watched Ben tear up the stairs—clearly with excess energy to work off—and smiled.

"Are you sure this is temporary?"

Lacey's question broke into her reverie. "You sound like Mom."

"Yeah, but I'm asking based on preponderance of evidence, not wishful thinking."

She groaned, as much over the lawyer speak as the comment itself. "What evidence?"

Lacey gave her a bland look. "I know you. Also, I'm very observant."

"Mm-hmm. Well, it doesn't matter. That's not the arrangement." The arrangement didn't even include sex yet, and sharing a room with Cody and Ben had her relegated to the rollaway cot.

"She's hot, though."

Understatement of the century. "Not the foundation of a long-term relationship."

"Ben seems to adore you."

She'd fallen for him as much as his mom at this point. "You realize the implication of that, right?"

Lacey shrugged. "I could say that I do, and also that I know you want to be a mom but feel ambivalent about being pregnant."

"But you won't?"

"I won't. One, because it's heavy-handed and that's more Mom's style than mine. Two, because you've only been seeing each other for a month and I only met her about two hours ago."

Jess blew out a breath. All the things she reminded herself of on a daily basis. "And three, because we mutually agreed to break up on Valentine's Day."

"No, not and three."

"You object?" She wasn't a lawyer, but she'd watched enough courtroom dramas to know the lingo.

"Yes." Lacey's expression was smug. "Relevance."

"Overruled." She elbowed Lacey gently but laughed.

"Let's take a recess until I see how she handles the chaos that is Archer family Thanksgiving dinner. We'll reconvene tomorrow before bedtime."

Jess rolled her eyes. "I'm going to go put on my snow pants."

Chapter Sixteen

"Can I bring Papa Bruce his pie?"

Cody nodded, surprised again at how confident Ben was around Jess's family. "Ask him what type he wants. Pumpkin, pecan, or apple."

Ben tugged her arm. "You come too."

Okay, not entirely confident. Still, he'd come a long way in the short twenty-four hours they'd all been in Breckenridge, and she was proud of him. True, Jess's family made it easy. Her parents and her grandparents were sweet and welcoming. Her sister and sister's wife were fun, not to mention funny. What was even better, their kids created enough chaos that Cody didn't stress about Ben making messes. And Jess was so happy around them. It all seemed exactly the way Thanksgiving should be and almost too good to be true.

"Papa Bruce, do you want pie?"

"Do I want pie?" Bruce grinned at Ben. "Do ducks quack?"

"Ask him which type he wants," Cody whispered.

Bruce glanced up at her and winked, then waited for Ben.

Ben cleared his throat. "Would you like pumpkin, pecan, or apple?"

Bruce rubbed his belly. "I don't know if I can pick."

"We can probably convince Jess to cut a little slice of each," Cody offered.

"I knew I liked you." Bruce looked over at his wife. "Hon, we have to tell Jess this one's a keeper."

"Oh, I've been telling her that all day." Elaine pulled Ben into a sideways hug. "We're keeping him too. Even if he managed to scare me with that fake snake. Where did you find that thing?"

"Not telling." Ben laughed and wiggled away when she pretended to look for the plastic snake in his hair. He'd been soaking up grandparent attention all day. Cody loved to see it, even if it was a painful reminder that her own parents had never had the chance to lavish a grandkid with love.

"If I'm eating a slice of each pie, I guess I better go get my extra stomach."

"You have an extra stomach?" Ben looked intrigued but also a little grossed out.

"Well, cows have four stomachs," Cody said. "But I don't think he's a cow. What do you think?"

Bruce let out a convincing moo, then mooed again when Ben clapped his hands over his mouth and giggled. "You go tell Jess that Papa Bruce is a cow and wants a slice of pie for each stomach."

"Four slices?" Ben's eyes got big.

"Nah, just three. Moo. The first stomach's full, remember?"

Ben looked at Cody as if wondering if she was going to let him get away with it. Cody only smiled. "Okay, we got our order. Three slices of pie coming up for Papa Bruce."

As they made their way back to the kitchen, Ben said, "Papa Bruce only has one stomach, right?"

"Yeah, buddy. People only have one stomach."

"He's gonna have a tummy ache later."

"Probably. That's how it is on Thanksgiving. There's too much good food to pass up." Although Cody wondered if Ben even remembered having a big Thanksgiving. They'd had their share of Friendsgivings, but this was different.

"It's not fair we get our pie last," Ben said, passing Jess's grandparents who were tucking into a shared slice of pecan and looking not only adorable but an awful lot like Mr. and Mrs. Claus in matching red.

"Sure, it's fair. It's our turn to serve. But don't worry. There's no way we're going to run out of pie." Cody had recruited Ben to help with pie delivery while Jess was cutting and serving in the kitchen with Lacey. More than wanting him to help, she'd wanted a moment to check on him. Since he had virtually no experience with big family gatherings, she'd half expected him to act out at some point that day. Fortunately, he'd bonded with Jess's nephew, and the two had played nonstop until dinner. "You and Joshua seem to be having fun. Everything going okay?"

"He's my best friend."

"That was fast." Not surprising, though. That was how things went with him. By the end of the trip, he'd be attached to every member of Jess's family—not to mention a lot more attached to Jess. A little part of her worried about that attachment, but she pushed it away for now.

"I want pumpkin pie. With extra whip cream," Ben said. "Same as Joshua."

They'd gotten back to the kitchen and Jess chuckled. "Another kid wants extra whipped cream?"

He gave an enthusiastic nod to Jess. "Yes, please."

"One more delivery to take to Papa Bruce. Then I'll have your pumpkin pie ready for you. With extra whipped cream." She handed Ben a plate laden with a slice of each pie. "Think you can carry this one by yourself?"

Ben stared down at the plate. "How'd you know he was gonna want all three?"

"I can read minds." Jess tapped her temple.

Ben opened his mouth in amazement. "Really?"

"If she can, we better watch what we think, huh?" Cody sidled up to Jess as Ben headed off with the last delivery. Lacey was busy putting leftovers into containers and not looking their direction and Jess was in the process of adding a generous dollop of cream to a slice of pumpkin pie. "So, what do I have to do to get my own slice?"

"I could give you a list." Jess dipped the spoon back into the bowl of whipped cream and held it up to Cody's lips. In a lower voice, she added, "Or you can just eat whatever I put in front of you."

Anticipating Jess might teasingly take the spoon back before she got any, Cody caught her wrist and held tight. She opened her mouth and licked the tip of the spoon, then took the whole thing into her mouth. A sound between a moan and a gasp slipped out of Jess's lips.

Lacey whistled. "Damn, you two need a room."

Earning a whistle from Jess's sister probably should have been embarrassing, but Cody couldn't help laughing. With her mouth full of cream, the sound came out more as a snort, which got Jess laughing too.

"We do need a room." Jess dropped the spoon in the kitchen sink and got another from the drawer. "You got that hotel reservation lined up, right?"

"One week from tonight."

"I wish we lived closer to you two," Lacey said. "Ben could have a sleepover with Joshua and you could have the whole night instead of only a few hours."

Ben returned to the kitchen just as Cody wondered how much Jess had told her sister—not only about the hotel plans but about all of it.

"Sleepover?" Ben's eyes darted to Cody. "Can I have a sleepover with Joshua?"

"You hear everything, don't you?" Jess handed Ben a plate and tapped his nose. "This one's yours. Extra whipped cream as promised. Maybe someday you and Joshua can have a sleepover but not next week. He lives in Boulder. It's a little too far away and we'd worry about you."

She liked the way Jess didn't hesitate to help set boundaries and wondered if it really would be a shared worry. Something told her it would. Ben wasn't the only one who'd gotten attached.

"What about a sleepover tonight?" Lacey suggested. "Instead of you sleeping in your mom's room, you could sleep with Joshua and the girls. There's an extra bunk bed."

Ben hesitated. A sleepover in theory was apparently easier to imagine than a sleepover that night. Cody had hoped to convince him to sleep in the kids' room the first night, but he'd refused. So instead of having at least some snuggle time with Jess in the double bed, Jess was stuck on the cot. She'd promised it was fine, but Cody knew she was disappointed.

"You don't get many chances to sleep in a bunk bed." She tried to be encouraging without nudging.

Ben nodded slowly. "Okay."

"When it's lights out, you and Joshua have to sleep though." Lacey knew kids, that was for sure.

"We will," Ben promised.

Cody didn't know if he'd actually fall asleep, but having even a little time alone with Jess would be worth it. She glanced at Jess hoping she had the same thought. Jess gave her a coy smile. *Oh, yeah. She can read minds.*

❖

"I still want a hotel room," Jess said.

"Me too. And I don't know how long Ben will last in there." Cody gestured to the closed door. The sounds of kids chattering had started up again.

"My sister promised she'd be on call for the night."

"Yeah, but…"

"I know. We should make the most of our time."

Jess slipped her hand in Cody's as they made their way down the hall from the kids' room to theirs. Everyone, adults included, had decided to call it an early night in anticipation of tomorrow's skiing. She'd been happy to go to bed for other reasons entirely.

"You know, you're getting this kid thing down pretty well." She meant it. Over the course of the last two days, she'd lost count of the number of times Jess had made exactly the same parenting call she would've. "It's like it's intuitive to you when the rest of us take years and years to figure it out."

"Thank you. I'll happily take that compliment. I like kids." Jess paused in the hallway outside the closed door of their room. "But that's not the only thing that's intuitive to me."

The change in Jess's tone made her smile. Since dessert, Jess seemed to go out of her way to brush against her or casually touch. Not only had each caress felt amazing, they kicked her arousal into overdrive. She'd been enjoying the anticipation but now she couldn't wait to get Jess undressed. "So what else is intuitive?"

"This." Jess stepped forward and pressed into Cody's lips.

Even knowing it was coming, Jess's kiss took her breath away. She stumbled back a step and bumped into the closed door, then fumbled for the handle as Jess continued the kiss.

They made it through the door, then tumbled onto the bed. Jess landed on top, but laughingly accepted getting flipped. Cody pushed a pillow under Jess's head and braced herself above her. "Hi."

Jess smiled. "Hi yourself."

A charge raced through her knowing Jess was waiting for her next move. "It's been a while for me. Which isn't to say I'm feeling shy about what comes next, but I'm not sure I'm going to be able to go slow."

"I can tell." Jess brushed a finger across Cody's lips. "The way you've been looking me up and down all night. You're like a kid who knows what present they're getting and can't wait to unwrap it."

"That's a really good description." Cody's clit pulsed. Damn, it was nice having Jess under her. She wanted to hold on to the feeling and at the same time her body hummed with eager anticipation of what to do next.

Jess narrowed her eyes. "What are you waiting for?"

"Maybe for someone to tell me I can unwrap my present."

Jess pushed up to whisper right into her ear. "Unwrap your damn present, Cody."

Cody had imagined their first time more than once: slowly stripping Jess with gentle kisses, their skin meeting like two palms lightly pressing together. But that wasn't what she wanted tonight. Need overpowered her.

In practically one move, she pulled Jess to a sitting position and had her sweater off. She unclipped Jess's bra, and warm, full breasts fell into her hands. Cody nearly moaned her own pleasure. She'd fully intended on taking the rest of Jess's clothes off but she couldn't resist the dark pink nipples that perked with only a light caress. She bent her head and sucked one between her lips.

Jess gasped and found Cody's shoulders. She gripped tight and her gasp became a moan. "Oh, God. You know what you're doing."

Cody chuckled, letting Jess's nipple slip out of her mouth. "You were worried I might not?"

"I mean, you never know."

Jess's playful look made Cody want to pull out all the stops. "I'll have to show you all the things I'm good at."

"You should." Jess stroked her hands down Cody's arms. "I like this side of you. Confident is even sexier than strong and stubborn."

"Still calling me stubborn? Hmm. You might like that about me after a while." Cody needed Jess all the way naked then. She had to feel all of her, every bit of smooth skin, every taut muscle, and then she'd show Jess exactly what she was capable of.

Even in bed, Jess's skirt came off easy once the side zipper was taken care of, and it wasn't any trouble to get her underwear off either. Once she was naked, Cody managed one moment to appreciate her body before desire overwhelmed her.

She started at Jess's neck, kissing all the way down to the apex of her thighs and then back up to her swollen nipples. Desire made her delirious. Delirious to everything except how good Jess felt. The strength of her body was undeniable and yet she was responsive to even the lightest touch. The combination felt like ripples of challenge that only made her hotter.

"I want you naked too." Jess tugged at Cody's pants. "Get these clothes off. I've been waiting too damn long. I want to feel you on me the right way."

"There's a right way?"

"Yes. Naked."

Cody grinned. "So demanding."

"Oh, you have no idea. Just wait."

Cody laughed. She nipped Jess's shoulder and then rolled off to strip. Jess watched, propped up on one elbow.

"Do you prefer handsome or pretty?"

"Guess."

"You're both, but I'm going to call you handsome tonight."

"Good call." Cody shifted back onto Jess. When her skin pressed against Jess's, she couldn't hold back her moan. "God it's been too long since I've felt a naked woman under me."

"Just any naked woman would do, huh?"

"No. Definitely not." She stopped smiling as Jess's beauty struck her. It wasn't only how gorgeous she was, though. It was everything else about her, too. How amazing she was with Ben, how funny she was, how sharp-witted, and how she challenged Cody in all the right ways. "I don't know how I got lucky enough to date you, but I'm going to make the most of it for as long as I get."

Cody leaned down and met Jess's lips. Each time felt even better than the last. Her lips had found a perfect match and she didn't know if she'd ever like kissing anyone else near as much. She moved from Jess's lips to her neck and then down to her breasts—again sidetracked by Jess's nipples. But then she shifted and her leg moved between Jess's. As soon as she felt Jess's wetness against her thigh, she knew she needed more.

She scattered kisses along Jess's soft belly and inched lower until she was between her legs. The thought of going slow was tempting. Of drawing everything out for as long she could. But as soon as Jess's faint musk caught her attention, she didn't want to hold back.

She dropped her head and coursed her tongue between Jess's folds. Jess drew up her legs, moaning and clutching at Cody's hair. She loved having her hair pulled and groaned her own approval. Maybe later she'd tell Jess to feel free to grab harder. *Later.* She found Jess's swollen clit and sucked it between her lips then let it slip out, only to repeat the move again.

"Fuck. Do that again and I'm going to come."

"That easy, huh?" Cody wanted to give Jess more pleasure. She had a list of other things she wanted to do. But she couldn't help herself. She circled the spot and then sucked again. Jess bucked her hips and gripped Cody's shoulders. Nails dug into her skin and a half growl escaped her lips. She'd been thinking her trusty vibrator was enough. How had she forgotten how much she loved pleasuring someone else? She lowered her head and gave all her attention to Jess's clit.

"Oh yeah...yes...yessss."

Jess's thighs clamped together as she rode out the orgasm, and Cody almost laughed at how strong her legs were. She filed away the thought of asking Jess about her other job. The one that didn't involve writing about their relationship and instead gave her a kick-ass body.

"Shit, am I hurting you?" Jess parted her legs and Cody shifted up to kiss her lips.

"I'm tough, don't worry. But you've got amazing legs."

"You have an amazing mouth." Jess shivered and then wrapped her arms around Cody. "Can you relax all the way? I want to feel your weight on me."

Cody had been holding herself up, but when she lowered herself all the way on Jess, she definitely wasn't relaxed.

"Give me a minute here and I'll return that gift you gave me."

"You know you aren't supposed to return gifts."

Jess laughed softly and the feel of it rumbled through Cody. "Then I won't return it. I'll give you something entirely different."

"Can't wait." She found Jess's lips but had no sooner started the kiss than Jess turned her face to the side. "What's wrong?"

"I think someone knocked on the door. Did you hear that?"

Cody listened for a moment, hoping Jess was wrong. A more distinct knock and Cody wanted to pretend she was imagining it, even as she got out of bed and tugged on the shirt she'd tossed to the ground not long enough ago.

She opened the door and Ben looked up at her, eyes puffy and red. "Oh, buddy, what's wrong?"

"I don't want to sleep in the kid room. Where's Jess?"

"She's in here. But—" She felt Jess's hand on her arm. She'd come up behind her and managed to grab a T-shirt and pair of pajama pants along the way.

"It's fine," Jess murmured when Cody started to apologize.

Ben pushed past Cody to wrap his arms around Jess's legs. "I want to sleep with you guys. Please?"

Jess gave her a pleading look. But it wasn't a get rid of him kind. It was more of a we can't say no.

Cody sighed. She kind of figured he'd be in at some point. If only they'd had a little more time. One dose of Jess was nowhere near enough to sate her desires. "All right, you can sleep in here but no kicking Jess."

CHAPTER SEVENTEEN

Jess woke to something pressing into her left shoulder blade. Had Rascal sneaked into her bed again? She opened her eyes. Realizing where she was gave way to remembering who she was sharing a bed with. But why was Cody pushing her away? She rolled over, only to discover it wasn't Cody's hand shoved against her but Ben's foot.

Oh. Right.

Details of the night before flooded her still drowsy brain. Being with Cody. The amazing orgasm. The interruption. Ben's tear-streaked face lighting up when she said he should climb into bed with them. Of course, he'd wanted the middle and fell asleep almost instantly. She and Cody had made eyes at each other for a while, managing to convey humor, frustration, desire, and resignation without uttering a word.

She'd been hesitant about being able to sleep with a kid in the bed—fear of squishing him as much as fear she'd subconsciously reach for Cody and get Ben instead—but she'd drifted off and slept soundly. And now sunlight peeked in around the curtains and Ben, who'd managed to turn himself upside down and practically sideways, had his foot wedged against her with far more force than a sleeping five-year-old should be able to muster.

Since she literally had no room to scoot over, she tried to shift him into a slightly more up-and-down position. He mumbled but didn't otherwise stir. Cody didn't either, giving her the luxury of studying them both.

The more time she spent with Ben, the more she could see Cody in him. Even if they weren't biologically related, they shared the same sandy blond hair that had a tendency to go every which way. His mannerisms were like Cody in miniature most of the time, even in sleep. It made her wonder about Cody's ex, Ben's other mom. Was she really out of the picture completely? Ben hadn't gone to see her once in the time she'd known Cody—at least that she was aware of— and Ben never mentioned her.

Not that it was her place to think about such things, except maybe to judge the woman for walking out on both Ben and Cody and seeming to not look back. Even if she hoped to be part of their lives when this whole experiment ended, parenting wasn't part of the deal. Yet, Ben had wanted her last night. Did he miss his bio mom? If she got closer to Cody, and things didn't end come Valentine's Day, what would her role be in Ben's life?

She shifted her gaze from Ben to Cody and, despite having Ben sandwiched between them, let her mind wander to easier topics. Like what she and Cody had been up to before he knocked on their door. Cody was hotter—and better at giving pleasure—than even her most salacious fantasies. And they'd only just gotten started. Just the visual of Cody between her legs had her pressing her thighs together and squirming slightly.

Ben mumbled again and turned, thwacking Cody across the stomach. She cringed, convinced the force of it would wake them both. But no. Which was funny because she was pretty sure the sound of Ben's voice a room away would wake Cody in a heartbeat. The fact that Cody didn't even flinch made her smile.

Since she was fully awake, she slid from bed as quietly as possible. She threw a hoodie on over the pajamas she'd managed to scramble into last night and headed downstairs. The aroma of coffee greeted her before she even made it into the kitchen. She found her mom and sister at the kitchen island, already sipping their first cups. "Morning," she said, making a beeline for the pot.

"Did you and Cody sleep well?" Lacey's tone was pure innocence, even if the insinuation in the question was anything but.

She poured herself a cup, adding her holiday levels of cream and sugar, before joining them. "We did, or at least I did. Better than I would have expected with a kid taking his half out of the middle."

Lacey laughed and Mom gave her a sympathetic look. "Did Ben not make it through the night in the kids' room?" Mom asked.

"Not even close." Though, as disappointed as she was to be interrupted when they were, perhaps it was for the best. Well, better than in the middle of what would have been happening next.

"Welcome to life with little ones." Lacey lifted her cup.

It was a gentle tease, but it made her think. Less about how she wouldn't want that to be her everyday life and more about how, if being with Cody was her everyday life, she wouldn't mind the occasional interruption.

Oof. Her brain was about two thousand steps ahead of where she should be this morning.

Lacey gave her a gentle nudge with her elbow. "Oh, don't worry. You get used to it. You also get a lock for the door."

Deciding this was a safer topic, even with Mom there, she lifted a shoulder. "Or you get a hotel."

"Bow-chicka-wow-wow." Lacey did a little dance in her seat.

Mom, who'd gotten awfully quiet, stared into her coffee cup. Jess reached over and squeezed her arm. "Sorry. No more sex talk."

Mom looked up, exasperation on her face. "Oh, that doesn't bother me. You two are grown women. I know what you get up to. And I'm not a prude."

Jess put up her hands in a show of concession. "Okay, okay. Didn't mean to insult your cool mom rep. You looked uncomfortable is all."

"I'm just wondering again how temporary this temporary arrangement really is."

She groaned, not because she didn't want to talk about it but because she didn't have an answer. Again and again, she'd questioned whether things would really be temporary. This morning she couldn't stop her mind. She'd even started noodling ways to broach it in her column. "We've already discussed this."

Mom offered one of her don't try to pull one over on me head tilts. "Yes, but that was before I had the chance to meet Cody."

She blew out a breath. "And you like her. And Ben, of course. I'm sure you'd love to add him to your brood of grandkids. There's more to it than that, though."

"There's a hell of a lot more to it. Like the way Cody looks at you in ways that have nothing to do with a passing attraction. Or the way you clearly adore Ben as much as he adores you."

"It still doesn't mean we're going to settle down and be a perfect little happy family."

Mom lifted her chin. "But it doesn't mean you couldn't."

She looked to Lacey for backup, but the look on Lacey's face said her sister had sided with their mother. "Never mind. Don't say anything."

"Did you apply for that job you told me about? The one in Philadelphia?" Mom's seeming abrupt change of subject was anything but.

"Not yet." She'd dusted off her résumé but had yet to draft a cover letter, telling herself she needed to finish this week's column and get ready for the long weekend instead.

"Are you going to?"

She'd been on the fence about it from the get-go. It was a higher profile staff writer position at *Q*, one of the leading LGBTQ magazines, one that had print circulation twice that of Sapphisticate's digital audience. More money for sure, and more prestige. Assignments about current events, not dating dos and don'ts.

But also a hell of a lot more pressure. Oh, and a relocation. A big, across the country, East Coast relocation. She adored Philly the few times she'd been, but the prospect of moving there—or anywhere, really—filled her with a vague sense of sadness. And that was before things with Cody.

Of course, she hadn't said any of that to Mom or Lacey. She'd only told them that her former boss sent her the posting with some encouragement to apply. It had been so flattering, she'd shared the email without thinking. Before the reality of what it would entail set in. If she tried to explain that now, they'd be convinced it was because of Cody. Convinced she was holding out hope that things with Cody would become permanent.

"I am. Yes. Next week. As soon as I get home."

Lacey's raised brow made her think maybe she'd overplayed her hand with the eagerness, but it was too late to take it back. Fortunately, a flurry of footsteps on the stairs meant at least some of the sleeping kids were now awake. A few seconds later, Joshua, Ava, and Addy appeared in the kitchen. Keisha followed a moment later.

Several conversations started at once and she took it as her cue to go check on Cody and Ben. But before she made it to the stairs, they appeared at the top and started down. "Good morning, sleepyhead."

"Jess!" Ben jumped from the bottom step into her outstretched arms.

She gave him a squeeze, using the opportunity to look over his shoulder at Cody. "Good morning."

Cody's smile was sheepish. "I hope we didn't drive you away with kicks or snores."

"Nah." She shook her head. "Early riser."

"Usually we are, too."

Ben leaned back. "I always sleep better with Mom. Do you?"

If he only knew. "I did sleep really well, so maybe." She put him down and offered Cody a wink. "Who wants coffee?"

Ben made faces and various noises of disgust as they headed into the kitchen. She poured Cody a cup before asking Ben what he might like instead. He was already deep in conversation with Joshua about whether Spiderman or Batman was a better superhero. She was glad to see that Ben abandoning the kids' room hadn't dampened their budding friendship.

Dad came in with firewood, Mom started making French toast, and Keisha queued up a Christmas playlist because it was the day after Thanksgiving and therefore time. In almost every way, it was identical to so many post-holiday mornings with her family. The familiarity of it, the tradition, meant almost as much as the holiday itself.

She'd wondered if having Cody and Ben there would make it feel different, strange. In truth, the strange part was just how not strange it felt. With Ben and Joshua vying for Ava's and Addy's attention and Cody engrossed in conversation with Keisha, it was like they'd been there countless times before. At the very least, it felt like they belonged. Considering she hadn't ever had a girlfriend serious enough to join her, it felt…significant.

Well, significant or potentially disastrous. She had such a habit of falling for the wrong people or letting herself get caught up with someone whose feelings went way deeper than her own, it was hard to imagine she'd magically broken her string of bad relationship luck. Having Convenient Arrangement Cody fit perfectly into her family was probably just one more way the universe had devised to pull a fast one on her.

Enough. Cody was here. Everything was going better than she could have imagined. Slipping into a funk would be pointless. Besides, the slopes beckoned. And no way in hell was she going to let getting ahead of herself ruin a perfectly good day of skiing.

She added extra butter and syrup to her second piece of French toast and helped herself to another slice of bacon before turning her attention to Cody. "So, am I going to talk you into strapping on a pair of skis?"

Cody hesitated. "I don't know. Ben's never gone and I don't want to slow everyone down."

"Nonsense," Dad said. "We all take turns. A couple of grown-ups on the bunny slopes with the kids, one or two in the lodge in case anyone has enough, and a couple enjoying the bigger runs."

Redoubling her commitment to just relax and have a good time already, she elbowed Cody lightly in the ribs. "So, are you worried about Ben slowing us down, or you?"

Cody elbowed her back. "You found me out."

"Don't worry, I'll go easy on you." She didn't mean to make it sound suggestive, but it totally did.

Cody's expression only confirmed it. "Not too easy, I hope."

"Never." She kept her words subtle if not her voice.

"I'm glad to hear it." Unlike herself, Cody's tone gave nothing away.

She indulged in one smirk before turning her attention to her breakfast before things got out of hand. But when she looked up, Mom and Lacey were sending her matching knowing looks. So much for subtlety. She swirled her bacon in syrup before taking a bite. That was okay. She'd never been good at fooling them anyway.

With Cody giving Ben a bath and everyone else lounging and lazing after the day of skiing, Jess found herself with a quiet moment alone. She settled on the sofa next to the fireplace with a blanket and her laptop, thinking she'd maybe take a stab at a cover letter. If for no other reason than to say she'd tried. But she'd no sooner finished the business letter formatting than she found herself clicking over to the Cuffing Chronicles folder.

She'd created a document for her Thanksgiving column but not decided on the angle. Fortunately, the last day and a half gave her plenty of options. Sure, the prospect of broadcasting her feelings to the universe gave her even more pause than writing about having sex, but that was the whole point of her column. She set her tea aside, cracked her knuckles, and started typing.

> You don't really expect your first time with someone to be at a cabin you're sharing with your parents and grandparents, but in true Carrie and Jess fashion, we don't seem to be doing anything by the books. Of course, we didn't get very far before a certain adorable five-year-old insisted he needed to sleep with us and not in the kids' room. But what we did get to? Hoo boy.
>
> I know, I know. You want more. I'll give you more. But first we need to talk about Thanksgiving proper. One, because it was fantastic. Two, because if I have to live by the mantra of good things come to those who wait, you do, too. And three, because I'm pretty sure, dear readers, that I've caught a case of the feels.

Before she could decide whether to lead with Ben thinking Grandpa was Santa Claus or the way Cody looked at her over the pile of potatoes they'd been assigned to peel, Cody appeared at the top of the stairs. "You've been requested for story time."

"I'll be right there." She closed her laptop with a snap and extricated herself from the blanket just in time to catch Mom give her yet another knowing look.

"Requested, huh?" Mom's voice was quiet but lacked nothing in the insinuation department.

"I'll have you know I do really good voices."

"Right, right." Mom nodded and sipped her tea, a gesture that managed to convey she knew damn well it had nothing to do with Jess's acting.

She set her computer aside. "Well, I do."

"Yes, dear."

Dad looked up at the phrase usually reserved for placating him. Jess offered him a shrug and he returned his attention to his book on fly fishing. She padded up the stairs, enjoying the way her cushy wool socks felt against the wood.

Cody greeted her at the top with a smile. "You sure you don't mind?"

"Of course not. I love story time."

"Do you want me to come in with you?"

As much as she wanted to be near Cody pretty much any chance she got, having her around for stories made her feel a little silly about all the voices she did. And Cody rarely got a night off from bedtime. "I got this. The kettle is still warm if you want tea or cocoa."

Cody perked up. "Yeah?"

"And the bottle of ibuprofen is on the counter."

Cody cringed, then laughed. "Does it make me sound old to be excited by the prospect of hot tea and anti-inflammatories before bed?"

"Yes." She smirked. "But you're in good company."

"Oh, good."

"Keep my spot warm and I'll be down in a bit."

Cody brought a hand to Jess's cheek and kissed her. "You got it."

Cody headed downstairs and she headed into the room they'd all be sharing once again. Ben was tuckered out, but his eyes lit up at the sight of her. She picked up *The Mousetronaut*, which Ben had packed special for her, and thought about the column she'd started. Yep. Definitely a case of the feels.

Chapter Eighteen

Cody glanced around the room one last time, wondering if she should check under the bed for socks. Ben had a habit of flinging his everywhere, and there was a good chance when they got home and unpacked, she'd discover several singles. With a sigh, she got down on her knees and started a search.

"What are you doing down there?" Jess asked.

Cody looked up from where she'd half squeezed herself under the bed. Her luck that Jess would pick that moment to walk in. She held up a striped dinosaur sock. "Search and rescue mission. I have a sixth sense for missing socks."

"Why'd you wait till now to tell me this?" Jess folded her arms and gave Cody a mock disapproving look. "I'm going to need you to come over to my place pronto. You've got work to do."

Cody grinned. "Lots of missing socks?"

"You have no idea. I'm fairly certain it's my roommate's dog. Finn swears Rascal isn't a sock stealer, but someone's eating them. It's either the washing machine or the dog." Jess held out her hand and Cody passed her the dinosaur sock. She went over to Ben's backpack and squished it into one of the side pockets. "Just so you know, that's not the only reason I'd like you to come over."

"You think I'd be good for more than finding missing socks?" Cody got up from the floor.

"I'm also missing several gloves. Curiously only the left hand."

"Do I want to ask what you might only use one hand for?"

Jess tilted her head. "You can use your imagination. Or you could come over some time."

Her tone was flirty and light, but that didn't mean there wasn't a problem. As nice as the past few days had been, they'd barely had any time alone. Their one evening together had been cut short and Ben had been noticeably clingy the following night. "I'd hoped we'd have more time together—alone—on this trip. And I'd really like to be the kind of girlfriend, or whatever we are, who comes over to your place whenever. But with Ben I don't—"

"I didn't mean to make you feel bad. Or to make you feel like you have to explain yourself. I only wanted you to know I'd be happy with a little more of you." Jess sighed. "And now I feel silly admitting that."

"We'll have next Thursday all to ourselves. On a king-size bed." It wasn't enough and Cody knew it. But it was what she had to offer.

"Trust me, I haven't forgotten. You better show up at the hotel prepared for a lot of pent-up energy from me."

"I like the sound of that." A lot in fact. And yet it didn't get at the bigger problem. Jess hadn't signed up for a family. She only wanted someone to date. "I want to do a better job of one-on-one time. I can get a babysitter and come over to your place or we can go out. And maybe it'd be weird, but you could come over any night after Ben's asleep. He's usually out by eight."

"I like all those options." Jess reached for Cody's hand. "You gave me a little taste of something I want a lot more of. But I also like hanging out with you *and* Ben. Don't look so worried. We got this."

Cody wasn't sure, but she nodded anyway.

"The real question is whether you're ready for Thanksgiving good-byes Archer family-style."

"I think I've done pretty well with the Archer family so far."

Jess tugged Cody closer. "You have. Very impressive in fact. But we can be intense. Get ready for lots of hugs."

Good-byes were noisier than expected, and Jess wasn't joking about the hugs. Everyone seemed to hug everyone all at the same time. Ben's eyes got big when Ava—or was it Addy?—opened her arms and came toward him, but then Joshua intercepted the hug and it quickly turned into a game with everyone under seven chasing each other and zipping between the adults.

Jess's mom, Elaine, stepped forward to give Cody a hug last. After she let go, she caught hold of Cody's wrists and cleared her throat like she had something important to say. "So. Next year. I expect both you and Ben to be on pie duty again. What do we have to do to make that happen?"

Cody wasn't entirely sure who Elaine meant to include in "we" but the look of determination on her face reminded her exactly of Jess. How much did Elaine know? As much as she wished the cuffing thing could only be a funny sidebar to how they started dating, the truth was she didn't know what would happen in two months, let alone next year. What did Jess want out of this? Was she still only thinking of her column and what she'd write next? "I'll do what I can."

"Good. That's what I wanted to hear." Elaine released Cody's hands. "You're perfect for Jess. Let's hope she has the smarts to hold on tight."

"What do I have the smarts to hold on to?" Jess stepped away from hugging her sister and studied Elaine, clearly suspicious of what her mother might have said.

"Your father and I have decided Cody's a keeper." Elaine winked at Cody. "So, I'll expect a marriage proposal any day."

Cody and Jess both laughed. Elaine was clearly joking but pretended to act miffed before cracking a smile. "I can try, can't I?"

"Thanks for letting Ben and me crash your Thanksgiving. Jess was right—she's got the best family. You all made us feel like we belonged." From out of nowhere, she felt the press of tears and quickly clenched her teeth. Fortunately, Ben chose that moment to slam into her. He was being chased by Joshua, but it wasn't clear if he'd hit her on accident or needed to be rescued. She scooped him up regardless. For once, he had good timing in interrupting a conversation. "All right, time to go before someone starts crying."

"That's real." Lacey grabbed ahold of Joshua and pointed him to their minivan.

A chorus of "see you soons" followed as everyone tumbled into their respective cars, and a moment later, the rental cabin was in Cody's rearview mirror. She kept glancing at it, feeling ridiculous for being nostalgic for a place she'd only stayed for three nights. Nonetheless, a funk settled when the cabin dropped fully out of sight.

❖

"You okay?" Jess touched Cody's thigh.

"Just focused. I want to get us home in one piece." The snowy mountain roads were a plausible excuse anyway.

"You're a good driver. I'm not worried."

"Thanks." Cody smiled but kept her eyes trained on the car in front of them. They'd been driving for nearly an hour, but her mind hadn't taken a rest. Her thoughts circled from a recap of the week's adventures to sleeping with Jess to the parting words of Jess's mom. Promising to try to make it for next year's Thanksgiving had felt dishonest, but what else could she have said?

Jess turned in her seat and studied Ben, likely trying to decide if he was asleep or not. He seemed to be dozing, but he'd fooled them before. Jess was likely remembering that and weighing if a conversation was a good idea. She shifted back and looked out the window. A moment passed. "You're quiet."

"So are you."

"Because you are. Something's on your mind. You know I'd rather you just tell me what it is."

"I've heard that before."

Jess stuck out her tongue. "Whatever, Dr. Strong, Silent, and Stubborn."

"We can talk." Their mini vacation had been nearly perfect. She didn't need to screw things up now. "I had a nice time with you and your family. But I'm not really looking forward to going back to reality and grading all the exams I should have graded Tuesday night."

"That's what's on your mind?"

Cody found herself biting back the question that had nagged her all week.

"Come on. Out with it." Jess huffed. "You know I'll get it out of you eventually. You picked strong, right? So, you don't get to be silent too."

"I picked stubborn."

Jess smiled. "Fine. You can be stubborn. Start talking."

Cody took her eyes from the road long enough to roll them at Jess who playfully swatted her arm in return. She gripped the steering wheel and wondered what to say. Maybe asking the question was the right decision. It wasn't like she'd get it off her mind otherwise. "How much did you tell your family?"

"About us?"

Jess had to know that was what she meant, but she nodded anyway.

"They've all been reading my posts. Well, not my dad, but everyone else. And my mom tells my dad everything but in PG terms."

"Really? But your mom…" Cody stopped. She tried to recall Elaine's exact words after they'd hugged. "They know cuffing is temporary?"

"Yeah. They get it."

She slowed as the car in front of her swerved around a patch of ice. "They treated Ben and me like we were already part of the family."

"That's how they are." After a moment, Jess shrugged. "When they like someone."

She didn't want to ask how many women Jess had brought to Thanksgiving before her. Or how many the family had liked. They both had history, that was for sure, but Jess clearly hadn't written about everything she'd done with past girlfriends for the whole family to read. On one hand, Cody wished she knew what Jess had said about her. On the other, she remained relieved not to know.

"Mom, look! There's a farm where you can buy Christmas trees! Can we stop? Please?"

Cody looked over her shoulder. Ben was suddenly wide-awake and testing the straps on his booster seat. He bounced up and down with excitement and jammed his finger on the window. "Look! Right there! You promised we could get a real tree this year."

"I don't mind stopping," Jess said under her breath.

Cody looked from Jess to Ben. A Christmas tree definitely wasn't on the agenda and she did have a lot of work waiting for her, but...

"You drove past it." Ben made a sound that was closer to a dog whimper than a whine.

"Buddy, the exit hasn't come up yet. They have the billboard and the sign for the Christmas trees back there, but the exit's up ahead."

"Does that mean we can go?"

His question was so full of happy anticipation she didn't want to say no. Jess set her hand on Cody's leg again. What the signal meant this time wasn't completely clear, but it felt like a nod of support.

Cody exhaled. She needed to stop overthinking. Starting now. "Yeah, we can go pick out a tree."

Ben's squeal filled the car. "No fake tree!"

Jess smiled. "I take it this is your first real tree?"

"Ben's first real tree." Cody angled toward the freeway exit. "I keep promising him we'll get a real one, but each year we run out of time and I set up the plastic one instead."

"And it looks terrible," Ben said.

"How do you remember what our old tree looks like? You were only four the last time we put it up."

"I remember everything." Ben's tone was emphatic.

"Actually, we had a real tree the year you were born, but not even you can remember being a baby." Ben frowned and she wished she hadn't said anything. No one needed to know that Anastasia had embraced the excitement of at least some of Ben's firsts. Or that being left to fend for themselves was part of why the holidays felt like so much work.

Jess shrugged. "Well, I'm always going to vote for a real tree. Nothing smells better."

"I can think of a few things," Cody murmured.

"Ahem. I'm sure you can, but you better keep those thoughts to yourself." Jess's voice shifted to a whisper and her hand shifted up on Cody's thigh.

"Movie popcorn smells better than trees," Ben said.

"No way." Jess shook her head. "Not even close."

"So does chocolate." Ben looked up in contemplation. "And oranges. And...recess."

"Recess?" Jess's look was dubious. "What does recess smell like?"

Cody chuckled as Ben tried to defend that recess had a smell—and a good one at that. The Christmas tree farm came into view and Ben and Jess simultaneously let out a cheer. Cody couldn't help smiling. Whatever happened on Valentine's Day, she was at least eighty percent sure that Jess was good for Ben. And for her.

CHAPTER NINETEEN

Jess scanned the small studio to check everyone's form. "Okay, now that we're in our wide second, let's bend our knees and do slow pulses. Down for two, up for two."

She counted off the first few, then ran through the usual reminders to keep the movements small and maintain posture. She made a loop of the room to make small corrections, then returned to her spot in the center. "Now let's speed it up. Down, down, down."

She let the tempo of the music keep the pace for a minute and allowed her mind to wander. Just like the better part of the last week, it didn't wander. It made a beeline for Cody. And while some of her thoughts had been of the squishy and romantic variety, the majority were R, if not X-rated.

Despite the interruption, they'd managed to go further than on any of their previous attempts. And while she had no interest in being one-sided when it came to sex, she'd be hard-pressed to complain about being on the receiving end of Cody's attentions. All she had to do was close her eyes to see Cody's face between her legs. And the current exercise, with its focus on the inner thighs, reminded her all too well of how it felt to squeeze Cody's shoulders with those muscles.

The music changed, making her realize she'd forced her class to stay in one position far longer than usual. Not to worry. She'd make up the time in core section. She counted down the last four reps, ending with, "And we're out."

The groans from her regulars told her all she needed to know about just how long she'd lost track of time. "Let's come onto our mats for some stretching and show those thighs some love."

She kept her focus on her students for the rest of class, making her way through the remaining seat and core work, along with the final cool down and stretch. She reminded everyone to wipe down their mats and made a point of checking in with the newbie to her class, a gorgeously curvy college student who owned being both intimidated and a little terrified to try barre. "So, what do you think?"

Kari with a K nodded with enthusiasm. "I thought I was going to die during the plank section, but otherwise not bad. I mean, I still thought I was going to die, but in a good way."

"You held your own, way better than I did my first time."

Kari blushed. "That's nice of you to say."

"I mean it. You were a rock star. You should stretch more tonight if you can and know you're going to be sore tomorrow." She didn't want to scare people, but it was better to know what they were in for.

"Oh, I'm fully prepared for a long hot shower and some ibuprofen."

"Good. I hope to see you back."

Kari nodded. "You will. I like the class, but you're a great teacher. High energy without being manic."

"Aw, thanks."

"I mean it. That screaming, competitive thing gives me anxiety." Kari grimaced.

She laughed because she couldn't have described it better herself. "You and me both."

She wished Kari good night, then tidied the props for the next class before heading for the locker room. She grabbed her things instead of hitting the showers, wanting the comfort and full range of products of home before her night with Cody. On her way out, she bumped into Finn.

"Hey, stranger."

Finn lifted her chin. "Hey, yourself."

"You doing okay? I feel like I haven't seen you in a week."

Finn's smile said everything. "I'm good."

"I'm glad. You deserve it."

"You do, too. Speaking of, tonight's your sex date, right? You won't be home?"

Under normal circumstances, she'd give Finn a hard time about referring to anything she did as a sex date, but it would be hard to argue it was anything else. "Yes, but I might be home. Cody can't stay over because of Ben."

Finn nodded, more empathy than judgment. At least Jess hoped it was more empathy than judgment. "Bummer."

The difficulty they'd had getting past first base was frustrating to say the least. But other than those particular interruptions, she really didn't mind Ben being around. The truth of the matter was that she was pretty damn attached to him. And spending Thanksgiving with her family had only reinforced that. Since that wasn't a conversation she needed to have with Finn in the middle of the gym, she settled for, "Yeah."

"Well, I hope tonight is the six-hour sex fest of your dreams."

Again, she wanted to take issue with Finn's choice of words, but they were just a little too spot-on. "Catch up soon? At home, maybe?"

"You mean like civilized roommates?"

She laughed. "Exactly."

Cody had offered to pick her up, but since that would have cut a half hour into either end of the time they had, she suggested meeting there and using the time more fruitfully. She strode into the lobby just as Cody finished checking in, hovering off to the side to make it seem like they weren't together.

"All set?" she asked when Cody turned her way.

To her credit, Cody offered a nod and a casual smile. "All set."

They rode the elevator with a man and his two kids, clearly returning from a trip to the indoor pool. It didn't stop her from giving Cody's butt a surreptitious squeeze while the kids complained about being cold. The room had a standard three-star hotel aesthetic—nice linens, generic art, and a giant television.

"I have to say, this feels a little weird. Like I should buy you dinner first or something." Cody frowned.

She appreciated Cody's chivalry but hoped she'd get over it. "What if I don't want dinner?"

Cody raised a brow, a teasing gleam in her eye. At least Jess hoped it was teasing.

"Or, perhaps more accurately, what if I want you for dinner?"

"How long have you been working on that line?"

She laughed. "If I'd worked on it, I'd like to think I could have come up with a slightly better line."

"It's good to have goals?" Cody shrugged and it made Jess wonder if she really did have hang-ups about this whole hotel plan.

"Is not having dinner going to bother you? I swear I'm good, but I want you to be, too."

That seemed to get Cody's attention. She did this sort of shuddering gesture, like she was literally shaking off the hesitation. Or doubt. Or whatever it was. She closed her eyes and took a deep breath. When she opened them, she locked eyes with Jess. "It's not. I'm sorry. I don't know why I'm being weird."

The honesty, paired with the awkwardness that seemed to come just before they did anything physical, made her smile. "You're not being weird. Well, you are, but it's appropriate for the situation."

"So, you don't regularly book hotel rooms for sex rendezvous? Rendezvouses? What's the plural of rendezvous?" Cody winced. "Sorry. Now I'm definitely being weird."

And ridiculously charming. It was the charming, even more than the sexual attraction, that threatened to do her in. But since it was the sexual attraction that brought them to this moment, that's where she'd focus her attention. She slowly crossed the room to where Cody stood. "I'm pretty sure it's rendezvous."

Jess stopped short of touching Cody. She looked down at Cody's belt—resisting the urge to unbuckle it, at least for now—then at Cody's mouth. Cody swallowed. "Like moose."

She bit her lip and didn't even try not to smirk. "Yes. Like moose."

Cody nodded. "Thank you for being patient. I'm not sure how to, you know, start things off."

She placed a hand on Cody's bicep, loving how strong and solid it felt. "How about you start by kissing me?"

And just like that, Cody relaxed. Maybe it was because they'd kissed quite a few times now and she felt comfortable. Or maybe she needed permission. She seemed like the kind of woman who'd be very into consent. Whatever it was, the nerves that had seemed to be vibrating around her stilled. In their place, desire. It radiated from her and warmed Jess from the inside. She put one hand into Jess's hair, right at the base of her neck, and the other on Jess's waist. "That, I can do."

Despite the heat growing rapidly between them, Cody took her time with the kiss. But there was nothing questioning or hesitant about it. No, this was a deliberate sort of kiss, the kind designed to amp her up and melt her into a puddle at the same time. And holy cow did it ever work.

She tightened her grip on Cody's arm, as much to steady herself as anything else. She brought her other hand to Cody's waist, hooking a finger into one of her belt loops and giving it a gentle tug. Cody didn't stop kissing her, but she let out this little moan that reminded Jess of having Cody nestled between her legs.

She pressed her pelvis forward, not consciously exactly, but more in desperation to have Cody's body against hers. In response, Cody pulled her hair lightly, angling Jess's head. Jess let out a moan of her own and Cody's mouth found her jaw, her neck, the dip of flesh just above her collarbone.

Yep, definitely desperation.

She started tugging at Cody's shirt, wanting her naked but, at the very least, needing to feel her skin. Before she could get very far, Cody grabbed the hem of Jess's sweater and pulled it over her head. "No fair," she said with a laugh.

"I can't be held responsible for the fact that you chose not to tuck in your shirt."

Her clever comeback about the differences between butch and femme fashion vanished when Cody expertly unhooked her bra, slid it off, and tossed it on the bed. Instead, she attempted to focus her attention on unbuttoning Cody's shirt—not an easy feat with Cody's warm, slightly rough palms covering her breasts.

"Fuck." It was as much sigh as expletive, but it still gave her pause. She tilted her head just far enough to look Cody in the eye. "No swear jar tonight, right?"

Cody laughed—a sexy and relaxed sound that assured Jess any remaining nerves had melted away. "Cuss to your heart's content."

Cody kissed her again and it was pure confidence. Or competence. Both, really. She sank into it but resumed her efforts to rid Cody of as much of her clothes as possible. She managed to get Cody's shirt off, along with the snug A-shirt she wore underneath. Cody unbuttoned her jeans while she fussed with Cody's belt. It was a playful, if slightly frantic, endeavor but managed to get them naked and in bed in short order.

Cody pinned Jess's wrists lightly over her head and moved over her, against her. The sensation of skin against skin just about sent her into orbit, especially without Ben and the majority of her family a wall away. "This was a fantastic idea you had."

"I have them from time to time." Cody took one of Jess's nipples into her mouth.

She arched, pleasure shooting like electricity through her body and right to her clit. "See? That? That's a fantastic idea too."

"I'm so glad we're on the same page."

Cody released her wrists and began kissing her way down Jess's torso. As heavenly as it felt, she wasn't about to let Cody get away with going first. "Not so fast."

Cody stopped her progress and looked up. "What? What's wrong?"

It maybe wasn't fair to take advantage of Cody's concern, but it didn't stop her. She hooked one leg around Cody's and twisted her body, effectively reversing their positions. "Nothing's wrong. But I'm not about to let you go down on me again when I haven't laid a hand or mouth on you yet."

Cody regarded her with a mixture of confusion and concern. "Did you literally just flip me?"

Jess shifted her thighs and sat up, straddling Cody's hips. "Only in the most technical sense. You still get to be the top."

Cody gripped her hips—assertive without being aggressive. "In that case."

Since she didn't know how long, or how often, she'd get to be in this position, she milked it, circling her hips slowly and grinding against Cody in a way that seemed to be giving Cody as much pleasure as it gave her. Cody didn't loosen her grip, but she let Jess set the pace.

The movement, along with the friction it caused, brought her dangerously close to coming, so she shifted forward, bracing her hands on either side of Cody's head. Cody's eyes were dark with desire, but her gaze didn't waver. Jess kissed her, starting with her lips and then making a trail down Cody's torso. Cody's legs opened and she happily settled herself between them.

She placed kisses on the insides of Cody's thighs before sliding her tongue into Cody's wetness. Cody sucked in a breath, making her pull back. "Too much?"

Cody lifted her head and shook it. "No, just too long. It's been too long."

She smiled. "I can go easy."

Cody shook her head again. "Please don't."

It was all the invitation she needed. She pressed her tongue back to Cody's center and let out a contented sigh. She maybe hadn't been waiting for it as long as Cody had, but it felt like she'd been wanting to for ages.

Cody moaned and threaded her fingers into Jess's hair. Without words, she told Jess exactly what to do and Jess happily obliged. Jess licked and sucked, reveling in the way Cody's clit literally pulsed beneath her tongue.

Cody came hard and fast—faster than Jess might have liked, but she could appreciate the pent-up urgency. She rested her head on Cody's thigh, enjoying the way Cody's body continued to shudder. What were the chances Cody could go again?

"Get up here." Any force in the command was lost in the slight slur of Cody's voice.

She obliged but made a point of kissing Cody slowly and thoroughly. "I hope that doesn't mean you're done with me."

Cody chuckled. "Not a chance. I just need a minute. And maybe to do that to you."

She let out a happy sigh, crazy turned on but also sort of satisfied. "I approve this plan. Though…"

Cody regarded her with concern. "What?"

"I was hoping I could convince you to try a couple of other things, too."

The look of concern turned mischievous. Was there anything hotter than Cody post-orgasm and playful? "Obviously."

She imagined Cody moving inside her. "I wish I'd thought to ask you about strap-ons before this exact moment."

Cody rolled onto her side and propped herself on her elbow. "Yeah? What would you have asked me?"

She let her gaze wander the length of Cody's body. "If you liked to."

"And if I said I did?"

"I'd have asked you to come prepared."

"I see." Cody nodded slowly. "And if I said I didn't want to presume anything, but I came prepared, just in case?"

"I'd say your penchant for being prepared is quickly becoming one of the sexiest things about you."

Cody climbed out of bed. "Don't move."

"I'm not going anywhere." Jess flopped onto her back. Maybe there was something to be said for sex dates after all.

Chapter Twenty

"Good morning."

"If you called to ask if I'm sore, the answer's yes. And it's all your fault."

Cody could hear the smile in Jess's voice, and it was exactly what she'd hoped for. "Should I say sorry?"

"We both know you're not. Anyway, you should be proud of yourself. This doesn't happen often."

She laughed. "Well, I didn't call to ask that, but thanks for telling me. Unfortunately, now I'm going to spend the rest of the day wishing I could massage all those sore muscles of yours."

"You could come over. Finn's gone and I have the place to myself. I definitely could use a thorough massage." There was a pause and Cody imagined Jess stretched out naked in bed, maybe even reaching between her legs to feel one particular spot that might be tender from all her attention. "I'd even answer the door naked for you."

"Mm. That's not fair."

"You're one to talk about playing fair. Do you realize you only let me have one round with you last night? I was just lying here thinking about it."

"Are you really upset?"

"No. I can't remember the last time I was topped quite that nicely. But I'm making a list of things I want to do when I get you next. You sure you can't play hooky and come over?"

If only. Cody's imagination ran with the thought. She glanced at her watch. "I've got a lecture to give in twenty minutes. Maybe you could play with yourself and tell me after?"

"Is that an actual request? Because if so, I will."

Cody's breath caught. With one question Jess had taken them from light sexy banter to a place that pushed her hormones into overdrive. "Yeah, that's an actual request. I want a full report."

"Good. I didn't want to go into the office until later anyway. Now I have a good reason. I'll be working from home on a necessary project." Jess made a sound halfway between a purr and a contented moan, and Cody longed to ask for a picture of her in that moment.

She cleared her throat. "I want to let you get right to your work, but I did have a quick question."

"I thought you were being sweet and checking in on me after last night."

Cody felt a twinge of guilt and decided to put all of her cards on the table. "I was checking in on you but not because I didn't think you'd be fine. I wanted to hear your voice and so I came up with a question that seemed like a good excuse."

"And now you really want to know my answer."

"Exactly. Give me a sec. I need to unlock a door." Cody slipped the phone from her right ear to her left, then held her key card up to the scanner and waited for the lock to click. She pushed open the door to her office and set down her messenger bag. "You still there?"

"Yep. And getting wet with all the little sounds you're making."

"I let myself into my office. It's nothing sexy." Fortunately, none of her lab students were working that morning.

"Hmm. I don't know about that. So far, I've found pretty much everything about you sexy. Imagining you at work doing all your atmospheric chemistry stuff is definitely not a turn-off."

She couldn't help smiling. "Most of the time I'm analyzing data sets."

"Would you be annoyed if I came into your office and interrupted you? Told you I needed some of your attention?"

Cody ran her hand through her hair. It was way too early in the morning to be thinking of sex, but she was suddenly acutely aware of her clit. In fact, everything between her legs seemed to be at attention now.

"You had a question for me. I think I keep distracting you."

"Right. My question." Approximately three brain cells fired up. The rest were still entertaining the fantasy of having Jess in the office.

"Do you want to come over and decorate the tree tonight? I know we saw each other yesterday, but Ben's been asking me all week. We've been busy, but he also thinks you know more about tree decorating than we do. And he's probably right. I was also hoping maybe you could spend the night."

"So, Ben wants me to come over to decorate and you want me to come over so you can fuck me?"

She should have been mortified by the accuracy of Jess's succinct assessment, but the teasing tone had her laughing instead. "Pretty much, yeah."

"I like this plan. Could we do Saturday instead? I have a date tonight. Well, it's not a date. It's just a thing."

A thing? Jess's backpedaling stopped Cody from asking what she meant. They hadn't discussed dating other people. Of course, she could, but would Jess do that without a conversation first? And what would happen if her date went well? Was this someone Jess wanted a relationship with? She tried to temper the wave of disappointment with the desire not to jump to any conclusions. "Saturday would be fine."

"Any chance we can play Christmas music?"

"Sure. I could even make a fire. And popcorn."

"Ooh, I'd love that. Can you tell Ben I'm sorry I can't do tonight? And tell him not to sneak the star on the top before I get there."

"We should have a fire every night." Ben propped his chin on his two folded fists as he watched Cody poke at the logs. "When's Jess gonna be here?"

"Six."

"How much longer is that?"

Cody eyed her watch. "Five minutes." Actually, it was one minute till six, but she wanted Jess to have some grace and Ben wouldn't give her any.

"I want her to be here now." Ben pushed at the pile of LEGOs from a disassembled ice cream truck and grunted his frustration.

"Waiting's hard. How about we plan out what we want to do as soon as she gets here?" Even as she distracted Ben, her thoughts tumbled back to the question that had been on her mind all day. Should she bring up dating other people? As much as she wanted to tell Jess it was fine if she did, it would only add another layer of complication to their tenuous relationship. Regardless, they had to talk about it. Right? Or maybe she shouldn't bring it up until Jess did.

The doorbell rang and Ben scrambled to his feet, scattering LEGOs in all directions. "She's here!"

"Well, go answer the door, goofball."

Cody grinned at his contagious happiness. Maybe she wouldn't bring it up. Maybe the right thing to do was simply enjoy the evening. She hung the fire poker on the rack and brushed soot off her hands. As much as she wanted to see Jess, wrap her arms around her and kiss her, her chest felt tight. Would Jess have come tonight if she didn't want to?

Ben's boisterous greeting mingled with Jess's laughter and filtered down the hall. Cody rolled her shoulders, telling herself to loosen up. That's all she could do anyway. Enjoy the ride for as long as it lasted and trust Jess would tell her if she didn't want things to continue.

By the time Cody got to the entryway, Jess had Ben in her arms. She hadn't taken off her coat yet but was busy listening to Ben's monologue about the plans for the evening.

"And then we get to watch *The Grinch*. Have you seen it?"

"Hey, Ben, remember how we were going to ask Jess which movie she wanted to watch? And how about you let Jess take off her coat." She gave Jess a tentative smile and couldn't help being filled with warmth at the wide smile Jess sent her in return. Maybe they were fine. Maybe she was worrying over nothing.

"I am kind of hot. But I don't want to put you down. I missed seeing you all week. In fact, I think I'll keep holding you all night to make up for it. Except what happens when I have to go pee?" She gave Ben a tight squeeze and he giggled. "That would be a problem."

"You can move in with us and you'd see me all the time. We even have an extra room. Mom keeps her rowing machine and bike in there, but it's a big room. I have my train set in there too. You could play with it whenever you want. All you need is a bed."

Cody wondered how long Ben had been plotting this. She decided not responding was better than shutting his imagination down and having things be awkward. But they'd have to talk later. "Ben, let's give Jess a second to take off her coat. Come here."

She extended her arms and Jess let out a beleaguered sigh. "Fine."

She took Ben from Jess and set him on the ground. "Okay, when we have a guest over, we have to act fancy." She cleared her throat and straightened up. "Good evening, madam. May I take your coat?"

"Oh, yes, thank you." Jess winked at Ben, then took off her gloves and scarf, making a show of pretending to be extra proper. She handed them to Cody and took off her coat. "Kind sir, would you be so good as to place my things somewhere safe?"

"Why yes, of course." Cody bowed.

Ben scrunched up his nose. "You two are weird."

Cody laughed. "Just wait till you're a teenager. You're going to think we're really weird then."

Jess tilted her head and gave Cody a little smile. Did that mean she didn't mind being included? It was only a silly what-if to think of them together in ten years, but it wouldn't be the first time her imagination went there. Her thoughts swung back to the question of whether Jess wanted to be here tonight at all.

She wanted to kiss her. Needed to, in fact. One kiss and she'd be able to tell how Jess felt.

"Have you seen *The Grinch*, Jess?" Ben asked.

"I have. But it's been a long time and I think I should watch it again."

Ben started hopping around the room chanting yes. Suddenly, he stopped hopping and put one finger to his temple. "I'm gonna get the movie set up."

"Good idea. We'll be there in a sec." Ben tore off to the living room and she glanced at Jess. "He's a little excited."

"Really? I couldn't tell." Jess stepped forward and caught Cody's belt. "I'm excited, too. But not for *The Grinch*."

She didn't get a chance to ask what Jess was excited for. She tugged Cody to her and covered her mouth with a hard kiss. Cody barely managed to get her bearings before Jess went for another. All the second-guessing about whether Jess wanted to be here tonight came to an abrupt end. Jess's thing last night, date or otherwise, couldn't have gone that well.

Jess nipped Cody's lip before pulling back. "You better keep me busy hanging ornaments or I won't be able to keep my hands off you."

"As long as you're the one explaining that to Ben..." Her thoughts trailed as Jess went in for another kiss.

"You guys coming or not?" Ben hollered.

Jess ignored the summons and only deepened the kiss. Cody enjoyed it for a moment, let the arousal spread through her, but then stepped back. Ben would come for them any minute. "I don't know if I want to keep you busy hanging ornaments. I'm going to be thinking about better things your hands could do."

"Hands are nice, but I have other plans for you tonight." Jess fingered Cody's buckle. "I'll even give you a hint. It has something to do with me between your legs and you telling me where to lick."

"That's my hint?"

"Mm-hmm. Anywhere you tell me, I'll lick. But you have to tell me."

"Fuck. How the hell am I going to keep my hands off you for the next two hours?"

"Oh, I'm sure you'll figure it out. And you owe the swear jar two quarters."

Ben popped back into the entryway. "Why are you guys still talking in here? Jess, come see the tree. Mom put on the lights, but she said we had to save everything else for when you got here."

"It was hard waiting." Cody shrugged. "For both of us."

"Well, good things come to those who wait." Jess slipped her hand in Cody's when Ben took off again. "I can't wait to decorate the heck out of your tree."

Cody chuckled more at the eyebrow waggle than the innuendo. "Something tells me you're not going to be able to only use your tongue later."

"What do you mean?"

"I don't think you'll be able to keep your hands off me."

Jess shifted closer. "Is that a dare, Cody Dawson?"

"Maybe."

Jess let go of her hand when they got to the family room, oohing at the sight of the lit tree. "It looks even better than it did when we picked it out. You two found the perfect spot for it. And I love the fire." She went over to warm her hands.

"Don't get too close."

"I think she's got this, buddy." Apparently, he'd listened to the hundred or so times she'd said the same thing to him when he got too close to the flames. "Want to show her our ornaments?"

When Ben went to get the ornaments, Jess turned to Cody. "Just so you know, this is pretty much a perfect date."

"Better than a hotel room?"

"Different." Jess paused, looking between the fire and the tree before her gaze settled on Cody. "Turns out, I like both. Or maybe I just like dates with you."

"And what about your date last night?" The question tumbled out before she could stop it and she immediately wanted to kick herself.

"Last night?" Jess's brow creased. "Oh. Not a date date. Girls' night with some of my coworkers. We have a standing thing every month."

"Ah." Cody tried for a casual smile despite the massive wave of relief. And the kicking herself for freaking out in the first place.

Jess's eyes widened. "Did you think I was on a date with someone else?"

She winced. "Well, we never said we'd be—"

"What's a date?" Ben asked, suddenly back.

Jess gave her an *I'm so going to give you a hard time about this later* look before turning her attention to Ben. "A date is when you set aside a time to do something special with someone you like. Or two people you like."

"And you like us."

Jess ruffled Ben's hair. "Exactly."

He held up a shoebox of ornaments for Jess's inspection and she started to pick through them. Several were framed pictures of Ben that he'd made in day care and Jess graciously complimented each one, as well as all the handmade gingerbread cut-outs.

Ben pointed to a macaroni-framed picture he'd made in preschool two years back. "You can hang that one first, Jess. I made it myself."

"Really?" Jess picked up the ornament delicately. "You made this?" She waited for Ben's nod. "And I get to hang it anywhere I want?"

Another nod. "Except at the top. That's where we put the star."

"Okay. I'll hang this one and then you can hang the ornament I bought for you."

"You bought me one?"

"Yep. It's in my purse." Jess gingerly picked her way around Ben's LEGOs to get to the tree. She hooked the ornament on one of the middle branches, then stepped back and surveyed her work. "I think we need Christmas music before we hang anymore."

"On it." Cody pulled out her phone and started the playlist with Christmas songs. As soon as the music crackled through the house speakers, Jess smiled.

"This night keeps getting better and better." Jess tapped Ben's shoulder. "Let me go get the ornament I got for you."

Jess stepped out of the room and Ben came over to lean against Cody. "I like Jess."

"I do too, buddy." Cody sighed. All she had to do was not think about anything more than that because every time she did, she only seemed to get herself into trouble. A warmth filled her chest. The fire, the music, the sparkling lights, and the feel of Ben relaxing against her all helped. But she knew having Jess there was part of it, too.

Jess returned and held out a box for Ben. He immediately ripped into the present without remembering to say thank you. So much for manners. Not that Jess seemed to mind. Inside was a sleigh ornament with a tiny teddy bear riding it. "Ben" was printed on the sleigh in shimmering cursive.

It took a moment for him to notice the writing, but he gasped when he saw it. "My name's on it!"

"Amazing, right?" Jess lifted the sleigh by the thin red ribbon. "As soon as I saw it, I knew this one was for you. Let's find the perfect spot."

It didn't take long before all the ornaments in the shoebox—and the three other boxes—were hung. For the most part, Cody let Jess and Ben pick the spots and only assisted when her height was needed. She loved watching the two of them, heads together and debating the ideal location for each piece. Even at her most maternal, Anastasia never had that sort of patience.

Cody sighed. She loved everything about the evening. Including how her heart seemed to press against her ribs every time one of them looked at her and smiled.

"I think it's time for the star." Cody presented Jess with the sparkly gold star.

"She bought it for you," Ben added.

"I did. I saw it and thought of you." Maybe it was a little ridiculous, but it was true. "Just like you saw that sleigh and knew it was for Ben."

"Except the star doesn't have your name on it. She bought it 'cause it was pretty. She thinks you're pretty." Ben looked between Jess and Cody with a mischievous smile.

"What am I going to do with you?" Cody grabbed Ben's shoulders and playfully jostled him.

He laughed and tried to wiggle free. "Whatever. I'm right."

"Whatever? Where'd you pick up that one?" Cody let go and kissed the top of his head. "Maybe you are right. And maybe you're too darn smart for your own good." She glanced at Jess, wondering how she felt about Ben knowing.

Jess only smiled. "Let's see what this star looks like on our tree. Then it's movie time, right?"

"Yes!" Ben cheered.

"Then bedtime." She thought of Jess's promise earlier. As perfect as the evening was, Cody was ready to speed things up.

Jess pressed against Cody and whispered, "Remember, good things come to those who wait."

Chapter Twenty-one

Jess woke, not to Ben's foot jabbing her in the back, but to Cody's arm warm and snug around her. She'd never considered herself big on spooning, but this? This she could get used to. She wiggled her butt slightly, mostly to see if Cody was awake. Cody responded with a soft moan and squeezed her tighter. Nice, if not exactly an answer.

Since she wasn't in any hurry to break up the cozy and slightly sexual snuggle, she wiggled again and savored the press of Cody's entire body against hers. Cody nuzzled her neck. "Morning."

Jess let out a hum of pleasure. "Good morning."

The arm Cody had slung around her shifted and her hands started to wander. When she grazed the underside of Jess's breast, Jess rolled to give her better access. Could they get away with a quickie before Ben woke up?

"If I wasn't a hundred percent certain Ben was up, I'd ask how you felt about morning sex."

"It's so unfair to ask me that, to get me all turned on, and in the same breath tell me I can't have you."

Cody's hand stilled. "Sorry."

She rolled the rest of the way so they were facing each other. "Oh, I'm not telling you to stop. I'm telling you it's unfair."

"In that case..." Cody took one of Jess's nipples between her finger and thumb and gave it a squeeze.

She bit back a moan. "So unfair."

"Maybe I can talk you into another sleepover and wake you up earlier?"

The idea of Cody waking her up with roaming hands and kisses had both her pulse and her imagination going. "Yes, please."

"In the meantime, can I offer you breakfast and maybe some cartoons?"

She made a show of considering. "I suppose."

"I'm really glad you're okay with that."

The sincerity in Cody's voice made her think about how challenging it must be to try to date and be a single parent. "Of course."

They extricated themselves from bed and ventured downstairs, finding Ben occupying himself with his tablet. He looked up and let out a huge sigh. "Finally, you're awake. I'm starving."

"Good morning to you, too." Cody kissed the top of his head. "You could have had cereal, you know."

"Yeah, but it's the weekend and I want good breakfast."

She could appreciate that. "And what constitutes good breakfast?"

"Pancakes, waffles, French toast." He ticked them off one at a time with his fingers.

"Are you detecting a theme?" Cody asked Jess with a grin.

"Um..." She pretended to really have to think about it. "Maple syrup?"

"Syrup!" Ben thrust his fists in the air.

"How about pancakes?" Cody turned her attention to Jess. "Pancakes okay by you?"

"Oh, yeah. If you make coffee, I'll even help."

Cody bumped her hip to Jess's. "Sold."

It was more fun than it should be to putter around the kitchen with Cody. She made the batter while Cody prepped coffee, then set the table with Ben while Cody tended the skillet. In a matter of minutes, the three of them sat at the table, a giant stack of fluffy pancakes just begging to be devoured.

She took her time applying butter and syrup just so, a process that seemed to both fascinate and confuse Ben. She shrugged. "I take pancakes very seriously."

"I take eating pancakes very seriously." Ben stuffed a large bite into his mouth.

She took a bite of her own. "Mmm. Delicious."

"Mom makes the best pancakes."

"She does." She looked at Cody. "You do."

Cody sipped her coffee, seemingly more interested in the two of them than the pancakes in front of her. "Why, thank you."

"Did I hear you tell Joshua you like pancakes better than waffles?"

"Yes." Ben gave a serious nod.

"Why? Because I like them both, but think waffles are slightly more awesome." She glanced at Cody. "Although these are exceptional pancakes."

Ben frowned. "Waffles are okay. We just have them a lot and we never get pancakes."

"Really?" She raised a brow, but more at Cody than Ben.

"Yeah," Ben said before Cody could elaborate. "Waffles come frozen so Mom says they're easier."

"Ah." She nodded. "Your mom is really smart."

Cody chuckled. "That's the problem with kids. They tell all your secrets. We eat Eggos for breakfast maybe too often."

She lifted both hands. "Hey, no judgment here. I've been known to rock a Toaster Strudel, especially at certain times of the month."

Cody smiled. "Thanks for saying that. I think it makes us even."

"Happy to oblige."

"What's a Toaster Strudel?" Ben asked with his mouth full of pancake.

"Chew, swallow, then speak," Cody said.

He made a show of chewing and swallowing, then took a drink of milk and swiped his hand across his mouth. "What's a Toaster Strudel?"

She shot Cody an apologetic look and tried to explain in terms that didn't let on how delicious they were. She failed epically, leading Ben to insist they should have Toaster Strudel the next morning. "And you could sleep over again," he added.

It was hard to tell whether he was more interested in a new breakfast sweet or the prospect of another sleepover. She found both rather charming, even if she knew better than to let on. Fortunately, Cody was an expert in fielding Ben's requests and didn't miss a beat. "Breakfast treats are for the weekend and Jess has to work tomorrow, so we'll have to wait."

Ben let out a world-weary sigh—which proved utterly adorable—then turned to Jess with a "sorry, I tried" sort of look. "Will you come over again next weekend?"

Before she could answer, Cody's phone rang. Cody looked at it with a frown. "I should take this."

"No worries." She tried to make her smile extra reassuring.

"Thanks." Cody got up from the table and swiped her finger across the screen. "Hey."

Ben didn't seem fazed, so she decided not to be either. "More pancakes for us."

"Yeah!" Ben forked another onto his plate and drenched it in syrup.

She mirrored his movements but poured a more reasonable amount of syrup onto hers. She'd just taken a bite when the office door clicked closed. It gave her pause even as she told herself it shouldn't. It wasn't like she begrudged Cody a private conversation.

Cody had yet to emerge by the time they finished eating. Jess hesitated to clear the table in case Cody wanted more. But Ben had eaten his fill and remaining at the table seemed to be making him antsy. She glanced at the clock on the stove. Since she hadn't done that when Cody got up, it didn't provide any useful information. Was it Cody's boss? Someone in her lab? Was everything okay?

"Do you want to play LEGOs?"

Ben's question pulled her from the swirl of wondering who Cody was talking to for so long. "Sure. Why don't you go set them up and I'll clean up here?"

"Yeah!" Ben launched himself from his chair and darted upstairs.

She cleared her dishes and Ben's, rinsing them off and sliding them into the dishwasher. She washed the skillet and mixing bowl by hand, then poured herself another cup of coffee. Still no Cody.

Since there was no Rascal to go counter—or table—surfing, she left the remaining pancakes and Cody's plate and went in search of Ben. She found him in his room, literally surrounded by small colorful bricks. A rather large bin sat off to the side, empty. He'd definitely poured its entire contents onto the floor.

"Do you want to build something together or do you like building your own?"

The politeness of the question made her smile. "I'd love to build something together."

"We should build a spaceship since both of us love them so much."

"I like that idea."

"Cool!" He riffled in the pile, then held up a rectangular blue piece. "We should start with big ones like this."

"On it." She ran her fingers over the pieces, picking out a few more like the one he'd shown her.

He clicked them together with confidence, selecting components and instructing her to find more of each piece he required. It was a perfectly mindless activity, allowing her thoughts to wander to Cody. But instead of worrying and wondering about her mystery call, she thought about how nice it had been to stay over—falling asleep with Cody and waking up in her arms.

"There you two are. I thought I'd lost you for a minute."

Cody's voice pulled her back to the moment—to Ben's room and the mountain of LEGOs and a Sunday morning so unlike her usual.

Ben jumped up. "You were taking forever so we decided to build a spaceship."

He held it up for Cody's inspection and she nodded. "I'm sorry I was gone so long."

Even without knowing the who or the why of the phone call, Jess could sense it was something serious. The set of Cody's jaw, maybe, or the slightest hint of strain in her eyes. "Everything okay?"

"Absolutely." Cody's tone didn't quite match her answer and her smile seemed forced.

"Jess, I need five more red ones like this." Ben held up a narrow strip.

Cody's hands went to her hips. "Are you letting Jess play or are you just telling her what to do?"

Ben opened his mouth—either to protest or to apologize—but she cut him off. "I was happily playing assistant, I promise."

Cody narrowed her eyes but didn't press. "Okay."

She wanted to ask more about the phone call but not in front of Ben. "I wasn't sure if you wanted more pancakes, so I left them out."

Cody considered. "You know, I think I could go for one more."

"I can warm it up for you."

"No, no." Cody waved her off. "I can manage. You two keep playing and I'll be right back."

Cody disappeared and Ben reminded her of the blocks he wanted next. She rooted around in search of them, wondering if Cody's brushoff was intentional or because she didn't want it to seem like Jess was waiting on her. Ben chatted away, asking her opinion on wings and whether they should build a space for an astronaut to sit. She did her best to keep her attention on him, but it was a struggle.

Cody's return—smiling but distracted—didn't help. Ben finished his spaceship and they all admired it. Ben asked what they should do next, but Cody shook her head. "I'm sure Jess would like to go home and have a little bit of her weekend to herself."

"Oh." Ben frowned.

Again, it was impossible to tell if Cody was being overly considerate of her time or was subtly asking her to leave. She wasn't crazy about either, even if she had a stack of laundry waiting and needed to go grocery shopping on her way home. But since Cody showed zero signs of wanting to talk, she opted not to argue.

Ben pouted slightly, but a gentle nudge from Cody put him back into the role of well-mannered host. He thanked her for coming over and for helping to decorate the tree. Jess thanked him for including her, then excused herself to get dressed.

She'd thought Cody might follow so they'd have a moment alone, but no such luck. Was Cody being weird or was she being too sensitive? Apparently, temporary relationships weren't immune to such quandaries. Ugh.

Downstairs, Ben played with his Christmas train set while Cody looked on. She set her bag down and pulled on her coat and boots slowly, not ready to leave but not sure why. Ben came over to give her a hug but returned to his trains instead of lingering.

"Thanks again for coming." Cody didn't seem to intend the double entendre, which made Jess smile even more than if she had. Realization hit and Cody blushed, then offered a sheepish smile.

"Thanks for having me."

"I had a lot of fun. The tree, but also the grown-up time."

"Yes. Both were exceptional, in very different ways." She waited for Cody to suggest they do it again soon, but she didn't. "So, I'll talk to you this week?"

"Of course."

When Cody didn't say more, Jess reached for the front door, but paused before turning the knob. "Oh."

"Oh?"

"That concert is this week. The one I said we'd go to without asking you."

"Oh." Cody's tone was utterly noncommittal.

"I can talk to Shannon and get us out of it. Make it seem like I had something come up."

Cody shook her head perhaps a little too vigorously. "No. Don't do that."

She'd been looking forward to it, but still. She didn't want Cody to feel pressured, especially since it was essentially a social engagement with her boss. "It's okay. You weren't that excited about it in the first place."

"No, but I want to go. Definitely."

She wasn't convinced but equally didn't want to argue. Especially with Cody already acting weird. "You're sure?"

"Positive."

"Okay. We'd talked about grabbing dinner together before. Are you up for that, too?"

"Sure. As long as you arrange it. I don't really want to call the president's office to set up a double date."

Normally, she'd laugh and tease Cody about that, but this time she hesitated. "I'm on it. I'll sort out the specifics with Shannon and text you."

"Great. Thanks." Cody managed to look relieved if not enthused.

She opened the door and stepped through. Cody grabbed her hand, making her turn.

"Sorry again about having to take that call during breakfast. And for being weird about the concert. I swear I'm looking forward to it."

Part of her wanted to tell Cody she'd prefer an explanation to an apology, but she didn't. If Cody wanted to share more, she would. And if she didn't, she wouldn't. "It's all good."

"Thanks for that, too."

Cody leaned in and kissed her—briefly but on the lips. It made her feel better, if only marginally. "I'll see you soon."

"Can't wait."

Since Cody's smile seemed genuine this time, she returned it and headed to her car. It was fine. Cody didn't owe her an explanation. And maybe not sharing too much personal stuff was for the best. Like that job in Philadelphia. She'd submitted her résumé and cover letter more on principle than out of any real hope or desire she'd get it. And since she had no desire to hash through her ambition—or lack thereof—she had no plans to tell Cody about it.

Drawing a parallel made her feel better, both about her decision and whatever motivated Cody's reticence. It also allowed her mind to meander to more pleasant things. Like the way it felt to have Cody's fingers inside her. Or how nice it had been to fall asleep together. How Ben didn't come knocking even once.

By the time she got home, her mood had rebounded nicely. So much so that she pulled out her phone before going inside and dashed off a text to Shannon. They'd go to the concert and have a great time. She'd focus her attention on that, and on writing her column, and she'd stop borrowing trouble. And like so many things, that would be that.

Chapter Twenty-two

Cody tasted the Malbec Jess had picked and reminded herself to relax. "I have to admit, the concert was better than I expected."

Jess raised an eyebrow. "Not sure if that's a positive review or not."

"No, I enjoyed it."

"But you weren't expecting to?"

She hadn't exactly expected it to be bad, but she hadn't expected it to be good, either. "Um…"

Jess bumped Cody's shoulder, her eyes creasing with a smile. "If you're wondering if that's a trick question, the answer is yes."

Cody laughed. "Thanks for the warning. In that case, I'll only say that I'm glad you got us tickets."

"Good call." Jess's smile faded when she added, "I wasn't sure if you were having a good time earlier. You were quiet there for a while."

"Yeah. Sorry about that." She'd never been good at hiding her feelings.

"Want to talk about it?"

Cody closed one eye and tried for a lighthearted expression. "Not really."

"Why am I not surprised?" Jess shook her head but seemed more playfully exasperated than truly upset. She glanced at a group of women across from them—all laughing and clearly having a good time—and took a sip of her wine.

When the pause in their conversation stretched, Cody started to worry Jess really was upset that she didn't want to talk. She considered telling Jess what was going on but didn't want to create one more problem in a day already chock full of them. In fact, she'd nearly canceled their date simply because she was exhausted from putting out one fire after another.

"You said you weren't really a fan of Avis DeVoe, so I get that you weren't excited to come tonight. And this probably feels like more work than pleasure meeting up with Gillian and Shannon. I feel bad that I got you signed up for something you didn't want to do."

"Don't feel bad. You're right that I didn't really care about the concert, but I was looking forward to going out with you."

"You sure?" Jess shook her head. "Don't answer that."

Jess sighed and her attention returned almost pointedly to the group of women across from them. The wine bar was only a block from the concert hall and attracted a mixed crowd of after-concert couples winding down the evening and club-goers warming up for the night. President Toller—Gillian—had been the one to suggest it, but she and Shannon had been detained en route when a big donor to the university recognized Gillian. Shannon had suggested Cody and Jess go ahead and get a table, probably guessing Gillian wouldn't get out of the conversation quickly.

"Someone you know over there?" Cody asked, nodding at the group.

"No. They just look like they're having fun."

And we're not, Cody added silently. Though there was no real reason they shouldn't be. The concert had been good—Cody wasn't lying about that—and she did want to be out with Jess even if she was tired. But there was an unspoken tension between them that had settled in on Sunday. They'd had a few text conversations since but hadn't talked until Cody picked Jess up. Even then, they hadn't said much. "I'm sure that I wanted to come out with you tonight."

Jess tapped her wine glass against Cody's. "You weren't supposed to answer that question because I shouldn't have asked it."

"Doesn't matter. You did ask and I wanted to answer." Cody blew out a breath.

"Do you want to tell me what's really bugging you?"

"Tonight maybe wasn't the best night for me to make plans. The last few weeks of the semester are always stressful with grading and students freaking out about getting things in last minute, but on top of that I've had all these problems crop up in the lab. One of our computers has been punky and finally called it quits today. Two students in my lab need to have their senior theses in by the end of the semester and they're both depending on the samples we collected this past summer, but the equipment we've been using to analyze the samples is giving wacky results." Cody stopped and shook her head. "You don't need to hear all of this. I'm just frustrated. None of these things would be an issue if the funds from the grant I got had already been allocated."

Jess met her gaze. "You've got a lot on your plate. I get it."

Cody felt a twinge of guilt. Everything she'd said was true. Things in the lab were a mess and she was stressed about grading. But Anastasia's call and the decision she'd been forced to make was the real reason she'd been distracted and surly.

"This arrangement is weird for both of us. I think we both want to be here but we're also here for work reasons." Jess sighed. "Still, I want you to tell me when you don't have time to go out. You could have canceled tonight."

"I didn't want to cancel. I can get everything done. I'll just skip a few hours of sleep."

Jess tilted her head. "Do I need to tell you about all the studies showing how sleep deprivation is bad for your health?"

She tried a smile. "No, thanks."

"I thought maybe you felt bad leaving Ben with a babysitter to go out with me."

"No. Maybe I should, but I don't. We've spent plenty of time with him and I wanted one-on-one time with you."

Jess nodded slowly. "But you hardly said a word during dinner. Or when you picked me up. All the times we could be talking tonight you seemed miles away."

Cody hung her head. "I swear it's not because I don't want to be with you."

"I get that, but I don't want to add more stress to your world. If there's something I can do—or not do—tell me."

She considered simply telling Jess about the conversation with Anastasia. But talking about her ex-wife was the last thing she wanted to do on the one evening they had to spend together.

When Cody didn't answer right away, Jess continued. "Maybe we should send Shannon and Gillian a text and tell them we had to leave. We can use Ben as an excuse—say the babysitter called or something."

"I don't want to leave. Do you?"

"No. But I feel like there's something on your mind that you don't want to tell me, and you might think you're being subtle about it, but you're not."

She immediately wished she'd told Jess about the phone call from the beginning. She'd messed up their evening trying to pretend she was fine, but Jess could see right through her. "That phone call I had to take when we were eating breakfast Sunday was from my ex. Ben's other mom."

"Oh."

"Yeah." Cody felt the same weight settle on her shoulders as she had when she saw Anastasia's name pop up on her phone. "She almost never calls."

"Apologies." Gillian breezed up to the table. "That took much longer than I thought it would."

"I knew it would take exactly that long. Even with us both trying to cut the conversation short." Shannon winked at Cody and Jess as she let go of Gillian's arm to settle into the booth. "Which is why she keeps me around."

"Only one among many reasons." Gillian slid in next to Shannon. "Thanks for ordering a bottle of wine to get us started."

Shannon turned the bottle to survey the label. "Mmm. Malbec's my favorite and you two picked a good one. Have you tried the chocolate torte they serve here? It's to die for."

"Worth at least two hours on the elliptical. Maybe three." Gillian poured wine into the two glasses waiting for her and Shannon.

"Sounds like we need to order this torte." Cody glanced at Jess.

"I never say no to chocolate."

Cody rarely did either, but at the moment she wasn't interested in dessert at all. She wished they were alone—not at a busy wine bar with company. The unfinished conversation settled between them, and she'd managed to make the evening more complicated bringing up her ex.

"So, what'd you think about the concert?" Shannon asked.

"I loved it." Jess found Cody's hand under the table and gave her a gentle squeeze.

She met Jess's eyes. When Jess smiled softly, the tension in her shoulders eased some. They'd finish their conversation later. And maybe everything would work out.

"Any chance I can convince you to come home with me?" Cody jammed her hands in her pockets even as she wished she could link arms with Jess. "I promised Ben's sitter I'd be back before midnight, but I don't think we're done talking."

"It's a Wednesday."

She studied Jess's face, unsure if she should push or back off. "Is that a no?"

"We both work tomorrow."

"I know." She still wasn't sure of Jess's answer. They reached the parking garage and made their way up two flights of stairs, each step reminding her how long the day had been and how much her body wanted to curl up and sleep. Her mind, however, was a different beast altogether.

Dessert and drinks had gone smoothly, thanks mostly to Jess and Shannon carrying the conversation. Gillian had seemed even more exhausted than Cody, but they all loosened up with the wine. When they said good-bye, Cody realized she'd missed not only double dates but adult time in general. After everything, she was almost sad the evening was over. Still, she hadn't stopped thinking about what she needed to tell Jess.

Cody spotted her car and hit the unlock button as they approached. She went to the passenger side to open Jess's door.

"Thank you," Jess said without looking up.

Maybe they should call it a night even if things were left unfinished. Jess seemed tired too. Cody went around to the driver's side and settled in. As soon as she turned on the engine, a pop song blasted through the speakers. She hurried to hit the power button on the radio and bumped against Jess, who clearly had the same idea. When the song cut off as abruptly as it came on, she looked over at Jess. "Didn't realize I had the volume up that high earlier. Sorry."

"It's fine." Jess shifted to face Cody. "I want to go home with you."

"But?"

"No buts. We need to talk."

Cody backed out of the parking space. "What if we talk on the way?"

"So we can do other things when we get to your place?"

The hopeful tone in Jess's voice buoyed Cody's spirits. "I like your way of thinking. But we're both tired."

"Cuddling, Cody Dawson. That's what I was thinking about doing. What were you thinking about?"

Cody laughed. "Cuddling, of course."

"Good. Now spill. What was the call from your ex about?"

"Anastasia wants Ben to come out for Christmas."

Jess seemed to take a moment to take the information in—or maybe consider her response. "Where does she live?"

"LA. Well, technically, Santa Monica. She's got a place on the beach. Did I mention my ex is rich in addition to being completely self-absorbed and a shitty parent?" Cody shook her head. "I shouldn't say those things."

"I appreciate knowing you aren't pining for her."

"Oh, hell no. If Ben wasn't in the picture—" She stopped herself. "You know what, I don't want to go there. I'm usually better about not saying bad things about exes. Especially Anastasia since she's Ben's mom. I always worry what he might overhear."

"Ben's not here and you can be honest with me. I've had my share of nightmare exes." Jess rested her hand on Cody's thigh. "Why do you think I started writing a relationship column?"

She smiled, soothed as much by Jess's sympathetic look as by the steadiness of her touch. "Thanks for being understanding."

"So, I take it Anastasia doesn't usually have Ben for Christmas?"

"No. She hardly has any contact with him at all. Which is why we got into a fight about Christmas. And that's why it took me so long to get back to you and Ben." Cody slowed to a stop at a red light. "She hasn't talked to Ben since his birthday months ago. I used to set up weekly video call dates for them, but when I stopped pushing for that, she disappeared. I've suggested she come out and see us, even said we'd go out there for visits, but she hasn't been interested before now. It's been two years since Ben has even seen her in person. Then out of the blue she decides she wants Ben to come and stay with her for two weeks? It doesn't make sense."

"Two weeks is a long time. You think he'll want to stay that long?"

"I don't think either of us has a choice." Cody had the sudden urge to punch the steering wheel but instead only tightened her grip. It was exactly like Anastasia to pull a stunt like this, and Cody couldn't do anything but go along with it. In her twenties, it had been exciting. Anastasia was vibrant and brave and adventurous. She pulled Cody out of her too-serious shell and got Cody to let go and try new things and have fun. Now, it just felt immature and irresponsible.

"Why don't you have a choice?"

"We never formalized a custody arrangement. At any point, she could decide she wants joint custody of Ben and there's no reason she couldn't get it. If I don't say yes to this visit, I'm worried she'll get a lawyer. And I'm not saying I don't think it'd be good for Ben to know her, to have a relationship with her, but she's been checked out for years now. I don't want her to drop into his life and then disappear again."

"Oh, Cody. I'm sorry. No wonder you were distracted earlier." Jess paused. "How long ago did you break up?"

"She left when Ben was two. She'd started doing event planning here in Denver and met some celebrity at one of her events who invited her to put together this gala out in LA. That one led to another and the week in California turned into a month and then six and then she decided to stay there permanently." At first, she'd made a show of wanting Cody and Ben to join her, but like so many things in Anastasia's life, the familiar and tame always took a back seat to the new and exciting. Which was all well and good until it extended to their child.

Cody pulled onto the freeway, trying to focus on the other cars through a rush of emotion that made tears prick her eyes. What was wrong with her? One minute she was so angry she wanted to hit the steering wheel and the next she was so frustrated at her inability to protect Ben that she wanted to cry. She clenched her jaw, knowing she should probably have had this conversation with someone besides Jess.

"Maybe you should pull over and let me drive."

"I'm fine."

"You don't have to be fine. This is a lot, you know. Even I don't want Ben to go spend two weeks with someone who's practically a stranger." Jess folded her arms and looked out the passenger window. "What are you going to do?"

"I don't want to say no to her. Not outright." The fear of how Anastasia might retaliate made that impossible even to think of. "But I can't let him go alone."

"You're going with him?"

Cody nodded. "I doubt Anastasia will want him for more than a week—even if she says two—so I'm planning on staying nearby. I got a hotel not far from her house."

"So you'll be gone for Christmas?"

"Unless she's done with him in a week. Then we'll be back right before." She should leave it at that and let Jess digest everything, but she pushed on. "It might be a crazy idea, but I was thinking. Would you like to come with me? The hotel I booked is in Santa Monica right by the beach."

Jess nodded slowly, not giving away if she liked the idea or not. "And we'd both be there if Ben needed anything."

"Exactly. If he doesn't need us, we'd have a mini vacation." The thought of that much alone time sounded even more appealing than the idea of having a distraction while Ben was with Anastasia. Both at the same time? Hard to imagine anything better. But would Jess feel that way, or like she was only an addendum to the plan?

Jess squeezed her leg. "I want to come."

"You sure?"

"If you're sure I'm invited, then I'm sure I want to come."

Jess's quick agreement rushed away all her doubts. For the first time all week she felt like she could take a deep breath. "I want to kiss you right now, but I'm on the freeway."

"Get us home safe and you can kiss me all night. Or until we both fall asleep. It's been a long day."

"Thank you."

Jess narrowed her eyes. "For what?"

"For knowing this is hard. For wanting to come with me anyway."

"Okay, now you have to stop before I make you pull over so I can kiss you."

Cody laughed. "No more talking then until we park this car."

Chapter Twenty-three

Jess put the finishing touches on her "Ten Holiday Gift Ideas for the Woman You Just Started Dating" list and sent it to Cindy for copy editing. That left editing this week's cuffing column and finishing the bonus content, and then she'd be on vacation. Yes, she'd need to write a column while she was away, but Donna had let her off the hook for any other articles. Between that and the week she'd already planned off to see her family—complete with someone to cover her barre classes—she was looking at two weeks of practically no work.

She pulled up the draft of the bonus musings. While the main column had talked about offering moral support and looking forward to warm weather, she'd let her imagination wander here. Sexy daydreams, romantic walks on the beach, the whole nine yards. She knew she was getting ahead of herself, with her feelings as much as her sexual fantasies, but at least she could admit it—to herself and her readers. And since Cody remained adamant she didn't—wouldn't—read the column, it could be their little secret.

She dropped her chin onto her fist and let out a contented sigh. Maybe Cody would take her on a long walk on the beach. She was almost embarrassed by how few times she'd been to the ocean. Or maybe they'd stay in and order room service and have a nonstop sex fest. Would a week in bed be enough to get her fill of Cody?

On the heels of that delicious question came a wave of guilt. She was basically wishing for a week without Ben. No, that wasn't fair. She was hoping to make the most of the time Ben would be with his other mother. Nothing wrong with that, right? And probably more reasonable than the almost irrational protective—and maybe a little possessive—feelings she had over the thought of Ben spending time with someone who'd skipped out on him.

With that rationalization firmly in place, she returned to her sex-driven daydreams. With all the jokes about cuffing, she'd let herself wonder what it might be like if Cody tied her up. She hadn't been brave enough to suggest it yet, though. Despite the amount of time they'd spent together, relatively little of it had included sex and they hadn't really gone beyond the basics. Not that she was a full-blown kinkster or anything. She just liked to be adventurous—in bed and out.

"Archer. My office."

Donna's terse command yanked her from the thought of Cody bending her over the edge of the bed and plopped her unceremoniously at her desk, complete with the click-click of Silpa typing and Frida giving her a bemused smirk.

"Chop, chop, Archer." Frida angled her head in the direction of Donna's office.

Jess scrambled out of her chair. On the way, she smoothed her hair as though she'd actually been up to racy things and not just thinking about them. She squared her shoulders and took a deep breath. "Yes, boss?"

"I have an assignment for you."

Considering her last assignment from Donna had landed her in a relationship with Cody, she didn't know whether to cheer or cringe. "What's that?"

"Well, you're always carrying on about wanting to do serious journalism." Donna shook her head and let out a sigh. "Though I'm still not sure why. Your column got more views last week than mine."

Donna didn't seem overly bothered by that fact. If anything, it made her look at Jess with a touch more respect. Not that Donna didn't respect her before, but…well, she wrote a column about dating. No one would tally that under noble journalistic pursuits. "I love my column. I just don't want that to be all I leave behind."

Donna tutted but didn't argue. "Well, this isn't some big investigative piece, but it matters."

Still unsure whether she should be excited or apprehensive, she folded her arms. "I'm listening."

"We landed a two-day stint behind the scenes in Senator Lopez's office, including a face-to-face interview with the senator herself."

"Wow." Quite the coup for a startup lesbian lifestyle site, even if Sapphisticate was based in Denver and Gloria Lopez was Colorado's first lesbian senator.

"I know. I've been sucking up to her press secretary for months."

Jess didn't want to ask the obvious, but she needed to. "Why aren't you going?"

"Because the Christmas recital and play are next week."

In a lot of newsrooms, having an editor in chief hand off a big assignment because of a family obligation would be unheard of. But Sapphisticate wasn't a typical newsroom and Donna was certainly not just any editor in chief. "I'm honored that you would think of me."

Donna fixed her with a serious stare. "I know you think your column is fluffy, but you've turned it into something special. It's smart, insightful, funny, and honest. And deep down, most people care more about their relationships than what's going on in the world."

Unlike many of Donna's compliments—designed to get her writers to do something she wanted—this one seemed to stand on its own. Jess felt her cheeks flush. "Thank you."

Donna offered a decisive nod, bringing their brief moment to a close. She rattled off enough names, dates, and other details to make Jess wish she had something to write with. "I'll email you the logistics. I suggest booking your travel today."

If part of her wanted to respond with a salute and curt "yes, ma'am," she knew better than to press her luck. "I will. And thank you again."

"I'll look forward to your piece almost as much as your next column."

Donna's phone rang and she answered, effectively ending the conversation. Jess indulged in a double thumbs-up before hightailing it back to her desk. She flopped unceremoniously in her chair and let her head fall back.

"What's wrong? Did Donna yell? Or did she give you the 'I'm disappointed' bit that shouldn't be worse than yelling but totally is?" Frida asked.

She lifted her head and didn't even try to suppress the grin. "Nothing's wrong. She's sending me to DC."

Frida's concerned expression turned into one of alarm. "Permanently?"

"No, no. Nothing like that. She landed an interview with Senator Lopez and she's giving it to me."

"What?" Frida's voice held as much excitement as disbelief.

"I know. The senator wants the interview to be in person so she can show off the diversity of her staff, so it has to be before the end of session."

Frida nodded. "So, soon."

"Yeah, like next week." She'd never jetted off on assignment before, and the prospect made her a little giddy.

"Not that you aren't amazing and more than capable of doing a bang-up job, but why isn't Donna doing it herself? It's totally the kind of interview that would be a feather in her cap." Frida narrowed her eyes, as though looking for the catch.

Jess shrugged. "It conflicts with her kids' Christmas play. Or recital. Something like that."

Frida flicked her hands out with a flourish. "Of course. She's not going to neglect her kids—or the bread and butter of her column—for anything. Not even an interview with a senator."

"Fuck."

"What?"

How could she have been so stupid? "I have a conflict, too."

Frida arched a brow. "Well, I'm pretty sure whatever it is isn't more important than an interview that could take your career to the next level."

She had a fleeting thought of her sex fest fantasies before shaking her head sadly. "It's not."

Frida smiled. "Then it's settled."

Yeah. It was. Sigh.

She picked up her phone to call Cody, but a notification from her personal email account snared her attention so she tapped over to that instead.

Dear Jess,

Just following up on my email from a couple of days ago. We'd love to talk with you about the position but are committed to a timeline that will allow us to select a candidate by the end of the year. Please let me know no later than 5 p.m. EST if you are still interested so we may schedule your interview.

Best,

Maleeka Jones

Fuck. Fuck fuck fuck.

She'd gotten the first email, the one offering her the interview, two days ago. She'd been elated, anxious, indecisive, and in denial, pretty much in that order. She'd also been at Cody's, so she quickly shoved it to the back of her mind. When she'd finally gone home, she drafted a professional, grateful reply withdrawing herself from consideration. But she'd not brought herself to hit send. And now she'd waited so long that she looked flaky and unprofessional.

And yet.

Thanks to Donna's assignment, she'd now be in DC—not even a two-hour train ride from Philadelphia—during the exact timeframe they wanted to meet with her. She wasn't a big one for believing in fate, but it all felt a little too much like stars aligning to ignore. As much as she didn't want to disappoint Cody, would she forgive herself if she passed up the opportunity? Well, two opportunities, technically. Opportunities that would make her proud of her work, of how far she'd come. Opportunities that could change the trajectory of her career, and her life.

Opportunities that should make her excited.

"Girl, did someone die?" Frida's face appeared above her screen. "Or did Donna take back the assignment?"

Jess blew out a breath, realizing just how many times she'd done that today. A wave of self-loathing joined her roiling emotions. "Neither. Do you ever have one of those days where good things happen but then instantly become more trouble than they're worth?"

Frida offered a single, decisive nod. "Yes."

"Really?" For some reason, she hadn't expected that answer.

"Do you want to talk about it?"

Frida was a colleague, but the kind she could confide in. And vice versa. Jess knew about Frida's love life, her battles with anxiety, and the job at ESPN she almost got a few months prior. She looked around. Silpa typed away with her earbuds in. Donna emerged from her office and strode with purpose toward the cluster of cubicles that housed the IT department. "Not here."

Frida angled her head in the direction of the elevator. "Come on. These conversations are better with cocktails anyway."

She needed to finish this week's bonus column. She needed to talk to Cody. She needed to book a plane ticket. But the promise of an empathetic ear and some liquid courage won out. She grabbed her coat. "I'm buying."

Frida zipped her North Face. "You most certainly are."

Twenty minutes later, she sat at the bar of Calamity Jane's with an extra dirty martini and Frida's expectant gaze fixed on her. Jess raised her glass. "Cheers to colleagues who are also friends."

Frida tapped her glass to Jess's and took a sip. "Cheers. Now spill."

She started at the beginning. Well, the beginning of applying for the job she wasn't sure she wanted. "It was impulsive, you know. I didn't really think about it. Or, maybe, I did and I had mixed feelings so it felt easier to apply and imagine that would be the end of it."

"Well, it's also that you didn't want to think about Cody and how serious your supposedly not serious relationship was getting."

She made a face. "And that."

"So, do you want advice or empathy?"

She appreciated the distinction. "Advice, please."

"Don't borrow trouble."

When Frida didn't elaborate, she made a circular motion with her head. "I'm not sure what that means."

"It means don't worry about something until you need to worry about it."

"Pretty sure I need to worry about all of it." That was the problem—she couldn't figure out what to worry about first.

"You don't. Going on the interview isn't deciding on the job. It's wanting to learn more. If they offer it to you, then you have to worry about it. And you'll have more data about whether you want it, so it'll be an easier decision to make."

There was a certain logic to that argument. There was also a sense that she'd be doing little more than kicking the can, putting off the inevitable angst. Of course, if she didn't get it, the decision would be made for her. That had more appeal than she cared to admit. "You're right."

"I know." Frida plucked the olive from her glass and popped it into her mouth.

"Cheaper than my therapist, too." Not that she didn't love her therapist.

"Definitely keep her for the big stuff. This? This is easy-peasy."

She wouldn't go that far, but Frida did have a way of making it all seem rather simple. "So, I say yes to the interview?"

Frida shrugged. "I mean, you're already going to be there."

"Yeah." Because turning down the assignment wasn't on the table.

"Why do you still look so stressed?"

"Because I'm going to have to bail on Cody." And the prospect of more one-on-one time than they'd managed all put together thus far.

"She'll understand. It's work."

Given how focused Cody was on her career, she hoped that would be the case. And hopefully she and Ben would only be gone a week and she'd be able to coax them into Christmas with her family. "Yeah."

"You don't look convinced."

She wasn't, though she couldn't quite put her finger on why. Maybe it was because of how stressed Cody seemed by the prospect of dealing with her ex, and the fact that she'd wanted to offer moral support. Or maybe it was the fact that she'd essentially swapped a week of vacation for work and a job interview. Either way, it didn't feel great. And she wasn't looking forward to telling Cody about the last-minute change of plans.

Chapter Twenty-four

R arely did anyone knock on the lab office door. Cody wasn't even sure it was a knock at first. She looked up from the lines of data, then scrubbed her face, feeling bleary-eyed after an hour of reviewing numbers. The thump-thump-thump sounded again.

"Rashad, can you turn down the music? And, Keith, maybe you should take singing lessons, man." She loved spending enough time with her lab students that she could tease them.

Rashad turned the music down a notch and Danae laughed. Keith grumbled about his talent not being appreciated but stopped short when Maria said, "We keep him around 'cause he's nice to look at."

Keith went nearly as red as his shirt while Maria popped another Skittle in her mouth and squinted at her screen.

Cody squeezed between the sofa and her desk, picking her way between backpacks and knocking over someone's half-finished Starbucks in the process. At least there was a lid. When she leaned down to pick it up, she noticed popcorn littering the floor and two empty Skittles bags.

"You guys, we have to clean up this place. You keep the lab pristine, but this office looks like someone's dorm room and none of this is my crap." She resisted scooping up the trash. As much as she loved the fact that her students liked to hang out in the lab and spent time there even when they didn't have lab work to do, she didn't like their mess. She also wasn't sold on the sofa they'd insisted the lab office needed. Someone had clearly dumped it, and while it wasn't in horrible shape by college student standards, it was nothing pretty to look at and took up a quarter of the space in the already cramped office.

Cody opened the door and straightened. "President Toller. Uh, hi. How are you?"

"Fine. Good, actually." Gillian seemed undeterred by the music—still too loud—and smiled as she looked past Cody, no doubt taking in the popcorn and candy wrappers on the floor, the backpacks and scattered books, and the deer-in-the-headlights expression on all four of her students' faces. "I was just in a meeting with Professor Hayes and thought I'd drop by since you're on the same floor. It occurred to me that I've never actually seen your space. Is now a good time for a tour of your lab?"

"Yeah, definitely. Unfortunately, you have to go through the office to get to the lab." Cody stepped back from the door, giving everyone a look she hoped they would interpret as "let's not screw this up any more." Rashad hurried to switch off the music and Maria hopped up from the sofa.

"President Toller," Maria said, now blushing as hard as Keith had earlier. "We would have cleaned up if we knew you were coming. This mess is totally all our fault. Professor Dawson lets us hang out and study here when we don't have lab work to do, but—"

"They're messy but these four students are some of the best I've ever worked with," Cody said. Maybe it was a mistake, but she'd shared with her lab students how nervous she was about the upcoming tenure review and she knew that had to be on Maria's mind now. Still, it was her responsibility to make a good impression on the president, not Maria's. "All of them work their butts off. And they're all brilliant. Unfortunately, cleaning's not really their thing."

Gillian tipped her head and continued to smile. "It's okay. Cleaning's not my thing either."

A collective sigh of relief went through the office, and Cody almost laughed at Maria's audible "phew."

Cody motioned for Keith to pick up his backpack that was in the middle of the walkway while Gillian asked Maria about her role in the lab. Taking the cue, the others scrambled to pick up their things as well. Maria animatedly described her senior honors thesis project and how that fit in with the lab's overarching research goals, then pointed out each of the other students and what they were working on. Gillian was obviously impressed and hardly seemed to notice how many items got kicked under the sofa and the desks.

Maria continued. "If Cody—Professor Dawson—hadn't asked me to join her lab, I probably never would have gotten into research at all. And now it's what I want to do with the rest of my life. I thought I might like it, but I wasn't brave enough to ask a professor for a lab position. She left a note on my first exam in her class that said 'we need to talk,' and I thought I was going to fail the class."

"Have you ever even gotten a B?" Keith asked.

Maria lifted a shoulder. "I came really close once."

The others laughed and Cody said, "All right, President Toller. I think we've cleaned up enough that you won't fall getting to the lab. It's right this way."

Gillian followed, as did all four of the students. Cody brimmed with pride as each student stepped forward to show Gillian their area of the lab. When Rashad ran through the steps of setting up a sample to be analyzed—his job as newest member of the lab—Cody glanced at her phone. She'd felt it vibrating in her pocket but had ignored it earlier and realized she'd not only missed a call but a few texts as well. All from Jess. The first read simply *We need to talk* but the next was *I have bad news.*

Cody's heart sank. *Can't talk now. In ten?*

Jess immediately responded. *I want to talk in person. You free in an hour?*

"Shit," Cody said under her breath. If Jess wanted to talk in person, the news had to be really bad. Cody looked up from her phone. Gillian was facing the other way, fortunately, now getting a tour of Danae's section of the lab. *If it's an emergency, I can be free. But I've got a class to teach.*

Not an emergency. It has to do with work. How about tonight?

Cody wondered what work thing would involve bad news that pertained to her. She nearly stopped breathing when she remembered the Cuffing Chronicles. Funny how she'd almost blocked the column from her mind. She drummed her fingers on the back of the phone case. *Sure. But other than class I'm free. Call me.*

Cody slipped her phone back in her pocket and went over to pick up the tour where Danae left off. Gillian thanked the students and then followed Cody out of the lab and through the nearly tidy office. They got to the outer hallway and Cody closed the door behind them before turning to Gillian. "They really are an amazing group of kids."

"I can tell. And each one of them knows how lucky they are to be in your lab. I'm not surprised, but I am impressed." Gillian held out an envelope. "I may have had an ulterior motive for dropping by. Shannon normally mails these out, but I told her I'd hand deliver yours. We have a little party every New Year's. Nothing fancy, but we wanted to make sure we got on your schedule early. Do you and Jess have plans yet?"

Cody hesitated. "Not that I know of."

"Let me guess. Jess handles your social calendar?" Before Cody could answer, Gillian added, "I love that you are at Jess's whim exactly the way I'm at Shannon's. Talk with her and let me know. If she's already got you signed up for an all-night dance party, no worries."

"I'm going to say for the record that I really hope we can make it. I'm not much of a dancer."

Gillian left and Cody reached for her phone again. She ran through the text exchange, wishing Jess would simply tell her the bad news. Jess hadn't responded to her last text suggesting a phone call. Maybe the bad work news meant the Cuffing Chronicles were getting canceled?

Cody glanced down at the envelope Gillian had given her. *Cody and Jess* was written in perfect swirling cursive. Their names looked perfect together. Almost as if they belonged that way. But they were only dating because of Jess's work. Cody shook her head. That wasn't right. They'd started dating because of the column. What they had now was a lot more.

❖

"I don't want to go." Ben plopped down in the open suitcase. None of the items Cody handed him had made it inside, but he fit perfectly.

"We're gonna have a blast. It'll be so warm you won't even need this jacket probably."

"Then why do I have to pack it?"

"Good to be prepared." Cody handed him the jacket, but he tossed it on the floor along with everything else. When she gave him a look—not unlike the one she'd given her lab students earlier that day—he only shrugged. She didn't want to force him to go. In fact, she'd hoped he'd be excited about it. But maybe he could tell she didn't want to either.

"We can play in the ocean. You've never even seen the ocean, but I promise you're going to love it. We can even build sandcastles. That's my favorite part."

"You said the water's cold."

"Well, it isn't a bathtub, but you can run and splash in it. And the waves are fun."

"I want to stay at your hotel. With you and Jess." Ben folded his arms.

Now she wondered if she should have told him Jess was coming. Was that her bad news? That she couldn't come? Cody pushed the thought away. She couldn't worry about what she'd already told Ben. At the moment, she had to focus on getting him excited about the trip. She'd thought packing early might help, but so far that didn't seem to be the case.

"I know you'd like to stay with me and Jess, but we're going to be in a boring little hotel room. Anastasia—Mommy—has a big house with lots of rooms and a pool. It's way warmer than the ocean."

Ben's brow furrowed. "I don't like swimming."

"You loved swimming last summer. We went to the pool almost every day." When Ben didn't respond, she decided to change tack. "I bet if you ask, she'll play hide-and-seek with you. She'll probably play anything you want." Hopefully. Anastasia hadn't known what to do with a toddler, but maybe she'd play now that Ben was a kid. "She wants you to stay with her so you two can have time together. You're going to have so much fun."

"I don't want to have fun with her. I want to have fun with you. You're my mom."

"You've got two moms. You know that." When he merely pouted, she dropped down on her knees and crawled over to him. She flipped the cover of the suitcase onto his head. "Maybe I'll just pack you up like this. They won't even charge me a ticket."

Ben stuck out his tongue, but a smile followed. Then he giggled when she wrestled with him. She shifted back on her heels and stretched out her arms. "Come here."

It took a moment, and several grumbles, but he climbed out of the suitcase. He stood in front of Cody, not stepping into her arms and not looking up to meet her eyes. Cody tilted his chin up.

"Listen, if you're not having a good time, you can come stay with me and Jess. But I want you to try and spend some time with Mommy. Give her a chance to be fun. You're lucky you got two moms. Not many kids do."

"Jess could be my other mom instead of her."

What the hell was she supposed to say to that? Her plans to keep Jess as separate as possible from Ben's world had failed completely. He talked about her all the time and she could tell by the hopeful look on his face that he'd thought about this mom proposal before. On top of the generally tenuous nature of their relationship, she still had no idea what Jess's bad news was. Jess had finally returned her text to say that she preferred talking in person and would come by after Ben was in bed. Her heart had only sunk further at that. But none of that was for Ben to deal with. "Jess and I are friends. She loves hanging out with us, but—"

"Are you not gonna marry Jess?"

"Buddy, that's like a hundred steps from where we are. We're good friends and we like each other, but you have to like someone a whole lot to marry them." Except what if they didn't stay friends? If they broke up, it wasn't as if Jess would drop by to say hi to Ben. God, she should have planned this all out before now. "Do you understand?"

Ben nodded reluctantly.

"It would make me really proud if you give Mommy a chance. I'm not saying you have to like her as much as me. Maybe I don't even want you to." She made a silly face and got a smile from him. "But I want you to try."

"Okay." He nodded and stepped forward. Cody wrapped him up in a hug and he dropped into her lap. "What if she smells bad?"

Cody grinned. "Some of us think perfume smells nice."

"Blech." Ben pretended to gag. He didn't like strong perfume, and for some reason out of all the possible memories he could have of Anastasia, the one that stuck was that she was stinky.

"Even if she's wearing perfume, I want you to be nice to her."

He squeezed his nose. "I'll try."

"Thank you. You're the best."

Ben snuggled deeper in Cody's arms. She rocked him, and for a moment he wasn't five going on six but a little toddler again. The years had slipped by and they'd done okay on their own. Now everything felt full of unknowns. And none of it was his fault.

Her phone ringing broke the quiet moment. She kept Ben in her arms but reached into her back pocket to switch off the sound. Seeing Jess's name, she hesitated. She didn't want to let go of Ben now but wasn't sure she could mask her emotions entirely. Depending, of course, on what Jess had to say. She decided to call Jess back later, but before she could hit the decline button, Ben snagged the phone.

"Hi, Jess!"

Cody held her hand out for the phone, but Ben shook his head. She could hear Jess's voice but couldn't make out what she was saying. Ben listened for a moment and then said, "LEGOs. Or something cool. No clothes. Definitely no socks."

"What are you talking about?"

Ben held the phone away from his ear. "Jess wants to know what Joshua would like for Christmas. And what I want, too." He listened to Jess again and then held the phone out to her. "She wants to talk to you now."

If Jess was asking about Christmas presents, she wasn't planning on ending things. But it didn't stop her stomach tightening as she took the phone. "Hey."

"Turns out I can't come over tonight. I forgot I promised Finn I'd help her wrap presents for the foster kids. Her work does this toy drive every year and then she brings home a bunch of the toys and they all have to be wrapped before they get delivered tomorrow. Finn's freaking out about getting it done without me."

"What's wrong?" Ben asked.

"Nothing, buddy." At least with Ben there, she had to pretend that was the case. Later, when she was alone, she could process. She cleared her throat. "It's fine by me if we talk over the phone instead."

"Thanks." Jess sighed. "I really wanted to tell you in person, but…I can't come to California with you and Ben. My boss gave me this last-minute assignment in DC and I want to turn her down but it's a big deal that she asked me to do it and, well, I can't exactly say that I want to go on vacation instead."

"That makes sense." Cody took a moment to let the news sink in. Of the options she'd considered, it wasn't the worst. And yet it still sucked.

"What is it, Mom?" Ben asked.

"Jess, can you hold on?" Cody took the phone away from her ear. "Everything's fine, but Jess can't come to California and she's bummed about it."

When Cody put the phone back to her ear, Jess said, "I'm more than bummed."

"It'll be fine. Don't worry." Cody glanced at Ben and saw tears rolling down his cheeks. "Hey, Jess, I gotta go."

"Um, okay. Well, maybe we can talk more later?"

"Yeah. Sure." She ended the call and pulled Ben close, kissing away the tears on his cheeks. "I'm sorry, buddy."

Dammit. She should have known better. She shouldn't have invited Jess and she definitely shouldn't have told Ben about the plan. And all those boundaries she'd let get fuzzy, well, they needed to be put back in place. Lesson learned.

Chapter Twenty-five

Senator Lopez shook Jess's hand and gestured to the small seating area in the corner of her office. "Let's sit over here. It's much more comfortable."

Jess followed her lead and perched on the edge of a wing chair in deep blue. Then she remembered she didn't want to look like an eager teenager for the school newspaper and sat back. She crossed her legs and rested her notebook on her lap but leaned forward slightly to make sure her body language showed interest. "Thank you again for meeting with me. It's a real honor."

Senator Lopez sat back in her chair as well, crossing ankle over knee. Jess appreciated the casual refusal to adhere to gender norms as much as she'd appreciated the senator's perfectly tailored, perfectly androgynous suit. "I'll be honest. It's fun to do an interview with someone who doesn't have a hidden agenda or desire to back me into a corner."

She'd been so nervous about being taken seriously, it hadn't occurred to her the senator might actually appreciate the kind of article she'd be writing. "Well, I've sworn to find out who makes your clothes. Does that count?"

Senator Lopez laughed. "State secret."

She feigned a forlorn expression. "I guess I'll have to settle for asking what it's like to be the only openly lesbian woman of color in the US Senate."

"It helps that I'm not the only lesbian or woman of color. But let's be honest, politics is still a boys' club. A cis, straight, white boys' club at that."

Jess used that as a launch point for the senator's initiative to encourage public service careers in underrepresented communities, from the local level to the national. They talked about the senator's staff—more diverse than was typical for Capitol Hill and from non-traditional backgrounds. As expected, it posed a few logistical challenges. But it also informed both her platform and her political priorities. "We have to make the government look more like the people it's supposed to represent."

Jess nodded, no longer worried that she might look eager or excited. "I love that."

There was a terse knock and the door to her office opened. A black woman in a trim business suit smiled at Jess and then turned her attention to the senator. "Ten minutes, Senator."

"Thank you, Naomi. We're wrapping up here."

It was hard to believe they'd talked for close to an hour, even if her pages of notes said otherwise. She flipped back to her page of questions and tried to pick a good one to end on. Though, honestly, it was more about ending on a nice note than needing any more material.

"So, how's life in cuffing land?"

Jess's head jerked up and her mouth fell open. "What?" She mentally kicked herself, both for the reaction and the reply, before clearing her throat and trying to look like something other than a deer in headlights. "I mean, I'm sorry?"

Senator Lopez grinned, clearly amused at catching her so off guard. "I've been following your column and I was curious if it was going as well as you make it seem."

"Um…" It was hard to know what rendered her more speechless—the fact that Senator Lopez read her column or the tangle of feelings and questions that made up the current state of things with Cody.

"Sorry. Too personal?" For as sincere a person as Senator Lopez seemed, she was in no way sorry. At least not in this moment.

"It's complicated?" She tried for a playful shrug.

That got her a smirk. An honest to God smirk from a United States senator. "Isn't the point of cuffing to keep things uncomplicated?"

Since they'd gone this far off script, and she didn't have anything to lose, she decided to play along. "No, I'm pretty sure that's what one-night stands are for. Cuffing means you have to like someone enough to spend three months with them but not fall in love."

A simple explanation that drove home just how spectacularly she was failing with Cody. At least when it came to the not falling in love part.

"Well, when you put it that way." Senator Lopez raised a brow in lieu of finishing the sentence, making her sentiment obvious.

"Let's just say there's more to it than I initially anticipated."

Senator Lopez angled her head. "That I'll believe. Does that mean I'm not going to talk you into any spoilers? I could get you an 'I met a senator' button."

Jess laughed then. Who would have expected such a powerful woman to have such a wicked sense of humor? "I already snagged one from the basket on your assistant's desk."

"Hmm."

She had no way of knowing if she'd ever cross paths with the senator again, but she wanted to give her something, and not just so they'd part on good terms. "I'm missing a mini beach vacation with her to be here."

"Oh, really?" Senator Lopez leaned in like they were discussing international espionage instead of Jess's love life. "With or without the kid?"

She'd withheld as many of Cody's and Ben's personal details from the column as possible, but not Ben's existence. "Without."

"Well, that's a damn shame."

The comment made her wonder what she and Cody might be doing right now. But it just as quickly gave her a pang of missing Ben. Talk about complicated.

"Hey, you okay? I was mostly joking with you. I didn't mean to stir up anything."

Great, she'd gone from being teased by a senator about her love life to being coddled by one. "Not at all. Though don't tell my boss that you're the one who ended up asking the tough questions."

Senator Lopez laughed and stood. She put one hand on Jess's shoulder and extended the other. "Deal."

Jess accepted the handshake. "Thank you again for the time today, and for letting me shadow your staff for the last two."

"A pleasure." Senator Lopez walked her to the door. "And seriously, good luck with your project. I hope it turns out exactly how you want it to."

Jess smiled at the choice of phrase. "You and me both."

Jess picked at the remains of her Cobb salad before setting the container aside. She sort of hated herself for ordering room service in one of the top restaurant cities in the country, but between the day in Senator Lopez's offices and needing to catch a ridiculously early train to make her interview in Philly, she was beat. And more than a little anxious.

There was also the fact that Cody hadn't texted her once today. Yes, she and Ben were spending the day together in LA before the handoff to Anastasia, but still. It made her wonder if Cody was more upset about her canceling than she'd let on.

That was why she'd wanted to have the conversation in person. Not only because it was the sort of conversation that deserved to be face-to-face, but because she trusted her ability to read Cody's body language way more than her ability to glean subtext from their too-brief phone conversation. But there'd been no time between them leaving and her trip to DC. And now they were literally on opposite sides of the country and she didn't know if they'd even see each other before Christmas.

She got up to pace for a bit but grabbed her phone after only walking the length of the room a couple of times. She tapped the phone icon next to Cody's name and waited as it rang. And rang.

When Cody's voice mail greeting started, she almost hung up. But leaving a message felt somehow more personal than texting. "Hey. Hope things are going well. Thinking about you. Well, you and Ben, really. I'm sorry again I'm not there. I'd love to hear how things are going if you're up for it. Did the interview today and it went well. Apparently, the senator reads my column. How wild is that? About as wild as the fact that she asked about you. Anyway. Sorry to ramble. Talk to you soon."

She hit the red X to end the call.

"I miss you. I'm sort of in love with you. Oh, and I have an interview tomorrow for a very prestigious job that I'm pretty sure I don't want."

By the time she'd finished the unrecorded part of the message, her screen had gone black. She tossed her phone on the bed, only to pick it up a few lengths of the room later. She checked the volume to make sure she'd unsilenced it from earlier.

Of course she had.

Now that she'd managed to make herself feel pathetic on top of everything else, she grabbed her laptop. After setting up a pillow fort slash desk, she situated herself in the middle and booted up. She should probably start drafting the piece about the senator while everything was fresh in her mind, but she found herself navigating to the folder where she stored her columns.

Her most recent had teased the time away with Cody, complete with artfully vague references to Ben spending time with his other mom. She'd started drafting this week's on the plane, citing the interview and how adulting had a lot to recommend it, but sure did get in the way sometimes. Her goal had been to keep things light because the whole point of cuffing was to avoid the "are we serious?" and "what are our priorities?" conversations that plagued traditional relationships.

And yet, as she opened a blank document—wondering if she'd screwed things up with Cody the way she screwed up most of her relationships—those were the questions she couldn't seem to escape.

Going in, I imagined the biggest problem with cuffing was that many people did it without meaning to, or worse, meaning to and not being up front about it. I, of course, insured myself against both and figured I was good to go.

But here's the thing, readers. Your heart doesn't give a damn about whether you're supposed to fall for someone or not. Your heart is going to want what it wants and I'm pretty sure there's no way to stop it. What you do about it is another matter. You get some say there. Which should feel like a consolation of sorts but rarely does.

I'm falling for her. At least the parts of me that haven't already fallen are falling. I don't know what to do about it and I'm growing more worried by the hour I'm alone in that boat.

I'm pretty sure most of you are screaming at your screens about now. "Talk to her! Tell her how you feel!" Maybe you have a point. But I'm going to play the "it's complicated" card for now, and there's nothing you can do about it.

For better or worse, still crossing my fingers for Christmas.

She hit save and then stared at the darkened screen of the television opposite the bed. The setup made her think of the night she and Cody had booked a hotel so they could finally have sex uninterrupted. It was funny. She'd thought it would be hard to write about the sex part, when really, the difficult thing turned out to be all the feelings, laying her heart bare to her readers in ways she couldn't quite seem to with Cody. Tonight, though, in a hotel by herself and a couple thousand miles from home, it made her feel a little bit less alone.

CHAPTER TWENTY-SIX

The rain stopped early that morning, but the sky remained stubbornly gray, along with the ocean, and the line between the two blurred on the horizon. At least the scene fit her somber mood. Cody listened to Jess's message again, wishing her heart didn't rise at the sound of Jess's voice and wishing she didn't long to call her back.

When the message ended, Cody tossed her phone facedown on the damp sand. She felt silly making a sandcastle without Ben, but with nothing else to occupy her mind, she fell back on scooping handfuls of sand and patting a tower into place. The past three days without Ben had been productive but repetitive. Every day, she woke early and went for a run, then lifted weights in the hotel gym, before showering and having breakfast alone. She'd used the better part of each day to catch up on work interspersed with breaks to wander the beach across from the hotel. Unfortunately, that gave her plenty of time to think of how nice it would have been if Jess had come with her.

Cody could tell from the message that Jess really was sorry to be missing the trip. Work obligations came first—she understood that. Still, she wished Jess hadn't said yes in the first place. More, she wished she'd never asked. She'd gotten not only her hopes up but Ben's, too.

After Ben heard that Jess wasn't coming, he decided—again—he wasn't going either. It took hours of bargaining to get him on board. Fortunately, when they finally got to California, he'd been thrilled at the sight of the ocean and excited by the adventure of it all. Seeing him run in the waves, laughing and screeching at the cold, made it all seem worth it.

But then they'd gone to Anastasia's and Ben had begged her not to leave him. He bawled on the phone that first night and it took all the restraint she had not to run over. The next day was better. Anastasia had taken him to Disneyland and he happily told Cody all about the rides that evening. Cody didn't know what their plans were today—she wanted to give them space, so she hadn't asked. Maybe Anastasia wanted to be a parent after all, and Cody didn't want to get in the way if that was the case. For Ben, she'd do anything. Even step back.

She wanted to give Jess space, too, or at least that's what she told herself when she'd texted a quick response to Jess's call instead of phoning her. But maybe she was the one who needed space. If she talked to Jess now, she knew she'd tell her how much she wanted her in California. Not only for the adult fun part but because she needed someone to talk to. Being apart from Ben and trusting that Anastasia would take care of him was harder than she'd anticipated. She knew better than to call Jess up to discuss her ex-wife, however, or to try to describe how she was feeling. None of it was sexy. It was also all a reminder of how different they were and how it didn't make sense that they were dating in the first place.

The problem was, she'd fallen in love with Jess. She knew it and couldn't do anything about it. Even worse, she couldn't do anything to stop the countdown to Valentine's Day.

With a sigh, she put the finishing touches on the tower and leaned back to study her work. The tide was out and the castle wouldn't be swept away anytime soon, still she felt a rush of protectiveness. She'd fortified one wall with rocks and shells to break little waves, but it would all be swept clean at high tide.

Did Jess like the ocean? That was only the start of the questions she'd thought of over the past few days. She'd thought of Jess nearly as much as she'd thought of Ben. She stood and stretched her stiff muscles, then headed back to the hotel, not letting herself look back at the sandcastle.

Once she reached her room, she kicked off her shoes and sank down on the bed. She called Amelia and leaned back on the pillows, hoping she'd answer.

"Aren't you on vacation? Why are you calling me?"

"I am on vacation." Did it qualify as a vacation if she spent most of the time working and feeling lonely?

"You sound miserable. Thanks for reminding me vacations aren't all that."

Cody chuckled. "I'm not miserable. I'm, well…"

"Lonely without Ben?"

"Yeah." And Jess. Cody sighed. "I'm worried about him but trying not to be. Anastasia took him to Disneyland yesterday and everything seems to be going well so I told myself I'd give them space. I'm trying not to call him until bedtime."

"Let's hope Anastasia doesn't forget him at a restaurant before then. Remember that time?"

Cody groaned. "Can we not talk about that? I'm barely holding it together over here."

"I'm sorry but I don't know how you put up with her shit. The fact that she got you to drop everything and fly Ben out there when she hasn't even tried for the last three years—"

"Amelia, I've accepted that part. She screwed up, but she's still his mom. If she wants to try again with him, I have to support them both." It had been her decision to have a child with Anastasia in the first place.

"You don't have to." Amelia sniffed. "Whatever. We can argue this later. How's the beach?"

"Fine."

Amelia laughed. "Wow, you really are miserable. Is it just Ben and everything with Anastasia or is something else bothering you?"

"Yeah. Everything with Jess."

"Oh, good."

Cody chuckled. "Good?"

"Yeah. I want to talk about Finn. You tell me about Jess first and then I'll complain about how much I don't want to be falling for Finn."

"I thought things were going well with you two."

"They were. Then something came up with her sister and she skipped town. Totally bailed on plans we'd made and hardly apologized. And now I'm realizing I'm in way deeper than she is."

"Sounds like we've got the same problem." She realized how that could be taken and quickly added, "But mine's with Jess, obviously. Not Finn."

"You and Finn wouldn't make it two dates. You're both too damn guarded. I've almost decided relationships with butch women aren't worth it."

"They probably aren't. You know femme women aren't exactly easy either. But the sex…"

"Nice to know I'm not the only lonely horny one."

Cody laughed. It wasn't only the sex she was missing but having a hotel room all to herself and all the time in the world did drive home the point of what she could be doing.

The phone vibrated against her ear and she checked to see who was calling. She didn't recognize the number. Someone from LA. She started to hit the ignore but hesitated. With a sinking feeling, she realized it might be about Ben. It didn't make sense—if something was wrong, Anastasia would call, not a stranger. But still. "Amelia, I have to take another call. Can I ring you back in a minute?"

"Sure. You sound worried. Everything okay?"

"I'm probably being overprotective."

"Considering everything, I don't blame you. Go."

Cody breathed out, unable to fight the building tightness in her chest. She switched to the other call. "Hello?"

"Is this Cody Dawson?" The young woman's voice was strained.

"Yes, who's this?" Her heart pushed into her throat as she heard crying in the background. "Is that Ben?"

"He fell. I didn't think it was a big deal, but he's been holding his arm and crying and I can't do anything to make him stop. I didn't want to bother Anastasia, but I finally tried calling her and she didn't answer. I think his arm might be broken. She gave me your number as a backup."

Cody clenched her teeth. "Let me talk to him."

"Mom, my arm hurts. A lot." His shaky voice gave way to a choked sob. "Can you come get me? Please?"

She couldn't hold the tears back then. "I'm on my way."

The wait at urgent care wasn't long, but Ben fell asleep in her arms before they were even called into a room. He woke up for the

X-ray and fell asleep again as they waited for the doctor to return. He was clearly exhausted, making her wonder how much he'd slept in the last few days. She hadn't been able to reach Anastasia to ask that or to ask where the hell she was. The babysitter, who seemed nice enough and was clearly worried about Ben, had only said that Anastasia had left around noon and would be gone until late that evening. Cody hoped she had a damn good reason to leave Ben with a babysitter all day and not even tell her.

When her phone rang and Jess's name appeared on the screen, she answered without hesitating. Ben shifted in her lap, but his eyes didn't open.

"Hey. How are you?" Jess's voice sounded light and carefree. Like someone on vacation.

"I'm okay. At urgent care with Ben."

"Oh, shit. What happened?" The immediate shift in Jess's tone gave her some comfort and made her feel like crap at the same time.

"He broke his arm."

"While he was with your ex?"

"He was with a babysitter."

"She has him for two weeks and she leaves him with a babysitter on the third day?"

The same thought had gone through her mind more than once. "Yeah. I'm guessing she had to work."

"But she didn't tell you? He could have been with you instead of a stranger. I'm sorry. You've probably already had this whole conversation."

She had, of course, but only in her head. It was some small consolation to hear Jess say it aloud.

"How is he? Does the arm hurt a lot?"

"They gave him a sling to wear while we wait. His arm looks so little in it." And frail, like the rest of him. Cody glanced down and found Ben staring up at her, his eyes still rimmed in red.

"Is that Jess?"

Cody nodded.

"Tell her hi." That he didn't try to scramble for the phone tugged at Cody's heart. He was beat.

"He says hi. I'd pass him the phone but he's pretty tired."

"That's okay. I just wish I were there. You know I could get on a flight tomorrow morning. I could join you for the rest of the week…"

"What about your work?"

"I finished up here. I'm heading back to Denver."

Cody considered it. She wanted to say yes, but at the same time, she had no idea what the rest of the week would be like. Would Ben go back to Anastasia's? Before he'd fallen asleep, he'd made her promise she wouldn't make him. But what could she say to Anastasia?

"I want you to come, but I'm not sure what's going to happen here. I think Ben's going to need a cast. The nurse said that would have to happen tomorrow but I'm not sure what Anastasia had planned for the rest of the week or what Ben will be up for—"

"I'm not going back," Ben said, anger raising his voice. "You said I only had to try to like her and I tried."

"Buddy, we'll talk about it later. Maybe we'll stay there together or something."

"You're going to stay with your ex?"

She was caught between Jess's question, which didn't seem judgmental but had more than a twinge of concern, and Ben's glare. "I don't know what we're going to do, honestly."

"Okay. Sounds like I'd probably only complicate things, but let me know if you change your mind. I miss you. And Ben."

"I miss you, too." Was Jess thinking about complicating the matters at hand or did it go further? She wanted to tell Jess how often she'd thought of her over the past several days and how she was sorry about not calling her back. Jess didn't make things complicated—her life was already complicated.

"Tell Jess I miss her too," Ben said.

"Ben misses you too."

"Give him a hug for me. I can't wait to draw a heart on his cast."

The doctor came back into the room with a nurse at her side. "We've got to go, Jess. Doctor's back."

"Maybe we can talk later? I wish I could give you both hugs right now."

"I'll call you tonight," Cody promised. Whether it was a good thing, or only another problem, she wanted Jess's hug more than ever.

After the doctor quizzed Ben on what had happened—he'd tried to jump from Anastasia's sofa onto one of her loveseats and his socked feet had slipped on the expensive smooth leather—she showed them the X-ray and pointed to the two bones that had snapped. Ben's expression was stoic, but her stomach clenched.

"How long till it heals?" Cody asked.

"Kids heal quick and the breaks are clean. He'll probably only be in a cast for five or six weeks. Give him some Tylenol tonight and set up an appointment for the cast tomorrow."

The doctor handed her a card with the name of an orthopedic center and turned to say something to the nurse.

Ben tugged on Cody's shirt. "Can I swim in a cast?"

"Nope. No swimming."

"Then I want to go home. The only fun thing about the hotel is the ocean and the only fun thing about Mommy's house is the pool."

She didn't blame him. She wanted to go home too. "We'll talk about it."

Ben grumbled again about going home and the nurse looked over. The doctor had slipped out. "Give me a minute to wrap your arm in a splint and then you can go home. But no more jumping on that sofa." She winked. "Or if you do, at least take off your socks first."

In no time, Ben's arm was wrapped in bright yellow and fitted against his chest in the sling. As soon as the nurse said he was all set, he stood. "Let's go to the airport."

Cody spent the walk out to the parking lot explaining that the nurse didn't mean he could go home to Denver. His spirits sank further when he understood that the bandage on his arm was only temporary and the cast would come later. They reached the rental car and Cody's phone rang. She hoped to see Jess's name again, but it was Anastasia. Cody helped Ben into his booster seat before answering.

"I just got off the phone with the sitter." Anastasia sounded worried, which was a small consolation. "She said Ben might have broken his arm?"

"Yeah. He did. We're leaving urgent care now. Are you home?"

Anastasia hesitated and Cody noticed the background noise. Laughing and loud music. Maybe she was in the middle of an event. But then why would she have set up Ben's visit for a time she knew she'd be working? "Did you have to go into work today?"

"One of my friends is putting on a charity gala. I'm overseeing it. You wouldn't believe the guest list."

As Anastasia started listing actors' names, Cody's frustration grew. She didn't care about famous people. She didn't know half of them anyway. But that wasn't the point. "Look, Ben's tired. I can take him back to your house or he can come with me to the hotel. Are you going to be home soon?"

"Not before midnight."

It was half past seven. "Then you can call in the morning. If you want. We'll be at the hotel."

"I'm sorry, did I do something to piss you off?"

Anastasia's legitimately confused tone and non-apology did more to piss off Cody than anything else that had happened. She glanced in the back seat. Ben wasn't asleep but he stared vacantly out the window and didn't seem to be paying any attention to the conversation. "You didn't do anything." She could leave it at that. After all, the broken arm wasn't Anastasia's fault. But for once she wanted to say what was on her mind instead of simply making it easier for Anastasia to walk away from responsibility. "I wish you'd told me you were going to leave Ben with a babysitter."

"Cody, this gala is my job. I know you don't understand, and you've never cared about what I care about, but—"

"I care about Ben. I need to get him dinner. And some pain medication. He broke his damn arm and I hate that I wasn't right there when he needed me."

Anastasia went quiet. After a moment she cleared her throat. "Well, you seem to have everything under control now."

"Yeah, I do. Good-bye, Anastasia." Cody didn't wait to end the call. If she stayed on the line a moment longer, she'd only end up swearing and Ben didn't need to hear that. Maybe she should have simply told Anastasia that she and Ben were going back to Colorado. She didn't want to spend another minute in LA. The thought of a custody battle kicked that thought right to the curb, however. And Anastasia might not have admitted any guilt aloud, but her voice had been tempered at the end. Cody knew that she did care about Ben. She just cared about other things more.

She glanced behind her. "What do you feel like for dinner, buddy? Your pick tonight."

"Are we in trouble?"

"What do you mean?"

Ben looked down at his splinted arm and then up at Cody. "If we don't go back to her house, she'll be mad, right?"

"No, she'll understand. Don't worry." With luck, Anastasia would decide she'd had enough parenting for a while. She turned half around in her seat and touched Ben's knee. "Hey, I'm proud of you for staying at her house. It wasn't all bad right?"

"Disneyland was fun. Especially the teacup ride."

Cody smiled. "That's my favorite too. Maybe one day we can go back and you can show me all the other things you liked."

"Maybe with Jess?"

"Maybe." Cody had no idea what would happen with Jess. And yet a family trip to Disneyland with her didn't seem all that far-fetched, which might be the craziest thought she'd had all day. Whatever happened, she couldn't help feeling Jess was good for her—for them. Better than Anastasia ever had wanted to be.

Chapter Twenty-seven

G ah." Jess woke with a start, her entire body jerking to attention. Or, rather, having her body jerked to attention. She took in the seat back in front of her, the tray table in its upright and locked position. The rumbling beneath her told her the plane had landed. She looked at the college student in the seat next to her. "Sorry."

The guy pulled out his ear buds. "Huh?"

She attempted a steadying breath. "I was just apologizing for my flailing."

"It's all good." He offered her a nod and put his ear buds back in.

One of the flight attendants came on the intercom to announce their arrival at Denver International Airport and the local time, reminding everyone to remain seated with their seat belts fastened until the captain had turned off the sign. She turned on her phone, doing the math as it powered up. Thirty-one hours. That's how long it had taken her to get home. Not bad, honestly, considering the blizzard in Chicago and the very real possibility of spending Christmas in terminal C of O'Hare.

After three attempts at getting on a flight from the standby list, she'd succeeded. It was two in the afternoon on Christmas Eve, but she was home. She texted Finn, then Donna, then her mom. Then she pulled up her text thread with Cody.

Ben had gotten his cast and Cody made the decision not to force him to spend any more time with Anastasia. They'd gotten home the day before, around the same time Jess was supposed to before all the delays and cancellations. Cody had been sympathetic to her plight but hadn't said much else.

Was she busy? Disinterested? Still mad about Jess not being there?

Was dicey there for a bit, but I made it!

She wanted to ask about Ben, about whether Anastasia put up a fuss, about when she could see them both. She resisted, though, at least until Cody answered and gave her a sense of things. She sighed, hating her hesitation. For all her flirty confidence, when it came to feelings, she was little more than a garden variety chicken.

Hooray! Do you need a ride?

Cody's text shouldn't have felt like winning the lottery, but it kind of did. Even more than the prospect of seeing Cody, the offer made it seem like Cody wanted to see her, too. *No, no. It's out of the way and I'm a mess. But I'd love to stop by later.*

If we survive the mall, we'd love that. Takeout maybe?

Jess smiled at the mall comment, then freed her suitcase from the overhead bin and joined the line waiting to deplane. *Who goes shopping on Christmas Eve?*

The woman who's pandering to her kid out of guilt.

It was hard to tell if Cody was making a joke or genuinely blamed herself for what happened with Ben. *Stop. You still win the parenting prize in my book.*

Cody deflected the compliment and made a joke about buying her extra presents. Jess wished her luck and fortitude and promised to check in after a snack, a shower, and some clean clothes. She made her way through the terminal and to the taxi stand, glad she didn't have to drive herself home.

With Finn at her family's ranch in South Dakota and Rascal staying with Amelia, the apartment had an almost eerily quiet vibe. It hit her in that moment that she'd never lived alone. She'd gone from home to college dorms to apartments with a motley array of girlfriends and roommates. Finances motivated her as much as anything, but she liked having people around. It made her wonder if Cody had ever lived on her own, or if she'd wanted to.

She ate a container of yogurt standing at the sink before making her way to the bathroom, peeling off travel-crusty layers as she went. She cranked the heat in the shower, flicking the sprayer to the massage setting, and climbed in.

The pelting water managed to both relax and revive her. And as much as part of her longed for bed, the thought of seeing Cody and Ben gave her a burst of energy. Okay, maybe not a burst. But a recharge. Definitely a recharge.

Since she hadn't driven to the airport—or used her car in days— it sat encased in several inches of snow. She grumbled as she pulled out the snowbrush and started the ignition, but by the time she was done, she'd started humming Christmas carols and had visions of pepperoni and mushrooms dancing in her head.

She might have a million things to worry about, but Cody wanted to see her. That made everything about the last few days better. So, for the moment at least, she let herself simply be happy to be on her way to see them, happy for hot pizza, and happy to be home.

❖

"Jess!" Ben no sooner opened the door than he flung himself into her arms.

"Hey, Ben." Jess held the pizza box out for Cody to grab so she could accept the hug. She wrapped both arms around him and let herself soak in his enthusiasm and the kid shampoo smell coming from his damp hair. "I missed you."

"I missed you too. Mom said you were coming over after you took a bath so I took one, too. We had to wrap my arm in a Ziploc bag because it can't get wet." He grabbed her hand with his good one and pulled her inside. "Did you know casts can't get wet? I can't go swimming until it comes off, but since we aren't in California anymore and it's winter here, I don't even care."

"How about we let Jess take off her coat? She probably wants a minute before all of our stories and questions."

Jess looked up to find Cody regarding her with a half-smile and her heart tripped over itself a few times. "Hey."

Cody's smile grew. "You look pretty good for someone who's been traveling for two days and slept in an airport."

"I'm not sure that's a compliment."

Cody nodded. "It is."

"It's amazing what a nice hot shower and some fresh makeup can do. How are you?"

She'd directed the question at Cody, but Ben launched into how his arm hardly hurt at all anymore and he got to pick the color of his cast and that he didn't like breaking his arm but was glad it meant he got to come home. Jess nodded and tutted and exclaimed. She asked follow-up questions and declared that Ben had been very brave indeed. All the while, catching Cody's eye over the top of Ben's head.

Given the tense conversation before their respective trips, she wasn't sure what she expected now. But Cody seemed relaxed, and the way she was looking at Jess—a mixture of affection and desire—made everything feel right in the world. It also made her want to prod, to ask Cody exactly what she was thinking. And it made her wonder what would unfold after Ben went to bed.

But dinner first. They dove into the pizza and put Christmas cartoons on the television, debating the relative merits of *A Charlie Brown Christmas* and *Olive, the Other Reindeer.* When they'd finished eating, Cody tried to convince Ben to start winding down for bed.

"Are you gonna sleep over?" Ben asked. "I bet Santa would know to leave your presents here if you did. He knows everything."

"I think Santa is more focused on making sure all the kids get presents than worrying too much about the adults."

Cody tipped her head. "I don't know. I'm pretty sure Santa will bring you something."

The gleam in Cody's eye told her "Santa" had something for her already. It made her extra glad she'd had the wherewithal to bring Cody's and Ben's gifts with her. "Santa is pretty smart."

"I'm sure you're exhausted, and I don't know what your plans are with your family, but we'd love you to stay."

She'd expected Cody to demur. Or at least to qualify and caveat her invitation. The fact that she didn't made Jess want to say yes even more. It felt like Cody knew what she wanted, and that was her. "I usually go over on Christmas afternoon, but I'm pretty sure I'd get three cheers if I told them I was spending the day with you."

Cody narrowed her eyes slightly. "So, is that a yes?"

She looked from Cody to Ben, whose eyes were wide and pleading. And it hit her in that moment—more than when they'd been thousands of miles apart, more than when she'd learned Ben was hurt and she wasn't there—just how much she wanted to be exactly where she was. "It is."

Ben whooped his delight and Cody smiled in earnest. She offered to read him a story and Ben asked if they could all read in bed together. Cody let him pick out four since it was a special occasion, but he got sleepy halfway through the second one.

After good night hugs, they tiptoed from the room and Cody pulled his door most of the way closed. "I don't think he slept much with Anastasia."

The now familiar surge of protectiveness clenched her ribs. "I'm glad you came home when you did. It sounds like she's even more useless than I thought."

"She's not useless. She's...I don't know." Cody sighed. "I don't think she ever wanted to be a parent. For so long, I thought it was her idea but I'm wondering now if it was all me. Maybe I convinced her. I wanted kids—well, a family really—and she just loved the excitement of anything new. Still does. Anyway. I was trying to do the right thing, you know?"

She took Cody's hand and led them down the short hall toward Cody's room. "I do know. And you did."

"Did I? It doesn't feel like it."

It was hard to tell whether Cody meant coming home early or going to California in the first place. "It was good for Ben to see her and it was good to come home early. You acted completely and totally with his best interest in mind."

Cody gave a decisive nod, like having Jess say it made it truer. Or maybe like she could let herself believe it. "Thanks."

She imagined Cody alone in the hotel room they were supposed to share, getting the phone call from the babysitter. "I'm sorry again I wasn't there. I was sorry to miss a vacation, but I'm even sorrier you had to go through all that alone."

Cody studied her for a moment, as if she wasn't sure what to make of that. Eventually, she said, "I'd have felt terrible to ruin your vacation, but yeah. I missed you, too."

She shook her head, but the warmth of knowing Cody missed her spread in her chest. "It wouldn't have been ruined because we would have been together."

Cody took her free hand and held them both. "But you're here now."

"I am."

"And so much better for me and Ben than my ex. In so many ways."

Jess laughed. "I wasn't feeling insecure about that but thank you."

"Also, I wish I'd thought to hunt up some mistletoe."

Despite the endless hours in airport terminals, the exhaustion that almost left her asleep standing up in the shower, the idea of Cody's mouth on hers sent a hum of anticipation buzzing through her. "Who says you need mistletoe to kiss me?"

Cody leaned in. Jess closed her eyes in anticipation. But instead of taking her mouth, Cody feathered kisses over her eyelids, each of her temples, and her jaw. She eventually made her way to Jess's mouth, but the kiss she left was as gentle and fleeting as the rest. Jess opened her eyes just as Cody brought a hand to either side of her face. "I bet you're beat."

Maybe it was adrenaline at this point. Or maybe she'd crossed the line into that giddiness that comes with being overtired. Whatever it was, sleep was the last thing on her mind. "I can think of a couple of things I'd rather do than sleep."

"Is that so? Movie, maybe? I'd say we could open our stockings, but Ben would never forgive me."

Like before, this confident, playful side of Cody caught her off guard. And it turned her on. "We can't have that."

"Well, then. Maybe I should just take you to bed. In case you decide you're tired after all." Cody pulled her into the bedroom and closed the door, flicking the newly installed lock and making it clear she had no intentions of resting. At least not right away.

"So thoughtful. The lock, too." The lock made it feel like Cody had every intention of having her over beyond the next few weeks.

Cody grinned. "That's me. Let's get you out of those clothes, too. Much more comfortable that way."

Cody reached for the hem of Jess's sweater. She lifted her arms, letting the wanting ping through her. And if there were feelings way bigger than wanting mixed in, she let them. "Oh, yes. Let's."

Chapter Twenty-eight

Jess was sound asleep in Cody's arms, her naked backside nestled in the hollow made from the curve of Cody's hip to her chest. They'd been swapping memories of how they'd discovered Santa wasn't real when Jess's words slowed then faltered. A long, quiet minute passed before Cody realized Jess wasn't getting to the punchline—she'd been in the midst of describing her nine-year-old self climbing out of bed with a camera to try to catch a picture of Santa in the act. She hadn't minded that Jess was taking her time with the story. In fact, she didn't care what they talked about, if anything. She was too distracted by how nice Jess felt and the way Jess snuggled against her as if there was no other place she'd rather be.

Jess falling asleep in her arms was even more amazing than the sounds she'd made when she'd climaxed earlier that night. Or at least nearly as good. She loved how comfortable she felt with Jess and how comfortable Jess was with her—in her arms, in her house, in her life. It had happened quick, almost too quick to believe, but there was no point arguing that it had happened. The question was what to do about it.

She'd convinced herself that she needed to set better boundaries for the relationship—at least for Ben's sake—but as soon as they were all together that plan had gone out the window. Truthfully, she didn't want boundaries. She wanted to simply give in and accept that some good things were easy.

Everything about Jess felt easy. Maybe that's how it went with cuffing? No processing old baggage, no getting caught up with the what-ifs of the future, simply being present with someone and completely in the moment. But she'd also meant what she'd told Jess last night. Jess was good for her and Ben. They were both happier. She only hoped they were good for Jess.

She shifted away from Jess to glance at the bedside clock. A handful of gifts for Ben still needed to be wrapped and she hadn't put any of the "Santa" presents under the tree yet. Plus, the stockings were waiting to be filled. But she couldn't bring herself to get out of bed.

"What time is it?" Jess's words mumbled with sleep.

"A little after one." Cody settled back against Jess and kissed her neck. Santa could be a few hours late. No way would Ben be up until at least five. With luck, he might even remember the rule and stay in bed until sunrise. "Sorry for waking you."

"We have to do Ben's stocking, right?" She started to get up, then shivered and pulled Cody close. "It's cold out there, but we have to do it. We can't forget. It's important."

That something like Ben's stocking was important to Jess made Cody's heart swell. "You don't have to get out of bed. I can do it."

"I want to help. If that's okay?"

Cody kissed her again. "It's definitely okay. I'd like your help, in fact. But at the moment I don't want to let go of you."

"I don't want you to let go of me either, but I'm worried I'll fall asleep again if we stay like this." Jess yawned. "I think I fell asleep in the middle of our conversation. I'm sorry."

"It's fine. You were tired."

"We can pretend that's all it was. And not how you make me all woozy and noodly."

"Woozy and noodly?"

"Mm-hmm." Jess found Cody's hand and brought it to her lips. She brushed a kiss over Cody's knuckles. "Your hand smells like me. Have I told you how much I like it when you're inside me?"

"You mentioned it about an hour ago."

"I did?"

Cody smiled at Jess's mock gasp. She'd worried then that Jess's declaration, complete with a "fuck yes," might be loud enough to wake Ben. Fortunately, that hadn't happened. "But I think I like being inside you even more than you like me being there."

"Debatable." Jess tugged Cody's hand as she shifted to the edge of the bed. "Come on, Santa. We've got work to do."

Cody grumbled but climbed out of bed. She found a sweatshirt for Jess and a pair of sweatpants for herself, but her pick of clothing earned her an arched eyebrow from Jess.

"This is all we're wearing?" Jess pulled the sweatshirt over her deliciously disheveled hair.

"We'll work faster that way."

"So basically, you're angling to get me back into your bed shivering? Is that so I'll have to cuddle up against you again to get warm?"

"I hadn't really thought about it, but now that you mention it…"

Jess laughed. "That guilty look only makes me want to jump you all over again."

"All over again? I'm pretty sure I jumped you."

"Did you?" Jess tapped her chin. "Hmm. My memory of who grabbed who is apparently fuzzy. You might have to remind me of what happened."

"I could give you a reenactment."

"I like the sound of that. Can I expect a full play-by-play?" When Cody nodded, Jess hooked her arm. "Let's get these stockings filled. I don't know how long I'll be able to wait to have you again."

As much as she'd been ready to oblige Jess, by the time the stockings were filled and the last few presents tucked under the tree, they were both yawning and sleep caught them both.

Not enough hours later, Ben came flying onto the bed hollering "Santa came! Santa came!"

Cody tried to quiet him, but he launched into a full description of all the presents under the tree and Jess only encouraged him, laughing and asking "What else?" each time he paused for a breath. Bleary-eyed, Cody squinted at the clock. It was after six and they couldn't exactly send him back to his room. She turned to tell Jess she didn't have to get up, but Jess was already scooting out of bed, deftly wrapping the throw blanket around her and asking Ben to check to see if Santa had filled her stocking too.

There was no slowing down the morning then. They opened stockings first, then Ben picked one present from under the tree to open before breakfast, as was their routine. After that, Jess convinced Cody to let her make real waffles—not frozen ones—and the house soon smelled like maple syrup and butter.

They lounged after breakfast, curled up on the couch with second cups of coffee, while Ben opened the rest of his presents in a noisy messy rush. The cast didn't slow him down much, though he complained once or twice about not being able to untie the ribbon. Cody loved his never-ending excitement. He even cheered when one of his presents from Santa turned out to be socks, and Jess's smile didn't leave her face the whole time.

Jess snapped a picture of him surrounded by wrapping paper with a bow stuck to his cast and a goofy grin on his face. She showed the image to Cody and asked if she could text it to her mom. The question warmed Cody's heart, as did the follow-up texts from Jess's mom checking to make sure Ben got everything he wanted.

After Ben's presents were unwrapped, he didn't waste time admiring his cache. Instead, he immediately ripped into the LEGO set Jess had given him and started building right in front of the tree. As he worked, Cody waited for Jess to announce she needed to leave. But she only snuggled closer.

The rest of the day passed lazily. She hadn't planned any fancy meals, anticipating it'd only be her and Ben, so they heated up canned soup for lunch and Jess insisted it was completely reasonable to order take-out Chinese for dinner. She didn't bring up other plans or needing to be somewhere else, though she did FaceTime with her parents and siblings. When she was on with her sister, she asked Ben if he wanted to say hi to Joshua. She promptly lost her phone to Ben so the boys could show each other every single one of the presents they'd received.

"This might be the nicest Christmas I've ever had." Jess cozied up to Cody on the sofa again.

"Really?"

"You sound surprised."

"Well, I am. We're pretty boring here. And you're not with your family."

"It feels like I am." She didn't meet Cody's gaze, or notice the questioning look Cody gave her. Instead, she watched Ben jabbering away with Joshua. They'd both gotten the LEGO space station from Jess and were excitedly showing each other all the cool pieces.

"I wasn't sure if it was a good idea to get them the same present, but I saw that space station and couldn't resist."

"Oh, it was a good idea. Maybe sometime we can get together with your sister and the cousins can play again." Cody paused, shaking her head. "I don't know why I said cousins."

"It feels like they're cousins, doesn't it?" Jess brushed her hand down Cody's chest as she shifted closer. She rested her head on Cody's shoulder and sighed softly. "I've been going back and forth all day between wanting to bring up how happy you and Ben make me and not wanting to break the spell."

"Ditto." Cody wanted to say more but a lump formed in her throat. It wasn't only how perfect the day had been, how happy Ben was, or how content she felt. There was something different between her and Jess—something had changed since their respective trips. When Jess looked up and met her eyes, Cody was almost certain she felt it too.

"What are you thinking?"

"That I like you," Cody said. "Actually, I was thinking about how much I like you."

"I thought maybe you were trying to guess what your present is." Jess handed Cody the narrow silver box and smiled. "I've been trying to guess what mine is all morning and you haven't taken even one guess about yours. Nervous?"

"Well, now I am." She shook the box and held it up against her ear. "Is it a jump rope?" No doubt it was a tie and, in fact, she was more than a little excited to put it on for Jess later. "Or a magic wand?"

"It's not magical though I might grant you a few wishes if you're wearing it." Jess's eyes sparkled with mischief. She picked up her present from Cody and mimicked Cody's move, tipping the box back and forth and listening to the paper inside slide from one end to the other. "Flowers?"

"Close." Not at all, actually. Jess had opened the earrings Ben had picked out for her, but she'd waited on Cody's present, insisting she wanted to try to guess it first. So far, she'd been trying silly guesses, but Cody wondered if she had any clue.

To make it harder to guess, she'd put the envelope with the concert tickets and the hotel reservation in a big box. Avis DeVoe was having a concert in Boulder and she thought it'd be a good surprise to get tickets but also a night away with only the two of them. Jess's sister, who she'd called because Ben would need a place to stay for the night while they were there, had promised Jess liked surprises. Cody only hoped she liked this one.

"Is what I said a problem? That I was thinking about how much I like you?" She hadn't minded Jess's deflection earlier, but maybe it made Jess uncomfortable. If that was the case, planning something for after Valentine's Day—something all the way in March—had been a mistake.

"It wasn't a problem. I was thinking I'm starting to more than like you." Jess swallowed. "And maybe that's a problem?"

"More than like me, huh?" She couldn't help smiling but didn't want to make Jess feel like her words were a joke. At all. She tilted Jess's chin up so their gaze met again. Her heart raced in her chest as she considered telling Jess the truth about all the stirrings in her chest. She hadn't fallen for many women, and so far, she'd regretted it each time. But everything about Jess was different. "Thank you for telling me. And it's not a problem. It makes me pretty darn happy, actually. I like knowing I'm not the only one who more than likes someone."

"Someone? Wait, who do you more than like?" Jess teasingly narrowed her eyes.

"You. Only you."

Jess touched Cody's lips with her fingertip. "You do that a lot."

"Do what?"

"Look at me that way and make my heart do a flip. That one was more like a triple twist." Jess glanced at Ben and then back at Cody. "I really want to kiss you right now."

"He knows we kiss." Ben was still chatting with Joshua, though now their LEGO figures were attacking each other through the phone screen. "Besides, he's distracted."

Jess leaned in but didn't go for a kiss. "How would you feel about me staying another night?"

"I'd like that. Maybe you could spend the weekend, too."

"You wouldn't mind me in your space for that long?"

Cody wrapped an arm around Jess and pulled her closer. "Turns out I like you in my space."

Jess eyed Ben again. "At some point we're going to need to tell him that friends don't usually kiss the way we kiss."

"You still thinking about kissing me?"

Jess smiled. "Yes."

Cody closed the distance to Jess's lips. If she could keep kissing Jess, it'd be worth all the tricky conversations she'd need to have with Ben. And somehow it would all work out. She was sure of it.

Chapter Twenty-nine

A re you sure you don't need to go to the office?" Cody angled her head, looking more worried than disapproving.

Jess looked up from her computer, raised a brow, and smirked. "Is that your subtle way of trying to get rid of me?"

Cody's eyes got huge. "Oh, God. No. Of course not. I love having you here."

She folded her arms and continued to smirk. "You're cute when you're freaking out."

"I'm not freaking out."

"You're even cuter when you're pouting." Cody was almost too easy to tease. She'd forgotten how nice that was in a partner. The fact that Cody took it so well, that she could dish it as well as she could take it, made it even better.

"I was trying to be considerate of your work and all you do is harass me." Cody tutted and shook her head in mock disappointment.

The fact of the matter was that she'd spent every night since Christmas at Cody's house. With both Cody and Ben off from school, it had been so easy to have leisurely mornings and productive afternoons with her laptop, leaving only to teach barre and pick up clean clothes when Cody and Ben went to campus to check on something at her lab. She loved it, and she loved that her job—jobs—afforded her that flexibility. "I'm sorry, you're being very sweet."

Cody angled her head at the concession. "Thank you."

"Honestly, though, as long as I'm getting my work done, it doesn't really matter where I do it. Especially this week. My boss is mostly off to be with her kids." And since she'd also picked up her outfit for the New Year's party at Shannon and Gillian's last time she was out, she pretty much didn't need to go anywhere.

Cody's smile was conciliatory. "I trust you. And we'll all have to get back to real-life routines soon enough."

She let her head fall back with a sigh. "Don't remind me."

Cody's features softened. "It's been nice having you here. Maybe that part doesn't have to change too much."

"I'd like that." More than she wanted to admit.

Cody returned her attention to her own laptop and Jess studied her for a moment. If neither of them wanted things to end at Valentine's Day, there was no reason they needed to. Cody's Christmas present of a weekend away in March pretty much made Cody's feelings on the subject clear. And even though her present to Cody was scheduled for before The Deadline—as she'd taken to thinking of it—a ski weekend in a private cabin with an outdoor hot tub hardly said let's break up in the next couple of weeks.

She'd even gone so far as to broach the subject with Donna. Not that she needed Donna's permission or blessing when it came to her personal life, but Donna's enthusiasm for the prospect of a cuffing fail at the conclusion of the series took away any anxiety over how to deal with it in her column. Really, everything seemed to be falling into place. Not to jinx herself, but it was kind of nice.

She closed out of the document that would be her next column and did a quick check of her email. Her Sapphisticate account didn't offer much of note: her main password was expiring in a couple of weeks, a question from Donna about whether she wanted to interview a lesbian congresswoman from New Mexico who'd seen the piece on Senator Lopez and reached out. She switched over to her personal email, deleting junk and relishing the feedback she'd gotten on her article about President Toller. The local magazine didn't have the reach of Sapphisticate, but she loved its mission and the chance to freelance for them from time to time.

She almost deleted the one from Maleeka Jones before the name registered. She clicked on it, already feeling relieved. Email invariably meant thank you, but no, thank you. And at this point, it was exactly what she wanted to hear. Or read. Whatever. Only the words in Maleeka's email didn't match her expectations. They were all but a job offer, ending with a request to chat by phone the next day.

"What's wrong?"

"Huh? Oh, nothing."

Despite the assertion, Cody continued to regard her with concern. "Wow. You're a worse liar than Ben."

She laughed. "I'm not lying. It's just an email I don't want to deal with and so I'm not going to."

The reassurance didn't seem to help. "Is it urgent?"

She closed her laptop with a snap. "Nothing that can't wait until tomorrow."

Cody wiggled her eyebrows. "It's hot when you're decisive."

"Stop."

"I mean it."

She set her computer to the side. With Ben at his friend Daevon's for the afternoon, she didn't hesitate to climb right into Cody's lap, straddling her thighs. "And now? Do you like me when I'm decisive about how much I want you?"

She'd mostly been kidding, but Cody's expression turned serious. "I really do."

"And if I asked you to take me to bed?"

Cody's hands went to her hips. "I'd say maybe you should take me to bed."

"Oh, really?"

Cody nodded. "Really."

"Because you'd totally let me be in charge once we got there." She meant it as a joke, but simply saying it out loud had her pulse racing.

"I mean, I'm not asking you to strap on, but you on top, doing exactly what you want? Yeah. That's hot."

It was hot. And the more they talked about it, the more she wanted it.

She wiggled her butt back far enough for her toes to graze the floor, then stood. She stuck out both hands and Cody took them without hesitating. Cody stood and Jess let go long enough to turn around. She held her hands behind her this time and Cody took them once again, inviting her to lead them upstairs.

Once they were in Cody's room, she expected Cody to turn the tables and take over. Only Cody didn't. She shed her clothes and Cody merely watched. She stripped Cody of hers and Cody let her, sliding her hands up Jess's sides and back down. She didn't make any other movements, no attempts to grab or tease or kiss. She merely waited.

The waiting sent Jess's senses into overdrive. She wanted to touch and taste everywhere at once, to have her fill of Cody and have Cody let her. Would Cody let her?

Cody's gaze didn't waver. And still, she waited.

Jess dipped her head, pulling one of Cody's nipples into her mouth. She used her finger and thumb to pinch the other. Cody let out a moan and her head fell back. She grabbed Jess's hips—possessive, but maybe also like she was trying to keep her bearings.

Any illusions Jess had of taking her time vanished. "I think you need to get your cock."

Cody lifted her head. "Yeah?"

"Oh, yeah." She looked Cody up and down. "Because once I get you in that bed, I'm not letting you out."

It only took Cody a minute to snag her harness from the locked case under the bed, but Jess barely let her finish tightening the straps before kissing her again. She gave Cody a shove and Cody didn't fight it, falling back onto the bed with a smile. Jess joined her, straddling her thigh for the moment instead of her hips.

She kissed Cody's mouth, her neck. She sucked Cody's nipples, one and then the other, using her free hand to stroke the cock and push the base against Cody's clit. Cody groaned her approval, arching into Jess and writhing in ways that had Jess dripping with want.

"I hope you're ready because I'm not sure how much more teasing you I can take."

Cody managed something resembling "uh-huh," but no words. Jess took that as all the consent and invitation she needed. She shifted her knees so they were situated on either side of Cody's hips and reached behind her to grab the cock.

"Lube?" Cody's question came out with a shaky breath.

"Oh, that won't be necessary."

She positioned the cock and settled herself on it, sitting back so that it filled her completely. "Fuck."

Cody swallowed, nodded.

She started to move, slowly at first. She'd forgotten how good it felt to be on top. Cody's hands once again found her hips. But instead of trying to control Jess's movements, her pace, Cody moved with her, followed her lead. She opened her eyes and found Cody staring at her with something resembling awe. It made her heart trip with something far more potent than pleasure.

Afraid her emotions might get the better of her, she closed her eyes and touched her own breasts for a moment rather than Cody's. But then Cody had to go and make this almost whimpering sound. Jess opened her eyes and smiled. She leaned forward, planting a hand on either side of Cody's head. "Fuck, you feel good."

Another nod from Cody. Jess took that as a cue to ride her in earnest, grinding forward and back in a way that hit every nerve ending she had. And if Cody's expletive-laced response was anything to go on, she hit a good number of Cody's as well.

Cody let out a ragged chuckle. "It's all I can do not to come yet."

"Well, don't hold back on my account."

She increased the pumping of her hips. Cody grabbed her hips with more force. "Fuck. Yes. Please."

The change in angle, paired with the sensation of her nipples brushing Cody's, pushed her to the edge. Cody's words, followed by her entire body trembling under Jess, nudged her over. The orgasm flooded through her with waves of pleasure. Cody's grip on her tightened and she rode it out, powerless to do anything else.

They stayed like that for a long minute—Jess unable to move and Cody seeming to be perfectly content with Jess on top of her. Only when one of her hip flexors started to protest did she ease herself away, collapsing next to Cody in a sweaty, satisfied heap.

Cody's arm came around her shoulders. "Wow."

"That was really okay?"

Cody kissed the top of her head. "I'm sorry. Was my begging unclear? Or maybe it was the swearing. You're not used to that, so I can see how it might have thrown you."

As much as she didn't want to move even a fraction of an inch away from Cody, Jess propped herself on her elbow to look Cody in the eye. "I'm serious. That wasn't too...toppy?"

Cody studied her and she braced herself for the inevitable. "I'm not saying I don't want to be the top. In fact, I'm quite fond of it. But there's something to be said for variety. For being topped by a femme who knows exactly what she wants."

"Oh."

"You seem surprised."

How could she explain? "I guess I'm used to being with people who have more rigid ideas of what they like."

Cody brought a hand to her cheek. "I like you, Jess. More than like. Way more, if you recall. That means I like all of you, not just bits and pieces."

"But—"

"No buts. I love how you are with Ben. I love that we can go out with other adults and have interesting conversation. And I love being in bed with you. All the ways of being in bed."

If a small voice in the back of her mind remained suspicious, she let the rest of herself believe Cody's words. Not only the ones about her taking charge in bed but all of them. The ones that let her believe she and Cody might have a future together. "Okay."

"Now come here so I can hold you like the strapping butch I am before we have to get up."

She laughed, then did as she was told. "So bossy."

Cody's arms came around her and held her close. "I think the word you're looking for is switch."

Strangely, she hadn't given it much thought before. Just that she liked butch women and most of the ones she fell for weren't interested in anything like that. "Um."

"Kidding." Cody kissed the crown of her head. "I remain a top at heart. But anytime you want to do that, you're not going to get a word of protest from me."

"I can live with that." It was essentially the sex dynamic of her dreams.

Cody let out a sigh. "Would it be wrong to take a nap before Ben gets home?"

"If it's wrong, I don't want to be right."

Cody gave her squeeze and she squeezed back. "See, you still follow my lead sometimes."

At the rate she was going, she'd pretty much follow Cody anywhere. Or, maybe more accurately, she'd happily stay put. Could it be as simple as that? Maybe not always, but she could pretend it was, at least for the moment.

Chapter Thirty

Cody squeezed through a narrow space between two groups of women, apologizing when she bumped someone's elbow. She breathed out when she reached the empty hallway between the living room and kitchen, but there was another crowd to pass through before she'd make it to the counter where the bar was set up.

This wasn't a small gathering by her standards, but maybe Shannon had added a few more to the guest list since the president had given her the invitation. Despite not being a fan of crowds, or even parties really, Cody was enjoying herself. She'd even let Jess convince her to dress up, and when she caught her reflection in the hall mirror, she couldn't help but smile. Bow ties and vests always reminded her of teddy bears, and she was caught between feeling slightly ridiculous and liking the look anyway. At least she knew Jess appreciated the outfit—she'd scarcely kept her hands off Cody all night.

Not that she'd done much better. In a silky black dress with an open back that showed off her toned shoulders, Jess was truly a knockout. Cody had been ready to find a bed the moment she'd seen her in the outfit. Unfortunately, Jess insisted they make it to the party on time and she was left feeling Jess up surreptitiously while dealing with being wet and horny in a crowd of strangers.

Hopefully, they could escape right after midnight.

"Going for a refill?" Gillian held up an empty glass as she nodded at the two Cody held. "Apparently, we had the same thought."

"Yep. Jess and Shannon found each other and started chatting so I figured it'd be a good time to slip away for a minute."

"You weren't hoping that'd be a quiet minute, were you?"

"No, not at all." Cody grinned.

"Oh good. Because quiet isn't happening tonight. For the record, this is a few dozen more people than I originally agreed to." Gillian offered a what are you going to do shrug. "I'm not a fan of big parties, but Shannon is amazing at making friends—and remembering to invite them all over."

"Honestly, I'm having a great time. Jess makes things like this easy. She handles all the small talk and I just get to smile and nod at people."

"Not a bad gig."

"Plus, I know she loves parties." She'd enjoyed watching Jess's face light up when they arrived and she hadn't stopped smiling yet. "My introvert self can go out for her sake every once in a while. Besides, this crowd is kind of amazing. I didn't know there were this many lesbians in all of Denver."

"Shannon knows everyone. And who they've dated. If you didn't have Jess, she'd probably be setting you up with any one of her forty best friends right now."

"Good thing I'm not single. I don't think I could handle having my choice of forty women."

Gillian laughed. Two women passed through the hall and Gillian lifted a finger to signal Cody not to go anywhere. She exchanged pleasantries with them, pointed them in the direction of the bar, then returned her attention to Cody. "So, you and Jess. Everything going okay?"

"Yeah. We're great." As confident as Cody was about that fact, something in the tone of Gillian's question gave her pause.

"Good. You two make a great couple." Gillian bit at the edge of her lip and seemed to consider how to phrase what she wanted to say next. "I only ask because even if two people are great for each other like you and Jess, a lot of outside things can put a strain on a relationship."

Cody wanted to ask what Gillian meant, but she couldn't bring herself to say the question out loud. Instead she nodded. It was true, of course, that outside influences could turn a good relationship bad, but things were fine with her and Jess—better than fine.

"Oh, before I forget, I wanted to let you know that I got your file to review. It's fine but it came in a little late and I haven't had a chance to look at it yet."

Late? Instead of feeling any relief at Gillian's explanation, she was left more anxious than before. Had her department chair done something to sabotage her after all? Were letters of recommendation missing? With the trip to California and everything with Anastasia, she'd been out of the loop and hadn't thought about her file beyond knowing she'd submitted all her pieces on time.

"I'm certainly not worried about what will be in your file." Gillian put a reassuring hand on her shoulder. "Just wanted to explain why you hadn't heard anything. I'll probably have news for you in a week. I'll be back to work day after tomorrow and the full tenure and promotion committee meets before classes start."

"No rest for the weary?" Cody hoped her tone played down her fear.

"Keeps me out of trouble." Gillian gave Cody a conspiratorial wink and gave her shoulder a squeeze. "Go find your gal. I was trying to relieve your stress, not add to it. And, of course, we didn't have this conversation."

"Of course." Cody took a deep breath, aware of how shaky she felt. She suddenly did want to find Jess. She needed to talk through things and hear the words "you're freaking out for no reason" from someone besides the president.

She refilled her and Jess's wine glasses and headed back to the sofa where she'd left Shannon and Jess. She'd barely made it out of the kitchen when she felt her back pocket buzz. Since it could be the sitter, she set one of the glasses down and reached for her phone.

She stared at the name on the screen. A moment of relief that the text wasn't from the sitter gave way to anxiety. *I know this is probably going to come as a surprise.*

The rest of the words in the message block blurred. She took a steadying breath, reminding herself not to freak out prematurely. Unfortunately, her blood pressure still hadn't dropped from Gillian's news about her tenure file. And now Anastasia. Cody took another deep breath and forced herself to keep reading.

I'm getting married in February. On Valentine's Day. I was going to tell you when you were here but you left early—obviously. Since we never formalized the divorce, I need you to sign some documents. My lawyer will be sending you an email. Most of this is a formality, but we do have to talk about Ben.

Cody swallowed, then read the long text all over again. She didn't care about Anastasia remarrying, but was this her way of asking for joint custody? Anastasia often had a hidden agenda, and she felt sick with all the possibilities spinning through her head. Why had Anastasia texted tonight? Wasn't she out partying with her new fiancée?

If she wanted to put a damper on Cody's New Year's Eve, she'd accomplished her goal. The Valentine's Day wedding only added weight. Cody had stopped thinking of that particular day as the breakup day with Jess, but just when things were going better than ever, Gillian's words had her doubting her conviction on that too.

This was silly. Jess was nothing like Anastasia. Sure, she was spontaneous and adventurous—traits she'd once ascribed to Anastasia—but she was also patient and present and better with Ben than Anastasia had ever been. No way was Jess going to pull the carpet out from under her. And Jess was exactly the person she needed to talk all this out with now—before she messaged Anastasia back.

Cody tucked her phone away and picked up the wine glasses. She looked through the crowd trying to spot Jess. She couldn't see Jess or Shannon or even the sofa from where she stood. It didn't seem possible, but the living room had gotten more crowded.

She made her way over to the sofa but found it filled with women she didn't know. She looked around and finally spotted Jess with Shannon in the dining room. Shannon was replenishing the trays of food while Jess arranged napkins and silverware. Cody guessed Shannon and Gillian hadn't prepared all the food, but there were no caterers in sight. She watched Jess and Shannon—heads close together in what appeared to be an intense conversation—and wondered if she should wait till they'd finished.

"Lost your date?" Gillian asked, a smile on her lips.

"Not exactly. She's with your wife." Cody motioned to the dining room.

"Oh, I promised Shannon I'd help set up the carving station." Gillian's chin dropped. "We didn't want the caterers to have to work all night, so we let them off early. And then I forgot about the roast beef. I swear I don't know why she puts up with me." Gillian managed one step toward the dining room before someone called her name from the other side of the piano.

"I can do it." Cody shook her head when Gillian started to protest and insisted again, then got instructions for what needed setting up. She went to the kitchen to retrieve the roast from the warming box and made her way to the dining room.

"Tell me you aren't breaking up with her on Valentine's Day," Shannon said. "When I read that part, I broke down crying. No joke. You can't do it."

Cody's feet stopped of their own volition. She'd come up behind Shannon and Jess prepared to joke about joining the catering crew, but the words vanished. She should clear her throat or something to alert them to her presence but instead took a step back into the hall and out of their view as her pulse whooshed in her ears.

Shannon knew. Cody struggled to take a breath. If Shannon knew, Gillian knew as well. *Fuck.* Suddenly, Gillian checking in made sense. But was a breakup on Valentine's Day still on the table? Cody couldn't believe it and yet, really, what did she know? Would Jess do it for the sake of her column?

Shannon continued. "I still can't believe Cody is Carrie—and you're that Jess."

"You can't say anything. Promise you won't tell Gillian? If Cody knew that you knew, she'd freak out. But if Gillian knows, it could affect Cody's job. She's been worrying about that from the beginning. Gillian doesn't know, right?"

Shannon hesitated long enough for Cody to be certain it was too late to keep things from Gillian.

"She already knows." Jess's words mirrored the ones in Cody's mind. "Fuck."

"We've both been following it. I got Gillian into it, but we didn't know it was you and Cody at first."

"What am I going to tell Cody?"

"Maybe don't tell Cody anything. If you aren't breaking up on Valentine's Day, it doesn't matter, right?" When Jess didn't immediately respond, Shannon continued. "God, you've got to tell me. You aren't planning on breaking up with her, are you? I can't handle waiting until Valentine's Day to find out."

"Suspense is good for page clicks." Jess didn't budge even when Shannon whined.

"If you break up, are you going to put those details behind the paywall too?"

"Don't give my boss any ideas. I think she'd have me do this whole thing all over again next cuffing season with all the juicy bits behind the paywall."

Cody wished she could see Jess's face. She sounded serious, but she couldn't be. Unless she was. Cody stared down at the platter of meat, feeling nauseous.

"You do a good job teasing the juicy bits," Shannon said. "I have to admit I've been a little envious. Even told Gillian we should get a hotel room sometime to spice things up. I was bummed you couldn't go to Santa Monica with her. A whole week without a kid? I think I needed to vicariously live through that sexfest as much as you needed it in person."

Jess laughed. "Don't worry. We've caught up on the sex this past week."

"So I've read." Shannon's tone was teasing now. "But a week without a kid? That'd be priceless, right? I mean you said so yourself—you didn't get into this to be a parent."

Jess sighed. "You're right. A week with only the two of us would have been nice."

Cody couldn't listen anymore. She spun around, the half-carved roast beef teetering on the platter with the sudden move, and beelined back to the kitchen. She set the tray on the kitchen table, kicking a chair out of her way as she did. A cluster of women standing nearby gave her a look, but she only shrugged and turned back to the dining room.

This time, she didn't hesitate in the hallway. "Jess, can I talk to you?"

Jess's smile slipped off her face when she caught Cody's expression. "Is something wrong?"

Cody shook her head. So many things were wrong. Starting with the choice she'd made to call Jess in the first place. "Just need to talk to you for a minute." She smiled at Shannon. "I won't keep her for long."

"She's all yours. I've got to get the roast beef anyway."

Cody willed herself to remain calm. "It's on the kitchen table. I told Gillian I'd set it up in here, but I got distracted."

Jess tilted her head, a question forming on her lips. Cody wasn't going to keep it to herself that she'd overheard everything Jess had told Shannon. She couldn't. But she also couldn't say anything more with Shannon there.

"Is it okay with you if we go outside?"

"Sure." Jess's tone was uncertain, but Cody didn't tell her not to worry. She couldn't say everything was fine. Nothing was.

"Can I grab my coat?"

"Yeah, of course."

Cody led the way to the foyer and found their coats. She handed Jess hers without meeting her eyes and opened the front door. Jess followed her out, shivering at a gust of cold air and hurrying to button up her coat.

"What's wrong, Cody? You've got a look on your face that's got me freaked out. Is it Ben?"

"Why are you bringing up Ben now?"

Jess shook her head. "Because you're clearly upset. I can't think of anything that would get you this way except something happening to him."

"Nothing happened to Ben." Except she'd managed to not protect him at all, despite how she'd told herself that she would. "Did you overhear Shannon? About her reading my article?"

Cody nodded.

"Okay." Jess blew out a breath. "We can figure this out. I know you're probably worrying about what Gillian is going to do, but we can craft this the right way. We're not breaking up on Valentine's Day and it was a silly way for two people to meet, but what difference does it make now?"

"Would breaking up on Valentine's Day boost your site hits? Or would it be better for your job if we drag this out a little longer?"

"Are you seriously asking me that?"

"Yeah, I'm serious." The anger that had reared up inside her was at a tipping point. She should stop talking but couldn't. "Because if that's where this is going, I'm thinking we should just rip the Band-Aid off now and move on."

"I don't want to break up at all. I was joking with Shannon about it, and I'm sorry you overheard, but if I was even considering it, I wouldn't have just turned down my dream job. I like you. I like us."

"Your dream job? Did you get a job offer somewhere?"

Jess's shoulders dropped. "Yeah. In Philadelphia. I wasn't going to tell you because it doesn't matter anyway since I'm not taking it."

Despite just reassuring herself Jess was nothing like Anastasia, her mind started drawing more parallels than she could process. "When did you get the offer?"

"Day before yesterday."

"When you were at my house? And you didn't mention it?" Cody shook her head. Like Anastasia had agreed to those first gigs in LA without telling her. "So you interviewed too, right? I mean no one offers a job without an interview. Was that part of the DC trip?"

"Yes, but—" Jess started and then stopped. "I should have told you, but with everything going on with Ben and Anastasia, I figured you had enough on your plate." Jess tried to reach for Cody, as if the contact might make things right, but Cody sidestepped and Jess's hand fell to her side.

"I think we need to not touch right now." She took a deep breath, realization setting in. It didn't matter what Jess said to gloss over things. It didn't matter that she'd kept things to herself—important things—exactly as Anastasia would have done. It didn't matter how good Jess felt in her arms. Or what she wrote in her damn article.

"Cody."

"We don't make sense together, Jess." And she'd been fooling herself to pretend otherwise.

Jess's jaw clenched. "I don't agree, but why do you think that?"

"Because you aren't in a place to be a parent. You wanted a week alone without a kid—which is completely reasonable. Hell, I wanted it too. But Ben, and being a parent, is my reality. I'm not going to ask you to keep doing this when it isn't what you want. I made that mistake before and I'm not doing it again. I want to be something good in your life. Something you really want. Not a work assignment that you got caught up in."

Jess shook her head, but Cody continued. "I'd rather you walk away now than regret it later. No one should give up a dream job for a relationship that's not supposed to last more than a few months."

"Maybe this started out as cuffing, but we both know it's more than that now. I don't want to end this. Or I didn't five minutes ago." Jess looked at the door as if thinking of going back inside, then cussed softly. "Cody, if you read my column, you'd know how much I love being with Ben and figuring out how to be a parent. I didn't expect that part, and maybe I wasn't ready for it—and maybe I'm not that great at it yet—but that doesn't mean I don't want it."

"How long before you regret it? Before you realize playing parent isn't always Christmas morning? Before you realize I'm not all that cool and Ben is a ton of work? How long before you split?"

Jess shook her head to every question Cody posed and was still shaking her head now, but tears welled in her eyes as well. "Where the hell is this even coming from? Did you not hear me tell Shannon that I love Ben? Can't you see it when he hugs me?"

"I heard you tell Shannon that you wanted a week without him—and apparently wrote about wanting a weeklong sexfest. And the president of my university read all of that." But Gillian knowing wasn't the real problem. "Jess, I like you, but who are we kidding?"

"Do you actually like me? I don't think you do. Because if you actually liked someone, you wouldn't be treating them the way you're treating me right now. And you keep bringing up my column and my job, but we didn't get into this arrangement just because of me. You're freaking out because you're worried about your fucking tenure. Fine. I get that. This is you freaking out about maybe losing your job. And I'm sorry about that, but don't make this about whether or not we should be together."

Cody opened her mouth to argue, but Jess held up a hand. "I'm not done. When you say that I don't care about Ben..." She swallowed, her lips squeezed together as she fought back crying. Cody started to interrupt but she only raised her hand higher. "I get to finish. Sometimes I'm not sure which one of you I fell for first. And it makes me livid that you can callously say things like I don't care about him."

"I know you've gotten close to Ben. But that shouldn't have happened. I shouldn't have let it happen. And now he's going to get hurt all over again."

"You know what? You're right. It was a selfish move. If you knew you were going to walk away, you should have protected him. You shouldn't have ever had me over. But you didn't do that and now he's attached. And so am I. Nice going."

"Fuck you."

Jess threw up her hands. "What the hell do you expect me to say?"

"I don't expect anything at this point. Anything you do say, I won't be able to trust anyway. It'll all be for your column, right?"

Jess swore again, then swiped angrily at the tears falling down her cheeks. "I don't know what I was thinking falling for you. So, we're ending this?"

"What's the point in waiting? Cuffing isn't forever." Cody clenched her jaw, fighting back the press of her own tears. "Maybe next season you'll find someone who's better at the fun parts. Someone who can take you on a weeklong sexfest whenever you want."

"Cody, I don't want that. I want..." Jess looked up at the dark sky, clouds hiding any stars, and shook her head. A moment later, her eyes leveled on Cody. "It doesn't even matter now. I shouldn't have let myself get close to you. But you're right. There's no point dragging this out if you're someone who walks away when shit gets hard."

The front door swung open and a couple came out, laughing and bumping against each other. They glanced at Cody and Jess, realizing at the same moment that they were interrupting something. "Sorry," the taller woman said. "We were coming out for a smoke."

"It's fine. We're done here." Jess didn't look at Cody before pushing past the couple and slipping inside.

CHAPTER THIRTY-ONE

Three whole days passed without a peep from Cody. Jess had thought she'd calm down after a day or two and reach out, but nada. She didn't know whether to scream, cry, or throw something.

As tempting as those options were, she settled on fumbling through work like a zombie, writing and editing anything and everything but the next installment of her column and teaching barre on autopilot. At home, she hid in her room, only emerging to make peanut butter toast and take Rascal for runs when Finn wasn't home. All while checking her phone obsessively.

With the column deadline looming, she knew better than to think she could keep putting off the inevitable. But in addition to having no idea what to say, she also had to contend with knowing that—whatever it was—it wouldn't be what Donna wanted or had in mind. Jess needed to tell her and hopefully, not fall apart into a sobbing heap in the process.

She got up from her desk, sad that Frida was once again off on assignment and she had no one to commiserate with about the sorry state of her existence. She headed to Donna's office, but as she so often was, Donna was on the phone. She considered going back to her desk, but given how long it had taken to screw up her courage in the first place, it was entirely possible she'd waste hours. And she didn't have hours.

She went over to the story board that hung on the adjacent wall, an old school bulletin board where any of the writers or editors could post pictures or half-baked ideas for future articles. But rather than inspire her, the jumble of images and phrases made her even more restless. She wandered back in front of Donna's door, trying to be subtle and knowing she wasn't.

She stretched. She paced some more.

"Archer. Get in here."

She'd been pacing in front of Donna's door for so long, she'd gotten lost in her thoughts—thoughts of Cody and just how ugly their fight had been—and managed to look like a total flake. Once again. She scurried into Donna's office. "Can I talk to you for a minute?"

"Well, I didn't imagine you were prowling back and forth for exercise." Donna's smile took the sting out of her words. "What's up?"

She took a deep breath, willing herself not to vomit. "Cody and I broke up."

Donna's eyes narrowed in confusion.

"Carrie. Sorry. Carrie and I broke up."

Donna's lips formed a perfect O and she nodded slowly. "Okay."

"We weren't supposed to break up until Valentine's Day, but we were at a New Year's party and…" She hesitated, not wanting to relive the conversation but also not wanting to air all her relationship woes to her boss. "We had a fight and both said some awful stuff and, well, it's done."

Donna lifted her chin. "How are you holding up?"

She lifted both hands and waved them a bit more frantically than she intended. "I'm not looking for a shoulder to cry on. I was worried about the column ending earlier than we agreed it would."

Donna flipped her wrist dismissively. "The column is a hit. And honestly, the relationship lasted longer than I expected it would, given the kid and all."

Just the vague reference to Ben had her stomach twisting. She shoved it aside and told herself to focus on the issue at hand. "So, you aren't mad?"

Donna's features softened. "Close the door. Sit down."

She did as Donna asked, the knot of sadness in her gut turning into one of anxiety.

"You're my best writer, Jess, hands down."

She swallowed, waiting for the shoe to drop. The inevitable and soul-crushing *but*.

"You've managed to make a column that could have been superficial and seedy a must-read on the site. You did that by being vulnerable, with the woman you were dating and with your readers. And you did it with absolutely no way of knowing how it would go or how it would end."

Tears pricked at her eyes, but not for the reasons she'd expected. "Thank you."

"I'm guessing from the look on your face you're nursing quite a broken heart."

Ha. "You could say that."

"I'm sorry. When I pitched the series to you, I didn't imagine the stakes would ever be so high."

She let out a rueful chuckle. "Me neither."

"Is it really a lost cause?"

Given Cody's refusal to talk in the moment, and absolute radio silence since, it was hard to imagine otherwise. "I think so."

"I'm sorry to hear it. More for your sake than the column's."

It was nice of Donna to say, even if she didn't mean it entirely. "About that."

"Are you asking for an out? Is that it? A quick disclaimer instead of pouring your heart and soul out all over again?" Donna sighed. "I don't suppose I could blame you."

As much as the thought of writing about the last couple of days made her feel sick, that hadn't occurred to her. "No, no. Not at all. I just, I guess I wanted to give you a heads-up that things were over. And that the column would be, too, sooner than we'd discussed."

"Well, the cuffing part at least. I have a feeling most of the readers you picked up are going to stick with you, whatever your next adventure is." Donna smirked. "I'm sure at least a few will celebrate the fact that you're back on the market."

A groan escaped before she could stop it, followed by a quick apology.

Donna waved a hand again. "I think you've earned a reprieve. Perhaps you could write about self-care. It'll resonate with the singletons and the New Year's resolutions crowd."

She swallowed the groan this time, if only barely. "I'm not going to tell people that the answer to their sadness or loneliness or whatever is to go to the gym and drop ten pounds."

It was snarky, even for her. Donna folded her hands and set them on her desk. "I'll indulge that since you're having a bad week."

She closed her eyes for a second, took a deep steadying breath, and apologized again.

"Think about what you need right now, what's going to set your world back to rights."

Cody showing up with a heartfelt apology and a bouquet of flowers? It was preposterous even to think it, but that didn't stop her from wanting it. "Um."

"What about a meditation retreat? Or a weekend at a spa?"

The thought of saunas and hot stone massages perked her up a bit. As did the thought of Sapphisticate footing the bill. "Are you offering to send me to a spa because you feel bad about this assignment breaking my heart?"

Donna angled her head slightly. "Honestly, I think you deserve it. Like any of our readers would if they were going through something similar."

Even as Donna's encouragement made her feel better, it made her feel shitty for an entirely different reason. "There's something else I need to tell you."

"Dear God, Archer. There's more?" Donna rolled her eyes, but her expression remained playful.

She contemplated saying nothing. It was possible Donna would never find out. It was also quite possible she would. "I interviewed and was offered a position at *Q*. I turned it down, but I know the queer publishing universe is small and I wanted you to hear it from me."

"Did you turn it down because of—what's her real name again?"

"Cody."

"Right. Did you turn it down because of Cody?"

Despite what she'd blurted out in the heat of the moment, it hadn't been about Cody. Or, maybe more accurately, it hadn't been about being offered her dream job. How could she explain to Donna what she'd so epically failed to explain to Cody? "It's more than that. When I was in DC, it was amazing. But it was intense and fast-paced, too. The senator's office, the city, everything. I realized moving to Philadelphia would be just like that. And even though it would be a once-in-a-lifetime opportunity, it filled me with dread. I know that sounds dramatic and maybe immature, but…"

When she trailed off again, convinced she'd made a thorough fool of herself, Donna merely offered her a sympathetic smile. "You like your life."

Was it as simple as that? "I feel like I'm supposed to be ambitious. Aren't smart, independent women supposed to be ambitious?"

Donna shrugged. "They can be. They can also value family and work-life balance and find a career that's satisfying and challenging without consuming everything they have to give."

She thought about Donna sending her to DC in the first place, passing up a high-profile interview so she could go to her kids' Christmas play. "Is that what you did?"

Donna smiled. "Most days it feels that way."

"And you're happy." It was a statement—an observation of the obvious—more than a question.

"I am. It helps that I have a supportive partner, parents who pushed me to find my own path more than they pushed me to be the best. Not everyone has those luxuries."

The irony of it all was that she did have those things, at least on the parent front. She'd been so busy deflecting her feelings for Cody, she'd backed herself into a corner of her own making. "I'm such an idiot."

"We all are, from time to time. I'd be sad to lose you, but if you decide you want that life, I have no doubt you'd crush it, and make it your own."

Once again, tears threatened. She bit the inside of her cheek to keep them at bay. "Thank you."

"Now go write your column. I'm guessing you haven't started and it goes live tomorrow." Donna winked and tipped her head toward the door, making it clear her words were equal part pep talk and dismissal.

Jess squared her shoulders and returned to her desk. She could do this. She was strong. She was resilient. And since she'd basically insisted to Donna she could, she had no choice.

Three hours later, her shoulders ached more than her heart, but she'd cranked out a column she could live with. Maybe, once the gloom faded, one she could even be proud of. She hadn't thrown Cody under the bus, but she hadn't taken all the blame, either. And as she read it through, she managed to laugh as well as cry. It was the end, really, that did her in.

I learned a lot of hard lessons this week. I'll be honest, dear readers, I wouldn't recommend it. But I know myself a little better, and I know that love isn't really love unless you're willing to be your whole, imperfect, messy self. I'll always regret blowing my shot with this one. I truly believe it could have been the real thing, you know?

The thing about relationships is that you never know. Sometimes you want to fall for someone and it just doesn't happen. Sometimes, you explicitly agree to the opposite and still manage to lose your heart along the way. I'm not sure cuffing is exempt from either end of the spectrum, so I guess the moral of the story is buyer beware.

I promise I won't pine forever, but this one's going to take a while to get over. I hope you'll stick with me, or at least give me another chance eventually. If you need a breather, trust me, I understand. I'm in need of one of those myself. Thanks for going on this adventure with me.

Xo
Jess

She read the whole thing through one last time before attaching it to an email to Cody. She resisted context or explanations or a request to talk. She'd said her piece. Cody would either accept that she'd contributed to this mess or she wouldn't. And if Cody wasn't willing to do that, well, maybe it was better to know sooner rather than later.

She gathered her things and headed home, exhausted but satisfied she'd done her best. At least as far as the column was concerned. But as she stalked around her empty apartment, the need to connect—to try—won out. She pulled out her phone and dashed off a text to Cody before she could talk herself out of it. *I sent you my final column for the cuffing series. I know you don't read them but wanted to give you the chance to see it before it went live.*

She changed her clothes and headed to barre. Her phone told her Cody had read the message, but there was no reply. No response to her email, either. Since everyone in class was a regular, she pushed them extra hard, forcing her body through the routine along with them. After, she went home and showered away the sweat and tried to stretch the soreness from her muscles. Still no word from Cody.

She sent her column to Cindy for edits and to Donna, swearing under her breath the whole time, only to be reminded of Cody's G-rated vocabulary and their running swear jar jokes. She contemplated a glass of wine or some of the chocolate Ben and Cody had stuffed in her stocking. In the end, she went to bed instead, pulling the blankets over her head and giving in to the tears she'd worked so hard to keep at bay.

Chapter Thirty-two

Cody rubbed her eyes and then focused again on the screen. Or tried to focus anyway. She'd lost track of the number of times she'd scanned the data set. Usually, it only took one quick glance and she had a good idea of what the results would be after the calculations were run, and yet this time, the numbers seemed to swirl on the screen, not lining up in any order or caring in the slightest about making sense. If only the numbers could analyze themselves for once.

She didn't need to be at work, but Ben had a playdate and she could only spend so many hours on the rowing machine. Unfortunately, the empty lab office, quiet enough to hear the buzz of the lab instruments on the other side of the wall, only provided a change of scenery. Her mood hadn't improved one bit. If anything, it was marginally worse. She missed her students and wished break was over already so she could get back to teaching—at least then she'd have something to think about besides Jess and everything that had been said.

When her phone rang, she risked hoping it was Jess, even knowing it wouldn't be. Jess had sent her a text the day before, along with an email Cody couldn't bring herself to read. Who wanted to read a recap of a breakup they hadn't wanted to happen in the first place?

She appreciated Jess giving her the chance to look it over, especially knowing her college president would likely read it, but she simply couldn't stomach it. And now there was no chance Jess would reach out again. Not unless Cody contacted her, and even then, she'd be unlikely to forgive New Year's Eve.

Even now, the ugliness of the fight made bile rise in her throat. She'd been so irrational, so worked up about Gillian's bombshell about her file and the cryptic text from Anastasia. The fact that the text was Anastasia's lead-in to essentially relinquishing her parental rights—so she and her new wife wouldn't end up on the hook for child support—was a huge relief, but it felt almost hollow knowing she couldn't share it with Jess. Or maybe she was simply too busy kicking herself over ruining things to enjoy it.

The phone rang for a third time before Cody found it in her messenger bag. "Hey, Amelia. What's up?"

"Oh, don't act like you don't know."

"Know what?" Clearly, Amelia was mad at her but why?

"I know you've done some stupid things, but I can't believe even you would have done something that stupid. So, tell me this is all to get readers riled up and you didn't really break up with her."

Cody pushed her chair back from the desk and exhaled. Was expecting Amelia to be understanding too much of a stretch? She wanted someone on her side even if she knew she didn't deserve it. "Did Finn tell you?"

"Finn didn't know until I told her. Apparently, Jess has been hiding out in her room or at the office. Finn guessed something was up but couldn't get anything out of her."

"But how'd you find out?"

Amelia gave an exaggerated sigh. "I read about it online this morning. Four days after the fact."

"You read Jess's column?"

"Yeah—don't act so surprised. Me and half the lesbian population have been hanging on every one of Jess's words for the past month."

"Half?"

"Only an estimate. I figure the other half are as dumb as you. You didn't actually end it, did you?"

Cody wanted to laugh at Amelia's teasing, but she didn't have it in her. "Yeah."

"Yeah, you broke up with her? Or were you agreeing to the dumb part?"

Cody sighed. "Both."

"You know what's annoying? You're not dumb at all. You're one of the smartest people I know." Amelia grumbled about smart dumb people for a minute. "What happened?"

"Jess didn't give all the gory details in her column?"

"Not enough for me to understand why the hell you would have done it. Which is why I didn't believe it. And why I'm calling."

It was some relief knowing Jess hadn't given an exact play-by-play of what had gone down, but then everyone reading would wonder what the hell was wrong with her. She was wondering, too. In the heat of the moment, she'd been certain breaking up was the right decision, the only decision. But within an hour of leaving the party, she'd wanted to take back nearly all the words she'd said.

"You know she's in love with you, right?"

"I don't know that, no." Cody thought back to the conversation Christmas morning. Neither of them had said love, though Cody had wanted to. Jess had hedged around the word, only saying she might more than like her. Not exactly words she could base a future on.

"I think you should hang up right now and go read the column."

"That's the last thing I want to do. Amelia, put yourself in my shoes. This crazy perfect relationship you're in just ended. Do you want to go back and read about how amazing it was and how it all imploded? No thanks."

"Do you love her?"

"Yeah." Tears welled. She looked at the ceiling, swallowed, and only when she was sure she could go on without emotion betraying her, said, "It doesn't matter how I feel. I should have been watching out for Ben. I knew this was going to be temporary and I shouldn't have let Jess and Ben get close. I messed up bigtime. It's just everything felt so right. So easy. I started thinking it wasn't going to be temporary, you know? Jess said that she didn't want to break up, but then she went on a job interview in Philadelphia and didn't even tell me. So, obviously she wasn't planning on the relationship lasting. And maybe she is staying here, for now, but what happens when another, better offer comes along? She says she wants to be a parent, but she doesn't know what it's really like. Not day to day. Not all the things you give up. Like job offers across the country and—"

"Cody, stop." Amelia's voice softened. "Jess isn't Anastasia. You're jumping to conclusions that aren't fair. And I get that you have to watch out for Ben. But you told me you thought Jess was good for Ben."

"Yeah…" She thought of Jess and Ben snuggled up together on the sofa the day after Christmas. Along with the LEGOs, Jess had given him a handful of books about space, and the two had pored over them for hours. She thought of how proud Ben was of the little heart Jess had drawn on his cast. And then she pictured Ben's confused expression that morning when she'd told him Jess wouldn't be coming over for a while. He'd asked where Jess was sleeping, seeming to have already decided they should all be living together after one week of it. Cody evaded the question and half a dozen more about Jess before Ben held up his arms for her to pick him up, clearly sensing that something big was wrong. She'd held him for a while, not saying anything more.

Was Jess good for him? Even if she might someday leave? And were she and Ben good for Jess or would they only hold her back from doing amazing things?

"If you really love her, go read her column. Start at the beginning and don't skip anything. Even if it hurts."

The line clicked and Cody glanced down at the phone, surprised Amelia had hung up. And yet not. That was how she proved a point.

Cody tossed the phone on her desk and stared down the computer for a long minute. Did she really want to read everything Jess had said about their relationship? She'd been tempted every night since New Year's but had resisted, knowing it would only make her more miserable to think of how good things had been. Then again, maybe she deserved feeling miserable.

With a heavy sigh, Cody minimized the data screen and pulled up a browser. In a few clicks, she had Jess's Cuffing Chronicles up on the screen. Instead of reading the last article, despite how desperately she wanted to, she started at the beginning.

An hour slipped away and Cody hadn't moved from her seat. She hadn't expected to laugh, but she did. She cried, too. And then laughed again.

When Jess recapped the trip to the Space Foundation, she hung on every word—more than a little surprised that Jess freely admitted she'd been turned on and wishing Cody would have surreptitiously felt her up while they were huddled under the picnic blanket at the park after. And when Jess recounted finding Cody on the floor of the rental cabin in Breckenridge, half under the bed trying to grab Ben's sock, she laughed until she got to the part where Jess admitted that not only did she want to jump Cody, she also was fighting back admitting she was falling for her. It was too soon, she said. And they were only cuffing.

A few posts later, Jess admitted she'd fallen in love anyway. Not only with Cody but with Ben, too. She'd placed the star on the tree they'd picked out together, looked at Cody and Ben, and known without a doubt.

Finally, she got to the last post. New Year's Eve. When she read the last line, the little x and o made her heart ache all the more. The xo wasn't for her. And yet the good-bye was. She stood and paced around the office, Jess's words—buyer beware—echoing in her mind. Was it true and Jess was in love? Or was it all for the column?

In some ways, she was no better off having read everything. Why would Jess tell the whole world what she wouldn't tell her directly? Maybe Jess thought she already knew? In fact, she had known. Or at least she'd been ninety percent sure of how Jess felt, but that hadn't stopped all the doubts.

When the office felt too small, she grabbed her jacket and headed outside. She didn't have a destination in mind, only needed a bigger space to think. It wasn't until she nearly collided with Gillian that she realized she wasn't even looking where she was going.

She slammed to a stop, catching herself only inches before taking Gillian out. "Oh, gosh, sorry."

"No worries. I'm used to professors with their heads in the clouds. Work hazard." Gillian held up her coffee mug. "Good thing these come with lids."

Gillian had stepped out of the café right as Cody was zooming past. Most of the campus was shut down for break, but the café kept limited hours primarily to serve the students that had nowhere else to eat with the cafeterias closed—and the staff that couldn't work without caffeine.

"Were you going for a coffee break too?" Gillian asked.

"No. I was thinking. And walking. And apparently not looking where I was going."

Gillian's smile seemed sympathetic. "You've got a lot on your mind. With Jess and everything else."

She didn't need to ask if Gillian had read Jess's last column. Her shoulders dropped. "Yeah."

"Maybe you need a coffee break?" Gillian nodded to the café. "I don't normally get coffee here, but it turns out it's quite good. My staff is off and I couldn't bring myself to make a whole pot for just me."

Cody eyed the café and then shook her head. "I don't think I can sit still right now."

"Then we'll walk and talk."

Gillian didn't give Cody a chance to get out of a conversation. She angled her head toward the arboretum path. "You were going this way, right?"

"I didn't have a plan really."

"That was your first mistake." Gillian started walking, not waiting to see if Cody would follow.

She had to agree. In so many ways, she should have at least had a plan.

They passed the empty student quad and turned right. Cody recalled the mad dash she'd made with Jess down the same path and felt a rush of nostalgia. So many things had felt so right with Jess. Then she'd ruined everything.

"When I started dating Shannon, I knew it'd be over by summer. We met when we were both on vacation in Costa Rica. I figured no way would the relationship survive after we got back to the real world. And that was fine. She was a fun distraction." Gillian stopped walking just long enough to point at Cody and add, "Don't you dare tell anyone I said that. Ever."

"Your secret's safe. What happened at the end of summer?"

"I broke up with her."

Gillian's simple declaration took Cody by surprise. "But—"

"But she's amazing? But she's the light of my life? But she changed me, made me a better person?" Gillian nodded. "All those things are true. And I thought she wouldn't want to be tied to my career. I didn't want to ask her to change her life to be with me. I didn't want her to give up anything. She was used to traveling all the time, going out dancing at clubs. All these things I loved about her would have to end if we tried to make a life together. I didn't want that."

This time Cody stopped walking. "What happened after you broke up?"

"I realized I'd made a huge mistake. I hadn't let her decide. I was scared she'd hate this life." Gillian waved her arm as if to include the whole campus. "Ending things before we were unhappy seemed like a better idea than having to go through being miserable only to break up later."

Cody nodded. "I think I would have made the same call. But you two are perfect together. Are you still worried about her being happy?"

"I am. She tells me she loves our life and I'm silly to worry. She says I make her happy and I'd make her happy anywhere." Gillian lifted a shoulder. "Opening up to Shannon and asking her for a second chance was the smartest thing I've ever done. Also the hardest."

They started walking again and soon reached the grove of bare trees. Gillian stopped when the main path split away from the arboretum path. "You know Jess loves you. Still."

"She never said she loved me. Told the rest of the world, but—"

"She was waiting for you. Waiting for you to be ready to let someone new into your life. She said it felt like you were holding back. Honestly, I don't blame you. It's hard to let someone close if you think they'll eventually be unhappy with you. Or with the life you have to share." Gillian let out a sigh. "I suppose I should get back to the office."

"Yeah." She should too even though any attempt at work would be fruitless now.

"By the way, the board of trustees doesn't meet until the first week of February, but that's only a rubber stamp. The committee and I have reviewed everything in your file and are recommending you for tenure. I can't think of a single reason they won't vote in your favor. Congratulations, Cody."

She thanked Gillian but was too taken aback to say more. All the stress and it came down to that. She was going to keep her job. She could keep teaching and continue her research. It was everything she'd wanted.

So why didn't she feel happy? She answered the question with one word: Jess.

Gillian touched her shoulder. "I know you've got a lot going through your mind right now, but I'm going to give you one more piece of advice. Groveling never hurts."

Cody managed a half-smile. "With flowers?"

"You're catching on. And go with a plan."

Gillian went on her way and Cody's weak hope wavered. It didn't seem likely that Jess would jump at the chance to take her back after she'd done such a stellar job of pushing her away. And Gillian was right—Jess had been waiting for her to say "I love you" first because she'd been holding back all along. She'd used the excuse of protecting Ben, but there was more to it. She was scared of risking her own heart all over again.

So much for being brave.

Even when Jess had said she'd decided to stay instead of taking her dream job, Cody hadn't believed her. She hadn't given Jess a real chance. She'd been so ready for the relationship to blow up that she'd lit the fuse herself.

Could she ask for a second chance? Their cuffing experiment was over, but maybe it wasn't too late to try for a real relationship. Maybe it wasn't too late to be brave, either. If she knew nothing else in that moment, she knew she had to see Jess. And if Gillian was right and groveling and flowers would do any good, she was ready to buy out the whole florist.

Chapter Thirty-three

I'm sorry about Carrie."

Jess whipped her head around, recognizing Silpa's voice but struggling to reconcile the comment with something Silpa would actually say. "I'm sorry. What?"

Silpa offered a soft smile that Jess had never seen before. "I said I'm sorry about Carrie. That things didn't end well."

"Thanks." She tried for a smile and only managed a shrug. She started to turn back to her desk but stopped. "You read my column?"

Silpa chuckled and shook her head. "I'm pretty sure every lesbian in the US with internet access reads your column."

Sympathy and now compliments. From Silpa. Either she was more pathetic than she'd realized and Silpa had a pity button, or hell was freezing over. "Pretty sure it's not that popular, but thanks for that, too."

Silpa shrugged this time, only it was that mix of playful and incredulous that came with admitting something you don't want to. "Everyone I know does."

She knew she shouldn't but couldn't help herself. "Not to be weird, but I didn't even know you were gay."

"I don't advertise it. I'm not in the closet or anything, I just keep my personal life separate from work."

In pretty much any other circumstance, she'd take that as a dig— that she wasn't as professional but also that her work wasn't, either. But Silpa's expression remained kind and, just maybe, laced with a hint of admiration. "Well, I'm sorry I made assumptions. I—"

Silpa's eyes went wide. "Jess."

She stopped talking, appreciating the interruption before she managed to put her foot in her mouth. But instead of saying anything else, Silpa angled her head at something behind Jess. She turned, expecting Donna or maybe Frida, giving her a look of comic disbelief for fraternizing with the enemy. But what she saw was a bouquet of flowers. A giant bouquet. And behind it, an anxious looking Cody.

Jess's breath caught and her stomach lurched, though it was hard to tell if it was nerves or excitement or dread. "Cody?"

"Damn. I'd hoped it was Carrie." Silpa shook her head. Then she gasped. "Cody is Carrie."

She glanced at Silpa long enough to offer a nod and a smile of acknowledgement. Then she turned her attention fully to Cody. Silpa faded away, as did her desk and the rest of the bustling office floor. All she saw was Cody.

"Hi." Cody gave her a tentative smile.

"Hi." She willed herself not to pass out. Or throw up. "What are you doing here?"

"Apologizing. Groveling if you'll let me."

Had she scripted this in her mind, she wouldn't have been able to come up with a better line. "You came to my work."

Cody winced. "Yeah. I was afraid you might not answer the door if I showed up at your apartment. Although now that I say that, I don't want you to think that you have to see me now. You can tell me to leave. Maybe apologizing in public is a bad idea because it puts you in the position—"

"Stop. You're fine." As angry as she was, she couldn't imagine shutting Cody out. "Also, I would have answered the door."

A trace of relief flashed in Cody's eyes. She cleared her throat. "The other reason I'm here now is that when I realize I've made a huge mistake, I want to try to fix it sooner rather than later."

Was Cody really there to make things right? Her heart leapt at the possibility even as her brain rattled off a dozen worries. Cody might just be there to apologize for picking a fight on New Year's. She might still want to break up. Or maybe she wanted to get back together but wouldn't be able to explain why she'd reacted so badly, leaving Jess to decide if she could risk her heart on someone who might never entirely trust her. Her mind swirled with the possibilities and the tangle of emotions that came with them.

"Can we talk? I mean, I understand if this is a bad time. But soon? I'll pretty much show up whenever and wherever you say."

She was scheduled to meet with Donna in an hour to discuss strategies for her column for the next few months. But if there was even half a chance she and Cody were going to make up, she had no intention of letting Cody out of her sights. She lifted a finger. "Now is good. Can you give me one minute?"

Cody nodded, still clutching the vase of pink and white roses, orchids, and lilies. "Of course."

She hurried over to Donna's office and, miracle of all miracles, found her not on the phone. She knocked lightly on the doorframe and Donna looked up from her computer. "Please don't tell me it's four already."

"No. I was coming to see if we could move—"

Donna stood abruptly, sending her chair rolling and breaking Jess's train of thought. "Who's getting flowers?"

She'd worked with Donna long enough that the inherent nosiness didn't surprise or bother her. "I am, actually."

Donna angled her body back and forth, not even pretending to be subtle in her efforts to get a better look. "Is that—"

"It is."

"Oh, this is going to be good." The relish in Donna's voice clearly had less to do with Jess's happiness and more to do with new installments of the Cuffing Chronicles.

"Ahem." She wasn't really angry, but given what she'd put herself through for Donna's grand idea, it only felt fair.

"Sorry, sorry. I mean, this looks promising. Are you going to talk? Take her back?" Donna's features softened enough to convince Jess of her sincerity.

"Yes, and I'm not sure. I'm not sure that's even what she wants."

"Of course that's what she wants. You don't show up with flowers to say, 'I'm sorry things went so badly and I hope you don't think I'm an ass for all eternity and have a nice life.'"

The specificity of the description made her laugh. It also gave her hope. "Well, I'm still not sure, then."

"Don't be afraid to make her work for it."

She pulled her eyes from Cody and fixed them on Donna. "Are you saying that as my friend or as my boss who's already imagining the column that's going to come out of this?"

"I'm saying that as a woman who has done her share of stupid things, and whose wife is forgiving but makes her a better person by not letting her off the hook too easily."

It would be hard to put into words all the ways this single assignment had changed her life. The obvious ones, of course: falling in love, confronting her mixed feelings on her career and ambition, realizing all the mistakes she invariably made in relationships. The deeper connection with Donna, well, that seemed as far out of left field as becoming friends with Silpa. But here they were. "Thank you for saying that."

"Whatever happens, trust your heart and you'll do fine."

A sniff of contempt escaped before she could help it.

"I'm serious, Jess. The fact that you've fallen for people who didn't deserve you doesn't mean your heart is faulty. It means you've had bad luck. And there are a lot of jerks out there."

She knew it was more than that, that she'd ignored warning signs in the past because she wanted things to work out. But maybe Donna had a point. Enough at least that she wanted to own her mistakes and see what Cody had to say for herself. "So, can we reschedule our meeting?"

Donna glanced at Cody again. "I think that's for the best."

"Thanks." Without waiting for Donna to say anything more, she went back to where she'd left Cody. "Okay. Let's get out of here."

"Yeah?" Cody seemed surprised by her answer.

"Well, we're not going to hash it out in the middle of my office, that's for sure."

"Where do you want to go?"

It was cold out but not frigid. Outdoors seemed preferable to a café or bar, or to either of their places. "There's a park across the street. Is that okay?"

"Absolutely." Cody looked at the flowers. "I wasn't sure if you'd want these."

"They're beautiful." And officially the nicest flowers anyone had gotten her. Ever.

"I had the florist put them in a vase so you wouldn't have to find something."

It was thoughtful, thoughtful in ways that had her softening even before they had a chance to talk. "Thank you. I'll leave them here so they aren't out in the cold."

Cody handed her the vase and she set them on her desk. She slipped on her coat and grabbed her purse. A quick look around told her Silpa was watching and trying to look like she wasn't. Donna, too. Along with half the staff of *Mile High Business Journal*. It made her wonder just how many of them were following her column and knew exactly what was happening. She shook off the weirdness of that and led Cody to the elevator. A few minutes later, they sat together on a bench as people strolled and pigeons pecked around them.

"I'm sorry." Cody turned to face her fully, eyes intense. "I'm sorry I picked a fight and I'm sorry I ruined New Year's and most of all I'm sorry I suggested we break up."

It was a start. More of a start than she'd expected. "Okay. Thank you for that. I think I need to understand why."

Cody huffed out a breath. "I overreacted. To be fair, Gillian told me my tenure file had been delayed and Anastasia texted me about getting married again and wanting to 'discuss Ben,' so I was kind of on edge to begin with."

"Anastasia wants to get married?" Jess looked at her with equal parts alarm and exasperation. "To you?"

"To her new girlfriend."

"Oh." Jess hesitated. "Why didn't you tell me either of those things at the time?"

"Because I was too busy picking a fight. They're both resolved now. I can give you the specifics later."

Jess sniffed. "Yeah, you will."

"Anyway. I spent so much time waiting for the other shoe to drop that I almost needed it to happen."

"I get that. The whole premise of our relationship implied it was going to happen. I also get that protecting Ben triggers all your fight-or-flight instincts." She looked down at her hands and sighed.

"There's a but, isn't there? I can tell. Is it knowing you'll never be my only top priority?"

If Cody didn't look like she might be on the edge of tears, Jess might have given in to the urge to punch her. In the arm, at least. "No. And honestly, fuck you for thinking that. It's that you don't trust how much I love him, how much I want to be in his life. You overheard one little comment about me wanting time alone with you and freaked. I can't do this if you're going to doubt me at every turn."

Cody let out a sigh. "I'm sorry. You've never given me reason to doubt how you feel about Ben. What I said wasn't fair and, honestly, you deserve better."

"Thank you."

"In my defense, Anastasia, who is literally his birth mother, decided parenting was a drag and bailed on us."

Even if she bristled at the comparison, she could appreciate the trauma of that. "I know. So I'll say 'and' instead of 'but' here. I'm not Anastasia."

"You're nothing like her. Nothing."

"If we're going to have a chance, you have to remember that."

Cody nodded. "I will."

"I'm not saying you can't ever worry, but you have to tell me. We have to talk about it."

"Yeah."

"Good. I'm glad we got that settled."

Cody nodded again but dropped her head and stared at her lap. There was definitely something she wasn't saying.

"Okay. We seem to be moving in the right direction, but you still look like I just kicked your puppy."

Cody looked up, misery in her eyes. "You interviewed for your dream job and you didn't tell me. Worse, you got it and didn't take it. You can't give that up for me."

Right. That. "It wasn't my dream job."

Cody closed one eye and tipped her head. "You literally said it was."

Thanks to her chat with Donna, she had words to explain all the ways it wasn't. She told the story, starting with the inadvertent pressure from her mom to apply. She went through her conversation with Frida, convincing her that applying would help her know what she wanted, and the one with Donna where she not only made peace with her decision but embraced it. "I like my life here. I like it a hell of a lot better with you and Ben, but I wouldn't have accepted the job either way."

"I believe you."

Given how this whole mess started, those three words packed quite a punch. Almost as much as "I love you" would have. "Good. I'm sorry I didn't tell you. I can't ask you to trust me if I don't share things that have the potential to affect us."

"Or you. I want to know what affects you, too. And I want to be good for you—you're good for me and Ben. I want to be the same for you. If I'm not, I want you to be able to tell me."

It was her turn to nod. "You're very good for me. And so is Ben."

"I don't want to cuff with you anymore. I want more than that. I want a real relationship, one that lasts. I love you, Jess, and I want it all."

She was wrong. Cody saying "I believe you" had been great, but it had nothing on "I love you." She reached out and caressed Cody's hand. The light touch sent a thrill through her and Cody's tentative smile made her ache all the more to wrap her arms around her. "I love you, too."

Cody's features relaxed fully. "I read your columns. I know. I feel foolish for avoiding them this whole time."

She blew out a breath. "I get how weird it was that I was writing about our relationship."

"And telling your readers things you didn't tell me." Cody didn't seem angry about that, but maybe a little disappointed.

"That, too. I'm sorry about that."

"Still. I get why you needed me to say it first." Cody held out her hand, palm up. As soon as Jess clasped it, she smiled. "I love you, Jess. I'm in love with you. All the way in love."

Had she not already been convinced, the last line, one she'd used in her column, sealed the deal. "Good because I'm really in love with you, too."

"I'm glad that's settled."

And just like that, joy replaced the sadness and the worry. "Are you going to kiss me now or what?"

Cody grinned. "The first."

Without another word, she did. And oh, what a kiss it was. It had all the fire, all the spark, of their first kiss, but with the depth that only comes with knowing, with feeling. With being in love.

"So, now what?" It seemed fair to ask, though her preference was to go home with Cody and not leave for the foreseeable future.

"Well, as much as I'd like to get you to myself for a few hours, I need to pick up Ben from a playdate." Cody paused, then gave an almost imperceptible shake of her head. "I'm sure he'd love to see you."

She didn't want it to, but suspicion won out. "Why did you shake your head?"

Cody cringed. "Because I hesitated and then I kicked myself for still hesitating."

"Pretty quick self-correction. I'll let it slide." Because she knew better than anyone that some habits were hard to break, even with good intentions.

"I love you, you know. Like, I know I said it a minute ago, but I really, really love you."

Jess's heart swelled at the words. It probably would for a while. "Good. Because I love you, too, and I'm not going to get tired of hearing it. How about I pick up a pizza and meet you at the house?"

Cody shook her head in earnest this time. "I don't know what I—what we—did to deserve you."

"That's easy. You love me, just as I am." It had seemed so hard, and yet when push came to shove, it was that simple.

"I do." Cody stood and pulled her to her feet.

Cody's arms came around her and she let herself sink into the embrace. Until Cody's mouth found hers and she wanted a hell of a lot more than Cody's arms. She stepped back and the look on Cody's face told her Cody's thoughts were in exactly the same place. "We'll get to that. In the meantime, the usual?"

Cody nodded. "The usual."

❖

Jess balanced the pizza box in one hand and used the other to ring the bell. Even through the door, she could make out the sound of running feet. Like the first time she'd visited. And exactly like the first time, the door swung open, but no one stood in front of her. At least no one at eye level.

"Jess!"

She'd thought Ben was enthusiastic that first time, but it had nothing on the look in his eyes now. Excitement, yes, but also love. Realizing that he loved her as much as she loved him had her own eyes filling and threatening to spill over. She bent down and pulled him into a hug with her free arm. "Hey, Ben."

"I missed you so much."

Cody appeared and relieved her of the pizza box. She wrapped her other arm around Ben and scooped him up. "I missed you, too."

She stepped the rest of the way inside and closed the door, putting Ben down long enough to take off her coat and boots. It was silly, but it felt almost as familiar as doing it at home.

"Are you gonna sleep over? I like waking up and you being here."

The comment, without design or pretense, tipped the balance of her self-control, and a few of the tears she'd held back rolled down her cheeks. She sniffed and tried to blink them away, feeling ridiculous for being so emotional.

"Are you okay?" Ben looked at her, eyes wide with concern.

She laughed. "I am. Sorry. I've had a lot of big feelings today and I think some of them are still swooshing around in there."

He nodded, as though that made perfect sense and he could empathize. "I had big feelings when Mom said we might not see you for a while."

She braved a look at Cody, who offered an apologetic wince, then returned her focus to Ben. "I was worried that might be the case, too. I'm glad it's not."

"Me, too." Ben's declaration was paired with a dramatic roll of his whole head.

"Who's hungry?" Cody asked. "I know I am."

"I am! I am!" Ben tore off in the direction of the kitchen.

Cody looked at her with uncertainty. "You okay?"

She thought about how her day had started, how the last few days had gone. Then she thought about the last two months, months she spent falling in love and figuring herself out and starting to build a family with Cody and Ben. All courtesy of Donna's wacky idea for the Cuffing Chronicles and her impulsive decision to say yes. "Depends. Do I get to sleep over?"

"If I had it my way, you'd spend all your nights here." Cody smiled. "It's probably too early to ask if you want to move in, isn't it?"

"Probably. But that doesn't mean I don't want you to ask." She wiped away the remnants of her tears and smiled in return. Then she kissed Cody long and slow. Long enough for Ben to run back to the entryway and insist they stop kissing and hurry up already before the pizza got cold.

Cody pulled away long enough to tell Ben to be patient, then turned back to Jess. "You sure you're okay?"

She looked at Ben before locking eyes with Cody. "Never better."

Epilogue

The following November

"Maybe don't run unless you want to eat that slice of pie off the ground," Jess said, deftly catching the edge of Ben's plate before the pie slid off.

"You know that wouldn't be a problem for him, right?" The cousins had been tearing around the cabin in a wild game of tag for the past hour and Cody knew Ben was too hungry to care about dirt. Not that he ever really did.

"She's right." Ben nodded earnestly. "Not a problem."

At Jess's raised eyebrow, Cody cleared her throat. "We all know it's not a problem, Ben, but how about you take a little break from the game and stand still while you eat."

"Both of you would eat pie anywhere it landed." Jess included Cody in her playful finger wag.

Cody let out a mock gasp before cracking a smile. "You're right. But only because you make the best pie ever."

"No comment about licking the rug?" Lacey murmured.

"Ahem." Jess gave her sister a stern look. "We're keeping this Thanksgiving PG-rated, remember?"

"Where's the fun in that?"

Cody laughed at Jess's exasperated groan, but Ben ignored all three of them, digging into his pie. As he chewed, Joshua crept up behind him. Right as Ben balanced a big bite on his fork, Joshua tapped his shoulder.

"You're it."

"Aw, man! Can you hold this, Mama?" Ben handed Jess his plate and didn't wait for an answer before zipping off after Joshua. He pushed through the kitchen door and disappeared from view.

Jess stood stock-still, plate of half-eaten pie in her hand. She looked at Cody. "Did he just call me Mama?"

It was good to know she hadn't imagined it. "Yeah."

Jess nodded slowly.

"Are you okay with that?" She'd planned to bring it up before the wedding, but she imagined having the conversation with Jess before broaching it with Ben. Jess had become a mother to Ben in every way that counted, ways Anastasia never had. Still. It should be her choice whether Ben called her that.

Jess continued to nod.

Jess seemed pleased, but the wordless response made her worry. "You sure?"

Jess's whole face broke into a smile. She sniffed. "Mm-hmm."

And that, it seemed, was that. A squeal from the kitchen broke the spell and confirmed Ben had tagged someone.

"I think they could keep this up all day." Jess set Ben's plate on the coffee table and settled on the sofa. Cody wrapped an arm around her and pulled her close.

"Let's hope they do," Lacey said. "They've got some sugar to run off."

The kitchen door swung again, and Ben appeared perched on Bruce's shoulders. Bruce grinned down at Ava, who was trying to leap up to tag Ben's dangling feet.

"You can't tag him now. I caught him." Bruce glanced at Ben. "How many slices of pie did you eat? You're getting heavy up there."

"Only one bite of apple pie."

"Only one bite?" Bruce shook his head. "Your grandpa better start lifting weights. You know that's a grandson's job right? You tell me to lift more weights so I can carry you around."

"Okay, Grandpa," Ben said, clearly taking the words to heart. "But you're pretty strong already."

Bruce chuckled. "I knew you were a keeper."

Joshua appeared in the hallway, hollering for his sister to try to catch him and then darting upstairs. Ben watched until his two cousins dashed out of view.

"You want me to put you down so you can follow them?" Bruce asked.

Ben shook his head. "I want you to take me over to my pie, please."

"Ben, you're a man after my own belly."

Bruce carefully deposited Ben on the sofa next to Cody and Jess. He glanced at the small piece—plenty for a six-year-old. "When you finish that one, come find me and we'll get you a real slice of pie."

"I knew you were a keeper, Grandpa," Ben said.

Everyone laughed at Ben's use of the phrase, but Bruce laughed the loudest. Much too fast, Ben polished off the pie and held out his hand to Bruce. "Do you have room for more pie, too?"

"Always."

They headed to the kitchen and Cody could hear Elaine agreeing to cut them both a slice of pumpkin pie, extra whipped cream. "Your dad and Ben are quite a pair."

"They are." Jess let out a happy sigh. "I love it."

"You and Ben are quite a pair, too."

Jess's expression turned serious. "I should ask if you're okay with Ben calling me Mama. It's a big deal for you, not just me."

She closed her eyes for a moment and let the reality of the last year sink in. So much better than she could have even imagined—for herself, but for Ben as well. "I was hoping we'd get there. I wasn't expecting him to do it on his own, though."

Jess beamed. "I love that he did."

She couldn't disagree.

Lacey stretched her feet up on the ottoman, as unfazed as the rest of Jess's family by the development. "So. You two going to let me help with the wedding plans?"

Cody tipped her head, deferring to Jess. Part of her still couldn't believe that Jess said yes—with no hesitation at all. Cody had sweated on when and how to ask. Was a proposal at a planetarium too nerdy? Would Jess mind if Ben was there? Then she'd worried about her ring choice. Would Jess like something simple and traditional or something flashy and fun?

In the end, she'd gone for fun. She'd waited until right before the show ended and then leaned over to whisper the question, her heart pounding in her chest so loud she could barely hear her own words. The lights snapped on a second later, and Jess's yes was loud enough to get everyone's attention. She'd wrapped her arms around Cody while Ben clapped his approval, which got the rest of the audience clapping as well.

They'd set the date for New Year's Eve, deciding it was the ultimate redo of the first one they'd spent together.

"I don't think we need to do too much more planning," Jess said. "But we could use some help in the kid department. Could you be in charge of the flower girls and ring bearers?"

"My pleasure." Lacey smiled. "I can't wait to see them all dressed up. I'm going to take way too many pictures."

"We will have a photographer, you know."

And a caterer, a DJ, and eighty guests. It was going to be a real wedding—and Cody couldn't wait. She reached for Jess's hand. "I'm glad I agreed to cuff with you. But I'm even happier you wanted to marry me."

Jess closed the distance between them. "Same."

About the Authors

Jaime Clevenger lives in Colorado with her wife, Corina; two daughters; two very hairy cats; and one golden retriever. When not working as a veterinarian or writing romance, Jaime enjoys family adventures, fostering furry animals, swimming, and practicing karate. Jaime has published many books with Bella Books and has won a Golden Crown Literary Award for the romance *Three Reasons to Say Yes*. Listening to rain and eating chocolate are two not-so-secret pleasures, but Jaime also loves walks on the beach and reading.

Aurora Rey is a college dean by day and award-winning lesbian romance author the rest of the time, except when she's cooking, baking, riding the tractor, or pining for goats. She grew up in a small town in south Louisiana, daydreaming about New England. She keeps a special place in her heart for the South, especially the food and the ways women are raised to be strong, even if they're taught not to show it. After a brief dalliance with biochemistry, she completed both a BA and an MA in English.

She is the author of the Cape End Romance series and several standalone contemporary lesbian romance novels and novellas. She has been a finalist for the Lambda Literary, RITA®, and Golden Crown Literary Society awards but loves reader feedback the most. She lives in Ithaca, New York, with her dog and whatever wildlife has taken up residence in the pond.

Books Available from Bold Strokes Books

A Convenient Arrangement by Aurora Rey and Jaime Clevenger. Cuffing season has come for lesbians, and for Jess Archer and Cody Dawson, their convenient arrangement becomes anything but. (978-1-63555-818-0)

An Alaskan Wedding by Nance Sparks. The last thing either Andrea or Riley expects is to bump into the one who broke her heart fifteen years ago, but when they meet at the welcome party, their feelings come rushing back. (978-1-63679-053-4)

Beulah Lodge by Cathy Dunnell. It's 1874, and newly engaged Ruth Mallowes is set on marriage and life as a missionary...until she falls in love with the housemaid at Beulah Lodge. (978-1-63679-007-7)

Gia's Gems by Toni Logan. When Lindsey Speyer discovers that popular travel columnist Gia Williams is a complete fake and threatens to expose her, blackmail has never been so sexy. (978-1-63555-917-0)

Holiday Wishes & Mistletoe Kisses by M. Ullrich. Four holidays, four couples, four chances to make their wishes come true. (978-1-63555-760-2)

Love By Proxy by Dena Blake. Tess has a secret crush on her best friend, Sophie, so the last thing she wants is to help Sophie fall in love with someone else, but how can she stand in the way of her happiness? (978-1-63555-973-6)

Loyalty, Love, & Vermouth by Eric Peterson. A comic valentine to a gay man's family of choice, including the ones with cold noses and four paws. (978-1-63555-997-2)

Marry Me by Melissa Brayden. Allison Hale attempts to plan the wedding of the century to a man who could save her family's business, if only she wasn't falling for her wedding planner, Megan Kinkaid. (978-1-63555-932-3)

Pathway to Love by Radclyffe. Courtney Valentine is looking for a woman exactly like Ben—smart, sexy, and not in the market for anything serious. All she has to do is convince Ben that sex-without-strings is the perfect pathway to pleasure. (978-1-63679-110-4)

Sweet Surprise by Jenny Frame. Flora and Mac never thought they'd ever see each other again, but when Mac opens up her barber shop right next to Flora's sweet shop, their connection comes roaring back. (978-1-63679-001-5)

The Edge of Yesterday by CJ Birch. Easton Gray is sent from the future to save humanity from technological disaster. When she's forced to target the woman she's falling in love with, can Easton do what's needed to save humanity? (978-1-63679-025-1)

The Scout and the Scoundrel by Barbara Ann Wright. With unexpected danger surrounding them, Zara and Roni are stuck between duty and survival, with little room for exploring their feelings, especially love. (978-1-63555-978-1)

Bury Me in Shadows by Greg Herren. College student Jake Chapman is forced to spend the summer at his dying grandmother's home and soon finds danger from long-buried family secrets. (978-1-63555-993-4)

Can't Leave Love by Kimberly Cooper Griffin. Sophia and Pru have no intention of falling in love, but sometimes love happens when and where you least expect it. (978-1-636790041-1)

Free Fall at Angel Creek by Julie Tizard. Detective Dee Rawlings and aircraft accident investigator Dr. River Dawson use conflicting methods to find answers when a plane goes missing, while overcoming surprising threats, and discovering an unlikely chance at love. (978-1-63555-884-5)

Love's Compromise by Cass Sellars. For Piper Holthaus and Brook Myers, will professional dreams and past baggage stop two hearts from realizing they are meant for each other? (978-1-63555-942-2)

Not All a Dream by Sophia Kell Hagin. Hester has lost the woman she loved and the world has descended into relentless dark and cold. But giving up will have to wait when she stumbles upon people who help her survive. (978-1-63679-067-1)

Protecting the Lady by Amanda Radley. If Eve Webb had known she'd be protecting royalty, she'd never have taken the job as bodyguard, but as the threat to Lady Katherine's life draws closer, she'll do whatever it takes to save her, and may just lose her heart in the process. (978-1-63679-003-9)

The Secrets of Willowra by Kadyan. A family saga of three women, their homestead called Willowra in the Australian outback, and the secrets that link them all. (978-1-63679-064-0)

Trial by Fire by Carsen Taite. When prosecutor Lennox Roy and public defender Wren Bishop become fierce adversaries in a headline-grabbing arson case, their attraction ignites a passion that leads them both to question their assumptions about the law, the truth, and each other. (978-1-63555-860-9)

Turbulent Waves by Ali Vali. Kai Merlin and Vivien Palmer plan their future together as hostile forces make their own plans to destroy what they have, as well as all those they love. (978-1-63679-011-4)

Unbreakable by Cari Hunter. When Dr. Grace Kendal is forced at gunpoint to help an injured woman, she is dragged into a nightmare where nothing is quite as it seems, and their lives aren't the only ones on the line. (978-1-63555-961-3)

Veterinary Surgeon by Nancy Wheelton. When dangerous drugs are stolen from the veterinary clinic, Mitch investigates and Kay becomes a suspect. As pride and professions clash, love seems impossible. (978-1-63679-043-5)

A Different Man by Andrew L. Huerta. This diverse collection of stories chronicling the challenges of gay life at various ages shines a light on the progress made and the progress still to come. (978-1-63555-977-4)

All That Remains by Sheri Lewis Wohl. Johnnie and Shantel might have to risk their lives—and their love—to stop a werewolf intent on killing. (978-1-63555-949-1)

Beginner's Bet by Fiona Riley. Phenom luxury Realtor Ellison Gamble has everything, except a family to share it with, so when a mix-up brings youthful Katie Crawford into her life, she bets the house on love. (978-1-63555-733-6)

Dangerous Without You by Lexus Grey. Throughout their senior year in high school, Aspen, Remington, Denna, and Raleigh face challenges in life and romance that they never expect. (978-1-63555-947-7)

Desiring More by Raven Sky. In this collection of steamy stories, a rich variety of lovers find themselves desiring more, more from a lover, more from themselves, and more from life. (978-1-63679-037-4)

Jordan's Kiss by Nanisi Barrett D'Arnuck. After losing everything in a fire, Jordan Phelps joins a small lounge band and meets pianist Morgan Sparks, who lights another blaze, this time in Jordan's heart. (978-1-63555-980-4)

Late City Summer by Jeanette Bears. Forced together for her wedding, Emily Stanton and Kate Alessi navigate their lingering passion for one another against the backdrop of New York City and World War II, and a summer romance they left behind. (978-1-63555-968-2)

Love and Lotus Blossoms by Anne Shade. On her path to self-acceptance and true passion, Janesse will risk everything—and possibly everyone—she loves. (978-1-63555-985-9)

Love in the Limelight by Ashley Moore. Marion Hargreaves, the finest actress of her generation, and Jessica Carmichael, the world's biggest pop star, rediscover each other twenty years after an ill-fated affair. (978-1-63679-051-0)

Suspecting Her by Mary P. Burns. Complications ensue when Erin O'Connor falls for top real estate saleswoman Catherine Williams while investigating racism in the real estate industry; the fallout could end their chance at happiness. (978-1-63555-960-6)

Two Winters by Lauren Emily Whalen. A modern YA retelling of Shakespeare's *The Winter's Tale* about birth, death, Catholic school, improv comedy, and the healing nature of time. (978-1-63679-019-0)

Busy Ain't the Half of It by Frederick Smith and Chaz Lamar Cruz. Elijah and Justin seek happily-ever-afters in LA, but are they too busy to notice happiness when it's there? (978-1-63555-944-6)

Calumet by Ali Vali. Jaxon Lavigne and Iris Long had a forbidden small-town romance that didn't last, and the consequences of that love will be uncovered fifteen years later at their high school reunion. (978-1-63555-900-2)

Her Countess to Cherish by Jane Walsh. London Society's material girl realizes there is more to life than diamonds when she falls in love with a non-binary bluestocking. (978-1-63555-902-6)

Hot Days, Heated Nights by Renee Roman. When Cole and Lee meet, instant attraction quickly flares into uncontrollable passion, but their connection might be short lived as Lee's identity is tied to her life in the city. (978-1-63555-888-3)

Never Be the Same by MA Binfield. Casey meets Olivia and sparks fly in this opposites attract romance that proves love can be found in the unlikeliest places. (978-1-63555-938-5)

Quiet Village by Eden Darry. Something not quite human is stalking Collie and her niece, and she'll be forced to work with undercover reporter Emily Lassiter if they want to get out of Hyam alive. (978-1-63555-898-2)

Shaken or Stirred by Georgia Beers. Bar owner Julia Martini and home health aide Savannah McNally attempt to weather the storms brought on by a mysterious blogger trashing the bar, family feuds they knew nothing about, and way too much advice from way too many relatives. (978-1-63555-928-6)

The Fiend in the Fog by Jess Faraday. Can four people on different trajectories work together to save the vulnerable residents of East London from the terrifying fiend in the fog before it's too late? (978-1-63555-514-1)

The Marriage Masquerade by Toni Logan. A no strings attached marriage scheme to inherit a Maui B&B uncovers unexpected attractions and a dark family secret. (978-1-63555-914-9)

Flight SQA016 by Amanda Radley. Fastidious airline passenger Olivia Lewis is used to things being a certain way. When her routine is changed by a new, attractive member of the staff, sparks fly. (978-1-63679-045-9)

Home Is Where the Heart Is by Jenny Frame. Can Archie make the countryside her home and give Ash the fairytale romance she desires? Or will the countryside and small village life all be too much for her? (978-1-63555-922-4)

Moving Forward by PJ Trebelhorn. The last person Shelby Ryan expects to be attracted to is Iris Calhoun, the sister of the man who killed her wife four years and three thousand miles ago. (978-1-63555-953-8)

Poison Pen by Jean Copeland. Debut author Kendra Blake is finally living her best life until a nasty book review and exposed secrets threaten her promising new romance with aspiring journalist Alison Chatterley. (978-1-63555-849-4)

Seasons for Change by KC Richardson. Love, laughter, and trust develop for Shawn and Morgan throughout the changing seasons of Lake Tahoe. (978-1-63555-882-1)

Summer Lovin' by Julie Cannon. Three different women, three exotic locations, one unforgettable summer. What do you think will happen? (978-1-63555-920-0)

Unbridled by D. Jackson Leigh. A visit to a local stable turns into more than riding lessons between a novel writer and an equestrian with a taste for power play. (978-1-63555-847-0)

VIP by Jackie D. In a town where relationships are forged and shattered by perception, sometimes even love can't change who you really are. (978-1-63555-908-8)

Yearning by Gun Brooke. The sleepy town of Dennamore has an irresistible pull on those who've moved away. The mystery Darian Benson and Samantha Pike uncover will change them forever, but the love they find along the way just might be the key to saving themselves. (978-1-63555-757-2)